ALSO BY J. F. POWERS

Prince of Darkness and Other Stories

The Presence of Grace

Morte D'Urban

Look How the Fish Live

*Wheat
That
Springeth
Green*

WHEAT THAT SPRINGETH GREEN

J. F. Powers

ALFRED A. KNOPF   NEW YORK   1988

THIS IS A BORZOI BOOK
PUBLISHED BY ALFRED A. KNOPF, INC.

Portions of this work were originally published in
The New Yorker.

The hymn "Now the Green Blade Riseth," words by
J. M. C. Crum from the *Oxford Book of Carols*, based on the
French medieval carol "Noël Nouvelet." This arrange-
ment is based on the harmonization from *The Hymnal
1982*. Copyright © 1985 by The Church Pension Fund,
New York. Reprinted by permission of The Church Pension Fund and Oxford University Press.

Library of Congress Cataloging-in-Publication Data

Powers, J. F. (James Farl).
 Wheat that springeth green.

 I. Title.
PS3566.O84W4   1988   813'.54   87-46104
ISBN 0-394-49609-4

Manufactured in the United States of America
Published August 31, 1988
Reprinted Once
Third Printing, October 1988

To
GGG and HFX for helping
OSB for providing
RAG for waiting
BWP for being

Now the green blade ris - eth

from the bur - ied grain,

wheat that in dark earth

man - y days has lain;

love lives a - gain, that

with the dead has been:

Love is come a - gain like

wheat that spring - eth green.

Words: John Macleod Campbell Crum (1872–1958)
Music: *Noël nouvelet*, medieval French carol

I

1

See Me

"See me," Joe said, in his pajamas and slippers now, coming into the living room to say good night to the party people again. "Oh, look who's here!" they said, glad to see him again. But Ivy came in from the kitchen and got him. "Good night," he said. "Good night, good night," they said, sad to see him go. In the kitchen Ivy said, "Roscoe," but Roscoe was just a cat, "whut I tell this boy?" (Ivy had told him what she always told him, "Don't do no bad stuff, boy.") She shooed him up the back stairs. He got into bed again. Then he came down the front stairs again, but stayed behind the portieres, peeking out. He wanted the pretty black-haired lady in the pretty orange dress to see him. "Oh oh," she said, "See Me's back again." He came out from behind the portieres, saying to her (he didn't know why), "I eat cheese." She and the other party people, and even Mama and Daddy, *laughed*. It was a joke! "I eat cheese! I eat cheese!" Uncle Bobby, Mama's brother, picked him up and carried him around the room, pinching his bottom, but not hard. "I eat cheese! I eat cheese!" But Uncle Bobby fooled him and carried him out of the room, up the front stairs. Uncle Bobby stood a silver dollar up on the table by Joe's bed. "Keep an eye on it, Sport, or it might run away." Joe didn't think it would. It didn't. So he came down the front stairs and stayed behind the portieres, not peeking out. "Last Sunday we took the boy to church," Daddy was telling the party people. "The new man was going on about the Dollar-a-Sunday Club, and I was going to sleep, when the boy, in that clear voice, says, 'Daddy, what does *she* want?' " The party people laughed, and Joe came smiling out from behind the portieres, and then didn't know what to say. But the pretty black-haired lady said, "And now you go to church, Joe?" "I go to church," he said. The party people *laughed*. It was a joke! "I go to church! I go to church!" The party people laughed, but not as much as before. "I eat cheese! I eat cheese!" The party people laughed, but not as much as before. "Good night, good night," they said, and Daddy said, "Good *night*." Mama took Joe up the front stairs. She told him to stay in bed. He told her he would. "Promise?" she said. "Promise," he said. Mama gave him a kiss. He gave Mama one. Mama liked him. Daddy did. Uncle Bobby did. The party people did. Ivy did. Roscoe didn't, but was just a cat. Frances, next door, didn't, but she didn't like boys or jokes. At her birthday party—no boys—when Frances and her friends were playing a game in the yard and Joe was sitting on the stone wall watching them, the birthday pony went poopy on the grass. "Poopy!" Joe yelled. Frances' friends and the maid *laughed*. It was a joke! But Frances yelled, "Shut up! You little squirt!" Frances didn't like jokes. Her friends did. The maid did. The party people did. They were sad Joe had to go to bed. No, if he went downstairs he'd break his promise, and that would be bad stuff. Stepping on ants was bad stuff. So was giving Roscoe a little kick. But Roscoe did bad stuff. He caught birds and ate them up, but not all the feathers. Joe had told on him, but Ivy had said, "Yeah, well, that's his business." Ivy said Roscoe could see God, but Joe didn't think he could. Ivy said Roscoe was thinking of God when he purred, but Joe didn't think he was. "Boy, can't you just *tell*?" Joe couldn't. "Ivy, what'll God do if I do bad stuff?" "Plenty." "What?" "You go and hurt yourself—fall down, bump your head, bite your tongue—*that's* whut." "Ivy, that's bad stuff." "That's whut *you* think." "Ivy, why does God do bad stuff?" "Boy, that's *his* business. Shut up." "Shut up's bad stuff, Ivy."

2

Carrying
the Cross

The little tower that bulged out of the attic was where Joe went when he didn't know what to do, where he'd gone to pray before and after Ivy died, where nowadays he went to smoke Daddy's Herbert Tareytons and Uncle Bobby's Camels and sometimes to be what he might be when he grew up—seeing one of Daddy's trucks (HACKETT'S COAL IS HOT STUFF) go by in the street below, he might call long distance, his fist the phone, his cigarette a cigar, and order a million short; hearing church bells, he might turn his baseball cap around, back to front, and show himself in the window (no balcony) and smile down upon the multitude below, his right hand busily blessing it, his left idly smoking behind him.

If he decided to be a businessman, he wanted to be one like Uncle Bobby and get a lot of fun out of life. (It was too bad, since he was Daddy's son, he didn't want to be one like Daddy, but he didn't.) The trouble wouldn't be, as it was now in sports and in crowds, that he was short for his age (nine)—so was Uncle Bobby (thirty-one). The trouble would be that he would be like Daddy and not like Uncle Bobby.

Uncle Bobby went to the barbershop in the basement of the First National Bank Building (eight chairs) and had his sideburns shaved down to points like check marks; Daddy went to the little neighborhood shop (two chairs) and had *his* shaved off. Uncle Bobby had a modern kitchen in his apartment, but ate out; Daddy drove home for lunch. Uncle Bobby was younger than Daddy (and Mama), but there was more to it than that. Uncle Bobby was a live wire and could come up with bright ideas; Daddy wasn't and couldn't. It was Uncle Bobby's idea to have HACKETT'S COAL IS HOT STUFF on the trucks and on the left-field fence at the ball park, and also HIT THIS SIGN AND WIN A TON (HOME TEAM ONLY)—the last part was Daddy's idea.

Uncle Bobby, who said of Daddy and himself, "He's coal, I'm ice," and of Joe, "He's a little of both," had built up the ice end of Hackett's by stopping home deliveries, by concentrating on hotels, institutions, and reefers (refrigerated boxcars), by moving into soft drinks (after consulting Joe) and now into near beer.

If Joe decided to be a businessman and someday stepped into Daddy's shoes, Uncle Bobby, only an employee now, would become a full partner in Hackett's.

Uncle Bobby and Joe were, as Daddy wasn't with either one of them, pals. When they were out in Uncle Bobby's Chrysler coupe, a tan one with a thin red stripe, wire wheels, and a rumble seat, they honked at chicks (what Uncle Bobby, from Kansas City, called them) in high-heel pumps and said "Hotsy totsy!" and "Hot ziggity!" to each other. But Joe was backward with people unless he knew them, and Uncle Bobby wasn't. At the barbershop in the First National Bank Building (where Joe now went), when Uncle Bobby said, "Whatcha say, Red!" to the old colored man who shined shoes, Joe said nothing, just smiled, as he did when Uncle Bobby said, "Hello, Beautiful!" to the manicurist who had a spit curl like Betty Boop and wore a uniform like a nurse, only pink, with high-heel pumps and no stockings. While she was doing him, Uncle Bobby would talk about how tired he was from his heavy dates and ask about his chances with her, winking at Joe and the barbers. (Joe wished he could wink like Uncle Bobby, so quick, like the tongue of a snake, but couldn't, he'd found, practicing it at home in front of a mirror, each time having to *wait* for it.) At the bakery shop in the Arcade, Uncle Bobby ate cookies right out of the showcase, passed some to Joe, and made the chicks who worked there (who at first said, "No! No!") laugh and squeal when he said he'd eat *them* if they weren't very careful. Hugging and kissing them, he'd say, "C'mon, Speed"—sometimes he called Joe that, or Ace—"get y'self some of this!" Joe wanted to, but didn't, just smiled. In the end, Joe paid for everything with Uncle Bobby's money, keeping the change, and sometimes the chicks, panting, fluffing out their hair, and adjusting their uniforms, would say, "What a pair!"

Uncle Bobby—a non-Catholic, he didn't have to go to church—got a lot of fun out of life. And if Joe did decide to be a businessman and not a priest, he could marry somebody he knew, maybe Frances, even if she was two years older, who could become a convert (as Mama had when she married Daddy) but probably wouldn't because she was so snippy and contrary (when Joe had tried "Hello, Beautiful!" on her, both times she'd said, "Shut up!"). Or he could be single like Uncle Bobby and have heavy dates. Either way, married or single, if he decided to be a businessman he could go on living in the house—and have heat piped into the little tower, which could be his den.

If he did decide to be a businessman, he would also perform good works, like Joseph of Arimathea, the rich merchant who'd paid for Our Lord's tomb.

If he decided to be a priest, he couldn't go on living in the house. That was one of the bad things about being a priest, having to move around and maybe live in a run-down neighborhood such as Hackett's plant was in because it had to be close to the railroad tracks. If he decided to be a priest in a religious order, though, he could live out in the country, at a college, and have invigorating walks and talks with students along the railroad tracks (different out there in the country), and maybe have some exciting adventures, and also do good, as often happened in the Father Finn books (" 'My God!' cried the atheist") that Sister Agatha read to the class at the end of the day if the class had been good. But Sister, though she belonged to a religious order herself, had advised Joe not to join one. Maybe if he decided to be a secular priest, as Sister was praying he and other guys in the class would, he wouldn't mind living in a run-down neighborhood if, like Our Lord, he loved the poor, as he would if he decided to be a priest. But that was another bad thing about being a priest—always having to try to be like Our Lord.

In the class play at Easter, when Joe was carrying the two-by-four cross, the hostile crowd was more hostile than it had been in practice—some guys were jealous of Joe for being Our Lord and even, in the case of Catfish Toohey, whose father was one of Daddy's drivers, for being Joe. By wagging the long end of the cross behind him, Joe managed to keep back the hostile crowd and, when falling for the third time, had managed to bring one of the arms of the cross down like a hammer on the foot of Catfish, who'd let out a yell and hopped around on the other foot, causing a few in the audience to laugh and Iggy Buker's father to call out, "Do it again!" After that performance, Sister Agatha had asked Joe to explain his conduct. "Catfish hit me a lot harder than he was supposed to, Sister, so I just hit him back." Sister had been disgusted with Joe. " *'So I just hit him back.' Any*body can do that! And with the *cross!* Joe, what *must* Our Lord *think* of you? Ask yourself *that*."

That might be the worst thing about being a priest, having to ask yourself *that*. Everybody had to, of course, but it wasn't the same for other people, even for nuns. Priests were in a class by themselves. To them alone, not even to Our Blessed Mother, had Our Lord given the power to turn water and wine into his body and blood, and to forgive sins. Such gifts couldn't be fully understood by us here below, in our fallen state, Sister had told the class. "But just remember this, class, the next time there's an electrical storm—thunder and lightning are as nothing, no more than the buzz of a fly, compared with the power of the priesthood."

That made up for all the bad things.

One afternoon that summer there was an electrical storm when Joe and Frances were smoking his cigarettes in her garage, once a stable, the smell of the pony and the horses before it still there, and he told her about the power of the priesthood.

"*Religion*," she said, crossing her legs so he could see her garters but not very well in the dark. "It's like Santa Claus, only it's for old people afraid of dying."

"Frances, you don't have to believe in it if you don't. But if you do and you won't—*that's* the sin against the Holy Ghost, Sister said."

"Screw Sister," Frances said.

Try to get a lot of fun out of life, then, and also perform good works? But not have the high place in heaven (if there was one; Frances said there wasn't) he'd have as a priest?

These were questions Joe couldn't answer that summer, and one evening when asked by the party people what he was going to be when he grew up, to be on the safe side, he said:

"A businessman or a priest."

"Oh, be *both* dear, like Father Stock," said Mama, the

party people laughing—for the same reason, Joe knew, that Father Stock, who talked so much about money in his sermons and whose first name was William, was called, but not to his face, Dollar Bill.

At the eight o'clock Mass that Sunday, Joe, the first server out of the sacristy, had to remember to ring the bell there on the sanctuary wall, which he did, but he must have pulled the chain too hard, or not let go of it soon enough, for the pierced brass globe that contained the bell and was the size of a basketball, came off the wall and crashed to the floor, spinning, the bell inside making a dying ha-ha noise. Joe stopped, wanting to put the thing back on the wall, or at least out of sight of the congregation, but Father Stock, behind Iggy, the other server, whispered, "No, no, boy, go ahead."

So Joe went ahead, to the foot of the altar, and with the thing there on the floor for everybody to see and blame him for pulling down, he was embarrassed all during Mass, even more when he didn't have his back to the congregation, during the sermon (Father Stock urged the congregation not only to attend the parish social themselves but to bring along their good non-Catholic friends and neighbors) and during Holy Communion (those waiting to receive got a closer look at the thing and also at Joe when he, attending Father Day, the new but not-so-young assistant from Ireland, held the plate under their chins).

In the sacristy after Mass, Father Day—he had a monkey face—smiled at Joe, but Father Stock, after sending Iggy to look for the janitor, frowned at Joe. "Put out the candles, boy. They cost a fortune." Joe made sure the candles didn't smoke and returned to the sacristy with the snuffer. Father Day smiled at him again.

"Hockitt's the name?" Father Day had a frosty voice.

"Yes, Father."

"Hockitt's Cull Iss Hut Stoof? That wan?"

"Yes, Father."

"Ah, so. Will we see yez at the beano, lad?"

"Father?"

"At the social, Jack."

Jack? "Yes, Father. I'm in the race."

"Ah, the race. That I'll have to see. Will yez win?"

Joe was sure he would, and would make up for pulling down the bell, but like Tom Playfair in the Father Finn books, said, modestly, "I'll do my best, Father."

"More power to yez, Jack."

"Yes, Father."

On the way home from church, Joe thought about his talk with Father Day (was glad Father Stock, with whom he'd never had one, had heard it), and at breakfast told Mama and Daddy about it (not about the Jack part, though, or anything about the bell), and repeated the funny part. " 'Hockitt's Cull Iss Hut Stoof? That wan?' "

"Drinks," Daddy said, and got up from the table.

"John." Mama followed Daddy out of the room, calling back to Joe, "Daddy's not feeling well. We won't be going to church today. Eat your prunes, dear."

After breakfast, after looking everywhere else, Joe went upstairs and, standing at the closed door of Mama and Daddy's bedroom, asked—reluctantly, because sometimes if you didn't ask, you found things—"Where's the paper?"

"Oh," Mama said, inside. "Oh. Has it come yet?"

"Course." It had been on the front porch when Joe left for Mass.

"Oh, here it is!" Mama handed out the funnies and the sport section.

Joe went down to the living room and was on the floor reading when Mama came in and sat down with a section of the paper, which, though, she wasn't reading whenever he looked at her. He thought she wanted the funnies (she read them; Daddy didn't), and so he hurried.

"Dear. If I have to call the doctor for Daddy, we may need something from the drugstore. So we want you to stay around the house this afternoon."

"I can't. I'm in the race." What Mama had said, the craziness of it, hit him again. "Call the doctor *now*. I'll go *now*."

Mama stood up looking sad, and Joe thought it was going to be one of those times when she said there was no use talking to him and left the room, but it wasn't—she gave him the section of the paper she hadn't been reading.

And there, on the front page, was a picture of one of Daddy's trucks—HACKETT'S COAL IS HOT STUFF. And over the picture, in big print, it said "HOT STUFF!" And under the picture, in small print, it said the truck had been seized with a load of Canadian whiskey.

"The truck was stolen, dear."

Not Uncle Bobby then.

"Or borrowed."

Uncle Bobby.

"Daddy's just sick about it, dear, and so am I."

So was Joe. It was worse than Tom Kane's mother swearing at Sister Agatha in front of the class, worse than Iggy Buker's father coming to the Easter play drunk, worse than—no, not worse than wetting your pants, what was always happening to Delbert Freeman (but wasn't mentioned to him because he was such a good fighter).

"We want you to stay around the house, dear."

"Because"—Joe was looking down at the funnies, not at

Mama—"you might need something at the drugstore?" *Chicken!*

"That's right, dear."

Not stopping at the stands for refreshments or to try his luck, though he had plenty of money, and changing directions whenever he saw guys from the class, though he was, or had been, fairly popular, Joe kept moving through the crowd. He wanted it to be seen that he was there, that he hadn't stayed away, but without attracting undue attention to himself until he won the race. That might make up for pulling down the bell and might even—but he was afraid it wouldn't—make up for the picture in the paper.

"Jack!"

"Afternoon, Father."

But Father Day, though Joe had kept moving, caught him by the arm and held onto it while listening to an old poor woman (part of his job, another bad thing about being a priest) and saying "Ah, yiss" and "Och, no" to her until he could get away.

"C'mon, lad. I'll trate yez."

Joe was embarrassed when Father Day said to the two women at the ice cream stand, "Ah, ladies, if you please, for Jack, here, my young friend, a crame ice." Crame ice!

Father Stock was making change at that stand, and Joe thought maybe Father Day wouldn't have to pay for the cone, since they were both priests, but he did. Joe remembered to thank him and was going off by himself (not impolite of him because Father Day was now listening to a young woman with a baby) when caught by the arm again. After that, Joe stood by whenever Father Day stopped to listen to people—some of them knew Joe and were probably surprised to hear him called Jack. Joe was embarrassed by that, but pleased with "my young friend" and with "He's vairrree fleeht of fooht."

It was keen being with Father Day, going from stand to stand, spending money (Joe changed his five-dollar bill), with people following the two of them around because wherever they went there was excitement. At one of the wheels Father Day ("I'm the monn that broke the bank at Montee Carrrlo!") won a half pound of sliced bacon and gave it to the old poor woman (who was one of the people following them around and who hurried off to put it in her icebox). At the stand where they threw lopsided baseballs at wooden milk bottles, Joe won a Kewpie doll and gave it to Frances, who was with a couple of Catholic friends. At that stand, though, Joe was embarrassed to see Father Day throw like a girl, *underhand*. And when they returned to the near beer stand and Father Day had another bottle ("A dozen of these min wouldn't make a piint"), Joe was embarrassed again, because of the picture in the paper, and was glad when they moved on.

"Crame ice, lad?"

"I better not, Father—on account of the race."

"Ah, the race! Ah, Sisters!" Father Day tipped his black hat to Sister Agatha and Sister Margaret. "My young friend Jack, here, he's in the race and vairrree flooht of fleeht."

Father Day laughed at his slip of tongue, and so did Joe, but Sister Agatha and Sister Margaret didn't—they moved up to the ice cream stand.

"Two cones, please," said Sister Agatha.

Father Stock called out to Father Day, "Mind stepping over to the rectory, Father? Saucers and spoons for the Sisters."

"Oh, bother," said Sister Agatha. "Two *cones*, please."

"Or Es*kee*mo Pies," said Sister Margaret.

"No, no," said Father Stock, shaking his square head.

"Not a-tall, not a-tall," said Father Day, and hurried off to the rectory.

Sister Agatha, looking put out, came over to Joe and whispered, "Father Day knows your father's name is John— he thinks that's your name too—*that's* why he calls you *Jack*."

Joe, embarrassed, whispered, "Sister, I *know*."

Sister Agatha whispered, "Then you should've corrected Father—it should've been done right away—it *wouldn't* have been impolite. Remember that in future."

"Yes, Sister," Joe whispered.

Sister Margaret whispered to herself, "Oh, what people must *think!*"

Father Stock called out, "You, boy!"

"Yes, Father."

"Run and tell Father Day I said to give *you* the saucers and spoons."

"Yes, Father."

"And tell him I said not to hurry back."

"Yes, Father."

"Run, boy."

"Yes, Father."

"*Go!*"

"Yes, Father." And before Father Stock could delay him again (not to speak when spoken to was impolite), Joe *went*, ran.

He met Father Day coming out of the rectory with the saucers and spoons wrapped in a napkin, and told him what Father Stock had said.

"Said that, did he? Not to come back?"

"Not to *hurry* back, Father."

"He's the buss," Father Day whispered to himself, his monkey face looking different, old*er*, and giving Joe the saucers and spoons, turned toward the rectory.

"Father, you're not coming back?"

"I am not."

"But you'll miss the race, Father."

"I'll be watchin' from me window above. God speed yez, Jack."

"Yes, Father."

Joe ran back to the stand, holding the saucers and spoons so they wouldn't rattle. Father Stock unwrapped them, stuck the napkin in his hip pocket, motioned Sister Agatha and Sister Margaret up to the stand, and said to one of the women behind the counter, "Double dips for the Sisters. No charge."

Joe moved away from the stand, away from an old smelly man who looked like a tramp and said to the woman who'd handed him a cone, "No charge." A joke?

"Pay Father," the woman said.

The old man licked the cone.

"*Father*," the woman said.

Father Stock said, "Five cents, mister."

The old man licked the cone. "Try and git it."

Joe was astonished to see Father Stock lie across the counter and, like a swimmer doing the breast stroke, swat the cone to the ground, the ice cream, only one dip, coming out of the cone and settling in the grass.

"No way to do," the old man said, squatting down—Joe saw he wasn't wearing socks—and was trying to scoop up the ice cream with the cone, but couldn't, and was going to use his fingers when Father Stock helped him to his feet and pointed him toward the rectory. The old man still had the cone and was chewing on it with his gums.

"I'm turning this bird in," Father Stock said to the women behind the counter, and to Joe, "Make change while I'm gone, boy."

So Joe, warned by the women to watch out for Canadian

coins ("Somebody tried to give *Father* one!"—"The very idea!") and shown the cashbox, made change while the women filled orders and discussed the saucers on the counter (Sister Agatha and Sister Margaret had disappeared), one woman for putting the ice cream back in the freezer, the other one for letting it stay right there, where Father could see it when he returned. There wasn't so much business. One woman could've handled it, and the other one, though she'd have to wash her hands if she went back to filling orders when Father Stock returned, could've made change. Joe wanted to say this to the women, but was afraid it wouldn't do any good, and so said nothing. Then, when he couldn't wait any longer—he'd been watching the crowd gathering over by the church—he blurted out, "I have to go now." "Oh, dear!"—"Can't you *wait?*" Knowing what *that* meant—he *couldn't* leave now—and too embarrassed to say anything, he turned away from the women so they couldn't see his face. He wanted to cry, but didn't, just snuffled. "Oh, dear!"—"Did you *go?*" He was even more embarrassed, staring down at the cashbox. "Did somebody give you *one?*"—"A dime or a *quarter?*" He shook his head, not embarrassed, just annoyed. "Did somebody *say* something?"—"Oh, you poor kid!" He realized then that they knew who he was and had seen the picture in the paper.

"Here, what's this?" said Father Stock, returning and seeing the ice cream melting in the saucers on the counter, but wouldn't listen to the women, said "Shhh!" to them, for Sister Agatha was also returning to the stand. "Sister," Father Stock said to her, "you and Sister didn't eat your ice cream. Where's Sister?"

"Over in *church*," said Sister Agatha. "*Praying.* For *you*, Father. Oh, *how* you treated that poor old soul!"

"Now, now, Sister. Gave him a good talking-to and let him go. Gave him a dollar."

Joe was astonished to hear this and thought Sister Agatha would be, but if she was she didn't show it.

"And that's not *all*, Father. You made Joe, here, miss the race with your—your *moneychanging*."

"Sister, that was *not* my intention—and that's what counts, fortunately for *all* of us here below. Come with me, boy. Make change while I'm gone, Sister, and eat your ice cream. Eat Sister's too."

Joe followed Father Stock through the crowd, over to where, alongside the church, the race had been run, where Sister Martina was assembling the contestants for the next event, and where Joe gave up the idea that Father Stock, who could do it, would order the race rerun.

"Sister, this boy, through no fault of his, missed the foot race. Please see that he gets one of those sacks."

"I'm sorry, Father, but they're all taken. Unless"—Sister Martina raised her voice—"someone would be willing to give up his or hers?"

A girl who wasn't in hers yet, a sixth-grader who wore tortoiseshell glasses, said, "*I* would, Sister."

"Good for you, Dolores," said Sister Martina (who taught the sixth grade).

Father Stock smiled at the girl, at Joe, said (to Sister Martina), "I have to get back to my stand," and left.

Joe went over to the girl and whispered to her, thinking she'd be pleased to hear it: "It's all right. I don't want your sack. I'm not in this race."

"Sister*rrr*!"

Sister Martina came. "*Now* what?"

Joe got in first. "Sister, it's all right. I don't want her sack. I'm not in this race."

"Sister, he *has* to be!"

"I *don't*!"

"Father *said*!"

Joe reeled back. "Father *didn't!*"

"No," said Sister Martina, "but Father *expects* it."

Joe could've cried, but didn't. "Sister, I don't *want* to."

"Sister, he *has* to!"

"Nobody *has* to, but *one* of you *should*." Sister Martina moved away from them, calling to the other contestants to line up.

"You *know* you're the *one*," the girl said to Joe, stuck her tongue out at him, threw down the sack, and *walked* on it. "Thanks for taking my place. *Half Pint*."

"*Four Eyes*."

Joe knew, when he picked up the sack, why the girl hadn't got into it—it was dusty, which he didn't mind so much, but damp at the bottom, which he did, and said BIG BOY POTATOES on it.

Joe went over to the starting line, carrying his sack to save energy, which other contestants were wasting by hopping around and falling down in theirs, but he also wanted to put off the moment when it would clearly be seen that he was one of them. When the moment came, he was laughed at by guys who knew he was the fastest runner in the fifth grade (and probably in the whole school), and by some of the girls, including one who'd been in love with him last year, and by Frances and her friends. Frances held up the Kewpie doll and said to it (really to her friends), "See Daddy!" Joe just smiled at Frances and everybody, so they couldn't tell how he really felt about being in the sack race, so he wouldn't get mad and cry and fight and maybe lose if he fought the guy he wanted to fight—Delbert Freeman, who was stumbling around, making believe his orange pop was whiskey, looking cross-eyed, and saying, "Hic!"

"*Piss Pants!*"

Delbert Freeman didn't hear it, but Sister Martina did and yelled:

"On your mark, get set, go!"

Joe broke fast and—he'd been in sack races before—watched out for early fallers. When he was clear, he eased up some to save himself for the stretch, concentrated on his sack, jockeying it, grabbing it up when he jumped, letting it out when he came down. (The noises from the crowd, the screams and groans, were not for him.) Lying third, breezing, gaining on the big seventh-grade girl who looked like Powerful Katinka in *Toonerville Folks* whose movements were erratic and might bring her (and him) down, he gave her more room, lost a little ground, gained it back, drew even, passed her. (Now the noises from the crowd *were* for him, cheering him on.) Closing on the leader, a big eighth-grade guy who smoked Wings (ten cents a pack) in the boys' washroom during recess and might not stay, Joe drew even, and was going ahead in the stretch, driving, when he fell.

"His old man's a bootlegger!" Delbert Freeman.

"His *uncle!*" Catfish.

Joe jumped up and out of his sack. He was heading not for Catfish but Delbert Freeman when, seeing and hearing Sister Agatha ("Joe, *don't!*"), he changed directions . . . and ran away . . . all the way home, where he went up to the little tower and did what he'd wanted to do all that day, cried.

3
Looking Up
Skirts

At the last meet that spring, Joe won his events, the hundred and the two-twenty dashes, and ran anchor in the four-forty relay, won by the team. But then, because the team's second best distance man had twisted an ankle in the broad jump, Joe—against the conscience of his coach, Father "Germany" Zahn, an old dash man—was entered in the *mile*. After setting a pace intended to tempt and kill off the opposition, he faded as expected, but miraculously came again and got up for a third, a point, which proved to be the margin of Immaculata's victory over hated Cathedral.

Joe was a hero to the faculty and student body for what remained of the school year—not much, summer vacation depriving the track star, as it didn't the football and basketball star, of his admirers all too soon. But Joe had lettered in a major sport as a sophomore, something seldom done at Immaculata, where standards were high, and he made the most of it, wearing his sweater of pale blue with its snow white *I* as long as the weather permitted, or a little longer— he was hoping for an unseasonably cool summer. And was looking forward to fall and football because, though he didn't care for the game and was small for it, Immaculata could use his blazing speed in the backfield—the head football coach, Father "On" Wisconski, present at the last meet, had been heard to remark (by the student manager of the track team, one of Joe's admirers), "I'd like to turn that little fart loose on Cathedral."

With that in mind, Joe was in training that summer. Instead of sharpening pencils and practicing his typing at Hackett's, he stayed home and cut the grass, about two acres of it, with a hand mower, weeded the flower beds, practiced fast starts and broken field running, did pushups, chinned himself on the apple tree, and ate a lot.

By July, though, it had become one of those summers that melt the streets, and Joe was spending more time in the cool of the cellarway. Here, in a deck chair, he read the *Sporting News* regularly, keeping track of players he'd seen before they went up to the majors, or after they came down; also read *Anthony Adverse*, a very long book, regularly; and occasionally dipped into Butler's *Lives of the Saints* and Rumble and Carty's *Radio Replies*, this (a gift from Sister Agatha, now stationed in Green Bay) answering questions he might be asked by the laity or enemies of the Church if he became a priest, which he wasn't sure about that summer.

Early in July, when the heat had reached into the bricks of the cellarway and was wilting the moss, he said good-bye to the horseflies and moved the deck chair inside, into the cellar, and shut the door. Here, sitting under a dusty light bulb, he smoked (English Ovals, exhaling into the open furnace to avoid detection) and drank (beer and ale, there being, or having been, a good supply in the cellar). Here he discovered what, until that summer, had been a mystery to him, why some stars stay out all night, experienced himself the special pleasure, the thrill, there is for the athlete in dissipation, in tempting fate—imagined himself in the fall (*"Fumble!"*) being taken out, hooted at.

And while smoking and drinking away these days in the

cellar, abusing his body, he also abused his mind and spirit with the little magazines he bought with embarrassment at a downtown cigar store, to which he'd return for more of the same, he knew, though regularly disappointed by the art ("Pensive," "Nocturne") and the fiction ("Concealed from the other merrymakers by a potted palm while the band played on, Randy cupped one of Diane's creamy cherry-tipped orbs").

He couldn't trust himself these days.

If he suddenly shoved his reading matter into the furnace and rushed out into the heat of the day, it might appear that he'd suddenly resolved to amend his life and that he just happened to be occupied in the front yard, moving the sprinklers, raking the gravel driveway, for a brief period in the morning and afternoon. The truth was, his reading matter could be retrieved from the cold furnace and he'd availed himself of the trial offer made to adults only for a limited time only by Seemore Products of Hollywood, to be dispatched to addressee in a plain brown envelope posthaste. Weeks had passed since addressee enclosed a dollar and signed himself J. Hackett—not such a good idea as he'd thought, since it meant meeting the mailman twice a day if the uncensored poses ("Kind Men Like! Nuff Sed!!") weren't to fall into the hands of the other J. Hackett at that address. Write and say that Seemore should cancel his order and give the money to the poor? Or that he'd moved to a nonexistent address in a distant city? Or that he'd recently married and was no longer interested? Or that he'd recently passed away, yours truly, Mrs J. Hackett?

It didn't just happen, either, that he'd be occupied in the backyard when Frances and Dora, the new maid (over twenty-one and built like a brick . . . as the guys at Hedblad's service station would say and Joe wouldn't, even there), came out to sunbathe by the stone wall—on which a friendly young neighbor, as he might appear to be, though seldom speaking or spoken to, would soon be leaning, with an erection, considering the possibilities in the bodies below and sometimes in the conversation.

When Dora said, as she frequently did, "Rex, he don't care if I go out with other parties, just so's I don't go steady, and I don't care, just so's he don't," Frances seemed to understand. But Joe wondered about this, since Rex and Dora (she seemed to meet these other parties while working at her other job, relief cashier at the Orpheum and the Palace) were engaged and planning to get married right after Rex had done his hitch. Joe also wondered about the property that Rex and Dora were hoping to buy with his winnings (craps) and her savings, which Joe thought could not amount to much. Dora called the property ("propitty"), which was in "easy reach" of Fort Bone, where Rex was stationed, a roadhouse—something Joe knew little about, only what he'd learned from his reading that summer (Randy had met Diane at a roadhouse, the Red Rooster) and from movies in which babes in high silk hats and black silk tights sold cigarettes to merrymakers at small tables with bed lamps on them. Joe thought that some of the places he heard swing music emanating from on his radio late at night, places like "Frank Dailey's Meadowbrook" and "the beautiful Glen Island Casino," might be roadhouses, real ones, but that what Rex and Dora had in mind was only a highway tavern with a name like Dew (or Do) Drop Inn stencilled on a beer sign. Even that was putting it too high, Joe thought when he heard that Rex would tend bar and keep order there while Dora kept order among the hostesses and doubled as one of them on busy nights, at least until the roadhouse got on its feet. "It won't take long. Rex says we'll be chargin' a dollar for a ten-cent bottle of beer, and maybe more after hours. All his old buddies'll come."

"*Dora!*"

"Whut?"

"What you *said!*"

"Whut?"

"*Come!*"

At such times they'd laugh, and even when they were lying with their heads down and their bottoms up (how Joe most liked to see them), he'd gaze off in the distance as if not listening to the conversation—he didn't know whether Frances thought he couldn't understand it, didn't care if he could, or was trying to embarrass him. Sometimes she'd suddenly look up at him and say: "*You* still here?" Once she'd said, but hadn't looked up at him, fortunately, because it had made him blush:

"Dora, what about this Peeping Tom here?"

"Whut? Who?"

"Joe. He drinks, you know. What if *he* came in drunk some night?"

"Whut? Where?"

"The *road*house."

"Whut if he did? So whut?"

"*Dora!*"

"Whut? Not old enough to do business with?"

"Dora, he plans to enter the *priesthood.*"

"Do tell."

"Maybe," Joe said, "I'll just enter the family business."

"Anytime, kid," Dora said.

And Frances laughed.

Until that summer, Joe had visited Hedblad's only as a customer, in the Reo or the Pierce-Arrow, usually in the daytime, but late in June, still wearing his letterman's sweater, he began what was now his routine in the evening (unless he drove out to the ball park in the Reo), dropping in at the station to talk sports with the night attendants. Dale, the younger one, had gone to Immaculata for a while, but wasn't the kind of guy Joe had known, not an athlete and not much of anything else, just one of the guys you see around school and then don't. Rock, over twenty-one, was from Chicago and thought he was so great—claimed that he'd once seen Ralph (not Al) Capone, whom he called Bottles, and that he'd lived near Wrigley Field, Home of the Cubs.

If Rock and Dale were busy, Joe was now trusted to answer the phone, to hand out road maps, to hose down the pavement, and the talk was now less of sports, more of cars and babes. Joe didn't pretend to know much about cars, couldn't say what the Reo or the Pierce would do if opened up, and wouldn't have pretended to know much about babes if it hadn't been thought (by Dale, not Rock) that he did because he was so blasé. ("You're Blasé" was one of Joe's favorite songs.) Dale, if not Rock, was impressed by the neighborhood Joe lived in, the clothes he wore, and probably by the way he'd casually pick up a dirty cartoon book and toss it aside unread, the way he'd casually point out that a car was waiting for service when the talk was about babes, and the way, recently, he'd casually bought (as if they were cigarettes) a pack of "cundrums" at the station. "Ever lose one on the job, Joe?" "Can't say I have, Dale. You?" Blasé.

So if Joe asked for advice on how to do business with Dora, he had plenty to lose at the station, at least with Dale, who, though, was a very serious guy for a guy with nothing on his mind but cars and babes and wouldn't laugh at him, as Rock would. But what if Joe asked for advice and Rock found out from Dale? Rock was a crude character. At first he'd called Joe Dash Man—"Hey, Dash Man!"—but now it was Gash Man. Joe, though embarrassed by this, was also flattered by it, as he wasn't when Rock asked him how often he beat his meat, pulled his pud, or when Rock held his hand out limply, palm up, as though the fingers were broken, and whispered, "Smell my *new* babe," which Rock had done nightly until Joe replied, "Sorry, Rock, I've got a cold." Blasé.

Some of the things Joe heard at the station were hard for him to believe. It was a sure sign of recent sexual activity if a babe's eyes were all black underneath, Dale said, and as often as not, after a babe whose tank he'd filled, oil he'd checked, windshield he'd cleaned, and eyes he'd inspected, drove away, he'd shake his head and say, "Goes another one," drawing from Joe, at most, a nod. Blasé. According to Rock, when Mr Hedblad was there during the day, hot babes phoned the station, even in the summertime, to say they couldn't get their car started—*that* was the *code*—and off Mr Hedblad (whom Rock called Horse Cock) would go in the wrecker. "You seen him in it, Joe." "Oh, sure." Blasé. It was hard for Joe to believe this of Mr Hedblad, an old bald-headed married guy who wore a black leather bow tie. But from other things Joe heard at the station and did not doubt, many more people than he'd imagined—not just young guys like himself, and certainly more babes—were having trouble with the Sixth Commandment.

It showed Joe what the world was like, what he'd be up against if he became a priest.

It also showed him he wasn't so bad, made him feel better about himself, but not much.

He was what St Augustine (who'd asked God to make him chaste but not yet) had been before he straightened out—a vicious youth.

One night Joe promised God that if the uncensored poses came the next day he'd burn them sight unseen and go to confession (to the Italian church downtown), but they hadn't come, fortunately.

So, early in August, in thought, word, and deed, Joe was still sinning away.

On the evenings he drove out to the ball park (the sign on the left field fence now said HACKETT'S QUALITY COAL, nothing about hot stuff, or win a ton—Uncle Bobby was selling real estate in California), he sat alone in the family box and appeared to take a lively interest in the flight of foul balls over the grandstand, but was really looking up skirts.

Late at night, wearing only his pajama bottoms because of the heat, he lay in the dark, listening to his radio, to dance music emanating from Frank Dailey's Meadowbrook, from the beautiful Glen Island Casino, the Aragon, the Trianon ("Lee Bennett steps forward to ask the musical question 'Who?' "), the Cotton Club ("Duke Ellington and his famous orchestra continue the program with a number captioned 'Caravan' "), but when the lights went on across the way, in Dora's living quarters over the garage, he got up to use Mama's opera glasses.

In the afternoon, leaning on the stone wall, he was still the friendly young neighbor with an erection, now waiting, however, for a chance to speak to one of the sunbathers alone, a chance that finally came.

"Dora."

"Whut?"

"You know what you said."

"Whut?"

" 'Anytime,' you said."

Silence.

"Dora."

"Whut?"

"You know."

Silence.

"Dora."

"Cost ya, kid."

"O.K."

"Ten dollars."

"O.K."

"I mean twenty."

"O.K."

Silence.

"Dora."

"Whut?"

"When?"

Silence.

"Tonight, Dora?"

"I don't get off till nine thirty."

"That's not late."

"I might be real late if somebody gives me a ride."

"I'll give you a ride. I'll pick you up in the Reo."

"No, the big one."

"O.K., the Pierce. Orpheum?"

"Palace."

Blasé but sweating in a white linen suit, parked—no parking —in front of the Palace with the motor running, he sat smoking, the big vertical sign going off then, the street a shade darker then, and she came clicking out of the air-cooled lobby in her black high-heel pumps and would have opened the *back* door if he hadn't reached over and opened the front one. She got in beside him, saying "Hot," and he pulled away from the curb, smelling her perfume and thinking they weren't a couple of kids off to a sock hop in a gym, they were a vicious youth and a hot babe off to an assignation (French), but the problem was the same—what to say?

"Have to turn off the sign when you leave?"

"I don't have to do *nothin'*." She was feeling around in her handbag. "Gimme one of them things."

He produced his English Ovals, pushed in the dashboard lighter, pulled it out, but not too soon, and held it away from her mouth, making her come for it—all while driving in traffic. Randy couldn't have done better.

"Phew! You *like* these lopsided stinkers?"

Not what Diane would say, he thought, and was silent.

Cheerfully: "Know why I like this boat, kid?"

"No."

"Looks like a hearse." She laughed at the idea.

"Uh-huh."

"Smells like one, too."

"Uh-huh." He produced his (really Mama's) little silver flask. "Scotch, babe?"

She turned on him. "You crazy kid! You shouldn't drink when you drive! *You* shouldn't drink! You wanna get us *both* arrested?" She was panting, arousing him.

He took a nip from the flask and put it away.

"And don't call me babe," she said.

"Don't call me kid," he said.

"Call you what I like."

"Call you what I like."

She shut up then, so he did, and they rode in silence. He'd meant to stop at the drugstore, but stopped instead at the station, which he wouldn't have done if he hadn't seen Dale out in front, hosing down the pavement. "Carton o' Luckies," Joe called to him—knew her brand from his afternoons in the sun with her and Frances, from being so observant then—and Dale hurried into the station.

"I got some in my apartment."

"Get you some more."

When Dale came out of the station, Rock did too, and while Dale collected for the carton and cleaned the windshield, especially the passenger's side, and talked about the weather, failing, though, to bring the passenger into it, Rock did the pavement, holding the hose between his legs, about a foot from the nozzle, all the time looking over at the car solemnly, which was embarrassing. When Joe drove away, he could—fortunately, she couldn't—see the attendants standing together in the rearview mirror, Rock laughing, Dale shaking his head.

"Them jerks know you?"

"They know the car."

He drove down the alley so she'd be on the right side to go into her place when she got out of the car, and then he reached across and opened the door, his arm resting for a moment on her legs above the knees but not much.

"Thanks for the ride and ceegrettes, Joe." Joe, not kid.

Yes, but he was afraid she was saying good night to him, had changed her mind about doing business with him, and the laugh was going to be on him—there wouldn't be anything, as there might have been, to keep her from telling *Frances* what had happened that night.

"Gimme a few minutes 'fore ya come up, Joe."

"O.K." *Blasé.*

He put the car in the garage, went into the house, washed his hands and face, his armpits and crotch (into which he shook talcum powder), combed his hair, urinated, and retired to his room to top up his flask from a bottle of White Horse on loan from the pantry, then returned to the garage, to the car for—it was on the floor in back—the bouquet of roses.

The door at the top of the stairs was wide open—on

account of the heat or him?—and he could hear the shower running, but he politely knocked—no response—before entering. Her apartment (what she called it) was just one big room with kitchen facilities and a bathroom, the door of which was wide open—on account of the heat or him or both? A small oscillating fan was playing on the opened-out couch, her bed, a pillow and sheet on it. He didn't want to sit there, naturally, or in the overstuffed chair, on account of the heat, and chose a straight-back chair from which he could see straight into the bathroom. It then occurred to him, sitting there with the bouquet wrapped in green wax paper, how he might look to her—like an old-fashioned beau, Harold Lloyd or somebody, in the movies—and so he put the bouquet on the floor. Then he got up to draw the shade of the window into which it was possible for a Peeping Tom to see, but not very well, from the house across the way. He returned to the straight-back chair, took a nip from his flask, and was reaching for his cigarettes, but forgot all about them when she stepped out of the shower wearing, it seemed, because of her tan, a white bathing suit.

"Oh, hi," she said.

He nodded. Blasé.

She held up a towel. "Do my back."

He went, *not* hurrying, into the bathroom and did her back—she was softer than he would have thought. Down below, where he wanted to do her, but did not, she was whiter, bigger than he would have thought, and was probably softer.

"Do my bottom too."

So he did, and she was.

"Do it good." She spread her legs and reached around to feel him down below. "My."

He—it was strange—*enjoyed* his embarrassment and

reached around to cup one of her creamy cherry-tipped orbs.

"You *nasty* man!" She snatched the towel away from him and held it crushed to her body, above the waist, and spoke to him, but down below. "Should be *ashamed* of ya'self! Go stand in the corner!"

He knew she was kidding, but he left the bathroom, blasé, stiffly though, somewhat hobbled by his erection, and stiffly stooped down for the bouquet, in it a little envelope—this was something he'd worried about and wanted to get over with.

She came bouncing and jiggling out of the bathroom in her black pumps only. "For *me*! Oh, hon, ya *shouldn'a*!"

"It's in the envelope."

"Whut?"

"You know."

After she counted it—he'd made it thirty—and she gave him a hug, a loose quick one because she had the bouquet in one hand and the envelope in the other, she stood back and stared at him down below. "My, my."

Enjoying his embarrassment, but blasé, he offered her his flask. "Drink?"

"*Now?*"

"Not now?"

"Later, hon."

He had one anyway.

"You're bad as Rex. I gotta put these in water." She went bouncing and jiggling over to the sink with the roses. "Take off your clothes, hon."

This was something else he'd worried about and wanted to get over with and was why, because there was something funny about a man in underwear, he wasn't wearing any. There was something funny, too, about an otherwise naked man in shoes and socks but he kept his on, not liking the look of the floor.

"*My.*" She had put the roses in a papier-mâché vase such as undertakers use and had set it on the end table by the couch. At the other end of the couch, the open end, she spread a towel. "Bring any safeties?"

"Oh, yeah." He hadn't forgotten them, he just hadn't known exactly when he'd need one, and went over to the straight-back chair, to his coat. She helped him on with one, kneeling down to do it. "*My.*" She stood up and bumped her bottom into him.

"I better shut the door," he said.

"No. That's part of it."

"How d'ya mean, Dora?"

She laughed at him. "Oh, nobody'll come—'cept you, I bet." And plopping down on the couch where the towel was, she raised and cocked her legs back so he could see her bottom very well, also the soles and heels of her pumps, and then, using both hands, her fingers pressing down and fanned out, she parted the hair at her crotch and the lips there. "See?"

"Uh-huh."

"Move the light closer."

He moved the floor lamp closer.

"See more now?"

"Uh-huh."

"What ya see?"

"You know."

"Like it?"

"Uh-huh."

"Like it a lot?"

"Uh-huh."

"Kiss it."

He hesitated.

She laughed at him. "You don't have to." She put her legs down and cupped one of her creamy cherry-tipped orbs. "Kiss it."

He did.

"Suck it."

He did.

"Now this one."

He did.

"Double feature, huh?"

He raised his head—"Uh-huh"—and put it down.

"Betcha'd like *another* girl."

He shook his head, not raising it.

"You're sweet. I mean another girl *and* me."

Silence.

"Two at one go, I mean."

Silence.

"Wouldja?"

He nodded, not raising his head.

"Cost ya."

He nodded, nuzzling.

"See whut I can do. That's enougha that. Put it in."

He and she did.

Silence.

"Grunt," she said.

He did.

"Growl," she said.

He did.

Silence.

"Dora, I don't know how long . . ."

"That's all right, hon. You'll last longer next time."

"*Tonight?*"

"Sure. Go ahead."

"O.K." *O.K.!*

"*Not yet!*"

He looked where she was looking, behind him, and seeing *her*—she'd been hiding behind the curtains in the closet thing and was naked except for brassiere and pumps—he panicked and pulled out of Dora and out of the condom too!

"Oh, *shit!*" Dora said, fishing for it.

Frances laughed at her and said to him, "Do *me*."

He'd done her a little later, with Dora watching, and then, a little later, Dora again, but from behind, with Frances watching, and then, a little later, Frances from behind, but standing up, with Dora watching and making coffee. Before he left that night, remembering "Cost ya," he asked, "What's the damage?" And Frances said, "We'll send you a bill at the end of the month." A joke? No, and of course it was all Frances' idea, he had received a bill at the end of August, in the mail, an *itemized* bill for services rendered, for Frances' on the first night, for hers and Dora's on the following nights. During that three-week period, at the start of it, he'd dropped in at the station only once in the evening, briefly, for condoms—a gross. To meet his expenses, he'd had to resign from the Christmas Club at the First National and dip—no, *dig*—into his regular account. The night he paid up (before Frances arrived), Dora, who was sitting on his lap, said, "I *hate* to set ya back so much, but it wouldn't be *fair* to charge less for her." "My pleasure, and I expect to pay for it. I enjoy doing business with you both," said the tipsy, vicious youth with the wisdom of Solomon, improving on it by copping a feel. He was getting all he'd bargained for and more from both babes, as they were from him—they called him "Arm and Hammer."

There wasn't anything the three of them could think of doing they hadn't done, though at first he'd hesitated, but only at first, and now he really was blasé.

Then it all ended.

"Like a runny nose, that's right, Dick, only it's his penis," said Father Zahn and, putting his hand over the mouthpiece of the phone, asked Joe, "How long?" "How d'ya mean, Father?" "How long's it been acting up?" "What? Oh. About a week." Father Zahn repeated this over the phone. "Well, what's the usual, Dick? I see. So football's out. Can't say I'm sorry, but On Wisconski will be. He's been after the boy, which is why the boy had the nerve to come and see me. I'll tell On something—pernicious anemia, maybe—anything but the truth. You know how he is. He had to get rid of another pup. 'They're never the same, once they get a taste of it.' *I* wouldn't exactly know. But the boy should definitely be fit in the spring? Good. Dash man—my best. Afraid so." Father Zahn put his hand over the mouthpiece. "He asked if it was *you*, Joe. He'll treat you right and this'll all be strictly confidential." Father Zahn repeated that part over the phone. "His folks mustn't know, Dick. No, no, I understand the other party's being seen to—parties, actually. No, he won't give you their names, Dick—would *you*? Thanks, Dick. I know you will. And send me the bill. He'll be right over." Father Zahn hung up. "Well, you heard that, Joe. Dr Leonard's expecting you. Physicians and Accountants Building. Better run. Oh, by the way, how long since your last confession?"

"*Madre di Dio!* You married man?" "No, Father." "You work—got job?" "No, Father." "What you do?" "Nothing,

Father." "You student?" "Yes, Father." "How old you?" "Fifteen, Father." "*Madre di Dio!* You sick?" "No, Father." "In a good health?" "Yes, Father." "For a your penance you pray rosary every day till next confession." "Yes, Father." "That a not all. You run mile morning, mile night. Make good act contrition. God bless."

4
At the Sem

Joe knew from his reading that some of the best saints had worn hair shirts. Catherine of Siena. Bernard of Clairvaux. And that Thomas à Becket, when murdered in the cathedral, had been wearing one that was crawling with vermin. (That, though, was pushing the penitential idea too far, Joe thought.) He had heard that hair shirts were still being worn, even in this country, by the tough contemplative orders—the Carthusians, the Trappists. But he had never seen one until he and a few of his fellow seminarians were invited to "take tea or beer" in the Rector's study one evening, it being the policy of the Rector, a stylish grey man, new at the job, to have everybody in at least once during the academic year.

The hair shirt—actually, this one was sleeveless, not a shirt but a vest of a coarse black-and-brown fabric that Joe later learned was goat's hair, woven like chain mail or a Brillo pad—was on a coat hanger hooked to an arm of the floor lamp by the Rector's chair, and not a pleasant sight. It was there to be asked about, Joe thought, and for that reason he wouldn't ask about it. But Cooney, his best friend, did.

"My *cilicium*—my hair shirt," said the Rector. "Back from the cleaner's." Seeing that Hrdlicka (a simple soul) believed him, the Rector said to Joe, "No, I'm afraid an old friend sent it to me as a joke"—as if Joe (pretty sophisticated), and not

Hrdlicka, needed help, and for this Joe had to admire the Rector.

The next time Joe saw the hair shirt, three months later, he didn't see it as a joke at all. Joe in those months, during and after the annual retreat—six days when the seminarians, lectured by an outside expert in the field, considered the state of their souls—had taken a big step up, spiritually. Oh, he still had a long way to go, but could now look back and down, like a man climbing a mountain, and see where he'd been. He could see himself as he'd been when he entered the seminary, down there in the foothills of sentimentality, sound asleep and dreaming that he would someday do great things for God, the Church, and his parishioners, and would thus, incidentally, make the world a better place. He could see himself as he'd been later on, on the lower slopes of reality, waking up and fearing that he, too, would poop out when put to the test, as others had, to judge by what was happening and not happening in parishes he knew about, to say nothing of the world. And now he'd changed again—this time for good, he believed. He had grown up. Now he knew what he was doing, or, anyway, what he was trying to do— simply the hardest job in the world: getting to know God, growing more like God, growing in holiness. Holiness, as the retreatmaster had said, was the only ambition worthy of the priest and therefore of candidates for the priesthood. Holiness was the point of all the lives of the saints, the point where all those glorious lives converged, and what the whole world was crying for. "And," the retreatmaster had said, "you can't give what you haven't got, lads."

So Joe and some others, in quest of holiness, had gone into spiritual training, which had its physical side. "Detachment!" the retreatmaster had cried, and they gave up their attachments—smokes, sweets, snacks, snooker, and handball were Joe's—and haunted the chapel. They were a dozen or so in number, kneeling in prayer and meditation by the hour, some, though, sitting from time to time—Mooney and Rooney, for example; not Joe, though, and not Cooney, and not Hrdlicka. But the way of the world is also the way of the seminary, and the number of those who kept vigil in the chapel, kneeling or sitting, daily diminished—down to five only a week after the retreat.

The five of them—Joe, Cooney, Hrdlicka, Mooney, and Rooney—came in for a lot of headshaking from their peers, were called quietists, "detachers," and so on (only to be expected if you knew anything about the history of the Church, the intramural dogfights between ascetics and time-servers), and were also a source of concern to some of the high-living faculty and the Rector. It was believed that the Rector enjoyed the favor of the Archbishop but not of his reverend consultors, who remembered their days in the seminary and were unhappy about the way the place was being run now—as a club, they said. So the ingredients were there, at the seminary and close by, for trouble—which Joe did all he could to avoid.

He counselled the members of the little band (they seemed to regard him as their spiritual director) to use their heaven-sent opportunities, which were many, to turn the other cheek. And he gave good example whenever he could, as when he was called "Holy Joe" or just "Holy." ("Hi, Holy!" Deadass Boekenhoff greeted him every morning in the lavatorium, and Joe, though tempted to answer something else, would murmur politely, "Good morning, George.") But not all members of the little band did so well. Mooney and Rooney, who were both sorry later but cited St Peter's bad example in the Garden of Gethsemane in extenuation of themselves, had exchanged sharp words and shoves with their persecutors. Mooney and Rooney had also fallen behind in their studies, as had Hrdlicka, owing to the hours they spent in the chapel. The three of them had to be tutored by Joe and Cooney, who were excellent students, and Mooney and Rooney were now keeping up. Things still looked bad for Hrdlicka scholastically—*he*, however, was making great progress spiritually. There were times in the chapel when Hrdlicka appeared to Joe to be out of this world, in a state of mystical ecstasy, reminding Joe of an old picture of St Aloysius with halo, lily, scourge, and upturned eyes.

And then, one evening early in December, Hrdlicka came to Joe's room and said, "I'm thinking of leaving the sem."

"*What!*"

"For the Trappists."

"Oh," said Joe, less gratified than relieved. "That's *different*, Al. That makes sense in your case. Well, well. The Trappists. Pretty quiet about it, weren't you?"

"I didn't know if I'd get a reply when I wrote. That's why I didn't say anything."

Hrdlicka handed Joe the reply from the Trappists, and Joe read it, surprised to see that they had a typewriter. "So now you need a letter of recommendation from the Rector, Al. Told *him* yet?"

"Not yet, Joe. I thought I'd tell you first."

This pleased Joe, as spiritual director of the little band, but, mindful of higher authority, which he knew from his reading was where so many good men had gone wrong, he said, "Better tell the Rector, Al. Tell him right away."

Hrdlicka went off to do this, but he soon returned—so soon that Joe assumed the Rector was out. Then he saw what Hrdlicka had in his hand—the hair shirt.

"Joe, he says I should think it over for two weeks. He'll

give me a letter of recommendation then, if I haven't changed my mind. Says in the meantime I can wear this."

Joe felt the hair shirt, as he hadn't that evening in the Rector's study, first with his fingers, then with the back of his hand, and said, "Whew!"

"Joe, I think the Rector figures I wear it I'll change my mind."

"You won't," said Joe, and he was right.

A few days before Christmas, on a Wednesday afternoon (Wednesday afternoons were "free" at the seminary), Hrdlicka departed for the Trappists with a letter of recommendation from the Rector and also with the hair shirt—a going-away present from the Rector. Joe accompanied him to the railroad station.

Since they were there early, Joe having hailed a cab while they were waiting for a bus, they sat down and talked. Presently, Joe was asking Hrdlicka for the hair shirt! He said there would be God's plenty of such where Hrdlicka was going. Hrdlicka was willing in principle to oblige Joe but not in fact, because he was *wearing* the shirt. (Joe had thought it was in Hrdlicka's suitcase.) Joe agreed that it might be awkward for Hrdlicka as a novice, even before he took the vow of silence, to ask the Trappists to mail the hair shirt to a friend, but neither Joe nor Hrdlicka liked the idea of just giving up. Then "Hey!" cried Joe, and told Hrdlicka his plan. They went to the men's room, into adjoining stalls, where they undressed from the waist up, and Hrdlicka passed the hair shirt over the top of the partition to Joe.

That was how Joe got the hair shirt. The only bad thing—something that made Joe ashamed of himself when he thought of Thomas à Becket—was that he'd succumbed to fastidiousness in the stall, and had emerged from it with the hair shirt in a pocket of his overcoat, and had then deceived the simple Hrdlicka by squirming and saying, "Whew!"

For his penance, Joe had walked back to the seminary, three miles against a north wind, ears freezing all the way, save for a minute or two in a little grocery where he stopped to purchase a box of Rinso.

Wearing the hair shirt was like coming from a really careless barber and being pricked by clippings on a hot summer day, only much worse, and so Joe, being human and not a masochist, was glad when he could take the thing off. This he did at night, hand-washing it in the utility room—too much traffic in the lavatorium—and leaving it to dry on his radiator, over a towel, as he would a woollen sweater.

As a discomforter of the flesh and a strengthener of the spirit, the hair shirt probably did the job, but Joe was still where he'd been before with respect to growth in holiness— still stuck in the first stage of his hoped-for spiritual evolution, in the purgative "way"—and was afraid he'd never enter the contemplative way, not to mention the unitive. The little appetizers of spiritual delight that Joe had read were not infrequently vouchsafed to the beginner—though they were not to be mistaken for the banquet itself, for they would soon be withdrawn—were not vouchsafed to him. He wasn't giving up, though. He was still in there—in the chapel for hours every day, trying, praying.

Mooney and Rooney were also doing hard time in the chapel, but they, unlike Joe and Cooney (who said, however, that wearing a hair shirt was taking an unfair advantage, like wearing brass knuckles), were openly complaining, wanting results—especially Mooney.

"Joe, I'm not getting anywhere."

"Let's go for a walk, Chuck."

During this period of crisis with both Mooney and Rooney wavering, Joe often took one or both of them for a walk around the seminary grounds. When it was really too cold to go for a walk, as it often was those days in January, Joe would say they'd be *better* for it, for the discomfort, and then Mooney, if not Rooney, would go gladly. Mooney could see that mortification was not an end in itself but a means to an end, a smelting process that got rid of what was worst and left what was best in a man, which was something that guys much brighter than Mooney, guys who called the little band "spiritual athletes," just couldn't see, or wouldn't. Unfortunately, in his reading, and he was not a great reader, Mooney had a taste for the flashy—Blessed Angela of Foligno punishing herself by drinking the water in which she had washed the sores of a leper, St Ben Joe Labre retrieving the lice that left him and piously putting them up his sleeve, that sort of thing—a taste that Joe did not share (and hoped he never would, however much he grew in holiness). "Chuck, your eyes are bigger than your stomach," Joe told Mooney, and quoted Pope Pius XI: " 'Sanctity is the chief and most important endowment of the Catholic priest,' Chuck. 'Without it other gifts will not go far; with it, even supposing *other gifts to be meagre* [Joe's italics], the priest can work marvels.' " Joe prescribed more prayer and renunciation for Mooney. "I saw a Baby Ruth wrapper in your wastebasket, Chuck."

In this manner, his words vaporizing in the icy air, Joe spoke to Mooney, and sometimes to Rooney, on their walks around the seminary grounds, stopping here and there to make a point. His favorite place to stop was a spot from which they could view, across the road, a billboard advertisement showing an amiable old clergyman (obviously Protestant, but no matter) sniffing the air as he passed under a windowsill on which a freshly baked pie was cooling. "There you are," Joe would say. "That's how most people see the clergy. And they're *right*."

It seemed to Joe that the billboard, taken with his commentary—he was scathing on the subject of the beery little evenings in the Rector's study—had a steadying effect on the wavering Mooney, but as time went on it was hard to get Mooney to stop at that spot, and impossible when Rooney was along. In any case, the billboard was changed. And Rooney—saying, "I'm sorry"—resigned from the little band.

The next evening, as Joe was about to leave his room for a siege in the chapel, Mooney dropped in.

"Joe, I'm not cut out for this," he said. "I just want to be a good priest and maybe work with the poor."

"Chuck, you can't give what you haven't got—even to the poor."

"Yeah, I know, Joe."

"So there you are, Chuck. And Thomas Aquinas tells us, Chuck, that 'to fulfill the duties of Holy Orders, common goodness does not suffice; but excelling goodness is required; that they who receive Orders and are thereby higher in rank than the people may also be higher in holiness.' "

"May?"

"He means 'must'—you know how cagey he is."

"Yeah. But I'm not getting anywhere, Joe."

"Chuck, *I'm* not getting anywhere. And Cooney—I happen to know he's not getting anywhere. So there you are."

"What d'ya mean, 'So there you are'? Joe, I wish you wouldn't always say that."

"We're all in the same boat, Chuck. That's what I mean."

"Joe, maybe we don't all want to be in the same boat with you. Ever think of that?"

"Rooney, you mean?"

"I mean *me*. I've had it," said Mooney, and turned away. "I'm sorry."

"*I'm* sorry," said Joe, sounding smug, but really hurt.

And so the little band was down to two—if that. The next evening, at a lecture in the auditorium, Joe asked during the question period, "Father, how can we make sanctity as attractive as sex to the common man?" (after all, the speaker had quoted Léon Bloy: "There is but one sorrow—not to be a saint"), and *Cooney*, who was sitting beside Joe, laughed right along with the rest.

Early the next morning Joe was summoned to the Rector's office, where the tobacco clouds were already building up, churning in the winter sunlight, and the Rector, like a nice old grey devil in his element, head smoking, hand smoking, waved Joe to a chair.

"Joe, I understand you have my hair shirt."

Joe weighed the Rector's words before replying, "No, Father."

The Rector smiled. "I'll try again. Joe, I understand you have the hair shirt I gave Mr Hrdlicka."

Joe was weighing the Rector's words when the Rector interrupted. "Yes?"

"Yes, Father."

"Well, Joe, I want it back."

Joe was weighing the demand in the light of his circumstances. "*Now*, Father?"

"You're wearing it, Joe?"

"Yes, Father."

"Tomorrow morning, then. Same time, same place." And the Rector smiled, ending the interview.

Joe rose and left, thinking how well he'd handled himself

and that the Rector had probably expected his ownership of the hair shirt, his right to impound it, to be disputed. This was far from Joe's mind, armed as it was with examples of heroic obedience—the example, say, of St John of the Cross (among mystics one of the all-time greats, perhaps No. 1), who had been jailed by his superiors and fed stinking fish.

That he had been summoned to the Rector's office was widely known, Joe discovered between classes that morning, though he'd told nobody but Cooney, and he'd asked that Cooney keep to himself what happened at the interview. Evidently Cooney did, for the questions that Joe fielded throughout the day, though probing, were uninformed. Whether he'd been called to Rome to defend himself—that sort of thing—and the usual half-serious references to Mani- chaeism, Jansenism, "detachismus," and so on. The hair shirt was mentioned, but not significantly.

As Joe washed it that evening, he speculated on the possibility of keeping the hand-over to the Rector a secret from everybody else (except Cooney), at least until such time as the event would have lost its news value. Wouldn't that— keeping it a secret—be best for all concerned? "Hair shirt? Oh, I no longer wear it, and haven't for some months now. I'm just like you now, Deadass."

The next morning, at the same time, same place, Joe dutifully appeared with the hair shirt (concealed in a plastic bag) and then learned that the Rector had suffered a heart attack in the night and was in the hospital. Saying a prayer for the Rector, Joe returned to his room with the hair shirt and, leaving it in the bag, put it in the bottom drawer of his dresser, where he'd once kept some of his attachments— peanuts, popcorn, candy, cigars, cigarettes—and then he visited the chapel, as was his practice nowadays before going to his first class.

Between classes he read the notice on the bulletin board stating that prayers were requested for the Rector, who, if all went well, would be back at the seminary "soon"—which Joe interpreted to mean weeks. Saying another prayer for the Rector, Joe dashed up to his room, and shortly thereafter dashed down to his next class, itching again, wearing the hair shirt.

Early that evening the news broke—Cooney told Mooney, and Mooney broke it—that the Rector had on the morning of the night he was stricken ordered Joe, under pain of sin, to forswear and deliver up the hair shirt. This was substantially true, but Joe toned it down for his visitors. He had a number of them later that evening after the news broke—the last being Mooney, who had been avoiding Joe ever since he apostatized from the little band.

"Oh, to think that the Rector wanted you to give it back!" Mooney said. "And *now*! Joe, are you wearing it now?"

"For the time being, yes."

"Keep it on, Joe. Don't take it off."

"At night I have to. I have to wash it."

"Joe, I *wouldn't*."

"I would, Chuck."

"But Joe—*for the Rector*!"

Earlier visitors had made it clear to Joe that they were no less wary than before of his hard-core spirituality but now considered him deserving of some sympathy, which Joe had assumed was all anybody had in mind where he and the hair shirt were concerned, when along comes Mooney with this crazy—what if it spread?—this superstitious idea that the Rector's life might depend on Joe's wearing the hair shirt.

"So I *wouldn't*, Joe. Oh, to *think*!"

"Don't," said Joe, silencing Mooney, and went down to the chapel, where, for a change, he was not alone. Evidently Cooney was still suffering from "bursitis of both knees," for he was absent, but there were quite a few others on hand that evening—a dozen or so, among them Rooney and Mooney.

Joe was the last man to leave the chapel that evening, the only one to stay very long. So it seemed that the others had only dropped in to say a few prayers for the Rector, and what Joe had feared, after hearing what he had from Mooney, that clunkhead—that the little holiness movement had revived and was drawing its strength from his not taking off the hair shirt—was not the case, thank God.

Joe washed it that night, as he would have done in any event, and when asked the next morning by Mooney if he'd slept in it said, "No," curtly. And likewise when asked the following morning. The next morning he wasn't asked.

"I hear the Rector's out of danger," Mooney said.

"Thank God," said Joe.

The days passed, and as far as Joe could tell nobody but Mooney, who was now acting as if he hadn't, had ever expected him to wear the hair shirt constantly for the Rector's sake. In fact, the hair shirt wasn't mentioned to Joe these days, even lightly, which was odd. And there was something else odd—easy to detect, hard to define. Joe noticed that certain guys never really looked at him—they looked to one side of him, or over his head, or down, but never in the eye. He went to see Cooney about it.

"Did somebody say something?" Cooney asked.

"No. I wish somebody would."

"Don't let it worry you."

"Then there *is* something!" said Joe. Even his best friend wouldn't look him in the eye!

"Joe, there are those . . ."

"Yes?"

"Who have never *approved* of you for wearing the hair shirt—for reasons you already know. 'Singularity' and so on."

"Yes? Yes?"

"And now there are those—they're the same ones, plus quite a few more—who *dis*approve of you for wearing it. Am I right in thinking you're wearing it now?"

Joe nodded.

"Well, the idea these guys have is that you were ordered not to wear it, and are therefore *in flagrante delicto.*"

"Not so!" said Joe, and gave Cooney a true account of the interview, as he had before, and again spoke of his attempt to comply with the Rector's demand—"request," he said, was probably a better word for it.

"Look, Joe," Cooney said. "As far as I'm concerned, you can go right on wearing the hair shirt, although I still say it's taking an unfair advantage, like wearing brass knuckles. But the idea these guys have—the reason you're *more* unpopular these days, and of course the heart attack, coming when it did, is also a factor in that—is that you're going against the Rector's *intention.*"

Joe thought about *his for a moment. "I see," he said, and went away to think some more.

As it happened, he had to think for three days before he arrived at a firm decision. Then he had to wait for Wednesday afternoon to come, and when it did he took a bus downtown. He was carrying the hair shirt in the plastic bag. At the hospital he found the Rector in a private room, in bed with a paperback.

"Ah, what's this?" the Rector said.

Joe, afraid the Rector was referring to the bag and was under the impression that it contained a gift for him, said, "No, Father," which made sense only in the context of Joe's thoughts. "I was just passing by, Father."

"*Were* you now?" replied the Rector in a marvelling tone, and looked Joe in the eye.

"As a matter of fact, Father, I wasn't."

The Rector smiled, and Joe felt foolish but better.

"Sit down, Joe."

Joe managed to sit down. "How've you been, Father?" Oh, great! "I mean, how *are* you, Father?"

"I'm better, I'm told."

You're greyer, Joe thought, and, the way he'd been going, did well not to say so.

"What's on your mind, Joe?"

Joe looked down at the floor, where he'd put the bag because it called attention to itself in his hands, and then back at the Rector. "Remember, Father, I was supposed to bring you the hair shirt?"

"Now that you mention it, Joe, yes."

"Father, I want you to know I did bring it to your office that morning, but you . . ." Joe felt foolish again.

"I didn't keep the appointment," the Rector said, and smiled.

"Not your fault, Father." As if that needed saying. Joe reached down for the bag and stood up with it. "Father, the hair shirt's inside," he said. "And it's nice and clean. I washed it."

"Not now, Joe. Not here. When I'm back. Soon enough then."

So Joe, about to place the bag on the bed at the Rector's feet, held on to it. He hadn't anticipated this development, but it didn't divert him. "Father, I have to ask you a question," he said, and got a funny look from the Rector. "It's about your intention, as to the hair shirt."

"I thought you should stop wearing it, Joe, or I wouldn't have asked for it. But in the circumstances—you've been wearing it, have you?"

"Yes, Father."

"And you want me to say whether you were right or wrong to do so?"

"Yes, Father."

"Well, I can't, in the circumstances, Joe. You're the one to say. I will say I was worried about you, Joe. That question of yours at the lecture!" The Rector shook his head at the thought of it. "After that, I *had* to ask for the hair shirt. But now I don't know. Things look different to me now, here. And you do, Joe. So I'd say do as you think best about the hair shirt. Wear it, or don't. I trust you. Now I'm tired. You'd better leave."

Joe asked for the Rector's blessing, knelt for it, and left with it, carrying the hair shirt in the plastic bag.

In the following days—the Rector had died that night—- Joe sensed that he was being blamed, as a puppy might be blamed for causing an accident in which it had escaped injury and someone had died, and that more guys than before liked the sight of him less. "When," he imagined them saying, "when will he repent and take off the hair shirt?" For he hadn't said anything to anybody about his visit to the hospital, and would not.

Mooney, one of the few who still spoke to him, asked, "Are you getting anywhere, Joe?"

"Can't say I am, Chuck."

"Still wearing it?"

"Yes."

"But not at night?"

"No."

"That could be why you're not getting anywhere, Joe. Ever think of that?"

"Yes."

Yes, Joe had thought of that—oh, not as a cure, as

Mooney meant, but as a pointer to the nature of his failure. He was, by the standards of saints, too fastidious, he knew— not enough of a slob. Why, for instance, should guys going about the corridors in their bare feet, or in their socks, which was somehow worse—why should this bother him so much? He kept his slippers handy by his bed and wore them or his shoes, preferably his shoes, when he went into the corridors. Yes, that could be his trouble—in a sense, the reason for his failure. Even if he did wear the hair shirt day and night—and he could—what about his feeling for others, his fellow men, who, next to God, should be his first concern? The seminary was a community, and a tight little one at that, and just wasn't the place for all-out mysticism, for growth in holiness beyond a certain point—a low point by the standards of saints. No place he'd ever be, no parish, would be the place for that. And just this, for him, knowing what he did about the life of the spirit (not much but something) and not being able to give himself to it—wouldn't that be a hair shirt of sorts? The Rector could have been wearing that kind for years day *and* night—probably all old priests did—and Joe, in feeling its prickliness already, before he was even ordained, was ahead of his time, he thought. Maybe it had been foolish to hope that he could go all the way, could get in touch with God directly, to think that he could bypass humanity, but he wasn't giving up yet. No, he would continue to wear the hair shirt (unless asked not to by the new Rector, whoever he might be), would wear it during the day and wash it at night, until it wore out. If, by then, he was still not getting anywhere, he would simply make do with the hair shirt that so many were wearing.

5
Ordained

Joe had been in the congregation the last time a new priest celebrated his first Mass in the parish church. That was some years back, but there hadn't been a change of pastors. So Joe—and doubtless Toohey—knew what to expect when they reported to the rectory that Saturday night, to hear Father Stock's arrangements for the next morning.

"Now, you, Michael"—Toohey—"will have the ten o'clock, and you, Joseph, the eleven. And as is the custom here"—and, to Joe's knowledge, nowhere else in the diocese—"a special collection will be taken up by the new priest, or priests. What I mean is, since you'll serve each other's Mass and are both priests—don't worry, I'll make that clear to the congregation—server will help celebrant take up the special collection. That way, we'll save time. Any questions?"

Just one, Joe thought, Why?

"No questions. Good. Now, right after the regular collection (to be taken up by the ushers, of course), the two of you'll come down from the altar. The communion rail gate will be open, an usher waiting for you there with the baskets. Celebrant takes one, server the other. Celebrant does one side of the middle aisle, server the other. Now you're at the back of the church—go over to the side aisles, celebrant to one, server to the other. Remember, the two middle sections are wide and you've only done *half* of these—you still have the other half to do from the side aisles. (I've known ushers to forget this.) But don't start at the back of the church, don't come up behind people. Go to the front of the church and work back as before, so people can see you coming. The same when you do the side sections—go to the front and work back. When you've done those sections, come up the middle aisle *together*. Leave the baskets at the communion rail, on the other side, the altar side. Don't worry, someone'll come out of the sacristy and take the baskets away before Communion. Well, that's about all. Any questions?''

''Just one. Why?''

''*Why*, Joseph? Why *what*?''

''Why should *we* take up the collection?'' Joe looked to Toohey—foolishly, he saw—for support.

'' 'We'?'' said Father Stock. ''Does Joseph speak for you, Michael?''

''No,'' Joe said, dissociating himself from Toohey before Toohey did it for him. ''I don't speak for myself, either. I speak for the Church.'' *Wham!*

From the walls of Father Stock's office, the photographs—mostly group pictures of clergy at class reunions and annual retreats, but a few individuals, bishops and popes—watched and waited, as Joe did, to see what would happen next.

Toohey stood up. ''I'll run along, Father, if that's all.''

Father Stock nodded. ''Be in the sacristy early tomorrow, Michael. Good night.''

So Toohey, who was being sent to Rome for further study, which could mean he'd be a bishop someday, left, and Joe, who was being sent to a parish as a curate, which could mean he'd be a pastor someday, sat tight.

Father Stock answered the phone—"Eight-nine-ten-eleven-it's-in-the-parish-bulletin"—and hung up. "All right, Joseph. I'm listening. Speak for the Church."

"Maybe I shouldn't have said that, Father. But for us to take up the collection is to cheapen the Mass and the priesthood, I say."

"I wouldn't say that."

"Well, I would, and I don't think I'm alone." The clergy on the walls, even the bishops and popes who'd frowned when Joe spoke for the Church, were now all for him, especially the dead ones. "Father, won't it look like we're cashing in on the occasion? Or that *you* are?" *Wham!*

"I'll make it clear that you aren't."

Joe had to like the man for that. Even vice, it seemed, in this case greed, could bring out the good in people. But the man was still wrong. "Father, maybe I shouldn't ask this, but what do you—what does the *parish*, I mean—stand to gain? Three hundred dollars? Four hundred? Five?"

Father Stock seemed to think it a fair question, no more than one priest might ask another, and replied with unconcealed regret, "Not five."

Joe was reluctant to go on, to say what he had in mind, afraid the man would be stung by it and sting back, which was how Joe himself might respond to what he had in mind—which, though, was well calculated to free the man's will (temporarily) from its long enslavement to merely monetary considerations, enabling him not only to do the right thing but to profit by it. *How often, here below, did such an opportunity arise?* "Father, I have some money from my folks to buy a car—I'll need one now that I'm ordained—but I don't care what I drive. So what would you say—what would the *parish*, I mean, say—to five hundred?"

Father Stock said, gravely, "The parish is always happy to

accept an offering made in good faith, without qualifications. Be in the sacristy early tomorrow, Joseph. Good night."

Joe was in the sacristy early the next morning, before Toohey, and put away the vestments for Father Stock's assistant, who'd had the nine o'clock and who, on leaving the sacristy, said, "Don't take any wooden nickels." But Joe looked on the bright side and hoped that his proposal—his exalted but not exaggerated regard for the Mass and the priesthood—had disturbed Father Stock's sleep, had perhaps so disgusted the man with himself that he'd decided to call off the special collections, or, if not, to employ the ushers. It even occurred to Joe, when Father Stock and Toohey entered the sacristy together, that Toohey had already been told the good news (that the special collections were off, at least as far as the new priests were concerned), and that the situation, though it could perhaps no longer be improved by an offering from Joe, was still intended to teach him a lesson in faith and hope, in both of which he'd been found wanting, as he would in charity too unless he acted blindly, swiftly, before it could be construed as payola.

"My offering, Father. It's made in good faith, I hope, but anyway without qualifications."

Father Stock accepted the unsealed envelope with a nod, but didn't peek inside or pull out the check, jump up and down, and yell "Yea!"—just put it aside, on the counter of the many-drawered cabinet in which vestments were kept flat, and got busy with the water and wine cruets, topping them up.

Joe—he'd expected something more reassuring than a nod—slipped into his surplice and cassock. He'd brought his own, rather than take a chance on what the sacristy might stock in his size, Men's 36 short, and maybe wind up in snotty, not to say boogery, altar boys' issue. And before Father Stock, now lighting candles on the altar, returned to the sacristy, Joe asked Toohey, "Did the man say anything about the special collections?"

"Grow up," said Toohey, the fink.

Father Stock returned to the sacristy, checked his pocket watch, and gave the word. "Now."

Server left the sacristy, ringing the bell in the pierced brass globe by the door (but not pulling it down), and led celebrant to the altar, *"Introibo ad altare dei,"* and so the ten o'clock began.

Celebrant, like server, had practiced saying Mass in the chapel at the sem, but celebrant, unlike server, was a born master-of-ceremonies type, his command of rubrics daunting in the classroom, likewise his quarterbacking, his finger-snapping at rites in the chapel, and so celebrant was in his element.

When it was time for the sermon, celebrant and server settled down on the sedilia, while preacher (Father Stock) came out of the sacristy and climbed into the pulpit. He read the announcements, the last one to the effect that both celebrant and server were newly ordained priests and former members of the parish—nothing about special collections. The sermon, though predictable (happy the parish that gives God and the Church two new priests in a single year, their high calling a difficult one in times like these), was, like the announcements, suspenseful, but like them, in the end, gratifying—nothing about special collections.

The Mass resumed, with celebrant still doing fine, with server, though, distracted by the sounds of the regular collection, never having heard those sounds—the scrape and shuffle of ushers' shoes, the rustle and clink of dough—so clearly before.

After the ushers retired, there was silence in the body of the church—gratifying to server. Father Stock had returned to the sacristy after the sermon, but he was one of those pastors who, when not conducting services themselves, are all over the place, opening and closing windows, shooing standees into pews, checking the front steps for smokers during the sermon, and evidently he'd left the sacristy by the outside door, gone around to the front of the church, and reentered it there, for server could hear him making a disturbance, crying, "The new priests will now take up a special collection. I've asked them to do this. So be generous, good people," whereupon server turned away from the altar (but so that it was hardly noticeable that he had) in an easy, flowing movement, and saw an usher with two baskets moving up the middle aisle, and heard celebrant, now alongside him, facing the other way (server was facing the altar), whisper to him, "Let's go, buster."

So, coming to the usher, celebrant took one basket, server the other. While celebrant went down one side of the middle aisle, doing it, stopping and starting, server went nonstop down the other side—he hadn't planned this, or this— holding a hand to his mouth as if sick and about to be sicker, and kept going ("Now you're at the back of the church"), an usher relieving him of the basket and pushing the inner door open for him, into the vestibule.

He ran down the stairs there, shoved the fire door open, and was in the dark tunnel that led to the school, the tiles amplifying and multiplying the sound of his passage so that he didn't know until he stopped to open the door at the other end, and the lights came on, that he was not alone.

"*Joseph!*"

He kept going, the fire door taking its time closing behind him, now in a corridor lit only by night lights, and with a number of doors to choose from, he chose BOYS, rather than the obvious but daring alternative, and in darkness ducked into the nearest stall, bolted the door, and in the act of stepping up on the toilet, an old-style institutional high one, was nearly thrown by the skirt of his cassock, hiked it up, stood and then crouched down on the seat.

Footsteps in the corridor, coming in, lights going on.

"Joseph?"

Silence.

"Joseph!"

Silence.

"Joseph, I know you're in there."

Silence.

"Joseph, you should be ashamed of yourself."

Silence.

Footsteps going away, lights left on.

He wanted to come out, the sooner the better, but not too soon. When he did come out, all the way out, into the corridor, he was expecting to meet the man there, but did not; in the vestibule then, but did not. Rather than call attention to himself and, possibly, distract the congregation further, he went out the front door and around to the sacristy, certainly expecting to meet the man there, but did not. Probably, in view of where and how server had last been seen, it was a pleasant surprise to the congregation when he came out of the sacristy and took up his duties again.

Joe had expected—and wanted—to meet the man in the sacristy after Mass, but did not. "What happened after I left?" he asked Toohey. "Have to do it all yourself, or what?" But Toohey gave Joe the silent treatment, and moved away when Joe tried to assist him in unvesting. So Joe, minding his own business, made the change from server to celebrant—

could have used a little help with the alb and cincture. By that time, Toohey had left the sacristy in his new—too new—black suit for the church lawn, where he would be giving his blessing to those near and dear to him (and to those who made a point of collecting the blessings of new priests), and where Father Stock would be playing the part of the popular pastor he wasn't, when he should have been in the sacristy clarifying the situation for Joe, or Joe for him.

What *was* the situation now? Had the man, after what had happened at the ten, changed his mind? Was loath, though, to admit it, being a pastor? And hence his absence? Or did the envelope (it was still there on the counter) mean something—that the situation was unchanged? The same again at the eleven? If so, now was the time to have it out with the man. Look, Father, better call off the special collection at my Mass, or let the ushers handle it. Otherwise I'm not going on. *Wham!* Now, now, Joseph. Now, now yourself, Father. Though small for my age, I'm a big boy now, a priest, no less. If you want to take this to the Chancery, Father—well, I wish you would. Actually, *I'm* the one who should. *Wham!* Whether I will or not, depends on what happens at the eleven. I'll wait and see how it goes. O.K., Father? [Toohey returned to the sacristy and selected a surplice and cassock from the stock there—no problem, he was average.] Comparisons are invidious, I know, Joseph, but look at Michael, here, *he's* not complaining. Michael's a fink, Father. Michael sucks, Father. And what about . . . No, say nothing about the offering—it spoke for itself. And nothing about the man's breach of faith—too vague, that, but not the man's obduracy and greed. No, say nothing about them—they spoke for themselves. But have it out with the man, clarify the situation, while there was still time. Yes, but *how*? Where the hell was the man?

Toohey, standing by the doorway to the sanctuary, suddenly moved out into it, ringing the bell, but Joe, while dialoguing with the man, had also been keeping an eye on the fink, and wasn't left at the post. And so the eleven began.

Celebrant read the right prayers, made the right moves, but fortunately for him and the congregation (and for celebrants and congregations everywhere) the efficacy of the Mass depends on a gift of God as irreducible as it is unreturnable, and not on the mental state of the celebrant, who, in the case of this one, deficient, distracted, was like a man drifting down a river in a boat without oars, blind to the scenery along the shore, hearing the roar of the cataract ahead.

When it was time for the sermon, celebrant and server settled down on the sedilia, while preacher came out of the sacristy and climbed into the pulpit. He read the announcements, he preached, he returned to the sacristy—all as before.

Celebrant returned to the altar and soon heard, as before, the sounds of the regular collection. After the ushers retired (the dangerous time), there was silence in the body of the church—gratifying to celebrant. Celebrant then heard, of all people, *server* addressing the congregation: "Father and I, both of us newly ordained and from this parish, will now take up a special collection. The pastor has asked us to do this. So be generous, good people," whereupon celebrant turned away from the altar in despair, saw an usher with two baskets moving up the middle aisle, saw server open the gates in the communion rail and then stand there waiting for celebrant.

Who, coming to the usher, took the basket from him (server having already taken the other) and did one side of the middle aisle (Hi, Mom; hi, Dad) while server did the other. Returning to the front of the church by the side aisles, celebrant by one, server by the other, not forgetting that they'd done only half of the wide middle sections, they worked back as before so people could see them. And likewise they did the side sections, front to back after which they came up the middle aisle *together*, left the baskets at the communion rail, on the altar side, making it easier for someone (at this Mass, Father Stock's assistant) to come out of the sacristy and take them away, and harder for someone in the congregation to run up and grab them. Then the Mass resumed.

After Mass, in the sacristy, nothing, just nothing, celebrant's silence saying, "You win, I lose, you fink," server's saying, "Did my duty and, thanks to me, you did yours, buster," server leaving first, celebrant about to leave—people were waiting for him and his blessing on the church lawn—when he reached out and reclaimed (it was still there) the envelope. Oh, that he hadn't! For the envelope, like his offering now, was empty. And to stoop further, instead of wadding up the envelope and throwing it on the floor, he put it back on the counter, just so.

6

Out in the World

Joe was generally avoided during his last years at the seminary—sometimes referred to as a gadfly, which he didn't mind, sometimes as a pain in the ass, which he did. His unpopularity was flattering in a way—in the light of "If the world hate you, know ye that it hath hated me before you," but that was pushing it in Joe's case. Besides, too many freaks and losers took comfort in Scripture, and Joe didn't see himself as either. Coming from a family more than just well-to-do, and unlike most of his classmates (but like St Augustine) having lived some before entering the sem, he couldn't be looked down on, nor could his views be gainsaid on the ground that it was a species of pride for him to cite Doctors of the Church in support of them, though this was often tried by his critics. "Pride?" he'd replied. (He'd *replied* a lot at the seminary.) "I'd cite you guys if you ever said anything worth citing." That was his style.

It wasn't so much his all-around unpopularity as something said to him in the confessional ("We have to watch ourselves. A holier-than-thou attitude toward others doesn't become us in the sight of God") that made Joe decide, about a month before ordination, to show more charity toward others. Maybe there hadn't been time enough for others to notice the change in him, though, for he was still generally avoided.

About a month after ordination, at the class's first little get-together, to which he *had* to be invited (he did see it like that) and which was held in a private room in a restaurant, Joe watched himself (that is, shut up) and listened to the clerical shoptalk. He enjoyed it, too, though not as much as some of the others at the big table for twelve. Mooney and Rooney gloried in it. But it went on too long, and thinking, Oh-oh, here I go again, Joe said, "W. G. Ward. That name mean anything to you guys? No? Well, Ward, and *not* Newman, was the first convert from the Oxford Movement. He says any priest without personal knowledge of Christ, *which knowledge can only come from contemplation*"—Joe had supplied and stressed that part to make his point better— "ought to seek out some desolate island so as to live alone and do no harm."

"Words," said Cooney, these days cultivating a worldlier-than-thou attitude. "Hard words, Joe."

"No harder than those of Our Lord to Martha," Joe replied.

"But *you're* not Our Lord!" cried a couple of deep thinkers at the table. Joe ignored them. He quoted from Luke 10, where Martha complains that she has her hands full serving Our Lord and the Disciples and could use some help from Mary, who sits listening to the conversation, and Our Lord replies, "Mary hath chosen the best part."

"Try telling that to the Chancery," said Rooney, who had earlier been complaining or bragging about having to do all the work in the parish where he was the assistant.

"Contemplation's all very well," said Mooney. "Some of the saints, I know, went in for it. But it's still an extra. We have to make a distinction, Joe, between following the counsels of perfection and doing the job—and a mighty big job it is— we've been ordained to do. How many of us can do both?"

"That so-called distinction is the biggest out in all theology," Joe replied. "Why *not* do both? At least *try*."

"You're doing both at Holy Faith?" said Rooney.

Cooney cut in, "According to Lefty Beeman" (a problem priest, always on the move; formerly at Holy Faith, he was now a curate at St Isidore's with Cooney), "the assistant at Holy Faith does the job, the pastor does the contemplating."

Joe replied, "Well, of course, I haven't been there as long as Beeman was. How long was he there? Six months?" This was not only cruel but wasted, and Joe, regretting it, shut up and listened to the others discuss the situation at Holy Faith.

"Two oddballs in one parish."

"Certainly an odd appointment."

"Crazy."

"Not fair to Joe—as a new man, I mean."

"Not fair to the pastor, you mean."

"Not fair to the *parishioners*."

"The Archbishop's slipping."

His appointment to Holy Faith, as assistant to Father Van Slaag, the only known contemplative in the diocese (among pastors), was not crazy, Joe believed. No, the Chancery must have heard of his hard times at the seminary, where he'd been the only known contemplative—he didn't really qualify as such, he knew, unless maybe by desire, but he did have that reputation—and the Archbishop must have decided to make it two of a kind at Holy Faith. It was an odd appointment, perhaps, but it appeared odder than it was to those who recalled the efforts of the old Archbishop to strike a balance in parishes by pairing athletes with aesthetes, scholars with dunces, fat kine with lean. The new Archbishop was said to believe that his priests had enough to do without working out on each other; not that it was his policy to accommodate *everybody*—poker players, hi-fiers, photogra-phers, astronomers, activists, liturgists—and not that some of his appointments didn't smack of old-fashioned therapy: a lush in the suburbs who'd lost his driver's license could find himself walking the corridors of a five-hundred-bed hospital in the city as a chaplain under the thumb of nuns; a big spender could find himself operating under the buddy or commissar system, with an assistant empowered to act for him and the parish in all money matters over two dollars and fifty cents.

Joe believed that his appointment, in a similar way—not, of course, in the same way—showed special concern on the part of the Archbishop, by whose wisdom and grace both pastor and assistant at Holy Faith were spared that heckling suspicion that is the lot of contemplatives, and even more of would-be contemplatives, in the modern world. With no need to apologize or explain, as each would have had to do with almost any other priest in the diocese, they could get on with or, in Joe's case, down to the job of working and praying for their personal sanctification and salvation (and their parishioners'). And that was what they were doing, though not everything was perfect at Holy Faith.

There was the problem of the housekeeper, Mrs Cox, a plump tough-talking TV fan, who called Father Van Slaag Van to his face and Slug to her friends on the phone. (And Joe was pretty sure he was the one she referred to as Shorty.) There was the problem of Mrs Cox's dog, Boots, a female bull terrier that would go for your ankles unless you carried a weapon. ("She's all right," the housekeeper would say with a hearty laugh. "She just hates men.") Joe had found a cane in the umbrella stand and took it with him whenever he left his bedroom.

There was also the problem of Father Van Slaag. Joe, for his part, had hoped to spend most of his free time in the church, in the presence of the Blessed Sacrament, but Father Van Slaag was already doing this—the man practically lived in the church. Pastor and assistant at first were absent from the rectory for long periods, until Joe asked himself, "Shepherd, what of the sheep?" This question, which could have come from Satan (who would doubtless employ any means to get a priest off his knees and out of a church) or from the Archbishop, was resolved for Joe after he discovered that he couldn't concentrate, let alone contemplate, when Father Van Slaag was in the church, as he was whenever Joe went there. Not wanting to ask when his free time was, or when Father Van Slaag's wasn't, Joe moved an old prie-dieu, which had been serving as a plant stand, into his bedroom. He now carried on from there with his spiritual exercises, and also—not the least of his duties—answered the phone there, more often than not while kneeling at the prie-dieu.

So, though not in the church much, Joe was on his knees a lot. When he discovered the state of his knees, however, which were only lightly callused (nothing like those he'd once seen on a visiting Trappist monk in the showers at the seminary—horny grey growths like the chestnuts on the legs of a horse), Joe felt he had a long way to go. The question was whether a diocesan priest—not the really rare one, like Father Van Slaag, but the merely unusual one, like Joe—with his ministry in and to the world, which would rub off on him, could ever go very far; whether in time, after constant, close association with parishioners and coming under their subtle influence, he wouldn't cease to be spiritually, perhaps even mentally, an adult. What was true in other fields of human endeavor at the highest level, in the arts and sciences and sports—namely, that success involves a hell of a lot of slogging—just had to be true, Joe believed, in the field of spirituality: not a crowded field but the trickiest of all to get anywhere in. The notion, so popular nowadays, that the best kind of spirituality just happens and is the by-product of routine apostolic activity, or, as some of Joe's critics at the seminary had claimed, is actually the same thing—well, Joe hadn't believed it then and didn't now.

"The priest's life," Joe said at the class's next little get-together, to which he'd received what had seemed to him a last-minute invitation, "*any* priest's life, *anybody's* life, in order to be fruitful in this world, to say nothing of the next, has to be rooted in contemplation. This is especially true of *our* life, which otherwise becomes one of sheer activity—the occupational disease of the diocesan clergy."

"Look," Rooney said. "I don't want to listen to that stuff tonight. I'm here to relax. You guys don't know what it's like to run a four-hundred-family parish all by yourself."

"That so?" replied Joe. "Happens to be what I'm doing at Holy Faith."

"Another parish heard from," said Cooney.

"Bob," Mooney said to Rooney, "we all have our crosses to bear."

"I *still* don't want to listen to that stuff tonight," Rooney said. "I had a tough day." So Joe shut up, and the clerical shoptalk, which he'd only cut into because it had gone on too long, continued.

At the very end, when Joe was leaving the restaurant for the parking lot, he was approached by Rooney. "Sorry, Joe," Rooney said. "But I had a tough one today."

"Bob, I know what you mean."

They went out to their cars together.

In the weeks that followed, Joe and Bob saw more of each other than they ever had before, except for that short time at the seminary when Bob had embraced the contemplative life.

Joe hoped that Bob was having second thoughts about the active life, that it wasn't only their plight as overworked assistants that had drawn them together again, but in any case he had a friend in Bob. They knew each other's phone number by heart, and frequently met in the course of their duties—Bob pausing at Holy Faith on his way home from downtown, Joe at St John Bosco's, Bob's parish, after visiting the hospital nearby.

St John Bosco's, unlike Holy Faith, was a new plant, with paid secretaries, the latest in equipment, and programs and organizations galore, many overlapping. The parish was too much for one man—even for him, Bob said, unless he was there every minute, which he couldn't be. The pastor, Monsignor McConkie, or Mac, as Bob called him, a handsome silver-haired glad-hander, who had long ago joined everything joinable and now acknowledged when he got up in the morning, if he did, that he was in too deep and had a serious drinking problem, expected Bob to "represent" him and the parish at functions that Mac was under both doctor's and confessor's orders to stay away from. The worst ones—worst because there was no end to them—were service-club luncheons at downtown hotels. Bob attended three or four of these a week, and it was usually after one of them, in the middle of the afternoon, in high spirits or low, that he paused at Holy Faith.

Joe, usually in the office at that time of day—he'd moved the old prie-dieu down there—would make a drink for the visitor, as was the practice at St John Bosco's, and they'd discuss what was uppermost in their minds: Boots, if she'd gone for Bob on the way in; Mrs Cox, if the TV in the living room was coming through well; or problems of universal concern. One of these was church finance, a subject that Bob had ideas about and that Joe, though he'd scorned it and clerical bookkeeping at the seminary, now felt he should interest himself in. To judge by some correspondence from the Chancery in the files, nobody else at Holy Faith had done so in recent times. What could be said of the take at Holy Faith—not enough—could also be said of organizations: only two, the Holy Name Society (men) and the Christian Mothers (their wives). Reluctantly, Joe would agree that something should be done about Youth or, anyway, about Young People and Young Marrieds—Bob had ideas about all these—but then Joe would renege and say he didn't want to bite off more than he could chew: a veiled reference to the situation at St John Bosco's.

"Heaven forbid!" Bob said. "Still, we're in the same boat, Joe."

That they were in the same boat (a commonplace in their discussions) and that Bob was having a rougher ride Joe would accept, but he couldn't agree that there was so little to choose between those responsible for their plights—between, if you didn't count the Archbishop, a mystic and a drunk—as to make no difference. One afternoon, Joe told Bob that it was the Father Van Slaags, oddly enough, and not the Monsignor McConkies, who kept the world going, who, by their feats of prayer and abnegation, stayed the hand of God. This, though he didn't like to hear it—noncontemplatives never did—Bob knew to be the accepted and time-honored belief of the Church.

Joe would have made his point even better had he spoken of what he'd seen the night before, when he'd gone to Father Van Slaag's room to complain about Boots and Mrs Cox's TV, only to change his mind and ask permission to order Sunday-collection envelopes from another supplier, and then to retire to think, as he'd been doing ever since, on what he'd seen through the gaps in the old, almost buttonless cassock that Father Van Slaag wore for a nightshirt—the horny grey growths on the knees, the dogtooth wounds on the ankles. Dear God! What Joe had wondered about ever since coming to Holy Faith was clear to him then: why Father Van Slaag did nothing about Mrs Cox's dog and TV. He was using them, these crosses, as a means to sanctification and salvation—making life make sense, which it otherwise wouldn't. Out of prudence, and out of reverence for Father Van Slaag, Joe didn't tell Bob or anyone else what he'd seen that night, but thereafter, whenever Bob said that their pastors ought to be put away—Mac in a sanitarium, Van in a cloister or cave—Joe was silent, brooding on those ankles and knees in awe and humility. He had decided that Father Van Slaag was—and not just in the sense that the word applied to anybody in the state of grace but in the sense that it applied to the big-time mystics and martyrs—a saint.

Before that night in Father Van Slaag's room, Joe had tried to do the job he'd been ordained to do for God and humanity while also trying, for the sake of the former, to preserve himself to a degree from the latter, but afterward there was a change in him. Without exactly going ape, Joe let down the barrier and no longer distinguished as he had before, sharply, between the religious and the social demands of parishioners. Mrs Cox noticed it. "What?" she'd say. "Stepping out again?"

In this change in him there was a certain despair, a giving up on himself and the contemplative life. Why not? When he tried to look down as God must and saw one man fending off Boots with a cane, the other allowing himself to be savaged by her, amortizing the world's great debt of sin a little, deferring foreclosure—really, there was no comparison. In that kind of company, Joe just didn't figure. Still, you never knew where you were in the spiritual life; that was the hell of it—only God knew. Joe's hope had to be that he was, without knowing it, a sleeper. He thought of Cardinal Merry del Val, who, as Pius X's secretary of state, was another overworked assistant to a saint, and perhaps one himself; among his personal effects, after his death, had been discovered (a shock to his friends in high places and low, these instruments of penance) two barbed-wire undershirts and a scourge with dried blood on it. But that sort of thing, though still nice to know—edifying—was discouraging if dwelt on, intimidating, like Father Van Slaag's ankles and knees. Joe took more comfort in Scripture—in "Whosoever shall seek to save his life, shall lose it," in "Greater love than this no man hath, that a man lay down his life for his friends," though this, too, was pushing it in his case. The truth was, *he* hadn't sacrificed his spiritual life—it had been done for him, by his appointment to Holy Faith. All he'd done since then, and might deserve credit for, was to stop grudging the time spent in doing the routine work of the parish, the time he might have spent in prayer. The old prie-dieu, which he'd been carrying back up to his bedroom one morning when the office phone rang, was still where he'd left it then, on the stair landing where he'd first found it, and since Mrs Cox had come along before he could get back to it, it was serving as a plant stand again. He didn't mind. Though praying a lot less these days, he prayed harder when he did (as recommended by Merry del Val), and though working harder and seeing more people, he had more appetite for them. The truth was, he'd always had a weakness for people, a weakness suppressed at the seminary but now indulged and transformed into a strength, a virtue.

He was good with people when he wished to be, as he did now. He sparkled in maternity wards ("Bring us another round of orange juice, Sister, and this time put something in it"); sparkled at parish meetings, of which there were more since he'd decided to come to grips with Youth, Young People, and Young Marrieds ("What are we waiting for? I'm here"); sparkled at home ("My compliments to the chef, Mrs Cox"). Occasionally, he even sat with Mrs Cox in the evening if there was a game of some kind on TV; at first he had to get her to switch channels and to instruct her, but now he had to do neither, and it was gratifying to see her interest in sports quicken and to know it was genuine (with so many women it wasn't)—to come in from a meeting and find her and Boots watching the NBA playoffs. With Boots, however, Joe was still persona non grata, and still went about the house with his cane, which he left on the back porch when he stepped out and picked up when he returned.

But the best times for Joe were those times when he could be of real use to people as a priest—those times of trial, tragedy, and ordinary death—into which he entered deeper than he had before. "After years of trying to walk on the water, you know," he told Bob, who was increasingly impatient with parishioners (and Mac), "it's good to come ashore and feel the warm sand between my toes."

This was not to say that Joe couldn't get enough of people. He could. And when he did, after a tough day, or when he just craved faster company, he went to play poker with Cooney and the gang at St Isidore's, a hard-drinking rectory, and the next morning it wasn't easy for him to get going. (He did not believe in Beeman's solution: "Weak drinks, more of 'em—that way you get more liquids into your system.") All in all, though, he felt better about himself both as a priest and as a person, as others appeared to these days—certainly Mrs Cox, and even Cooney, who was becoming his best friend again.

"Joe," Cooney said one night at St Isidore's, "know who you are?"

"Who?"

"Lemme put it another way. Know who Van is?"

"Who?"

"Mary. You're Martha, Joe."

Only now and then, late at night before he got to sleep, or early in the morning before he got going, did Joe look back and regret the change in himself.

A tough day. Coming to breakfast, talking to himself, Joe had simply said, "Somebody ought to poison that bitch," meaning Boots, and now Mrs Cox wouldn't speak to him. Later that morning, while trying to sparkle in a maternity ward, he'd simply said, "So *that's* the little bastard," and had been asked to leave by its mother. That afternoon, he had a visit from a young lady in real estate whom he'd just about enticed into fleeing the world and joining the Carmelites, and learned that she'd received a big promotion and would be staying in the world after all. Early that evening, two converts in the making, Tex and Candy, who'd been taking instructions with a view to marrying Margie and Mike, failed to show, and it developed after a couple of phone calls that they'd eloped together. While Joe was working this out for Margie and Mike in the office, on hold in the living room he had an old parishioner who was upset over a nine-dollar error in his account—under Joe's new system, actually Bob's, receipts were mailed out to contributors at the end of the fiscal year—and who, though Joe tried everything, even offering to reimburse the old devil on the spot, wouldn't go away until he'd seen the pastor.

"He's in the church," Joe said, and fled.

Later, Joe went over to St Isidore's for poker, and it

turned out to be a tough night, too. He was there to relax, but the others wouldn't let him. Bob, who had just come from driving Mac to the sanitarium (and felt a little sad about it, though it was all for the best), kept after Joe to talk to Van about checking in to a cloister. Beeman, not for the first time, advised Joe just to look Boots in the eye, which was what he'd always done at Holy Faith. "And don't let her see you're afraid of her," he said, and suggested (though he admitted he had only heard about this, hadn't done it himself), "Chuck her lightly under the jaw. Try it." When Joe mentioned the nine-dollar bookkeeping error, Beeman advised him in future just to say, "We all make mistakes. That's why they put erasers on lead pencils," which was what he always did in such a case. "Try it." When Joe mentioned the young lady who'd received a big promotion and let him down, Bob said, "Hell, you can't blame her," and then, presumably referring to his two weeks as a contemplative, had the nerve to misquote Joe without attribution, "It's kind of lonely out there, dangerous too, trying to walk on the water, and it's good to come in and feel the warm sand under your feet." Joe was grateful for Cooney's comment, "Bob, you never went out without your water wings," but a moment later he applied it to himself, with remorse. And Cooney, perhaps sensing this, tried to do his "Know who you are?" business with Joe again, but Joe foiled him by answering right away, "Martha." Then Cooney's pastor, one of the few really good poker players in the diocese and MC of its weekly TV program, said to Joe, "Found y'self, baby," and asked him if he'd ever considered how much he owed the Arch for sending him to Father Van Slaag at Holy Faith. Joe said he had, but unfortunately didn't leave it at that.

"Just one thing wrong with Van," he said. "Not doing his job." Joe had never said this, or anything like it, before, and immediately regretted it. Only the truth, yes, and they all knew it, but from him a betrayal.

From that point on, Joe, who hadn't taken a pot, won steadily. Later, much later, after a lot of standing around, though Joe himself was sitting down, and a lot of talk about cars and driving, Joe left St Isidore's with Bob, he thought, and the next thing he knew, not counting a bad dream—"Mrs Boots, come and get Cox!"—he was in bed and it was morning. He couldn't remember how the night had ended, and didn't want to, but had the presence of mind not to phone the police after he looked out the window and saw his car was missing from its usual place in the driveway. He took a hot bath, and in the course of it, soaping himself, he discovered and examined the marks on his right ankle—superficial wounds, five in number. They made him think of Our Lord but otherwise didn't hurt. He painted them with antiseptic, dressed, and went downstairs, armed only with a ruler (his cane was on the back porch), and got going again.

7
Carrying
On

The end of another day, another month, another year, the afternoon of New Year's Eve, and the rest of the staff at Archdiocesan Charities had left early, or so Joe had thought until Mrs Hope looked in on him.

"A young priest to see you, Father."

Joe was glad to see a young priest dressed like a priest.

"Ed Butler, Father."

The name meant nothing to Joe, but for the young man's sake he said, "Oh, yes. Sit down."

"It's not about Charities, Father."

"Good."

"Father, I'm here to ask your advice."

"Don't."

"Don't?"

"That's it—my advice."

Father Butler frowned, disapproving of such levity or taking it seriously, in either case proving that he was, though properly dressed, of his generation. "Then I'm afraid it's too late, Father."

"Yes, well, it usually is."

Father Butler frowned. "The pastor's retiring, you know."

Joe nodded, hoping the pastor's identity would soon be made known to him.

"I got the idea"—the young man seemed to regret the

idea—"of collecting a purse for him. The opposition—Father, you wouldn't believe it—from the people."

Thus the pastor's identity was, almost certainly, made known to Joe. "I'd believe it," he said.

Father Butler frowned. "Reason I came to you, Father, you're from the parish, the pastor says."

"Hold it. Is *he* in on this?"

Father Butler blushed. "Oh no, Father."

"Didn't put you up to it?"

"Oh no, Father."

"But knows about the purse?"

"Father, that's what makes it so bad—so *sad*."

Yes and no, Joe thought. "Seen Toohey yet? *He's* from the parish, you know."

"Just talked to him at the Chancery, Father. Form a committee was his advice. Only I already tried that. Nobody'd be on it."

"Hah. What'd Catfish say to that?"

"Beg your pardon?"

"What'd Toohey say when you told him that?"

"I didn't tell him that, Father."

"Should've, Father. You had him and you let him get away. He give you anything—except advice?"

Father Butler blushed. "That's all I went to him for, Father. That's all I'm here for, believe me."

Joe did. "O.K. The advice here is forget the whole thing. This could be one of those odd times when the voice of the people really is the voice of God. They still call him Dollar Bill?"

"They may."

"They do, you mean."

"Father, if you'd been the pastor there as long as he has—thirty-six years—and this happened to you . . ."

"I can think of worse things."

"Maybe you have to be in parish work to see what I mean."

Joe sniffed, resenting the young man's proud humble attitude—it was typical of men in parish work and had once been his own. "I was in it for a while, Father—not long, only five years. How long you been in it?"

Father Butler frowned. "Seven months and thirteen days," he said solemnly—then had to laugh at himself.

Joe liked him for that. "Doing hard time, Father?"

Father Butler smiled and got up. "It's been nice meeting you, Father."

"No, it hasn't, and I'm sorry about that."

Joe walked the young man to the elevator and pushed the down button for him. "Seven months and *how* many days?"

The elevator came down. "O.K, Father. I'm doing hard time."

"Yes, well, you're not alone."

When Joe had been due for a change the last time, after five years at Holy Faith, the clergy all—all of the few who gave Joe a thought—said he should be given a parish of his own. His youth, though, was against him—and the Archbishop's patriotic but idiotic practice of making pastors of honorably discharged chaplains. So Joe, the clergy said, would probably be sent out as an assistant again, probably to a big plant where the pastor was slipping, or fighting with his curates, or both. (One such pastor, with three curates, was known to be in the market for Joe, offering the Chancery two for one.) So, in view of the pastoral promise Joe had shown at Holy Faith, it made no sense, the clergy said, when Joe was sent to Charities, *unless* he was destined to take over the Director's job there—in which case, though, wouldn't it be better if he had a degree in social work? A good question, Joe had thought at the time, *unless* he was destined to move on and what the Arch had said to him (they'd run into each other in the barbershop in the First National Bank Building) meant that he'd been sent to Charities as a troubleshooter.

"Fresh battles, fresh victories, Father?"

"We'll see, Your Excellency."

Battles? Was the Arch thinking of Joe as he'd been in his last years at the sem, when a character sketch of him might have read, "Bright, good family, dough, but unbalanced on subject of sanctity (also pacificism), gets on your nerves," when feeling against Joe had run high—high enough, though, to reach and engage the archiepiscopal mind? *Victories?* Did the Arch maybe talk like that to any man taking up a new appointment, unless the man was a rolling stone, or boulder, like Lefty Beeman, and maybe even then? Was Joe's idea—that he'd been sent to Charities as a troubleshooter—maybe not the Arch's idea at all?

Possibly not, but Charities had never had two priests on its staff before, which suggested that the trouble, if trouble there was at Charities, might be with the other one, the Director.

"Paddy says use his office for the time being," Joe had been told on his first day at Charities, and was still using that office, Paddy's, the Director's, now, seven years later. (Joe had immediately made a point of calling Paddy Monsignor in front of the staff, but hadn't kept it up and had himself become Joe to the staff, which he found he preferred to Shorty and the like behind his back and no longer heard.) He had discovered that the Director was both liked and respected (two very different things where clergy and laity are concerned and working both ways), that the trouble with the Director, a trim diabetic when Joe arrived and now a wispy one, was that even when he wasn't in the hospital or convalescing at the Athletic Club, where he lived, he wasn't often at Charities (a bad thing in any concern), and that certain members of the staff, as Joe learned, not from the Director, were into him for "loans" (a bad thing in any concern, not excepting charitable ones). Not that there weren't instances in Scripture of favoritism, not that there was any question of peculation.

Paddy, with family money (oil), was very well off, which Joe, unlike some of the clergy, didn't hold against him. And Paddy, to Joe's knowledge, was the only priest in the diocese who called the Arch by his first name—this, since it was Albert, said plenty, in Joe's opinion. So Paddy had a thing or two going for him. And really, except for his absenteeism and favoritism, Paddy couldn't be faulted as Director.

Evidently Paddy's connections, a must for one in his position, were excellent—always an anonymous gift at the end of the year to cover the deficit to the penny.

It was also to Paddy's credit, after seven years, that Joe still liked him (and probably vice versa). Joe, after seven years, couldn't see that replacing Paddy with a younger man, or, for that matter, that *anything* would make any difference at Charities. Its mission was large, actually, as things were nowadays, preposterous—the rehabilitation and preservation of the family—and its means were small, a shoestring operation against the heartbreaking realities of life here below. Charities was just doing its best, no better and no worse than it had before Joe arrived.

What Joe had seen—"We'll see, Your Excellency"—was how little he could do (as the Arch must have known). Except for adding a couple of phones, getting in some new second-hand desks, increasing the face value of meal vouchers for derelicts (inflation), and putting up a suggestion box for clients ("Drop dead"), Joe had changed nothing at Charities. It, though, had changed him. It had certainly played hell with any idea he might have had of himself as a trouble-shooter.

"Joe, your time'll come," Lefty Beeman said early that evening, New Year's Eve, in the Robin Hood Room of the Hotel Garrison, while, instead of dessert, they were having another drink, after which, if they didn't have another, they'd go on to St Isidore's for poker. "Sure, you were let down when this kid, What's-his-name, that was getting his degree in social work, went over the hill. Never should've been ordained, of course. ["Or, anyway, allowed to travel without a companion," Joe said.] Joe, when I heard he had his own apartment in D.C.—Joe, the greatest occasion of sin in the world today is the apartment, not the parked car. Could do more good, they say, these kids, if they didn't live in rectories. Depends what you mean by good, I tell 'em. Too bad, I tell 'em, St Francis Assisi, and the other one, the Apostle of the Indies (they never heard of him *or* the Indies), didn't have their own apartments—could've done more good. Not criticizing you, Joe, though I was surprised when you moved out of Trinity, but that was before I got transferred *there*. I'd move out and live at the Athletic Club myself if beggars could be choosers, which they can't under our lousy system. Don't get me started on that. ["I won't," Joe said, beckoning to the waitress before asking Lefty, "Care for another?"] Thanks. Joe, be happy where you are. And don't think you'd be happier in parish work. You wouldn't. Lots of changes since you were in it, all for the bad. I fear for the future of our parishes. So be happy where you are, Joe. *I* would. I know, I know, don't tell me—it'd never do to have a radical at Charities. Don't get me started on that. ["I won't."] Joe, when you were sent to Charities after you did so well at Holy Faith (and, frankly, I didn't), I said to myself, 'Joe was born with a silver spoon in his mouth, and Big Albert' "—the Arch's middle name was Magnus—" 'wants him to have a taste of the other.' But that doesn't explain why you're *still* there. [Joe shook his head.] Joe, you must be the only guy from your class still without a parish, not counting that prick Toohey at the Chancery. [Joe nodded.] Well, Joe, I think I may have the answer. You see, something you said a while ago started me thinking— about this anonymous gift that comes in every year about this time and takes care of the deficit to the penny. Oh, sure, it could be some kind of bequest—some angel, dead or alive—that Paddy's keeping to himself. But that's not what figures, Joe. You know what figures, Joe? ["What?"] Paddy. An inside job. And I'll tell you why—*anonymous* and *to the penny*. Are you runnin' with me, Joe? [Joe shook his head, and before the waitress, about to drop the check on the table halfway between him and Lefty, could do so, Joe took the check from her and palmed it.] Thanks. Here's what it comes down to, Joe. Big Albert just wants somebody that's not a radical and can pick up the tab. Not a bad idea, Joe. And you're the best he can do. You'll never be in Paddy's class as a capitalist, but you're—correct me if I'm wrong— you're an only child. And under our lousy system—maybe in your case it's a good thing—you should be rolling in it someday. By the way, how're the folks? ["Fine. In Florida now."] Good for them. So, when this *other* kid, What's-his-name, gets back from Catholic U. with his degree—and there's a good chance he will—I understand he doesn't have his own apartment—he'll step into your shoes and you'll step into Paddy's. That's my prediction, Joe. Sort of a bombshell to you, huh?"

*   *   *

Joe treated Lefty with a certain respect, uncommon among
their brother clergy, because he felt sorry for the man (a
two-time loser as a pastor and now busted to curate again)
and because the man was older (ten years older, looking ten
more), and also because Lefty, in his youth, had caught the
eye of the immortal Connie Mack and had gone to spring
training in 1930 with the championship A's, with all-time
greats like Grove, Earnshaw, Cochrane, Foxx, Dykes, and
Simmons, about whom Joe had learned little from Lefty.
"Earnshaw on his day was harder to hit than Grove, they
say." "They do?" "Ever pitch to old Double X?" "Old Who?"
As was true of many players, some of the best, the history
and mystique of the national game evidently meant little to
Lefty, as the history and mystique of the Church evidently
did to many priests, some of the best. Joe wouldn't be
surprised at the Last Judgment, though, if Lefty was sent to
the right, with the sheep—another reason for treating the
man with a certain respect. In the meantime, however, Joe
doubted that their association was good for them, their vices
being the same, food and drink. Joe, if expecting to dine
alone, flinched when Lefty rose from his table to welcome
him to the Robin Hood Room and, later, suggested that they
have their coffee in the adjoining bar, the Little John Lounge,
where he was chaplain, he said, since he'd been in on the
death of a prominent judge there—"Gave him conditional
absolution." Lefty was good company, but he might have
been better. Joe sometimes lost patience with him, as he had
on New Year's Eve, when they hadn't gone on to St Isidore's
for poker, when Joe had begged off, not wanting to hear
Lefty's prediction repeated in the presence of others, and
claiming an upset stomach—mind, actually. Joe had seen in
the new year alone in his quarters at the Athletic Club with

Guy Lombardo and the Royal Canadians, at one low point seeing himself (if Lefty was right) as the little kid who gets to play with the big kids because it's his ball.

In the following days, in the course of his duties—Mass at Trinity early in the morning; court during the forenoon; Charities until quitting time or later—Joe carried on as before, but his life now looked and felt different to him because of Lefty's prediction. He could believe that he'd been sent to Charities for a reason and that he was still there (held over by the first What's-his-name's defection?) for the same reason, but not that this was the reason advanced by Lefty. Even if proved right in his prediction, Lefty could be wrong in his thinking: if Joe did become Director, might this not be for *another* reason? Such as? Well, *somebody* had to be Director when Paddy retired. Let's start over. Lefty, in his thinking and therefore in his prediction, was *wrong*. Was there any evidence to suggest that Joe would become Director, apart from the circumstantial evidence of his original and continuing appointment? No, none. Was there any evidence, apart from the circumstantial (*"anonymous* and *to the penny"*), to suggest that Paddy, whose directorate antedated the Arch's episcopate, was picking up the tab? No, none. *Ask* Paddy? No, because, even if he answered the question, the answer, if yes, would diminish the quality of his alms ("Cast thy bread upon the waters"), and if no, would embarrass him, seem to condemn him for not doing more. No, no good.

In any case, whether or not Paddy was picking up the tab was beside the point, as Joe came to see his own situation— as that of the rich young man in Scripture who, when told by Our Lord to sell what he had and give the proceeds to the poor, had taken a powder. Joe could say that he wasn't rich now and never would be, would only be fairly well off, and that he couldn't dispose of what he didn't have yet, but not that he couldn't declare himself now by intention, by desire. That was what counted, and counted for just as much, in the eyes of God and the Church, when to act materially was impossible—otherwise, religion, for most people, would be a spectator sport.

So what, in the matter of his inheritance, was his intention, his desire?

He didn't know and didn't, since his folks would have to die first, like to think about his inheritance, except, maybe, as a possible deterrent to some future archbishop. ("Watch it with old Joe, Your Excellency. He might retire on you. He's loaded, you know.") The truth was, he wasn't interested in money, or even in the things it could buy, apart from food and drink. The truth also was, since hearing Lefty's prediction he felt closer to the poor capitalists at the Athletic Club, some of them being bled white by greedy ex-wives and greedy radical offspring. He had no plans to cash in his annuity (without which he'd have to move back to Trinity) and give the proceeds to the poor. Was this to say that he couldn't readily accept the prospect of doing without his inheritance? No, only that he couldn't readily accept the prospect of becoming Director because "Big Albert just wants somebody that's not a radical and can pick up the tab."

"Odd you should mention the tax angle," Joe said to Lefty some nights later, in the Robin Hood Room. "Somebody was telling me about it the other night. ["It was me."] Whoever it was ["It was me, Joe"] said I should get the folks to make their moola over to me now ["But not *all* of it"], but not *all* of it. I don't want to leave 'em penniless. ["Right. Joe, *I* was the one talked to you the other night. That was *my* advice."] That so? So many give me their advice these days. Guys I haven't seen for years drop in at the office, or stop me on the street, and give me their advice. The word's going around—I don't know why—I'll be the next Director. ["It figures."] It figures, they say. They're all happy for me. [Lefty nodded.] Pleased, you might say, as Punch. [Lefty nodded.] The problem is— how do I tell the folks? I can't just say, 'Hey, folks, Guess what? I'm your—correct me if I'm wrong—your only child, and it looks very much like I'll be the next Director of Archdiocesan Charities, but if so I'll need your moola—but not *all* of it.' Afraid they may not take it so well. ["I see the problem, Joe. By the way, how *are* the folks?"] Fine. In Florida now. ["Good for them."] Hate to do it, but think I'd better go to the Arch—ask *his* advice. ["About what, Joe?"] Come right out and tell him I have a pretty good idea what's in store for me ["No, no"] and know why—that he just wants somebody that's not a radical and can pick up the tab. ["Joe."] But not yet, I'll have to tell him, not until the folks make their moola over to me—not *all* of it. ["Joe."] Afraid the Arch may not take it so well. He may want to talk to the folks himself. ["Joe."] Or he may want *you* to do it. ["Come on, Joe."] Actually, *Father*"—what Joe called Lefty when they weren't getting along—"it might be better if you both did, if you went down to Florida together, at my expense, of course."

"*Father*"—what Lefty called Joe when they weren't getting along—"here's how I look at it. 'From each according to his ability, to each according to his need.' But I can take a hint. You don't want to talk about it, right?"

"Right. No dessert for me."

"Drink?"

"No. But you go ahead."

"No, thanks."

So they rose from the table sooner than they might have, one man saying thanks when the other picked up the tab.

And then from one man, "Change your mind?" and from the other, "Well, all right." So they made for the Little John Lounge, one man smiling and nodding at diners along the way, the other ignoring them, until a woman, apparently sober, barked:

"Are you two father and son?"

Lefty stopped to talk, but Joe kept going, feeling sorry for Lefty for looking so old, until the woman howled:

"I *knew* it!"

Joe disappeared into the dimness of the Little John Lounge, feeling slandered as a priest and a person, a short one. Lefty, as he said, saw no harm in agreeing with people as long as nothing's at stake, and Joe had once heard him agreeing with some people, the kind who might think this, that *football* should be the national game. But what Lefty had just done was different, Joe thought, and he wasn't having any when Lefty sat down beside him and tried to interest him in an appeal that had gone out from Charities, producing a copy of it.

"Joe, when you're Director, I hope you'll do something about the letterhead."

"O.K., *Father*. What'd you tell that woman?"

"What woman, *Father?*"

"You know what woman. Tell her we're Protestants?"

"Why would I tell her a thing like that?"

"She didn't ask what we were?"

"No."

"O.K., *Father*. What if she *had* asked what we were?"

"*Father*, that's a hypothetical question, Joe."

Joe, silent, waited for Lefty to answer the question.

"Hell, I don't know. Greek Orthodox maybe, or that I was a late vocation."

"I see." But Joe wasn't (as Lefty appeared to think)

through with him. "O.K., *Father*. Why'd you say the other?"

"What other?"

Joe couldn't bring himself to say it. "You know what other."

"Father and son? Hell, *I* didn't say that. *She* did. I just went along with her. An old broad like that."

Marcia (the waitress) came for their orders.

When she'd gone, Lefty produced the appeal again. "Fat cats and tame clergy," he said, speaking of the Advisory Council whose names were on the letterhead. "And two of 'em dead. No balance, Joe."

"When I'm Director, I'll have your name on the letterhead—for balance."

"You *mean* that?"

Joe didn't, or anyway hadn't, but Lefty looked so *hopeful.* "I don't see why not," Joe said.

"Well, I'll be damned."

Marcia brought their orders.

"Here's to you, Joe."

"And you, Lefty."

After that, things gradually got out of hand. At one point, Lefty bought everybody a drink and put it on Joe's tab for the time being, which Joe didn't mind. At another point, while having a drink with a couple of college professors and their wives, Joe heard Lefty agreeing with them that "puritanism" might have figured in his vocation and might indeed color his thinking even today, which Joe did mind. "Some people," he said, "might indeed give up what they think of as thinking." At a later point, Lefty came back from the men's room with "Buzz"—somebody he either had or hadn't met before— who offered to give Joe an estimate on his new letterhead, Lefty producing the old one, now revised (in the men's room?), his name written in, Paddy's and those of the deceased crossed out. Paddy, thanks to Joe, was restored to the new letterhead first as a full member of the Advisory Council (not just an honorary one, as proposed by Lefty) and then as Director—in a version for *immediate* adoption because the old letterhead looked like hell with the names of the deceased on it and lacked balance, this crash version proposed by Lefty and seconded by Buzz and Marcia. That version was amended to show Joe, who'd had no title before, as Assistant Director. *That* version was amended to show Joe as Director and Paddy as Archdirector. At a later point—the last point that Joe clearly remembered—Buzz said he hoped in time to be doing all the Archdiocese's printing jobs, including Sunday envelopes, now shipped in from Indiana, to which Lefty had said, "I don't see why not."

The next morning Joe got up at the usual early hour, took a hot bath, and after Mass and a light breakfast (three orange juices), he got back in bed. But he couldn't sleep, or even rest—he had to find out, if possible without asking, whether he'd committed himself and Charities to Buzz and his firm. So he got up, took a hot bath, and went to his office, where he headed straight for the phone, but made himself sit down, thus disciplining himself, before using it.

"What's the name of Buzz's firm? In fact, what's *Buzz's* name?"

"Just a minute. His card's here somewhere." After a bit— "Here we are"—Joe was given the information, including the firm's phone number.

"Thanks, *Father*."

"*Father*, is something wrong, Joe?"

Joe hung up and called the firm. "Like to speak to Buzz."

"He's at a meeting."

"When'll it be over?"

"God knows."

"That's true. I'll call back."

Joe did this later that morning from Juvenile Court, between cases, but Buzz was still at the meeting. A little before noon, Joe tried again, but Buzz had gone to lunch.

Joe had his lunch in the Sawdust Grill of the Hotel Garrison, a roast beef on rye with two steins of Würzburger, which he took standing at one of the high tables with the idea of keeping his weight down, and was back at the office before one.

Mrs Hope, dressed to go out, looked in. "Father, would it be all right if I visited Monsignor?" (Paddy was in the hospital again.)

"Trouble, Mrs Hope?"

Mrs Hope gave Joe the latest bad news about her daughter's family, and he made her another loan. An hour or so later, he tried again, but Buzz hadn't come back from lunch yet. Before leaving for the bank, which closed at three, Joe tried again and was told by an unfamiliar voice, "Buzz didn't come in today."

While Joe was at the bank it occurred to him that the vibrator might help his head, and so he went downstairs for a trim.

"Ah, Father. Aren't you about ready for a parish?"

Joe just looked at the man under the sheet.

"Nothing to say, Father?"

"Tell you the truth, I thought you'd lost my file. I mean—*thanks*, Your Excellency."

That evening Joe went to the hospital to see Paddy about updating the letterhead, which also lacked balance.

"It'd mean a great deal to the man, Monsignor."

"In that case, Joe, let's do it."

Joe then told Paddy his good news.

"Oh, yes. Albert was asking about you, Joe."

"Thanks, Monsignor."

"No, no. I had nothing to do with it. You've had it coming, Joe—*too* long. I'm sorry about that."

Later that evening Joe called his folks in Florida and told them his good news (theirs too, conceivably, not that they would've been left penniless), and then he called Father Butler.

"I'll write a check in the morning. It'll be made out to you."

"To *me*?" said Father Butler.

"For reasons I won't go into. I don't want the pastor to know it's from me. Bread on the waters, Father."

"O.K., Father. Thanks a lot. Nothing's come in since I talked to you."

Joe wrote the check before he retired, in case he died in the night, and then went downstairs to mail it, in case he changed his mind in the morning.

II

8

The Rectory

and

Thereabout

At this time (1968) there were a half-dozen more or less new churches to be seen in the archdiocese, even a couple of new schools and convents if you were still thinking along those lines, but the prime movers, the clergy, were the forgotten men in building programs at this time, and you had to drive out to Joe's (Church of SS Francis and Clare, Inglenook) if you wanted to see a new rectory.

Architecturally it was tame stuff, in the same frosty orange brick as the school and convent, and did not interest the clergy, a rather advanced group architecturally. What did interest the clergy—since many a man had gone to the Arch and his reverend consultors with a more heartwarming project than putting up a house for himself and come away thinking himself a fool and a dangerous one at that—was why this roomy low-rise structure had risen at all in a parish where a glorified Quonset hut still did for a church.

Why?

Well, few men—none still active and building—could say with Joe: "I've always held the contractors to the original estimate and got everything called for in the plans, including copper plumbing." Or: "When those guys walk in here, they figure it's going to be like working for the U.S. government without inspectors—until I walk in." Once, after he'd walked in on some electricians and told them off for playing hell with his insulation and walked out, he'd been pleased to hear Steve, his janitor, respond to the question "What's wrong with that mother?" in kind, "Father, he don't take no shit." True. And Joe's school and convent were being paid for on schedule. As for a new church: "With more and more people moving out to the suburbs"—a big point in Joe's presentation to the Arch and his reverend consultors—"why not, I say, wait until everybody arrives?" "Bingo!" the Arch had said, his reverend consultors nodding away. So Joe, then living in a room in the school and quite prepared to go on living under such conditions if advised to build a new church but dearly wishing, as he'd told the Arch and his reverend consultors, to keep the best wine till last (*"Wine,* Archbishop? Did he say *wine?"*—"Means a new *church,* you dummy!"), had got his rectory.

Upstairs, the architect had simply gone about his business: pastor's suite (study, bedroom, bath), curate's bedroom and bath (for the curate Joe didn't have but hoped to get), guest room and bath (occupied on Saturday nights by Father Felix, the elderly monk who helped out on weekends), living room (seldom used), dining room, kitchen. (The housekeeper, Mrs Pelissier, a widow, was well paid, ran a car, and lived out, in her own little house.) Downstairs—that is, in the basement but surprisingly airy—was the rectory's outstanding feature, the office area: two offices (each with lavatory), waiting room, two conference rooms, and two (to use the architectural term) powder rooms.

The office area was all Joe's idea, which he could be passionate about, particularly with clerical visitors.

Just as the heart of the church is the altar, he'd say, so the heart of the rectory is, or should be, the office. *Offices,* rather, for pastor and curate don't sleep in the same bed, do they? No, but all too often, even in old rectories where space was not a problem, even where several men were in residence, what did you find? One office. And it a no-man's land, used by one and all, *or* a den for the pastor or whoever met the public, with everything in it pickled in smoke or otherwise smelling of him—no place to take a woman. (On the other hand, Joe knew of a rectory where, until recently, the office was also the housekeeper's sewing room.) There were still rectories where the action took place in the front hallway, with *everything*—Mass cards, baptismal and marriage certificates, pamphlets, rosaries, stoles, birettas, and *hats*—on the hat rack. There were still rectories where parishioners and salesmen, for want of a waiting room, waited in the dining room, roosted on the stairs, rectories where converts, Scouts, and sodalities, for want of conference rooms, conferred in ill-lit church basements with steam tables, echoes, and mice. "Fortune-tellers do better! I ask you"—so Joe in his presentation had asked the Arch and his reverend consultors, moving them visibly—"is this any way to carry on the most important business in the world? The only business in this world that'll matter a damn in the next!"

That morning in April Joe came out of the rectory with a beer case and two bags, a small one of brown cloth, a larger one of brown paper. He put the beer case in the trunk of his black Dachshund, the bags on the front seat, and got in beside them. He took the pen from the desk set above the dashboard and made a list on the memo pad there: BANK, BEER, DUMP, BOOZE, HOSP. He started the car and, with nothing coming from either direction, backed into the street. The next thing he knew he was almost run into by a speeder. He wasn't surprised when he saw who it was, Brad, and called to him out the window.

"After all you read about safe driving."

"Not in my column, you don't, Padre, and never will. That's a promise. *Ciao*."

Joe made an unscheduled stop in the next block, spoke to a child playing in the street, a boy, who then left his tricycle in the street, at the curb, and looked pleased with himself, saying, "Park car, park car." Joe pulled in to the curb, behind the tricycle, and the boy looked pleased saying, "Park car, park car." "Yeah, yeah," Joe said, getting out, lifted the boy onto the tricycle, and pushed it up the nearest driveway. When Joe returned to his car, the boy was saying to *his* (as Joe had taught him), "Park car on walk, not in street."

Approaching Inglenook's period shopping mall—cobblestones, gas lights, board signs—Family Grocer & Fruiterer, Apothecary, Ironmonger, and so on—Joe noticed that the weather ball, from which the mall took its name, Ball Mall, and for which a color code too often appeared in Hub's Column (Hub being Brad's nom de plume) in the Inglenook *Universe*—

> *When weather ball's red as fire,*
> *Temperature's going higher;*
> *When weather ball's white as snow,*
> *Down temperature will go;*
> *When weather ball's royal blue,*
> *Forecast says no change is due;*
> *When weather ball blinks in agitation,*
> *Watch out, folks, for precipitation*—

was grey, not working.

Joe turned into the Yellow Brick Road, the service lane that ran around the Mall and was roofed over with fiberglass, primrose dappled with daisies. He drove up to one of the bank's kiosks and dropped the brown cloth bag, the Sunday collection, into the chute. The teller on the TV screen, recognizing Joe, held up an empty bag, apparently a nice clean one. Joe nodded, saying through the voice tube, "Much obliged," meaning it. And wondered once again if there was anything in the idea of reviving the practice of coin washing—ladies' maids, he'd read, had done this in the past—a small service that banks could perform, and would if they *cared* as much as they said they did in their advertising. In any case, what about paper money? Before it was put back into circulation it could be dry-cleaned and pressed on the premises. If banks were looking for a new approach (as they should be, to judge by their advertising), a way to worm themselves into the hearts of depositors, one that would really work, well, there it was . . .

He followed the Yellow Brick Road around to the Licensed Vintner's, where, fortunately, the part-time employee, the old man, was on duty, and not the Licensed Vintner or his son—a couple of slobs to whom a beer case was a beer case. The old man removed the nice clean one from the trunk of Joe's car and was gone for some time. Joe, though he couldn't see him, could hear bottles clinking. When the old man returned with the case, he said, "Same one you had before, sir," and then of some stacked nearby, "No telling where *they* been, sir." "Much obliged," Joe said, meaning it, and after he'd paid, knowing the old man to be untippable, thanked him again, this time by name (Mr Barnes).

On the outskirts of town, Joe slowed down when he came to the dump, but saw Jim Gurrier prospecting, and drove on. He looked the other way until he'd passed the dump and the unfinished house in the next field. The Gurrier place—black with tar paper, still waiting for Jim to put on the siding; the PARTS sign in the front yard; the old cars multiplying in the weeds; the tire hanging from the big tree; the limp clothesline—depressed Joe. The Gurriers depressed him. He had moved Jim and Nan and their three (now there were five) children from the inner city. He had found the unfinished house for them and the down payment on it. He had thought that a suburban parish like his own needed people like the Gurriers, a leaven of God's poor. He had tried to see the Gurriers as the Holy Family, Jim and Nan as Joseph and Mary, only with more children. It couldn't be done, not by Joe anyway, not with the Gurriers. Jim, who Joe had hoped would shape up in time, still avoided all parish functions, including Mass, and Nan still went to everything—at first she'd inspired and embarrassed people with her talk of holy poverty in the inner city, now she bored them with it. If the Gurriers did move back to the inner city, as they said they might (to be close to the action), Joe wouldn't be sorry. It hadn't worked.

Joe was passing the Great Badger, "the discount house with a heart," which meant not only that the savings it realized through its wise volume purchases were passed on to you, the customer, in the usual manner of discount houses, but that your dependents in the event of your death would get to keep whatever you had been buying on time, with no further payments or charges of any kind. The Great Badger also hired the aged and handicapped. It was flourishing. Its real competitors were the big department stores in the city and other discount houses in fringe areas—and not the smocked and gaitered tradesmen on the Mall. *They* couldn't keep up, they knew it, and they were bitter. While they had more or less gone into hibernation after the Christmas rush, the Great Badger had staged a series of colossal interlocking sales during which it had stayed open, according to its ads, until ??? And now, to serve its customers better, it was staying open six nights a week until nine, Sundays until five. They were *very* bitter about this on the Mall, and Joe couldn't say he blamed them. The Great Badger itself, a forty-foot idol—its enlarged, exposed, red neon heart beating faintly in the sunlight that morning—sat up on its hunkers in the middle of the parking lot and waved a paw at cars going by. Joe did not, though he sometimes did if he had a passenger, wave back.

Joe was passing an industrial park, coveting the grass and geraniums, where once had stood the small machine shop that begat the medium-sized defense plant (Ketteridge Cartridge) that begat the giant Cones, Casing, Inc., which, with branches at home and abroad, was so important that it could afford to advertise not its many products—nose cones for missiles as well as ice cream cones, casings for bombs as well as sausages—but its humble birth, using only an artist's sketch of the small machine shop (looking like the village blacksmith's place of business in the poem) and three words, CONES + CASING = PEOPLE. Cones (as it was called) owned the corporation that owned the Mall, and was said to be so diversified that it was crisis-proof. Joe hoped that this was true, since many of his parishioners earned their daily bread there, but he also hoped that those who earned it by producing doomsday weapons could find other work. For Joe to say nothing, living among and off them and feeling as he did, was prudent but hard when a whiff of self-righteousness came his way, hinting that he was beholden to the freedom-loving military-industrial complex for protecting him from its opposite number in freedom-hating you-name-it. But then, running a parish, any parish, was like riding in a cattle car in wintertime—you could appreciate the warmth of your dear, dumb friends, but you never knew when you'd be stepped on, or worse.

Nearing the city limits and advocating as he did the

returnable bottle, Joe deplored the heavy fall of beer cans along the way, the shining fruits of the weekend. To his surprise, he drove *by* several big ammunition-depot-type liquor stores such as he ordinarily patronized when stocking up on the hard stuff (the Licensed Vintner and his son being Catholics and Mr Barnes a non-Catholic), and so, having shown a firmer resolve to amend his life than he might have if he'd stopped and bought a case of gin (though he might weaken when he passed that way again), Joe felt better about himself when he arrived at the hospital and knocked on the chaplain's, Father Day's, door.

"Ah, Joe!"

"Time to turn myself in again, Father."

Slowly, because Father Day had a game leg from one of his, now, rare sprees, they went up the corridor to the chapel and into a box where Joe knelt and waited for his old confessor to sit down and slide the wicket between them.

"All right, Joe."

"Bless me, Father. Sorry to say I'm still eating and drinking more than I should, especially the latter. And still not as good as I should be with the parishioners—they still give me a pain in the ass. I'm sorry, Father."

"Parishioners are people, Joe, and people have souls."

"I know, Father. I'm sorry."

"Don't be downhearted, Joe. Don't despair. Be on your guard there. Despair's really presumption, you know. Expecting too much. We can't change the world, Joe. Our Blessed Lord couldn't do it, Joe. But we can change ourselves. That's enough. Sometimes it's too much. Prayer, Joe, more prayer. Our best bet. Take it from me, though God knows, and so do you, I've made a bollux of my life."

"No, no, Father."

"Good of you, Joe. I *am* doing better these days." (Joe

heard his old confessor knock on wood.) "All right, Joe. For your penance, the same again—the holy rosary daily. Let's make that nightly, Joe. Pray for my intention. *Misereatur tui omnipotens Deus . . . ego te absolvo a peccatis in nomine Patris et Filii et Spiritus Sancti. Amen.* Love God, Joe, and have a trick in you."

After walking his old confessor back to his room, Joe looked in on patients from the parish. He planned to turn over the bulk of his practice to his curate if he ever got one, for this part of his job, with the growth of the parish, was getting to be too much for one man, the maternity cases alone. Sure, birth was a big deal—after death, the biggest deal—but what was there to say about either one of them, after a point? To pass the time that morning, Joe said to a nun who came in with a glass, "Sister, you still on the hard stuff?" and got a laugh. Top banana in the maternity ward, but he was tired of his routine and glad again to bow himself out and be on his way.

He drove by the ammunition depots again, all but the last one.

The dump was deserted, and so he drove in and disposed of the brown paper bag, his empties.

When he saw "car" parked not on walk but in street, at the curb, he wasn't surprised—the story of my priestly life and pastorate, he thought—and drove on.

9

In Jeopardy

That evening Joe was in the study having another beer and watching TV, the Twins, when Brad phoned.

"Suppose you caught my column, Padre."

Joe hadn't, but thought it safe to say, "Brad, why not give the weather ball a rest?" Joe hated it when Brad, off freeloading with what he called the working press at fun-sun resorts and military installations in hitherto unspoilt parts of the world, remembered the weather ball (so he wrote in his column) and got all . . . misty; or woke "betimes" in a strange but very comfortable bed (here a nice plug for hotel or base) and found the weather ball was only a . . . dream; or, circling at 10,000 feet, looked down and saw the weather ball like a lamp in the window and knew he was . . . home. "After all, Brad, it's not the Eiffel Tower or the Statue of Liberty."

"Who said it was?"

"Rather see Hansel and Gretel, or whoever they are, come out of their little house and say cuckoo."

"You kiddin'?"

"No."

"May I quote you?"

"No."

The Twins pulled in the infield, hoping to cut off the tying run at the plate. "Pretty busy here, Brad."

"Doing a survey of local churches—about HR 369." (A bill

before Congress containing goodies for Cones, Casing—its
NG3 missile was said to be far ahead of others in the field,
perhaps too far ahead, with *three* nostrils in its nose cone.)
"Will you be having public prayers for the success of the bill,
Padre?"

"No."

"*No?*"

"No. These things are best left to the lobbyists, Brad."

"May I quote you on that, Padre?"

"No."

"I understand you've been approached by your parishioners."

"Happens every day, Brad. Lost pets and so on."

"I wouldn't say this is the same thing, Padre."

"No." Unfortunately.

"I don't have to tell you, do I, that jobs're at stake?"

"No, and I'm sorry about that, more than I can say." To
you, you bastard.

"May I quote you on *that*?"

"No."

"This is *all* off the record then?"

"Yes."

"*Ciao.*"

The Twins were in a tight spot—bases loaded, nobody
out, a three-two count. Foul ball. Another. The phone rang.

"St Francis."

"If *you're* St Francis *I'm* Lyndon B. Johnson."

"Who's calling?"

"That's all right. Been reading the Good Book."

"Not a Catholic then?"

"That's all right. Don't like how you're running things
over there. Hate your methodology."

"Who's calling?"

"That's all right."

Joe had hung up. *Another* foul ball. Then a wild pitch! The phone rang again.

"Yes?"

"St Francis?"

"Hold on. I'll call him." Joe put down the phone. He picked it up when the inning was over—three unearned runs! "Still there? Hold on. He's coming." The Twins came to bat and went down in order, two swinging. To think these clowns had won the pennant only three years ago, Joe thought, and picked up the phone. "Hello? Hello?" Gone. Good. Joe was going for a beer when the phone rang again.

"Yes?"

"St Francis?"

"Hold on, will you? We're trying to trace your call. Hello? Hello?" Gone.

Leaving the Twins to their fate, Joe wandered over to the windows with his empty glass—maybe he'd switch to gin, but he was in no hurry—and staring out at the night saw, in the distance, the weather ball, royal blue ("Forecast says no change is due"), and farther away, on a hill, flood lit and sea green, the water tank, the new global type, around it blinking, spelling and respelling itself in neon white letters, INGLENOOK, which, though, Joe had to take on faith since only three letters were visible from the study windows or from any terrestrial point—*that* was planning for you. NOO, NOO, the water tank said to him (he was wishing the problem of public prayers for HR 369 would go away), and then the weather ball turned red as fire ("Temperature's going higher") and the phone rang again.

When Joe next caught Brad's column, read "Public prayers for the success of HR 369 to be offered in all local churches

. . . except one," he was tempted to sit down at his typewriter and have a go at the military-industrial complex, its pols and flacks. To the Editor of the *Universe* . . . and could already hear them at the Chancery. "Hey, what's with our man in Inglenook?" "Gee, I don't know. I pulled his file, but all it says is good hard worker fond of the sauce." "That could be it."

His vices, his eating and drinking, did tend to silence the prophet in him, but so did common sense. He would persevere in his difficult situation, however, and if asked to explain himself would do so (as he already had to a couple of parishioners such as he'd had in mind when complaining to his old confessor) in very general terms. "The Church tells us to pray for things that lead to salvation, for grace and so on, but for temporal things only insofar as they conduce to that end."

His situation had worsened, though, now that he'd been singled out and tied to the stake in Brad's column—only anonymously, yes, but how long only anonymously? Already he could feel the heat. This, in a small way, could soon be one of those times, all too frequent in the history of the Church, when one had to be wise as a serpent, simple as a dove—as when Our Lord had called for a coin and asked whose image it bore and when told, "Caesar's," had said in reply, "Render therefore to Caesar the things that are Caesar's and to God the things that are God's." That reply, which had made war and misrule easier for tyrants down through the ages and the Church a sitting duck, had heretofore struck Joe as uncharacteristic, even unworthy, of Our Lord. But then Joe hadn't heretofore been in Our Lord's position vis-à-vis Caesar.

In the following days, Joe, though he was used to being noticed in public—he dressed as a priest—did get the impression he was being *watched*. "There he is," he imagined people saying when he appeared on the Mall or, for that matter, at the altar, "the one who won't pray for the success of HR 369." All right. Those scandalized by him might be fewer than he imagined, but they weren't *all* in his mind.

Perhaps a dozen people had approached him, or phoned (one anonymously), to complain, and Nan Gurrier had assured him of *her* support in the hearing of a few of her, by now, many ill-wishers. On the other hand, several people had commended him, and he hadn't come under attack from Brad again, except for one glancing blow: "Our weather ball on a per capita basis . . . represents a greater community investment . . . and provides a greater public service . . . than the Eiffel Tower . . . or the Statue of Liberty."

Then, one evening, Joe had a visit from Brad and saw him in the study in order to keep an eye on the Twins.

"Bad news," said Brad, who, though pushing fifty, went around like a college kid with the sleeves of his cardigan shoved up to his elbows. "HR 369's in trouble—in danger of being returned to committee."

"That so?"

"Look, Padre. You had prayers for the crops last year and every year you have 'em for Hiroshima." (Brad gave Joe a dirty look, reminding him of their argument, some years back, which had gone on and on until Brad said, "But for Hiroshima and Nagasaki, *I* might not be here talking to you today," and Joe fell silent.) "O.K., Padre. I admit we have prayers for all kinds of stuff at our church too." (Brad was Episcopalian; his wife, Barb, and their sons, Scott and Greg, Catholic.) "Still, it *does* seem to me . . ."

"Brad, I still think these things are best left to the lobbyists."

"I guess I don't have your faith in lobbyists."

"Well, I don't have your faith in prayer."

"Hold it, Padre." Obviously Brad was scandalized, and delighted to be, but concerned that what he'd just heard might not be true. "*You* don't have faith in *prayer?*"

"I don't have *your* faith in prayer."

"But *shouldn't* you?"

Joe gravely replied: "The Church tells us to pray for things that lead to salvation, for grace and so on, but for temporal things only insofar as they conduce to that end." Much as Brad deserved it, Joe was sorry to have to hit him in the face with a custard pie of theology.

But Brad took it surprisingly well and, after wiping his eyes, said, "I see. May I quote you?"

"No."

"Look, Padre. What if I gave you a chance to put your case to the community in your own words? As you know, I sometimes open the column to guests when I'm off on an assignment."

Joe was afraid there was going to be more about the weather ball from far-off places. "No, thanks, Brad."

"Let me know if you change your mind. In the meantime"—from his shirt pocket Brad removed a folded sheet of yellow paper—"here's something for your church bulletin, a release I worked up from Scott's last letter from Nam. I'd run it myself, only it might sound self-serving, and maybe I owe you something."

"For giving me the business?"

Brad looked hurt but guilty. "If you're talking about the column, I kept it pretty vague, you know."

"Thanks."

"Anyhoo"—Brad, having smoothed out the release, handed it to Joe—"it's for your 'In the Service' department in the bulletin. Use it as you see fit, but *as is* might be best."

Joe was reading between the dots: ". . . elder son of the popular *Universe* columnist . . . is now executive officer at one of our bases in Viet Nam . . . with the grim duty of meeting and escorting VIPs . . . Sec'y of State Rusk, Generals Taylor, Westmoreland, et all . . . Scott awaits the arrival of his brother Greg . . . 'to help us end this mess in a hurry.'"

"We don't have such a department in our bulletin," Joe said, wondering that Brad hadn't seen copies of it around the house.

"About time you had one then, don't you think?"

"No."

Brad sighed. "Seems like all you ever say to me is no, Padre."

"Yes."

Brad smiled. "O.K. So I was wrong. Look, Padre. If you said yes to this it'd mean a lot to Scott, to Barb, to Greg, to me, to plenty of people. I don't have to tell you it'd help your image in the community."

"No."

"No what?"

"No, you don't have to tell me, and no, I'm not saying yes." Joe returned the release to Brad—at the risk, he supposed, of soon reading that "In the Service" departments appear in the bulletins of all local churches . . . except one.

Brad had got up and was leaving in a huff. "O.K., Padre. Go back to your game. I can find my way out. *Ciao.*"

"Same to you."

Early the next morning there was a phone call from the pastor of the local Lutheran church. "Father, is it true you're not having public prayers for HR 369?"

Not liking the sound of this, Joe stiffened. "It's true, Pastor. I'm not."

"Neither am I, Father."

In the spirited conversation that followed, Brad wasn't mentioned, but his column was, the Pastor referring to the little item that he, like Joe, had thought aimed at him alone. "A case of trying to kill two birds with one stone, Father," to which Joe (recalling Brad's "I kept it pretty vague, you know") replied, "You can say that again, Pastor." Joe and the Pastor promised to keep more in touch. Joe, hanging up, had never felt so ecumenical.

Later that morning there was a phone call from the Rector of the local Episcopal church. "I just got back from my vacation, Father, and I've discovered some of what's happened in my absence. When the cat's away, the mice will play, Father. I'm talking about public prayers for HR—or is it BS?—369." The Rector said he'd chewed out the substitute priest—a good person, really, but deficient in churchmanship—and had also dealt with Brad, but over the phone, and would do more of a job on him if they ever met again, to say nothing of what he had in mind for the vestry when next he and they convened. "None of which I'd be telling you, Father, if I hadn't spoken to the Pastor, who told me what you two have been through in my absence. My heart goes out to you both, Father." "Thanks, Rector." Joe and the Rector promised to keep more in touch. Joe, hanging up, had never felt so ecumenical.

That afternoon Joe ran into Brad on the Mall.

"Padre, you'll be interested to know I'm no longer a member of the Episcopal Church."

"That so? Excommunicated or what?"

"No, I left of my own free will."

Joe, remembering how Brad had begun the conversation

("Padre, you'll be interested to know . . ."), said, "Well, *we* don't want you."

"*We* won't get me. That's a promise."

"Promises, promises," Joe said, and left Brad standing on the Mall, but called back to him, "*Ciao*."

About a week later, Joe learned that Brad's wife, Barb, whose pleasure it was to sip cordials in the early afternoon while watching soap operas and then to go out shopping, had fallen and broken her left leg. That was bad enough. What made it worse was that Barb had fallen from a children's slide in the Humpty Dumpty department at the Great Badger. And what made it *worse* was that, only months before, the Draper's mother-in-law (like Barb, the Catholic party in a mixed marriage) had dropped dead at the Great Badger, in household appliances. Joe, who'd had the funeral, knew that the Great Badger's offer to pay the undertaker had been poorly received, and likewise the big wreath, by the Draper, his wife, and the Mall crowd. That Barb had declined the Great Badger's offer to pay her medical expenses was in her favor, but nothing else was. (Joe was thinking along such lines when he consented to autograph her cast.) Barb had bravely insisted that Brad not be told of her accident, but her son Greg had cabled him, and Brad had caught an early flight home (from Guam). Joe hadn't seen him, but had seen the column and had wondered whether Brad, perhaps from the strain of working off Barb's culpability with the Mall crowd (which probably couldn't be done), might be cracking up. "National Read Week . . . is fast approaching and . . . among the many fine things . . . to be read these days are . . . church bulletins"—there was MORE, but nothing about the local bulletins having or not having "In the Service" departments. There seemed to be even more than before about the weather ball, Brad now calling it "old girl" and "Spaceship Inglenook" and using more dots.

On the evening of the day that HR 369 was in the news— it *had* been returned to committee—there was a phone call from Brad.

"Father, did you know you belong to the first estate?" It had been a long time, Joe thought, since Brad had called him Father.

"How's that, Brad?"

"Yeah. As a member of the clergy. It came out in my research."

"Research, Brad?"

"I'm doing a think piece on the fourth estate—the press."

"Is this for the column, Brad?"

"No, no. It'll be too exhaustive for that."

"Brad, why not run it in the column as a—*serial?* Give the weather ball a rest."

In the ensuing silence Joe had time to regret his words.

"Father, I just thought you'd like to know you belong to the first estate. Did you *know* that?"

Joe did. "No, and it's good to know, Brad. Thanks."

"Yeah, well, I just thought you'd like to know, Father. *Ciao.*"

And that was all. Not a word about HR 369. Trying to mend fences. Poor devil.

10
Good News

In January, Joe had made it two to one against his getting a curate that year. Then, early in May, the Arch came out to see the new rectory and, in the office area, had paused before the doors PASTOR and ASSISTANT and said, "You're mighty sure of yourself, Father."

"I can dream, can't I, Your Excellency?"

The subject hadn't come up again during the visit, and the Arch had declined Joe's offer of a drink, which may or may not have been significant—hard to say how much the Arch knew about a man—but after he'd departed Joe made it seven to five, trusting his old gambler's instinct.

Two weeks later, on the eve of the annual shape-up, trusting his instinct again though he'd heard nothing, Joe made it even money.

The next morning, the Chancery (Toohey) phoned to say that Joe had a curate: "Letter follows."

"Wait a minute. Who?"

"He'll be in touch with you." And Toohey hung up.

Maybe it hadn't been decided who would be sent out to Joe's, but probably it had, and Toohey just didn't want to say because Joe had asked. That was how Toohey played the game. But Joe didn't think any more about it then.

He grabbed a scratch pad, rushed upstairs to the room, now bare, that would be occupied by his curate (Who?), and made—his response to problems, temporal and spiritual, that required thought—a list.

That afternoon, he visited furniture stores in Inglenook, in Silverstream, the next suburb, and in the city. "Just looking," he said to clerks. After a couple of hours, he had a pretty good idea of the market, but he was unable to act, and had to suspend operations in order to beat the rush-hour traffic.

On the way home he realized what was wrong. It was his list. Programmed without reference to the *relative* importance of the items on it, his list, instead of helping, had hindered him, had caused him to mess around looking at lamps, rugs, and ashtrays. It hadn't told him that everything in the room would be determined, dictated, by the bed. Why bed? Because the room was a *bed*room. Find the bed, the right bed, and the rest would follow. He understood where he was now, and he was glad that time had run out that afternoon. Toward the last, he had been suffering from shopper's fatigue, or he wouldn't have considered that knotty-pine suite, with its horseshoe brands and leather thongs, simply because it had a clean, masculine look that bedroom furniture on the whole seemed to lack.

That evening, he sat down in the quiet of his study (Twins rained out), with some brochures and a drink, and made another list. This one was different and should have been easy for him—with office equipment he knew where he was, probably no priest in the diocese knew so well—but for that very reason he couldn't bring himself to furnish the curate's office as other pastors would have done, as, in fact, he had planned to do. Why spoil a fine office by installing inferior, economy-type equipment? Why not move the pastor's desk and typewriter, both recent purchases, into the curate's office? Why not get the pastor one of those laminated mahogany desks, maybe Model DK 100, sleek and contemporary but warm and friendly as only wood can be? (The pastor was tired of his unfriendly metal desk and his orthopedic chair.) Why not get the pastor a typewriter with different type? (What, *again*? Yes, because he was tired of that phony script.) But keep the couch and chairs in the pastor's office, and let the new chairs—two or three, and no couch—go straight into the curate's office.

The next morning, Joe drove to the city with the traffic, and swiftly negotiated the items on his office list, including a desk, Model DK 100, and a typewriter with different type, called "editorial," and said to be used by newscasters.

"Always a pleasure to do business with you, Father."

The scene then changed to the fifth floor of a large department store, which Joe had visited the day before, and there life got difficult again. What had brought him back was a fourposter bed with pineapple finials. The clerk came on a little too strong.

"The double bed's making a big comeback, Father."

"That so?"

"What I'd have, if I had the choice."

"Yes, well." Joe liked the bed, especially the pineapples, but he couldn't see the curate (Who?) in it. Get it for himself, then, and give the curate the pastor's bed—*it* was single. And then what? The pastor's bed, of unfriendly metal and painted like a car, hospital grey, would dictate nothing about the other things for the room. Besides, it wouldn't be fair to the curate, would it?

"Lot of bed for the money, Father."

"Too much bed."

The clerk then brought out some brochures and binders with colored tabs. So Joe sat down with him on a bamboo chaise longue, and, passing the literature back and forth between them, they went to work on Joe's problem. They discovered that Joe could order the traditional type of bed in a single, in several models—cannonballs, spears, spools (Jenny Lind)—but not pineapples, which, it seemed, had been discontinued by the maker. "But I wonder about that, Father. Tell you what. With your permission, I'll call North Carolina."

Joe let him go ahead, after more discussion, mostly about air freight, but when the clerk returned to the chaise longue he was shaking his head. North Carolina had gone to lunch. North Carolina would call back, though, in an hour or so, after checking the warehouse. "You wouldn't take cannonballs or spears, Father? Or Jenny Lind?"

"Not Jenny Lind."

"You like cannonballs, Father?"

"Yes, but I prefer the other."

"Pineapples."

Since nothing could be done about the remaining items on his list until he found out about the bed—or beds, for he had decided to order *two,* singles, with matching chests, plus box springs and mattresses, eight pieces in all—Joe went home to await developments.

At six minutes to three, the phone rang. "St Francis," Joe said.

"Earl, Father."

"*Earl?*"

"At the store, Father."

"Oh, hello, Earl."

Earl said that North Carolina *could* supply, and would air-freight to customer's own address. So beds and chests would arrive in a couple of days, Friday at the outside, and box springs and mattresses, these from stock, would be on the store's Thursday delivery to Inglenook.

"O.K., Father?"

"O.K., Earl."

Joe didn't try to do any more that day.

The next morning, he took delivery of the office equipment (which Mrs P.—Mrs Pelissier—must have noticed), and so he got a late start on his shopping. He began where he'd left off the day before. Earl, spotting him among the lamps, came over to say hello. When he saw Joe's list, he recommended the store's interior-decorating department—"Mrs Fox, if she's not out on a job." With Joe's permission, Earl went to a phone, and Mrs Fox soon appeared among the lamps. Slightly embarrassed, Joe told her what he thought—that the room ought to be planned around the bed, since it was a *bed*room. Mrs Fox smacked her lips and shrieked (to Earl), "*He* doesn't need *me!*"

As a matter of fact, Mrs Fox proved very helpful—steered Joe from department to department, protected him from clerks, took him into stockrooms and onto a freight elevator, and remembered curtains and bedspreads (Joe bought two), which weren't on his list but were definitely needed. Finally, Mrs Fox had the easy chair and other things brought down to the parking lot and put into his car. These could have gone out on the Thursday delivery, but Joe wanted to see how the room would look even without the big stuff—the bed, the chest, the student's table, and the revolving bookcase. Mrs Fox felt the same way. Twice in the store she'd expressed a desire to see the room, and he'd managed to change the subject, and then she did it again, in the parking lot—was *dying* to see the room, she shrieked, just as he was driving away. He just smiled. What else could he do? He couldn't have Mrs Fox coming out there.

In some ways, things were moving too fast. He still

hadn't told Mrs P. that he was getting a curate—hadn't because he was afraid if he did, she'd ask, as he had, "Who?" Who, indeed? He still didn't know, and the fact that he didn't would, if admitted, make him look foolish in Mrs P.'s eyes. It would also put the Church—administrationwise—in a poor light.

That evening, after Mrs P. had gone home, Joe unloaded the car, which he'd run into the garage because the easy chair was clearly visible, protruding from the trunk. It took him four trips to get all his purchases up to the room. Then, using a kitchen chair, listening to the ball game and drinking beer, he put up the curtain rods. (Steve, if asked to, would wonder why, and if told, would tell Mrs P., who would ask, "Who?") When Joe had the curtains up, tiebacks and all, he took a much needed bath, changed, and made himself a gin-and-tonic. He carried it into the room, dark now—he had been waiting for this moment—and turned on the lamps he'd bought. O.K. And when the student's table came, the student's lamp, now on the little bedside table, would look even better. He had chosen one with a yellow shade, rather than green, so the room would look cheerful, and it certainly did. He tried the easy chair, the matching footstool, the gin-and-tonic. O.K. He sat there for some time, one foot going to sleep on the rose-and-blue hooked rug while he wondered why—why he hadn't heard anything from the curate.

The next day, Thursday, Mrs P. had the afternoon off, and so she wasn't present when the box springs, mattresses, student's table and revolving bookcase came, at twenty after four—the hottest time of day. Joe had a lot of trouble with the mattresses—really a job for two strong men, one to pull on the mattress, one to hold onto the carton—and had to drink two bottles of beer to restore his body salts. He took a much needed bath, changed, and feeling too tired to go out, made himself some ham sandwiches and a gin-and-tonic. He used a whole lime—it was his salad—and ate in his study while watching the news; Viet Nam, and people starving in Asia and Mississippi. He went without dessert. Suddenly he jumped up and got busy around the place, did the dishes— dish—and locked the church. When darkness came, he was back where he'd been the night before—in the room, in the chair, with a glass, wondering why he hadn't heard anything from the curate.

It was customary for the newly ordained men to take a few days off to visit and shake down their friends and relatives. Ordinations, though, had been held on Saturday. It was now Thursday, almost Friday, and still no word. What to do? He had called people at the seminary, hoping to learn the curate's name and perhaps something of his character, just in the course of conversation. ("Understand you're getting So-and-So, Joe.") But it hadn't happened—everybody he asked to speak to (the entire faculty, it seemed) had left for vacationland. He had then called the diocesan paper and, with pencil ready, asked for a complete rundown on new appointments, but the list hadn't come over from the Chancery yet. ("They can be pretty slow over there, Father." "Toohey, you mean?" "Monsignor's pretty busy, Father, we don't push him on a thing like this—it's not what we call hard news.")

So, really, there was nothing to do, short of calling the Chancery. Early in the week, it might have been done—that was when Joe made his mistake—but it was out of the question now. He didn't want to expose the curate to censure and run the risk of turning him against his pastor, and he also didn't want the Chancery to know what the situation was at SS Francis and Clare's (one of the best-run parishes in the diocese), though it certainly wasn't his fault. It was the curate's fault, it was Toohey's fault. "Letter follows." If called on that, Toohey would say, "Didn't say when. Busy here," and hang up. That was how Toohey played the game. Once, when Joe had called for help, saying he'd die if he didn't get away for a couple of weeks, Toohey had said, "Die," and hung up. Rough. If the Church ever got straightened out administrationwise, Toohey and his kind would have to go, but that was one of those long-term objectives. In the meantime, Joe and his kind would have to soldier on, and Joe would. It was hard, though, after years of waiting for a curate, after finally getting one, not to be able to mention it. While shopping, Joe had run into two pastors who would have been interested to hear of his good fortune, and one had even raised the subject of curates, had said that he was getting a *change*, "Thank God!" Joe hadn't thought much about it then—the "Thank God!" part—but now he did, and, swallowing the weak last inch of his drink, came face to face with the ice.

What, he thought—what if the curate, the unknown curate, *wasn't* one of the newly ordained men? What if he was one of those bad-news guys? A young man with five or six parishes behind him? Or a man as old as Joe, or older, a retread, a problem priest? Or a goldbrick who figured, since he was paid by the month, he wouldn't report until the first, Sunday? Or a slob who wouldn't give a damn about, or take care of, the room? These were sobering thoughts to Joe. He got up and made another drink.

The next morning, when he returned from a trip to the dump, Mrs P. met him at the door. "Somebody who says he's your assistant—"

"Yes, yes. Where is he?"

"Phoned. Said he'd be here tomorrow."

"*Tomorrow?*" But he didn't want Mrs P. to get the idea that he was disappointed, or that he didn't know what was going on. "Good. Did he say what time?"

"He just asked about confessions."

"So he'll be here in time for confessions. Good."

"Said he was calling from Whipple."

"*Whipple?*"

"Said he was down there buying a car."

Joe nodded, as though he regarded Whipple, which he'd driven through once or twice, as an excellent place to buy a car. He was waiting for Mrs P. to tell him more—and must have shown it.

"That's all *I* know," she said, and shot off to the kitchen. Hurt. Not his fault. Toohey's fault. Curate's fault. Not telling her about the curate was bad, but doing it as he would have had to would have been worse. Better she think less of him than know the truth—and think less of the Church. He took the sins of curates and administrators upon him.

That afternoon, he waited until four o'clock before he got on the phone to Earl. "Say, what *is* this? I thought you said Friday at the outside."

"Oh, oh," said Earl, and didn't have to be told who was calling, or about what. He said he'd put a tracer on the order, and promised to call back right away, which he did. "Hey, Father, guess what? The order's at our warehouse. North Carolina goofed."

"That so?" said Joe, but he wasn't interested in Earl's analysis of North Carolina's failure to ship to customer's own address, and cut in on it. He described his bed situation, as he hadn't before for Earl, in depth. He was going to be short a bed—no, not that night but the next, when his assistant would be there, and also a monk of advanced age who helped out on weekends and slept in the guest room. No, the bed in the guest room, to answer Earl's question, was a single—actually, a cot. Yes, Joe could put his assistant on the box spring and mattress, but wouldn't like to do it, and didn't see why he should. He'd been promised delivery by Friday at the outside. He didn't care if Inglenook *was* in Monday and Thursday territory. In the end, he was promised delivery the next day, Saturday.

"O.K., Father?"

"O.K., Earl."

11

Saturday

The next afternoon, a panel truck, scarred and bearing no name, pulled up in front of the rectory at seven minutes after four. Joe didn't know what to make of it. He stayed inside the rectory until the driver and his helper unloaded a carton, then rushed out, and was about to ask them to unload at the back door and save themselves a few steps when a word on the carton stopped him. "Hold everything!" And it wasn't, as he'd hoped, simply a matter of a word on a carton. Oh, no. On investigation, the beds proved to be as described on their cartons—cannonballs. "Hold everything. I have to call the store."

On the way to the telephone, passing Father Felix, the monk who helped out on weekends and was another who hadn't been told about the curate, and now appeared curious to know what was happening in the street, Joe wished that monks were forbidden to wear their habits away from the monastery. Flowing robes, Joe felt, had a bad effect on his parishioners, made him, even in his cassock, look second best in their eyes, and also reminded non-Catholics of the so-called Reformation.

"Say, what is this?" Joe said, on the phone.

"Oh, oh," said Earl when he learned what had happened. "North Carolina goofed."

"Now, *look*," said Joe, and really opened up on Earl and

the store. "I don't like the way you people do business," he said, pausing to breathe.

"Correct me if I'm wrong, Father, but didn't you say you liked cannonballs?"

"Better than Jenny Lind, I said. But that's not the point. I prefer the other, and that's what I said. You know what 'prefer' means, don't you?"

"Pineapples."

"You've got me over a barrel, Earl."

In the end, despite what he'd indicated earlier, Joe said he'd take delivery. "But we're through," he told Earl, and hung up.

He returned to the street where, parked behind the panel truck, there was now a new VW beetle, and there, it seemed, standing by the opened cartons with Father Felix, the driver, and his helper, was Joe's curate—big and young, obviously one of the newly ordained men. Seeing Joe, he left the others and came smiling toward him.

"Where the hell you been?" Joe said—like an old pastor, he thought.

The curate stopped smiling. "Whipple."

Joe put it another way. "Why didn't you give me a call?"

"I did. Don't know how many times I called. You were never in."

"Didn't know what to think," Joe said, ignoring the curate's point like an old pastor, and, looking away, wished that the beetle—light brown, or dark yellow, sort of a caramel—was another color, and also that it wasn't parked where it was, adding to the confusion. (The driver's helper was showing Father Felix how his dolly worked.) "Could've left your name with the housekeeper."

"I kept thinking I'd get you if I called again. You were never in."

Joe moved toward the street, saying, "Yes, well, I've been out a lot lately. Could've left your name, Father."

"I did, Father. Yesterday."

"Yes, well." Standing by the little car, viewing the books and luggage inside, Joe wished that he could start over, that he hadn't started off as he had. He had meant to welcome the curate. It wasn't his fault that he hadn't—look at the days and nights of needless anxiety, and look what time it was now—but still he wanted to make up for it. "Better drive your little car around to the back, Father, and unload," he said. "The housekeeper'll show you the room. Won't ask you to hear confessions this afternoon." And, having opened the door of the little car for the curate, he closed it for him, saying, through the window, "See you later, Father."

When Joe straightened up, he saw that Big Mouth, a neighbor and a parishioner, and Patton, his old bulldog, had arrived to inspect the cartons, heard Father Felix being questioned by Big Mouth, saw, too, that Mrs P. had decided to sweep the front walk and was working that way.

"I've bought a few things—besides the bed and chest here—for the curate's room," Joe told her, so she wouldn't be too surprised when she saw them. Then he gave her the key to the room, saying, perhaps needlessly, that she'd find it locked, and that the box springs, mattresses, and bedspreads would be found within. The other bed—the one that should and would have been his but for the interest shown in it by Father Felix and Big Mouth—the other bed and chest, he told Mrs P., should go into the guest room. "Fold up the cot and put it somewhere. Get the curate to help you—he's not hearing this afternoon."

Turning then to the little group around the cartons, he saw that his instructions to Mrs P. had been overheard and understood. The little group—held together by the question "Would he take delivery?"—was breaking up. He thanked the driver and his helper for waiting, nodded to Big Mouth, said "Coming?" to Father Felix, since it was now time for confessions, and turned toward the church slowly shaking his head. He took the sins of curates and administrators and North Carolina upon him. He gave another his bed.

That evening, while the curate and Father Felix were over in the church hearing confessions, Joe was in his office telling a thirtyish couple, the Lanes, about the fiscal system at SS Francis and Clare's, a system used in only two other parishes in the diocese and known among the clergy, variously, as the American plan, the California, the country club, the table d'hôte, the game sanctuary. "So I did away with Sunday envelopes and special collections except Christmas and Easter. No more yackety-yack about money from the pulpit. The Annual Offering covers everything. Tuition, pew rent, Missions, Peter's Pence, Bishops' Relief, Catholic University, and so on. Were you at Mass last Sunday? Here, I mean."

"No, we weren't," said Mr. Lane, a beefy type in a grey silk suit. "Not here."

"Well, we still have a flower collection—flowers for the altar—and if you toss in a quarter, that's plenty. That way it's still possible, technically, for parishioners to make an offering at the Offertory. And for visitors, children, and *others* to contribute." (Unfortunately, there were *others*—parishioners—who were against Joe's system.) "Some say the Annual Offering's too high—it's five hundred—but look what other goods and services run you today—a new car, country club membership, major, or even minor, surgery. St Francis," Joe said, answering the phone, and hearing the question dreaded in every rectory on Saturday night ("What time are Masses tomorrow?"), coldly replied, "Consult the church bulletin."

"Sorry—we're new here."

"Where's 'here'?"

The caller gave an address that put him in the parish—not always the case with Saturday night callers—and Joe's manner changed.

"Welcome aboard. This is your pastor, Father Hackett."

"Mike Gumball, Father."

Joe wrote it down and looked at it. "How do you spell your last name, Mike?"

"G-U-M-B-L-E."

"Got it. Any children, Mike? School-age tots?"

"No, Father. Just Nancy, and she's preschool."

"Good. Reason I say that, Mike—we're full up in some of the grades." (Joe had also said it for the benefit of the couple in his office.) "Mike, what we have to do now is get you and the family registered as members of the parish. You or your wife'll have to come in for that. It can't be done over the phone."

"I'll come in, Father."

"Don't put it off, Mike. You never know when somebody in the family might need a priest. It could be you. Right?"

"I guess so."

"That's the spirit."

"Father, I don't know if I can get over there tonight." (Mike sounded, though young, like a good old-fashioned parishioner to Joe.) "Would tomorrow be all right?"

"Tomorrow's Sunday, Mike. How about Monday at eight? P.M., that is."

"Fine, Father."

"Now, Mike, if you have the suburban directory there, you'll find the Mass times listed in the Yellow Pages."

"O.K., Father. I'll look 'em up."

"I can give 'em to you, Mike."

"No, no, Father."

"That's the spirit. G'night, Mike." Joe hung up, and saw that Mr Lane had his checkbook out.

"You said five hundred, Father?"

"Our fiscal year begins in January, Mr Lane. You can pay for the rest of the year, or you can pay for a year, or monthly, as many people prefer. It's entirely up to you."

"How do I make it out, Father?"

Joe gave Mr Lane the little calendar off the desk. "Every family gets one of these at Christmastime. No charge"—this to Mrs Lane, to no visible effect. She was about seven months pregnant and hadn't spoken to Joe yet. But he stayed with her. "Gives you," he said, producing another calendar from the bottom drawer of his desk, "the usual days and months, Mass times, confessions, rules for fasting (what's left of 'em), fire and police numbers, baseball, football, and hockey schedules—everything you need to know, ma'am."

Mrs Lane regarded Joe solemnly—she was hard to figure.

"Thanks, Father." Mr Lane handed the calendar to his wife. "She's French, Father. I was in the Company's international division when we met."

"*Comment allez-vous?*" Joe said to Mrs Lane, to no visible effect.

Mr Lane handed the check to Joe (who saw it was for five hundred dollars). "Just consider that for this year, Father. I'm sure you can find good use for the balance. I'll see you again in January."

"Very good of you, Mr Lane." But Joe didn't want the man to think he'd bought a piece of him. "You realize the balance goes to the parish, not to me personally?"

"Is that how it works?"

"Unless you specify otherwise, yes. The priest has to assume that whatever's given to him is given to him in his official capacity."

"Pretty strict."

"Yes, but a good thing, in a way. So I'll just put the balance in the building fund"—Joe checked the chart on his desk—"$291.62. Thanks, Mr Lane."

"Father, I've got a thing about building funds. If it's not too late to specify, I'd like the balance to be used as you think best—to be *yours*."

"Oh?" Joe showed more surprise and less concern than he felt. "Well, in that case, thanks again, Mr Lane." But Joe, more than before, didn't want the man to think he'd bought him. "Actually, it doesn't make much difference. I'm plowing my salary, if you can call it that, back into the parish, not to mention what little money I have of my own. A matter of bookkeeping, actually."

"What I was thinking, Father."

"This typewriter and the one in the other office, they're not what I'd have to buy if I were spending parish funds. This is a very nice machine." Joe turned to admire it.

"We have that model in our office, Father." But obviously Mr Lane wasn't interested in typewriters and chose that moment, though he'd been told over the phone that it wouldn't do him any good, to try again. "Father, you'd think now would be soon enough to enroll kids for school in fall."

"You would, yes, but you'd be wrong, Mr Lane. The boy, as I said, we can take—as of now. Tomorrow, or the next day, maybe not."

"I can't see putting the girl in a public school, Father."

"Oh, I don't know, Mr Lane." Joe wasn't a fanatic about education. All he'd wanted was a school where the emphasis was on studies and sports (*mens sana*, you might say, *in corpore sano*), where those who failed were not passed, where the boys wore dark green blazers and the girls dark green jumpers ("Down with the daily style show!"). But such a school stood out nowadays. Even Protestants and Jews tried to get their kids into Joe's school.

"Father, how about moving in another desk?"

"No, no. It wouldn't be fair to the other children in that grade, *or* to the Sister."

"What if *I* talked to the Sister?"

Joe didn't care for this at all. "No dice."

"You can't do *anything*?"

"What can I do, Mr Lane? Short of enlarging the school."

"Can *I* do anything, Father? Would it help if I gave you another check?"

So. But Joe wasn't *certain* he'd been insulted, and didn't want to be—he gave the man a possible out. "Toward enlarging the school? I'm afraid there are no such plans, if that's what you mean."

"No, it'd be *yours*."

So. "I'll put you down for a year, Mr Lane. You won't have to see me in January." Joe rose from his desk, moved swiftly to the door, opened it, and stood by it, waiting for the couple to go. When they passed him, he ignored the man (and was himself ignored) but nodded to the woman, feeling sorry for her—probably she'd been afraid all along that something like this would happen, and hence her silence, he thought. He went back to his desk and sat down to think.

People, he was thinking, have a right to be judged by their own standards until these can be raised, when he noticed that there were two calendars on his desk and no check.

Well, *he* wanted no part of it. Yes, the Lanes might attend Mass elsewhere. But they would discover when the time came, say, to have a baby baptized, that it couldn't be done elsewhere. The Church, to that extent anyway, was still the Church.

A bad situation, though—one of those situations from which the wise pastor ostensibly retires but handles in due course through his assistant.

Later that evening, after Father Felix had retired to the new bed in the guest room, Joe and the curate (whose name Joe still didn't know) sat on in the pastor's study. Joe, doing most of the talking, had had less than usual, the curate more, it seemed—he was yawning. "Used to be," Joe was saying, "we all drove black cars. I still do." Joe couldn't understand why a priest, even a young priest today, if able to afford a new car, would choose one the color of the curate's. "I guess it's not important. St Francis," Joe said, answering the phone.

"If *you're* St Francis, *I'm* Lyndon B. Johnson."

"Hold on, Lyndon. Don't hang up."

But Lyndon did.

"About phone calls, Father. Be sure you get the name and address before you give out any information, even Mass times. And don't settle bets. And don't discuss theology. Or you'll have drunks and worse calling at all hours. I've got a few more things to tell you, but they'll keep."

"In that case . . ." The curate swallowed a yawn. "Think I'll go to bed, Father."

Joe—he hated to go to bed—changed the subject. "How's the room? O.K.?"

"O.K."

Joe had been expecting a bit more and wondered if he had hurt the curate's feelings. "It's not important, what I was saying about cars."

The curate smiled at Joe. "My uncle's the dealer in Whipple. He gave me a deal on the car, but that was part of it—the color."

"I see." Joe tried not to appear as interested as he was. "What's your uncle call his place—Whipple Volkswagen? I know a lot of 'em do. That's what they call it here—Inglenook Volkswagen."

"He calls it by his own name."

"I see." Joe tried not to appear as interested as he was. "And this is your *father's* brother?"

"My mother's."

"I see."

"Think I'll turn in now, Father."

"Maybe we both should. Sunday's always a tough day."

12

Sunday

That morning, with Joe watching from the sacristy, the curate said his first Mass in the parish. He was slow, of course, but he wasn't fancy, and he didn't fall down, though he did stumble once. (This had made Joe think of the old pre-ecumenical, or triumphalist, joke about the curate who'd lost his footing at his first Mass, causing the pastor to whisper from the sacristy, "Get up! Get up! They'll be doing that down the street," and had also made Joe think the joke is on us now.) His sermon was standard, marred only by his gestures, and he read the announcements well. In one important respect he had been a disappointment.

"I should've told you," Joe said to him in the sacristy after Mass, "to introduce yourself to the congregation."

"Sorry. I'll do it next week. Father, what'd you think of the sermon?"

What have we here, a budding preacher? Let's hope not. "The sermon? Good enough. One thing I would say, Father. Your words and gestures were a little out of sync at times—looked like a bad job of dubbing."

The curate nodded. "Somebody said something like that at the sem."

Joe was pleased to have his criticism confirmed and taken so well. "Gestures—you have to feel 'em, or be a very gifted speaker. I gave 'em up."

"Maybe *I* should."

Joe nodded, pleased at the prospect.

"By the way," the curate said, "I'll be eating out today."

"Oh?" A little sudden, wasn't it?

"With one of my classmates."

"I see." But Joe didn't.

"Thought I'd better tell you."

"Good idea, but the word is *ask*."

"What I meant, Father."

"O.K."

That afternoon the Twins were rained out in Boston. So Joe and Father Felix were stuck with each other—and had at it in the study with the Sunday paper. Joe, by his good example, his tidiness, with the paper, had tried to make Father Felix mindful of the next reader, but had failed. The monk, whose glasses still needed changing, still held the paper open in front of him, as far away from him as he could, so that it was like the prow of a ship, until his arms gave out and the whole thing came crashing down in his lap—this was hard on the paper. Instead of smoothing it out while waiting for the strength to be restored to his arms, he cocked his head back and read what he could of the text in its collapsed and crumpled condition, the salient items or sentences thereof, noisily wrenching up more, shifting and tightening his grip like a dog with a bone—this was hard on the paper. If he'd read the funnies first (the only part of the paper he'd miss if it were missing), then Joe could have the other parts while they were fresh and intact. But no, the monk had to mess up the rest of the paper, it seemed, before he read the funnies.

Joe was that way about the sport section, keeping it to the last, sequestering it nowadays from Father Felix—that it wasn't missed said all there was to say about the monk as a sports fan, a role he worked at when there was a game on TV. "Struck 'im out!" he'd say in antiphon to the announcer, or, in the event of a home run, chant along with him, "Going, going, *gone!*" Or with the crowd, if it was football, "Dee-fense! Dee-fense!" All show. At crucial moments he'd get up and go to the bathroom.

Joe had hoped for some inside info when he learned that one of Father Felix's maternal uncles, now dead, whose name Joe remembered, had played tackle in pre-platoon days with the Packers and the Cardinals. "The *Chicago* Cardinals, Joe. You see, the team was later moved to St Louis or Kansas City." *Or!* That was the inside info. And: "Stan had a very nice wife, three very nice children—one a Sister of St Joseph—and a very nice business, a bowling alley in Kenosha." "Listen, Father. Stan lined up with the great Johnny Blood, with the great Ernie Nevers, and against the great Bronco Nagurski." "Joe, how old are you?" "Forty-four, why?" "Joe, you're going through a dangerous period for a man, especially for a priest. I've heard it called second puberty." "You have, huh? And was this by any chance at the monastery?" "It could've been." "I thought so. Luther was right about you guys." (Joe had been pleased to get that in, now that Luther was being fitted out with wings by ecumenists, some of them monks, and it sounded no worse to Joe in retrospect than what Father Felix had said to him.)

Joe had tried hard with Father Felix. In the beginning there had been afternoons at the stadium (spoiled not so much by the monk's ignorance and indifference as by his rather *amused* attitude), drives into the countryside to see the autumn foliage ("You should see it at the monastery"), visits to new churches of all denominations, since Joe would have to build a church someday (visits discontinued because the monk wasn't, as he put it, terribly interested in new churches, or, for that matter, old ones, and—it came out—disliked the bucket seats in Joe's car). So now, as a rule, they spent Sunday afternoons at home, in the study, sent out for seafood dinners, on which the monk's verdict was always "Very tasty," and watched television (which the monk didn't have in his cell at the monastery). This was all right when there was something on, by which Joe meant major sports, including golf, and also things like "Meet the Press" and "Face the Nation." But the monk wasn't so discriminating—he enjoyed quiz programs, bowling, water-skiing, government propaganda. At such times, after a beer or two, Joe would go down to his office and read the sport section in peace and quiet, or retire to his bedroom and drop off, float off, collar in hand.

On hot days, like this one, he might wake up in a sweat and wade through the study in a dazed state, startling the monk ("My!") but for whom Joe might have had his nap in the air-conditioned comfort of the study. That afternoon Joe kept moving, like a fighter in trouble, and made it to the kitchen, where he opened and reached into the refrigerator for a beer and then resisted it. Orange juice then? No. V-8? No. Tonic (*no* gin)? No. Ice water? No. Lukewarm chlorinated water from the tap? No, not even that. How about taking a much needed bath? No. A spot of mouthwash? No. How about just going to the toilet? No. Hey, I know—how about a *beer?*

Hey, what was he doing?

Ninety in the shade, and he was going out into the sun! *Why?* Hadn't he done enough? Hadn't he, though he'd lost points by opening the refrigerator, rallied, fought back, and won by a clear decision? Yes, he had, but the thing is not to let up, the thing is to pour it on, as every champion knows, be he (or she) athlete or saint, and that was what he was doing, pouring it on. Spiritually and physically—let's face it—he'd dropped too many decisions. He was on the way down. But he still had it at times. Call it guts, call it class. The great ones all had it—Sugar Ray, St John of the Cross, Man o' War, Stymie, and, not to forget the ladies, Gallorette . . .

From the can of nails in the garage, as from the ump, he took the official American League ball (a dog's ball of rubber, actually) and strolled out (about thirty feet out into the driveway, actually) to the mound in that hitter's heaven and pitcher's hell, Fenway Park, smelling the popcorn, the peanuts, the hot dogs, the cigarette and cigar smoke, the natural grass, hearing the chuckle of beer pouring into paper cups, the partisan but (he being what he was) reverent cries from the Bosox fans. After taking his warm-up tosses, these powdering the inside corners of the strike zone (chalked on the garage door of stadium green), he hitched up his trousers—a few clubs had worn dark uniforms in the past, the Chisox last?—and mopped his brow (one of the ways he doctored the ball) and glared at the hitter. It was the usual bases-loaded-nobody-out situation, or he, having worked and won at home the night before, after hearing confessions, wouldn't have got the call. Announcers up in the booth going on and on about him. "A picture-book pitcher!" "His delivery as, in the words of the Psalmist, oil being poured out!" "Yeah, and how he fields his position!" "He didn't learn *that* in books!" "Wire here signed Arch: 'MAY THE BETTER THAT IS TO SAY MORE DESERVING TEAM WIN.' How *about* that! That's America, folks!" "Understand Father said the ten o'clock Mass in his parish this morning." "Understand it was a *high* one." "Flown in by United." "Police escort." "Wire here signed Lefty: 'IF FATHER FIGURED IN A TRADE COULD BACKWARD CHURCH AUTHORITIES QUEER DEAL?'" "Well, as I understand it, they *could*, but probably wouldn't—in the national interest."

"The Bosox could sure use Father." "*Any* club could." He alone, with his knowledge of batters (encyclopedic), his stuff (world of), his control (phenomenal), had made the Twins a constant threat down the years. Forty-four now, ancient for baseball, he was perhaps best described as a short, fat, white Satchel Paige. Once a starter and consistent twenty- (make that thirty-) game winner, now used principally in relief. Iron Fireman. Little Engine That Could. His ERA still infinitesimal. Like Walter Johnson (the Big Train) and Ty Cobb and Rogers Hornsby, he was more respected than loved by players and fans, to say nothing, in his case, of his flock and fellow clergy. "Struck 'im out!" "Blew it past 'im!" "Father can really bring it!" "Wire here signed LBJ: 'HATE HIS METHODOLOGY BUT WILL SAY THIS FOR THE MOTHER HE DON'T TAKE NO CENSORED.' " "Wire here signed Backward Church Authorities, per Catfish: 'BOSOX CAN HAVE HIM GOOD RIDDANCE HIT ME WITH CROSS.' " Tough product of bygone era, up the hard way, sandlots, maximum-security seminary, buses, daytime ball. Boozer? A secret if so, but no secret—*vide* bios and centerfolds in *Playboy* and *Homiletic and Pastoral Review*—once wore no underwear on heavy dates and now chews Mail Pouch exclusively. Said to employ spitter (true), beanball (false)— Look out! Miraculously, his old sweat shirt, never laundered, dry-cleaned, or pressed (why not paper money?), gave off a pleasing odor, and his flapping right sleeve, denounced by batters and pruned by umpires, always grew back. The truth, known only to his confessor and the North American hierarchy, was that the garment in question, once without sleeves but no longer so, having grown them, was his old hair shirt. It would hang, when his playing days were over if they ever were, in Cooperstown, by the wish of the late Chaplain General U.S.A. and Cardinal Archbishop of New York (a recusant Bosox fan) in the pious and patriotic hope that it would settle for all time (sæcula sæculorum) the hash of un-American nativist hillbilly, and un-American pinko knee-jerk liberal, enemies of the Church.

"Struck 'im out!"

To a standing ovation from the all-too-loyal but ever-fair Bosox fans, he left the mound, returned the ball to its can of nails, and red of hand and face, dripping sweat, he passed through the kitchen, *by* the refrigerator (still pouring it on), through the study ("My!"), into the bathroom. Here he, now the ageing champ surrounded by handlers, press, police, and other well-wishers ("Had the little wife make a novena for you, Father"), stripped down to nothing ("Sorry, boys, no pix"), urinated—*any*thing to make the weight—and stepped on the scale. Something wrong with it? He turned on the bathwater full blast and sat down in it to save time (people spent what otherwise might have been the best part of their lives waiting for bathtubs to fill) and to get the benefits, if any, of hydrotherapy. He turned off the water with his toes to exercise the muscles and joints he might need to climb trees if civilization broke down completely, if there were any trees then and he was still around—the last man on earth a priest, Apostle to the Insects, if any, or business as usual. He used Dial soap, wishing everybody did, and emerged from the tub pink. He dried himself thoroughly—it was the *weight* of water that had kept the oceans, thank God, a mystery to man—and stepped on the scale. Something wrong with it? No, a man had a chance spiritually—it was more or less up to him—but physically, after a point, no. Still, he did feel better after he'd pitched an inning or two, enough to give him that old afterglow that only athletes know.

And so, deodorized, pink, immaculate in black and white, carrying his breviary, he passed through the study again ("Well!"), through the kitchen, and went over to the church. He chose a pew at random, knelt, and prayed. First for his parishioners, his first concern as pastor, then for his friends and relations living and dead, his enemies, if any, and then for, well, peace. The trouble was he believed that light would have to come first, that light even more than love was what was needed in the world today—light and the guts to act from it, the grace to gamble on it. Before people in general, including himself, and not just the assholes in high places (who know what people are like and profit by that sad knowledge) could lift up their minds and hearts there would have to be light. *"Let there be light."* So it was simpleminded, and not just simple-hearted, to pray for peace. But since that was the form—God knew he knew better—he prayed for peace. Then he sat back in the pew and read his office. If the text suggested a line of thought, he went along with it for a bit, not counting the time entirely lost. But he no longer hoped for a breakthrough, no longer forced himself to meditate, lest God and he both be bored.

He got on with the job, but not in unseemly haste, and when he finished, he'd leave the church, but not in unseemly haste, not breaking into a run, though headed for the kitchen, the refrigerator. He'd pick up a tray of ice and carry it through the study ("Well, well"), into the bathroom, his bar, where the hard stuff was kept in the same drawer with the shoe polish (and thus kept in its place). He'd make a couple of drinks—not undoing all he'd done that afternoon to deny himself but striking a balance. (You could laugh at the old via media, but it was still the best way—it had to be watched, though, or you'd end up in a rut.) After another drink or two, after their very tasty seafood dinner, he'd drive the monk to his bus. "See you Saturday, Father." "Okey-doke, Joe." And that would be it for another week.

*   *   *

That evening, after a surprise visit—"Just a social call, we live in Silverstream, you know"—from Earl, his wife, and two of their children, Joe washed the glasses in which he'd served them all 7-Up, finished the Sunday paper, read the *Catholic Worker* (and wrote it a check), switched the TV on and off at intervals, had a drink, two, touched it up once, twice—and all the time the likelihood that the curate would soon return got likelier and likelier.

Joe still hadn't written off the evening when, at eighteen after eleven, the curate returned. The door to the study was open, and the pastor was clearly visible within, in his Barcalounger, but the curate passed by without a word of greeting or explanation and could soon be heard taking a shower. When the drumming stopped, the pastor tried to get up, only to find his left foot asleep. While waiting for service to be resumed, he changed his mind about inviting the curate in for a nightcap. It was the curate's move. The hour, though late, was not too late, and the pastor's door was open.

To judge by the silence, though, the curate had gone to bed.

The pastor got up, shut his door, made himself a nightcap, switched on the TV, returned to his Barcalounger.

In some respects, with the pastor sitting alone, watching an old movie, it was like all those nights he'd known before he had a curate.

In one respect, though, it would be different: the pastor, not wishing to be heard foraging in the kitchen, would go to bed hungry.

13
Monday

Joe had the eight o'clock Mass, the curate the nine, and so they had breakfast at different times, Joe then going down to his office, the curate where?

Joe gave him a call. "Good morning. The time is ten past ten, the temperature is seventy-one, and the sun is shining."

"That you, Father?"

"That's right. Hope I didn't disturb you."

"No, I was just reading my office."

"Read it in your office, Father, or in church. That's what I do."

"Where you calling from, Father?"

"I'm calling from my office. You should be in yours."

"What's up?"—no immediate response—"I'll be right down."

Joe got a nasty shock, but concealed it, when the curate appeared before him in overalls and T-shirt, saying, "What's up?"

"What d'ya mean 'What's up?'? We open at nine thirty."

"We do?"

"As a rule. There'll be days when you have a wedding or funeral, but as a rule you should be in your office by ten when you have the nine o'clock Mass, by nine thirty when you have the eight. I was down here at nine today, but we open at nine thirty."

"For what?" said the curate.

Joe looked at him hard. "You thought your office was just a place to see people in?"

"More or less."

"Well, it's not, Father. That'll become clear to you as time goes on. Meanwhile, I don't want to see you got up like that."

"Around the house, I thought . . ."

"No good, Father. No overalls."

"Overalls? You mean jeans."

Joe did, but wouldn't use the word, hating the phony-cozy sound of it. "Look, Father. You may not be able to brighten the corner where you are, but why crumb it up? Why go out of your way to look bad? Everybody's doing it, sure, but you're not everybody, Father. You're not an old cowhand and you're not the boy next door. You're a priest, and that means, among other things, you dress like one. If you're traveling, say, and don't want to be bothered by people, that's different. But otherwise people have a right to know what you are. Don't be a snake in the grass, Father. Your feet sweat, or what?"

The curate, looking down at his feet, shook his head.

"O.K.," Joe said. "Sandals around the house, with a cassock, or with trousers and a shirt (either white or black), but not with a suit. I see somebody in a suit wearing sandals—and I don't only mean a priest—I mean *any*body—I want to throw up. Black socks, Father."

"Black?"

"Black. I hate these piddling little departures from the rule. I can understand a man leaving the priesthood, but wearing colored socks, including grey, no. No good."

"Breaks the monotony."

To show what he thought of *that*, Joe shut his eyes and

hung his head, simulating death, then snapped out of it. "You wouldn't say that, Father, if you knew anything about monotony. It's not that easy. But that's not the point. The point is, Why ruin a perfect color combination? Yes, perfect. *Any* man looks better in black and white. I don't say good; I say better. That's why evening dress is, or was, black and white. Actually, we're lucky that way, as priests. Look at the Buddhists."

The curate shook his head in, as seen on television, dismay.

Joe reread the message on the curate's chest ("Thou Shalt Not Kill, Bend, Fold, or Mutilate"), and said, "I've never worn T-shirts, even plain ones, but I have nothing against them as underwear. That's all they were ever meant to be, you know. Now, for Christ's sake—I mean that literally, Father—go up and change and come down again."

The curate came down in a cassock, but was still wearing the heavy grey socks with red toes and heels, which Joe said nothing about, however, hoping thus to give the young man pause, time to see where taking a stand against his pastor, if that was what he thought he was doing, had got him—out on a limb.

"Let's go over to your house," Joe said.

In the curate's office, about which the curate had said nothing on his first visit, on Saturday, and still said nothing, Joe went over to a cabinet and threw open its doors. "We're all right at the moment, Father, but it'll be one of your jobs to order supplies." Joe showed him the check writer. "Have to introduce you to the people at the bank"—assuming I ever find out your name—"and you can leave a specimen of your signature." Joe moved away from the cabinet, leaving the doors open, saying, "Oh, close those doors, Father," to involve him, and went over to the bank of files. He opened and closed a drawer, another, another, enjoying the smooth, gliding action, the bright colored tabs (new) on the folders. "Every family or household has a file. Parishioner comes in, you don't have to start from scratch—you know the wife's first name, how many kids, *their* names, and so on." Joe opened another drawer and, unable to control himself, enjoying the action so much, closed it, having meant to leave it open for the curate to close. "Parish correspondence. Strictly chronological"—Joe decided not to mention the stuff that came from Toohey undated, or dated, say, "Thursday." Joe went over to the bookcase, reached down to the bottom shelf, and slapped a big canvas-bound volume. "Parish register. Really something when I came here. Vital statistics on scraps of paper stuck inside, never entered." Joe handed a loose-leaf binder to the curate, involving him. "*Index* to the parish register. My idea. You don't have to hunt through the parish register every time somebody wants a baptismal certificate. Have to keep the index up to date, though, or it's useless. Be one of your jobs." The curate—involved?—put the index back in the bookcase. Joe, going over to the desk, caught himself before he sat down at it from force of habit, and went to one of the lemon chairs formerly in his office. "Sit down, Father. No, at the desk." After the curate had done this, Joe said, "You don't say much, Father."

"About what?"

"Anything. The office area. Weren't you surprised when you saw it?"

"No. I mean I'd heard about it."

Joe sniffed, assuming the worst. "There's been a lot of talk. Most of it pro, but some of it con. You know the clergy. Or maybe you don't. They come out here and sneer at the office area, laugh at my bathroom—it's orange and black tile, *bright* orange, an architect's error." Joe shook his head. "I've taken a lot, and not just from the clergy. 'Father, when will you build *God* a nice house?' One of the nuns—thank God they're gone for the summer." (What the nun had actually said was, "Father, when will you build *God* a nice house like *yours*?" to which he'd swiftly replied, "And like *yours*, Sister?") "But most of the negative comment comes from the clergy—from guys who wish *they'd* built the rectory first and now are afraid they'll never get it. It's not easy to sell people on a rectory after you've sold them on a church, especially if they're still paying for the church, especially if there's already a rectory of sorts. Fortunately, there wasn't one here, just the beginnings of one, a basement, where my predecessor lived, and I built the convent there. Fortunately, I say, because the rectory would've been like the church—on the small side, wartime construction, nothing like this. These guys"—coming back to his critics, and in case the curate was one—"like to forget I spent a year in a trailer and lived in a room in the school. And God'll get a new house, God willing. Just waiting until the time is ripe, saving the best wine till last." (This didn't, as it had the Arch and his reverend consultors, move the curate visibly.) "What I *don't* like about waiting, apart from the overcrowding at the late Masses on Sunday, is the way construction costs keep rising. And as I see it, money's going to get tighter. Don't suppose you know much about that—money."

"No. Not much."

"Well, you'll be glad to hear we don't talk about it here— in church. We just present the bill for services rendered, like doctors and lawyers." Joe explained his fiscal system. "Actually, it's just the old pew-rent system updated, with the option of time payments—something people today understand. I had the Sunday-envelope system, but they were killing me with their vacations. Summer *and* winter. In the history of the world there's never been a time like this for travel—everybody and his brother. With my overhead, I had to do something."

"Five hundred seems a lot."

"In most cases, in a parish like this, it's not three percent of the family income. The Mormons, I understand, get ten."

"Still seems a lot."

"It's not for every parish. Ideally, it should only be tried in new parishes, so you don't have the troublesome changeover period." Joe hadn't passed through that period yet.

"Still seems a lot."

Hey, *whose* side you on? "The old nickel-and-dime days are over, Father, but if it'll make you feel any better I'll handle that part for the time being."

"Thanks."

Joe got up, went to the desk, on which a light snow of paper had fallen since the curate's first visit, and dipping into it, selected an unimportant letter. "Answer this one right away, will you? I've made a note on the margin so you'll know what to say. Keep it brief. Sign *your* name—Assistant Pastor. Better let me have a look at it before you seal it." So the curate could get on with it, Joe headed back to his office.

"Does it have to be *typed*?"

Joe pulled up short. "How's that?"

"Can't *type* it."

"What d'ya mean?"

"Can't *type*."

Joe stood there in a distressed state. "Can't type," he said to himself, and then to the curate, "You mean at the sem you did everything in longhand? Term papers and everything?"

The curate, who seemed to think that too much was being made of his disability, nodded.

"Hard to believe," Joe said. "Why, you must've been the only guy in your class not to use a typewriter."

"There was one other guy."

Joe was relieved—at least the gambler in him was—to know that he hadn't been quite as unlucky as he'd supposed. "But you must've heard guys all around you using typewriters. Didn't you ever wonder why?"

"I never owned a typewriter. Never saw the need." The curate sounded proud, like somebody who brushes his teeth with table salt. "I write a good, clear hand."

Joe snorted. "*I* write a good, clear hand. But I don't do my parish correspondence by hand. And I hope *you* won't when you're a pastor."

"The hell with it, then."

Joe, who had been walking around in a distressed state, stopped and looked at the curate, but the curate—pretty clever—wouldn't look back. He was getting out a cigarette. Joe shook his head, and walked around shaking it. "Father, Father," he said.

"Father, hell," said the curate, emitting smoke. "You should've put in for a stenographer, not a priest."

Joe stopped, stood still, and sniffed. "Great," he said, nodding. "Sounds great, Father. But what does it *mean*? Does it mean you expect me to do the lion's share of the donkey work around here? While you're out saving souls? Or sitting in your room, waiting for something to turn up? Does it mean when you're a pastor you'll expect your curate to do what you never had to do? I hope not, Father. Because, you know, Father, when you're a pastor it may be years before you have a curate. You may never have one, Father. You may end up in a one-horse parish. Lots of guys do. You won't be able to afford a secretary, or public stenographers, and you won't care to trust your correspondence to nuns, to parishioners. You'll never be your own man. You'll always be an embarrassment to yourself and others. Let's face it, Father. Today, a man who can't use a typewriter is as ill-equipped for parish life as a man who can't drive a car. Go ahead. Laugh. Sneer. But it's true. You don't want to be like Toohey, do you? *He* can't type, and he's set this diocese back a hundred years. He writes 'No can do' on everything and returns it to the sender. For official business he uses scratch paper compliments of the Universal Portland Cement Company."

Depressed by the thought of Toohey and annoyed by the curate's cool, if that was what it was, Joe retired to his office. He sat down at his desk and made a list. Presently, he appeared in the doorway between the offices, wearing his hat. "And, Father," he continued, "when you're a pastor, what if you get a curate like yourself? Think it over. I have to go out now. Mind the store."

Joe drove to the city and bought a typing course consisting of a manual and phonograph records, and he also bought the bed—it was still there—the double, with pineapples. He was told that if he ever wished to order a matching chest or dresser there would be no trouble at all, and that the bed, along with box spring and mattress, would be on the Thursday delivery to Inglenook.

"O.K., Father?"

"O.K., Earl."

And that afternoon Joe, in his office, had a phone call from Mrs Fox. She just wondered if everything was O.K., she said—as if she didn't know. She was still dying to see the room. "What's it *like*!" Joe said he thought the room had turned out pretty well, thanked Mrs Fox for helping him, and also for calling, and hung up.

Immediately, the phone rang again. "St Francis," Joe said.

"Bill there?"

"*Bill?*"

"For *me*?" said the curate, who had been typing away, or, anyway, typing.

Joe tried to look right through the wall. (The door between the offices was open, but the angle was wrong.) "Take it over there," he said, and switched the call.

There were no further developments that day with respect to the curate's identity, but Joe was pleased to see the young man wearing black and white—black shoes, socks, trousers, and white shirt—at dinner, and afterwards, with a few more things to say to him, things best said in private (out of Mrs P.'s hearing), Joe took him into the study.

"Try one of these," Joe said, producing a box of baby cigars when the curate got out his cigarettes. "They're better for you. I don't say good; I say better."

"O.K. Thanks."

"Don't forget to put your little car in the garage tonight, Father."

"I'm not worried about it."

"*I'm* not worried about it, but we don't want the place looking like a trailer camp. Lots of miles per gallon, huh?"

"I can't say yet."

"Well, when you can, *don't*. Most small-car owners, that's all they talk about. I don't suppose you'll use any, but your gas and oil are on the house. Go to Smiley's Shell, here in town, and tell 'em who you are." *Tell me!* "Your dry-cleaning's on the house. Also laundry. Hard on it, sending it out, but don't try to economize. You'll have a liberal clothing allowance." Did the curate realize how lucky he was to have Joe for his pastor? Joe doubted it. "By the way, and I should've told you this before last night, the curfew blows at nine."

"You're kiddin'!"

"Afraid not."

The curate shook his head in, as seen on television, dismay.

"O.K., Father. Let's see if I can make myself understood. Let's say you're me, and I'm you, and this is my third day on the job. On the first day, I show up at the last possible minute. On the second day, I go out for dinner and come in eleven hours later. The next morning you have to call me down to the office. And now you sound like you want to stay out all night. *I* do, I mean. Remember, I'm you. I guess I expect to come and go as I please. I guess I think I'm old enough to look after myself—and maybe I am. Let's say I am, Father. But, Father—remember now you're me—*how do you know?*"

"I don't. I just assume you're an adult and I treat you like one."

"You do, huh?"

"Until I have reason not to."

"Until, huh? And then what—slam on the brakes?"

"If necessary."

"No good, Father. It's punitive then. This way, no. It's just one of the house rules—like black socks and no overalls. There's nothing personal about it. And look. Don't take it so hard. You want to go somewhere—a movie, a ball game— we'll work it out so you can. Maybe so we both can. So put your little car away, Father, and I'll make us a drink."

14

Revelations

On Thursday morning, as usual, Joe knocked out the church bulletin and, though it lacked something again, he was about to put it to bed when, inspired, he phoned the state highway department, was switched to the license division, and spoke to a voice that seemed to be coming out of a can.

"O.K.," it said. "Color and make?"

"VW beetle. Light brown, or dark yellow—sort of a caramel color."

"Brown VW beetle. O.K., who's calling?"

"I'd rather not say."

"Is this an accident case?"

"Oh, no."

"Sometimes people leave the scene of an accident. Then they get to thinking they might've been seen and reported. So they try and fix it up with the damaged car's owner before he or she goes to the police."

"Oh, no. Nothing like that. It's a long story, and I won't go into it, but I can tell you it's not an accident case. No damage of any kind. The car's right here."

"Where?"

"I'd rather not say."

"How long's the car been there?"

"Since Saturday, but that doesn't have anything to do with it."

"You have reason to believe the car's been abandoned or stolen?"

"No, no. I just thought you could tell me the owner's name if I gave you the license number. That's all."

"It's not the policy of this division of the department to give out information unless we know why we're doing it and who we're dealing with. We get a lot of calls—all kinds, mister. Some stud sees a broad, takes down her license number, and calls us. For all I know, you're one of *those*."

"This is Father Hackett, SS Francis and Clare's, Inglenook?"

"Oh, hello, Father. Captain O'Connell here. Sorry I didn't know it was you, Father. You see, we have to be pretty careful. I don't have to tell you why."

"No."

"Father, you say the car's there?"

"Yes."

"In your parking lot?"

"In my driveway."

"And you want it moved?"

"No, no, Captain."

"You don't want it moved, Father, or you don't want it moved by the *police*?"

"I don't want it moved, Captain. Believe me, I don't want it moved."

"Father, you know what I think?"

"What?"

"You want this information so you can ask the owner in a nice way to move his or her car."

"No, no. I don't want him to move it."

"Father, would you mind telling us why you want this information?"

"I'd rather not."

"Father, it's not the policy of this division of the department to give out information unless we know why we're doing it."

"I see."

"I know you wouldn't want us to make an exception in your case."

"If it's not the policy, no."

"Father, if you could give us *some* idea why you want this information."

"I'd rather not, Captain."

"Then all I can say, Father, is get in touch with your local police. They have access to this information. They'll ask why you want it, but maybe you wouldn't mind telling them."

"Thanks, but I think I'll just forget the whole thing."

"Nice talking to you, Father."

"And to you, Captain."

So Joe gathered up the bulletin copy, put on his hat, opened the door between the offices (had closed it before making the last phone call), and said to the curate (who was typing, so to speak), "Stepping out. Won't be long."

On the memo pad in his car he jotted down the purpose of his trip (BULL, BEER). But when he arrived at the *Universe*, where the bulletin was printed, he drove on. Thought he might, in the next hour or so, find out what he hadn't in more than a week? No, the odds were against it, about a hundred to one. But he still had an option or two—or three. Could go with the information he had, simply, chummily billing the curate as "Father Bill." Could call the VW people in Whipple, ask if they still had that light brown or dark yellow beetle, and take it from there. Could sneak into the curate's room and go through his books for one, probably a text, with his name in it.

At the Licensed Vintner's he exchanged his nice clean case for an unclean one (Mr Barnes not there).

Approaching Smiley's Shell he saw the lessee out by the

pumps, and drove in. "New customer for you, Jack, but a poor one, drives a beetle—my assistant. I'll pick up the tab."

"I know, Father. He came in yesterday."

At a hundred to one! "Have him sign for it?"

"Naw. I just put it down."

Joe sniffed. *"That* how we do?"

"How we do with you, Father."

Joe played out his losing hand. "Better have him sign for it in future."

"Wish you'd told me this before, Father."

"So do I."

Joe drove away, thinking O.K., that's it—he'd do the bedroom job that afternoon, Mrs P.'s afternoon off, as soon as she was gone.

He ran his car into the garage, out of the sun—another thing he'd have to tell the curate about, how hard it was on a car's finish, the sun. He left the unclean case in the trunk for the same reason he'd put the nice clean one there the evening before, after Mrs P. had gone, lest she think he had nothing to do but deliver beer to himself. He took the bulletin copy with him. He found the door between the offices closed now, and on his desk a typewritten note:

"INformation you re quested: William Alois Schmidt."

Only minutes later, while Joe was getting down to the job of thinking how the requested information could best be explained to the subject of it, a moving van from the St Vincent de Paul Society arrived (for his old bed, box spring, and mattress) prematurely—to put it mildly, which Joe didn't to the driver (no helper)—not, as promised, "sometime in the afternoon," when the whole operation (out with the old, in with the new) was to have taken place in Mrs P.'s absence. Yes, had this phase of the operation gone as planned, Mrs P.

might have had a shock or two in the morning when she didn't see the old bed and did see the new one, a double, but better that than this. "*I* don't know what's going on around here!" It was Joe's impression that the bed or beds operation was being associated, in Mrs P.'s mind, with the curate's appointment, perhaps because furniture had figured in it and because of the element of mystery in both matters. In any case, Mrs P. was upset, and with good reason, since nothing had been said to her about beds, new or old, and she probably thought she'd made the old one to no purpose that morning, not realizing that here was a case where ignorance was bliss and that Joe would've been happy to make the bed himself if the novelty of that small act wouldn't have upset her even more. "What'll happen next!" "Well, the store's bringing the new bed this afternoon." "But *I* won't be here!" "That's true."

After Mrs P. stripped the old bed, Joe and the driver (who said he had a bad back) tried to take it apart, Mrs P. standing by with the vacuum cleaner, impatient to do that part of the carpet (wall-to-wall) under the bed, which, ideally, couldn't be done until the bed was removed, which couldn't be done until it was taken apart, which couldn't be *done.* Joe was sweating profusely. "Hammer!" he gasped. Mrs P. brought the hammer, and Joe, wanting her elsewhere, told her to go ahead with making lunch, which she did, but kept making cameo appearances in the doorway. And when the bed came apart, she was there, on the scene, with the vacuum cleaner, and moved in like Gangbusters.

Joe and the driver loaded the bed, mattress, and box spring into the van, after which Joe served the driver (and himself) a cold beer on the back steps, tipped the man a fin for his trouble, and took a much needed bath, prolonging it, so that he had lunch alone, by design, not wishing perhaps to be questioned along certain lines by the curate at table, in Mrs P.'s hearing, in fact, not wishing to be so questioned period.

After lunch, he went down to his office—the door still closed—and wrote the story, entitling it "New Man/New Priest." He then put on his hat, said nothing to the curate, and delivered the copy. On his return (Mrs P.'s car gone), he brought in the beer, washed his hands, and went down to his office—the door still closed—to think. Explain. How could he? Not explain. How could he?

Presently he rose from his desk and opened the closed door, saying, "Stuffy," to which there was no response, and returned to his desk.

Presently from his desk: "Like to see you about something, Father."

When the curate came in, Joe had his head down and averted, in the confessorial position (though he was the penitent), and was fingering the typewritten note. "Father, when you got this . . . information . . . what'd you . . . say?"

"I said thanks."

Joe looked at the curate—no, he wasn't being funny (no, that wouldn't be like him). "Didn't say who you were?"

"No."

"He say who he was?"

"No. Who was he?"

Joe, for something to do in the ensuing lull, turned his hat (left upside down on his desk to cool) right side up, over the typewritten note. "Afraid I can't tell you that," he said, hearing the doorbell chime and:

"You order a bed?"

Joe and the curate went upstairs, and Joe, in view of his experience with Earl and the store, was glad that the bed—the right one, the double with pineapples—had come when promised, and the mattress and box spring too.

Joe and the curate and the two men from the store (who offered to help) assembled the bed, Joe supervising and otherwise doing more than his share, calling the men from the store by their first names (stitched on their shirts) and also, as he never had before, the curate by his. "Easy, Bill." Sam and George extricated the mattress and box spring from their cartons—these they offered to take with them, a load off Joe's mind. It was then, though, that Joe noticed—evidently the only one who had—that the mattress and box spring didn't match.

"Hold it," he said, and got on the phone.

"Oh, oh," Earl said. "Too bad you didn't catch it in time, Father."

"Too bad *I* didn't?"

"If you'd told the boys on the truck . . ."

"Earl."

"Yes, Father."

"They're still here."

"In that case, put one of 'em on, Father."

Joe gave the phone to Sam, who said, "Yup," "Nup," "Yup," and gave the phone to Joe.

"What's the deal, Earl?"

"All you have to do, Father, is specify the color of your choice. Choice of three—blue, pink, or silver grey. *That's* what I would've recommended in your case, Father. Silver grey."

"I don't care what color I get. Just so the mattress and box spring match."

"In that case, let's forget silver grey, Father. Blue or pink?"

"I don't care. All right. Blue."

"Blue. Now the mattress, or the box spring, is pink?"

"The mattress."

"That means the boys'll bring you a blue mattress on Monday."

"Wait a minute. Does that mean they'll take back the pink one today?"

"That's right."

"No good, Earl. I disposed of my old bed this morning."

"Oh, oh. M and B too?"

"What?"

"Mattress and box spring too, Father?"

"Yes, but they were for a single, Earl. My old bed was a single, remember?"

"Now I do. Father, how about using the new bed—the cannonballs—in the guest room? Just till Monday?"

"No good. I've got the monk coming on Saturday."

"Oh, oh. Forgot about *him*. Hey, how about the cot—or did you dispose of that?"

"No, it's still here somewhere."

"You couldn't use it—just till Monday?"

"You couldn't leave the pink mattress here till then?"

"Not very well, Father. No."

"Because of what it says on the label?"

"That's right. Public health measure. If you slept on it, we couldn't take it back and sell it. That's the law."

"You know what, Earl?"

"What, Father?"

"You can take 'em both back — the pink M and the blue B."

"And send out the silver grey?"

"And *not* send out the silver grey. I've had it with you people. I don't see how you stay in business."

"Father, just because somebody goofed . . ."

" 'Somebody,' huh?"

"Have her call me back. I'm talking to Father now. Sorry, Father. How's that again?"

"I have nothing to say."

"I don't care if she's the Queen of Siam. I'm talking to Father now. Sorry, Father. Now here's the way I look at it. Who's to know these units don't match? If you were a woman, it'd be different."

"*What* would?"

"Father, *you* don't care. You're a *man*."

"Yes, but what if I want to dispose of these units someday—to a woman?" (Joe was only thinking of what Mrs P. would say.)

"Father, you won't. These units'll last you a lifetime—and then some. All *right*, Foxie! I'll talk to her *personally*! Look, Father, you don't have to decide now, on the phone. Just let the boys know your decision."

Joe hung up. He let the boys know his decision, after which they left (with the cartons). Joe and Bill then made the bed. What was true of the bed pad was true, perhaps truer, of the sheets from the linen closet—all rather narrow, being singles, as Bill pointed out. Joe, who knew this but had been hoping that some sheets would be wider than they should be, said, "O.K., we'll buy some doubles, and also a pad"— so he wouldn't have to sleep right in the middle of the bed— "when we go out to eat."

" 'Lo, Ed," Joe murmured, waving back at Ed Smiley, pastor of St Peter's, Silverstream, who was at a table across the room with his curate and who, Joe had hoped, wouldn't see him.

"He was out at the seminary once, on a panel," Bill said.

"Ed was everywhere once, on a panel," Joe said. "Smiley, of Smiley's Shell, is Ed's brother, you know. Smiley runs a good, clean station. He has to. You can't mess around with Shell. Ed would be all right, or anyway better, if he didn't think of himself as a charismatic leader in this our time.

Hence the black leather jacket and the overalls he wears around the rectory ["Overalls?"—"You know what I mean"], the scooter he rides, the driv he talks ["Driv?"—"Drivel"]. Advised me to sprinkle grass seed in the snow and let nature do the rest. I believed him, too, because I *wanted* to. That's the trouble in the Church today. Too many clergy like Ed and too many people who want to believe 'em." Joe watched the waitress bring the check to Ed's table and give it to the curate. "The curate's running the parish, Bill. Ed's financially non compos." Joe watched Ed follow the curate out of the room. "That's the story on Ed, Bill. But his parishioners don't know. So keep it under your hat."

"Father, what's the story on that phone call?"

Since the matter hadn't come up when it might have—when they were making the bed, or when they returned to their offices, or in the car on the way to the restaurant, or during the meal until now—Joe had believed, because he'd *wanted* to, that Bill had decided not to pursue the matter, wisely and kindly, having perhaps seen the distress it had caused Joe earlier, that distress perhaps to be seen now. "It's a long story, Bill."

"You were hoping I wouldn't ask you again?"

"Yes. Sometimes we don't know what we're asking, Bill."

"I'd still like to know, Father."

"Yes, well." Until then Joe, who'd had two Martinis (Bill only one) and more than his share of the bottle of wine, might have done without a postprandial gin and bitters. The waitress, taking his order, looked unhappy (probably a Catholic or a non-Catholic), and Bill made it worse by abstaining and was obviously waiting to hear Joe's confession.

"Yes, well. It's customary for a pastor to be notified when he gets a curate, or change of curates. That wasn't done in your case—not properly. Toohey called up and said I was getting a curate, but didn't say who. 'Letter follows,' he said, and I haven't heard from him since. No letter. Nothing."

"That's funny."

"Yes, but that's how Toohey plays the game, and not just with me, though that may have something to do with it— that it's me. So I didn't know who you were when you showed up, and you didn't say—you didn't get a chance to, as it happened, which was my fault. For days, though, I'd been under a terrific strain, not knowing who was coming, or when, and that being so I couldn't tell anybody—Mrs P., Steve, Father Felix, the parishioners (in the bulletin). A hell of a situation."

"You should've called the Chancery."

"In the beginning, yes, but I was expecting the letter from Toohey. I was also expecting you to get in touch with me. All right. I was always out when you called. But if I'd called the Chancery, you might've been in trouble there."

Did Bill, drawing on his baby cigar, see, as he hadn't before, that Joe had protected him?

"A hell of a situation, Bill, and even worse after you came. I figured you'd introduced yourself to Mrs P., and Steve, and Father Felix, because none of 'em asked me your name. I hoped to hear one of 'em mention it, but I didn't. A hell of a situation, as I say, and it went on and on."

"You should've called the Chancery, Father."

"I told you why I didn't."

"After I came, I mean."

Slowly, Joe brought the glass down from his mouth. "You *mean* that?"

Bill looked as though he did.

"Use your nut, Bill. Put yourself in my place. Would you call up the Chancery to find out your curate's name—*after* you'd met him?'' Joe shook his head, trying to understand what Bill could have been thinking. ''You think just because it was all Toohey's fault, he wouldn't talk? It'd be all over the diocese and beyond. Father Felix would hear about it at the monastery. 'Hear the one about Joe Hackett?' The joke would be on me. On *us*. So, for God's sake, keep this thing under your hat.''

''You should've just asked *me*.''

''Yeah? When? A couple of hours after we met? The next day? This morning? What would you have thought if I had?''

''I don't know, but it would've been better than this.''

''Yes, but I didn't know it would be like this. I was trying to save us both embarrassment. I didn't want you to think what you would've—of me, of the Church, of yourself. I didn't want you to think you didn't matter, Bill. And I don't want you to think that now. So don't. This is all Toohey's fault. God help the diocese if they don't make a bishop of him pretty soon. He's doing untold harm where he is now. But I guess I don't have to tell you that, now.''

''You think he'll be a bishop?''

''Odds on. Oh, not here. Some two-bit see. I'm surprised it hasn't happened before this. I don't think the Arch likes him.''

''So what *did* you do?''

Joe was silent, thinking. They were back where they'd started, back to the phone call—it seemed unimportant now, after the embarrassing revelations. ''I called someone.''

''Who?''

The waitress moved in with the check and was, for some reason, about to drop it on Bill's side of the table.

''*I'll* take that,'' Joe said, annoyed with her.

''*Who?*''

''Look, Bill,'' Joe said, annoyed with him. ''I've told you

what I can—*why* and *how* this thing happened. Believe me, it wasn't easy."

"I realize that, Father."

"I'm damned glad to know your name, but I'm not about to say who told me. It wouldn't mean anything to you if I did, but to me it would. I'm sorry."

"I don't blame you, Father."

"You don't? Well, thanks. I can see how you might." Joe dropped some bills on the check, leaving more of a tip than he might have, in case the waitress was a Catholic or a non-Catholic, and swiftly departed, Bill following him.

15
Thereafter

Joe still had to do practically everything—all the accounts and correspondence—and he also had to think of jobs that Bill could do, quite a job. The future looked brighter, though, with Bill making good progress in his typing. Well, fairly good progress. He had turned against his manual, his records, even his phonograph—which at first, at the end of the business day, he'd lugged up to his room to play folk (in Joe's lexicon, "folks"), work, and protest songs on, but now, thank God, left down in his office. Bill was sweating it out these days, but so was Joe, and, really, Bill couldn't complain. It wasn't all business in the office area. With the door open between them, pastor and curate could carry on desk-to-desk conversation, and if the flow was more one way than the other, that was because there was so much Bill didn't know about practically everything—procedure and policy, the parish and the community, and the world in general. Here, too, Joe did what he could for Bill, mining a dozen periodicals that crossed his desk and passing them on with articles marked "Read" or "Skip." Sometimes Joe would go over to Bill's house just to smoke a baby cigar with him. And sometimes, Joe would put on his hat and say in the cawing voice of Edward G. Robinson in *Little Caesar* (to whom Joe knew he bore a growing resemblance), "Knock it off, kid." Bill would cover his typewriter (Joe was strict about that, as he was about not leaving the toilet seat up in Bill's lavatory) and off they'd go in Joe's car, the radio tuned to an FM music station for Bill. They had called at a number of rectories on business that could have been handled over the phone but wasn't because Joe enjoyed being seen with his curate—a pleasure he'd had to deny himself until he learned his curate's name. They had dropped in on a few parishioners, including the Gurriers—Bill enjoyed small talk, Joe didn't. At first, maybe after a visit to the hospital or the garage (in Bill's little car to bail out Joe's car, a habitual offender), they'd had a meal somewhere and gone on to box seats at the stadium— until it became clear to Joe that Bill, though he'd played in the outfield on his high school team and pitched in relief, was not greatly interested in the national game. One evening, at Bill's instigation, they had taken in a lousy foreign movie, after which Joe had stopped at a drugstore for aspirin and then, with the idea of keeping in shape, had bought a couple of catcher's mitts and a regulation ball. Now, when free in the evenings, they went out in the yard and pitched to each other. Bill had a honey of a fast ball, but Joe could hold him—better than Bill could hold Joe, who threw what is known as a heavy ball and was rather wild. Joe's change-up, too, was deceptive—as it was at such times in conversation. "You can say what you like about the Redemptorists, Bill, but don't forget St Alphonsus Liguori is a Doctor of the Church. You wouldn't remember Gomez. Tall like you, but frail. World of speed. With the Yanks." Sometimes the ball, streaking back and forth between them, going *pop* in Joe's mitt, *plunk* in Bill's, took part in their discussions, siding with the one who threw it last. *Pop.* "Get that junk off to Africa, Bill." *Plunk.* Joe hadn't realized, when he gave Bill permission to respond in a quiet way (nothing from the pulpit) to an appeal from an off-brand order of bearded missionaries for reading matter, T-shirts, and any spare change that might be lying around the house (toward the purchase of a "milch cow"), that parishioners would be involved to the extent they had, that Duz and Dash cartons would pile up in the office area. "Junk? No, you're right. We could and should be doing a lot more." *Pop.* "Don't put words in my mouth, Bill. Another operation like this and . . ." *Plunk.* "And what?" *Pop.* "And parishioners'll wonder what they're being protected from." *Plunk.* "Protected from!" *Pop.* "Under our system." *Plunk.* "Our system!" *Pop.* "Your bearded friends have their system. We have ours." *Plunk.* "So?" *Pop.* "They'll get their cow." *Plunk.* "So?" *Pop.* "I'm not so sure we will." *Plunk.* After they retired to the rectory—because of the failing light—and after a bath (Joe) and a shower (Bill), they might continue their discussion in the pastor's study, as they had that night, Joe in the end prevailing but contributing a twenty toward the purchase of the milch cow. Most of their evenings were spent together in the pastor's study, with drinks, TV if the Twins were playing away from home (but with the sound turned down), and good talk. Well, fairly good talk. Little interest was shown when Joe spoke of the remarkable personalities at the seminary during his era, and likewise when Bill spoke of his trials there, of piddling causes that already sounded like ancient history. Bill could say the usual things about the late Pope John, and about the present pope, but he couldn't discuss Frank Sinatra ("the Chairman of the Board") or Senator Dirksen ("the Wizard of Ooze"), and he hadn't even heard of figures like Fishbait Miller (the colorful doorkeeper of the House) and Nancy Dickerson (of all the media people, perhaps the one nearest and dearest to the President). Large, fertile areas of conversation—Capitol Hill, show business, sports—had therefore been abandoned. But what made the likeliest subjects unrewarding—the difference between Joe and Bill—was what kept them going when they got onto religion. Bill talked up the changes in the liturgy, lay participation, ecumenism, and so on, and Joe didn't. Bill claimed that religion had hit bottom in our time and had no place to go but up, and Joe questioned both statements. Bill said that religion (though not perhaps as we know it) was the coming thing, and that the clergy (though not perhaps as we know them) were the coming men. "Fuzzy thinking, Pollyanna stuff," Joe said, and advised Bill to stop reading Teilhard de Chardin (who—did Bill know?— had got a bang out of the Bomb) and other unpronounce- ables. So Joe was inclined to be bearish, and Bill bullish, about the future. As for the present, Joe could understand how Bill might be unhappy in his work, considering the satisfactions there were, or were said to be, in the priesthood—which, unfortunately, was not what it was cracked up to be in the seminary and not what *you* chose to make it. "Still, I'm sorry you don't like it here." "I like it all right." "But hoped for something better?" "Not better. Different." "Like what?" "I taught catechism at Holy Cross last summer." "So you know Al." (Al Fresco, not a friend, not an enemy, but also not a man to whom Joe was indifferent, was pastor at Holy Cross, a slum parish.) "I'm told he eats beans out of the can. O.K. I can see why you might want to go there, but what made you think you might?" "Father just told me he'd do what he could." "Probably meant he'd pray for you." Oh, Joe could see how it might be fine for the poor to have somebody like Bill ministering to their spiritual needs and confiscating switch- blades on the side, but why should a young man who'd more or less forsaken everything have the privilege of dealing with the world, the flesh, and the devil on his own terms? Might it not be better for another, one not so eager to share their lot, to go among the poor? Might it not be better for one like Bill to go to a place like Inglenook? These things didn't just happen. (Or why had Joe been sent first to Van and then to Catholic Charities?) ''Or is this Fruchtenberg''—one of Bill's classmates—''happy at Holy Cross?'' ''He thought he'd be studying abroad. He's a brain.'' ''Well, there you are.'' If Bill and Fruchtenberg had expected to labor in certain parts of the vineyard, and not in others, then they should have said so and saved the diocese the expense of educating them—and maybe the mistake of ordaining them if, later on, they jumped ship, as so many were doing these days. ''Bill, when you sign on this ship, you don't get out and swim, or try to walk on the water, because you think you should be doing more. You stay put. You do what little you can. You work on yourself.'' If Bill felt, as he said, thwarted and useless at SS Francis and Clare's—well, that was how men in slum parishes felt, probably Al too, if the truth were known. The truth was Bill had got what he wanted—a tough assignment, without the romantic props of a slum parish, bums, pigeons, and so on. ''This is a big old ship, Bill. She creaks, she rocks, she rolls, and at times she makes you want to throw up. But she gets where she's going. Always has, always will, until the end of time. With or without you.'' ''Man the lifeboats.'' ''Wrong again, Bill. No lifeboats on this ship—none needed.'' ''What would St Francis think of a parish like this?'' ''From what we know of him, I'm not sure he could hack it in a parish like this. But why do you ask? You might as well ask what Moses would think of space travel. Our means may be different, Bill, but the end's the same.'' ''We spill our seed on the ground.'' ''That so?'' ''I mean we waste our substance in spurious activity.'' ''I got you the first time.'' ''Suburban parishes are all the same.'' ''They all have money problems, if that's what you mean.'' ''Things like finance and construction shouldn't concern us at all. Or at least not as much.'' ''Turn it over to the laity, huh? That's the answer to everything nowadays. Turn it over to the laity." "Why not?" "Let 'em waste *their* substance?" "It wouldn't be the same for them." "Ho, ho." Sometimes Bill forgot himself and talked like the bad old clergy of dark, preconciliar times. "Look, Bill. We may be men apart and all that, but we still have to pay our way like everybody else. By the sweat of our brow, by doing things we don't want to do—like raising money. That's one of my jobs here. I don't ask the laity to do it. I don't even ask you. Look. This—*all* this—isn't my idea of the priesthood. But this is how it is, Bill, and how it's going to be. This is *it*, Bill—the future. I'm sorry." "I don't believe it." "You'd better, Bill. Al Fresco's living in the past. The corporal works of mercy have had it." "In this country maybe." "What'd you have in mind—Latin America?" "Well, I *didn't*." "What's *your* answer, Bill?" "You know I don't have one for a parish like this." "Well, there you are. For a parish like this, it's either yackety-yack about money all the time, or a system of some kind. The old nickel-and-dime days are over. (When I need repairs I know it's going to hurt, and if I weren't practically a master plumber and master everything else I'd get taken more often than not.) I have no choice. Pastors who think they can go along like the lilies of the field that toil not and neither do they spin—they find out differently. They find themselves out in the sticks." "Maybe that's better than this." "I wouldn't know. I do know one of the men from my class asked for and got a country parish. He couldn't stand the money worries in the city, he thought, and now he's collecting scrap iron to make ends meet. Farmers bring him their old rusty wheels. He doesn't find it any easier, I understand." " 'Easier' isn't what I want." " 'Easier' isn't what you've got." Naturally, Bill was finding it hard to adjust to reality after living in the rarefied atmosphere of the seminary. A slight case of the bends. That was all. Or was it?

"Pride, Bill." "Pride?" "Pride. You look down your nose at people out here because they aren't poor. They aren't poor enough, good enough, or maybe bad enough, to have you for a priest. Pride, Bill." All the same, Bill seemed to get along with them well enough. One evening at a cookout at Brad's place, after Joe said they had to be going, Bill wouldn't go, continued to sing along and play lead guitar around the campfire, and Joe had to drive home alone—a bad moment in the pastor-curate relationship. Late at night, in the pastor's study, Joe still accused Bill of looking down his nose at the parishioners because they weren't derelicts or great sinners, calling him an apostolic snob and a dreamer. In that connection, Joe had noticed that Bill had a faraway look in his eyes and had a head like a violin. Dreamers hadn't been so common in the Church back when he'd been one himself, hadn't constituted a working majority then, Joe was saying one night, when a picture of Rudolf Hess, the old Nazi, once Hitler's right-hand man and chosen successor, appeared on the TV screen, and Joe noticed that *Hess* had a head like a violin. Joe was beginning to develop his thesis, saying the fact that Hess had flown to Scotland in the hope of stopping the war, a war that still had years to run, certainly proved the man was a dreamer, when Bill interrupted: "The fact that you've got a head like a banjo, Father—what's *that* prove?" Well, Joe had tried not to show it, had smiled, but he'd been hurt—a bad moment in the pastor-curate relationship. On the whole, though, they were getting along. There were nights, yes, when Bill had to be called more than once before he came out of his room, before he left off strumming his guitar, listening to FM, or talking to his friends on the phone. There were nights, too, when Bill returned to his room earlier than Joe would have liked, when Joe had maybe had one too many . . . The truth was these weren't the nights that Joe had looked forward to during his years as a pastor without a curate . . . and still they weren't bad nights, by rectory standards nowadays. There had been some fairly good talk— arguments, really, ending sometimes with one man making a final point outside the other man's door, or, after they'd both gone to bed, over the phone. "Bill? Joe." And there had been moments, a few, when the manifest differences of age, position, and outlook between pastor and curate had just disappeared, when Joe and Bill had entered that rather exalted and somewhat relaxed state, induced in part perhaps by drink, that Joe recognized as priestly fellowship. One of the best things about the priesthood, he had been told in the seminary, is other priests—priestly fellowship. The words had sounded corny to Joe at the time, but he had believed in the idea behind them and he still did. For years, though, he hadn't had room in his life for those who should have been and would now be his intimates. Pursuing his building program as he had, he had been forced to associate almost exclusively with the laity—he wanted more from life now. And the truth was he wasn't getting it where he kept looking for it—under his own roof. Late one night, feeling content but also wondering if he couldn't do better, he invited Bill to have a friend or two in for a meal sometime, soon.

16
Priestly
Fellowship

When Joe discovered that surplus sod couldn't be returned for credit, he had put it down alongside the church, over the so-called flower beds—petunias, just a lot of dirt, really. And now he could walk in what shade there was during the last Mass on Sunday, read his office, and keep an eye on the parking lot. "The story is told . . ." And when the church windows were open, he could catch the sermon. He had heard Bill earlier, and now Father Felix was on. "Troubled by poor Mass attendance in one of his villages, the old duke, traveling incognito, wearing an overcoat, or cloak, buttoned up to his chin, arrived at the village in question just as the church bells were summoning the faithful to worship, yes, and just as the others were sitting down to a long table in the bar, or *Keller*, of the inn, or *Gasthaus*, where the old duke, tipped off by the local clergy, had known he'd find them at that hour. Asked to join them at the table—little did they know—the old duke seated himself beside what appeared to be the leader, an imposing individual, before whom was set an enormous jorum, or basin, of brandy, or schnapps, but with no ladle, glasses, cups, or steins. You see, at that time, in the Duchy of Brunswick, or Braunschweig, now part of Germany, it was the custom for friendly groups to drink from the same receptacle, in this case a jorum, or basin—a good idea, rightly understood, in that it made for *communitas*, or community, but in this case, of course, no, far from it. Well, after taking a big swallow from the jorum, or basin, the leader handed it to the old duke, saying, as was the custom, 'Pass that to thy neighbor.' The old duke did as directed (after only *pretending* to take a swallow), saying, as was the custom, 'Pass that to thy neighbor.' In due course, the jorum, or basin, came back to the first man, the leader, an imposing individual, who sent it on its way again, after taking a swallow, another big one. Again, the old duke only *pretended* to drink. And so it went, the jorum, or basin, going round and round the table until, finally, the old duke, furious, unbuttoning his overcoat, or cloak, and thus revealing his well-known uniform and insignia to the company, struck the leader with all his might, saying, 'Pass that to thy neighbor! And let thee beware and likewise any other here who striketh not his neighbor with all his might, for I will make an example of him and thee!' Well, the old duke's word was law, and blows fell hard and fast (none, of course, on the old duke) all around the table. Bim! Bam! Pow! At length, the old duke was satisfied with the penance he'd exacted (with good reason, need I say?) and departed for his castle, or *Schloss*. On the following Sunday, my good people, and on all the following Sundays in the old duke's lifetime, in that village, and in villages throughout his realm, attendance at Mass, it is said, and also at Vespers, was one hundred percent."

While Father Felix took it from there, Joe moved out of range, into the sun. Pausing before a little pile of cigarette butts in the gravel of the parking lot, he thought of inspecting the ashtrays of the nearest cars, thought again, and moved on, thinking, *As this church is the house of God, my good people, so this parking lot is*—forget it. "You're good people," he called out to a young couple heading for the church. "Good and late." No response. People weren't what they used to be.

Formerly able to take and even enjoy a little friendly needling from their pastor, like the customers in a nightclub where an insulting waiter is part of the show, people were touchy nowadays. They wanted their "rights." They wanted a priest to act like a minister, to thank them for showing up—"So nice to see you," "So glad you could come"—and still they emptied their ashtrays in his parking lot.

Joe entered the rectory by the back door, washed his hands at the kitchen sink, slipped into his illustrated apron (gift of a parishioner), which he wore inside out over his cassock so the funny stuff was hidden, and set about making Father Felix's breakfast.

When Bill, on his way over to church to help Father Felix with Communion, passed through the kitchen, Joe looked up from the breadboard, from sawing an orange, and said, "This isn't for me"—what he'd said to explain his continuing presence in the kitchen on Bill's first Sunday morning in residence, and what had since become a family joke, something to say when making another drink, when not declining dessert, or having a second—and when Bill went out the back door Joe intoned, "The story is told . . ." Another family joke. So far, there were just the two, but there should be more in time.

Father Felix sailed through the kitchen in his forest-green habit and sat down for his breakfast—or brunch, as he sometimes called it with a chuckle—in the dining room. (Joe and Bill had breakfast in the kitchen on Sunday, in Mrs P.'s absence, but Joe felt that Father Felix deserved better, as a man of the old school and as hard-to-get weekend help.) After serving him, Joe sank down at the other end of the table with a cup of coffee (what he really wanted was a cold beer). "How's everything at the Big House, Father?"

"About the same." Father Felix helped himself to the

strawberry preserves, praising the brand, Smucker's. He preferred strawberry to red raspberry, he said, and red to black raspberry, as a rule, and didn't care for the monastery stuff these days, as the nuns (who spent too much time in supermarkets) went in for short cuts, skimped on the natural ingredients. "And make too much plum."

"That so?" Joe had heard it all before. As a rule, he didn't sit with Father Felix at breakfast.

"My, but those were fine berries." Father Felix was referring, Joe knew, to some strawberries no longer grown at the monastery. "Little Scarlets. Small, yes, but with a most delicate flavor. And then Brother, he went and dug 'em out."

"Brother Gardener?" said Joe, as if in some doubt.

Father Felix, carried away by anger, could only reply by nodding.

"More toast, Father?"

"All right." Father Felix helped himself to more preserves. He kept getting ahead of himself—always more preserves than toast.

Joe produced another slice from the kitchen, and also the coffeepot. "Warm that up for you?"

"All right." But first Father Felix drained his cup. "You make good coffee here."

Joe poured, sat down again, considering what he had to say. (On his last trip to the kitchen, he had removed his apron as a hint to Father Felix that the dining room was closing.) "Father, I was thinking"—and Joe had been thinking this ever since Bill moved in—"you *could* go back on the one thirty bus."

Father Felix, who ordinarily returned to the monastery on the six thirty bus, gazed away, masticating, sheeplike. He seemed to be saying that there ought to be a reason for such a drastic and sudden change in his routine.

"Know you want to get back as soon as possible," Joe said. Monks, he'd often been told (by monks), are never happy away from their monastery. Between them and their real estate, there is a body-and-soul relationship, a strange bond. Monks are the homeowners, the solid citizens, of the ecclesiastical establishment. Other varieties of religious, and even secular priests like Joe—although he'd built a school, a convent, and now a rectory—are hoboes by comparison. That was certainly the impression you got if you spent any time with monks. So, really, what Joe was suggesting—that Father Felix return to his monastery a few hours earlier than usual—wasn't so bad, was it? "Of course, it's up to you, Father."

Father Felix folded his napkin, though it was headed for the laundry, and then he rolled it. He seemed to be looking for his napkin ring, and then he seemed to remember it was at the monastery and he wasn't.

Bill barged in, saying, "That was Potter on the phone. Looks like there'll be one more, Father."

Seeing that he had no choice, Joe informed Father Felix that a couple of Bill's friends—classmates—were coming to dinner, and that Mrs P. would report at three. "She's been having car trouble," he added, hoping, he guessed, to change the subject.

"Who else is coming?" Father Felix said to Bill.

"Name's Conklin. Classmate. Ex-classmate."

Joe didn't like the sound of it. "Dropout?"

Bill observed a moment of silence. "None of us knew why Conk left. I don't think *Conk* did—at the time."

"That's often the case, Bill. It's nothing to be ashamed of," said Father Felix, looking at Joe.

"Who said it was?" Joe inquired, and then continued with Bill. "So now he's married. Right?"

"No. Not exactly."

Joe waited for clarification.

"I guess he thinks about it," Bill said.

Father Felix nodded. "We all do."

"That so?" said Joe.

"Is it all right, then?" Bill asked.

Joe looked at Bill intently. "Is *what* all right?"

"For Conk to come? He's a pretty lonely guy."

Father Felix was nodding away, apparently giving *his* permission.

"It's your party," Joe said, and rose from the table in an energetic manner, as a subtle hint to Father Felix. "I'd ask you to stay for it, Father. Or Bill would—it's his party. But we plan to sit down—or stand up, it's buffet—around five. You'd have to eat and run." And somebody—Joe—would have to drive Father Felix to the bus.

"But stay if you like," Bill said.

"All right," said Father Felix.

Joe and Father Felix were watching the Twins game and drinking beer in the pastor's study when Bill brought in his friends and introduced them. The heavy one wearing a collar, which showed that he, or his pastor, was still holding the line, was Hennessy. The exhibitionist in overalls and a faded Brahms T-shirt was Potter. And the other one, the one with the handlebar moustache, a nasty affair, was Conklin.

"What's the score?" Bill asked, as if he cared.

"Four to one," Joe said.

"Twins?"

"No."

Potter and Conklin moved off to case the bookshelves, and Father Felix joined them, but Hennessy stood by, attending to the conversation.

"What inning?" Bill asked.

"Seventh."

"Who's pitching?"

Joe took a step toward the television set.

"Leave it on," Bill said. "We're going to my room for a drink."

Bill and his friends then departed, Hennessy murmuring, "See you later."

"Fine young men," said Father Felix.

"Uh-huh," Joe said. "Split a bottle, Father?"

"All right."

Joe carried the empties into the kitchen. "Everything O.K. in here?" he said to Mrs P., and opened the refrigerator— always an embarrassing act for him, even when alone. He had cut down on snacking, though, had suffered less from "night hunger" since Bill moved in.

"Sure you want to eat in the study, Father?"

"It's Bill's party," Joe said, although he felt as Mrs P. did about eating in the study.

But Bill had come out against eating in the dining room. "You at the head of the table, me at the other end—what a drag." Joe had offered to let Bill sit at the head of the table and not to sit at the other end himself, lest it appear to be the head, but Bill hadn't wanted that either. "All this formality— what a drag." Bill had proposed that they start off in the kitchen, get the food right off the stove, and go on from there. "Maybe finish up in my room. Be more natural that way." "Or out in the yard, like a dog with a bone. Be more natural that way." Joe had then proposed that they eat in the study, which was roomy and clubby and may have been what Bill had wanted all along.

"He's lucky he's got you for a pastor," said Mrs P.

"Oh, I don't know," Joe said, but didn't argue the point.

He returned to the study and poured half of the beer—more than half—into Father Felix's glass. "Hey. How'd that man get on second?"

Father Felix observed the television screen closely and nodded, as if to say yes, Joe was right, there was a man on second.

"The official scorer has ruled it a single and an error, not a double," said the announcer.

"Who made the error?" Joe said, more to the announcer than to Father Felix.

"According to our records, that's the first error Tony's made this season," said the announcer.

"What's so wonderful about that?" Joe said to the announcer. "He's an outfielder."

Father Felix got up and, as was his habit from time to time, left the room.

After a bit, Joe went to see if anything was wrong, but Father Felix, who used the lavatory off the guest room, wasn't there. Then, listening in the hallway, Joe heard the old monk's voice among the others in Bill's room, and returned to the study. Sitting there alone, finishing off Father Felix's beer, Joe asked himself, What's wrong with this picture? Nothing, really, he told himself. The curate was entertaining in his room so as not to interfere with the game, the visiting priest was a fair-weather fan, if that, and so, really, nothing was wrong—it meant nothing, nothing personal that the pastor sat alone. He didn't like it, though.

17

Priestly

Fellowship

Continued

For some time, Mrs P. had been bringing things into the study and arranging them on the library table, which had lost its somewhat refectory look (Bill's idea) when Mrs P. covered it with an ecru lace tablecloth. Joe, when he might have spoken up for the bare honest wood (Bill's idea), hadn't, and now it was too late.

"Should I call the others, Father?" Mrs P. sounded apprehensive—the others were getting kind of loud in Bill's room.

"No, I'll do it." But when Joe imagined himself at Bill's door, looking in on a scene he'd been more or less excluded from, he decided to phone. *"Bill?"* What the hell was this? Either Bill or Father Felix should've answered, or Hennessy or Potter, but *not* Conklin.

They came into the study like conventioneers, carrying glasses, and formed a circle that did not include Joe, who, on hearing Conklin say that his moustache was considered "cruel" by women, wanted to hit him. Then they were roughhousing, saying "Pass that to thy neighbor!" "Fine young men," said Father Felix, laughing to see such sport. "Uh-huh," Joe said, and moved in on them, ending a series of blows. Conklin, fist raised, appeared to entertain the thought of starting another series, beginning with Joe, but changed his mind, which was just as well, though it still made for nervous laughter at Joe's expense.

"Let's eat," Joe said. "Father Felix has to leave early."

"Oh, don't worry about me."

Joe bumped them over to the food and stationed himself at the end of the table, by the wine, ready to pour and, if possible, to enter the conversation. To Father Felix, first in line, first to reach the wine, Joe said, "Just like the monastery," referring to the nice display of food on the monk's plate.

"Yes." Father Felix had been saying (to Hennessy) that some days were perhaps better than others to visit the monastery if one wished to eat there. "We have a cafeteria now."

"Wine, Father?"

"What kind is it?"

Joe, speaking through his nose, named the wine.

"On second thought, no," said Father Felix, perhaps wisely, and moved off with his plate, holding it carefully with both hands but in a sloping manner.

Hennessy was next, and he also refused wine. But he complimented Joe on his building program, calling the rectory "a crackerjack," which suggested to Joe that the works of Father Finn were still being read and might have figured in Hennessy's vocation, as they had in his own. "You should see the office area," Joe said to Hennessy. "Maybe, if there's time later, I could show you around the plant."

"Oh, *no!*" said Conklin, next in line, and turned to Potter in disgust, but Potter was talking to Bill, and Hennessy ("Maybe later, Father") was moving off, and so Conklin, after more or less insulting Joe, had to face him alone.

"Wine, Mr Conklin?"

"*Si, señor.*"

Maybe it went with the moustache, but Joe wondered whether a priest should be so addressed, whether "reverendissimo" or something wouldn't be more appropriate, whether, in fact, Conklin had meant to pay him back for the "mister." At the seminary, as Conklin would know, there were still a few reverend fathers who made much of "mister," hissing it, using it to draw the line between miserable you and glorious them—which hadn't been Joe's intention. After all, what *was* Conklin now, and what was he ever likely to be, but "mister"? It didn't pay for someone in Conklin's position to be too sensitive, Joe thought.

And listened to Potter, who was saying (to Bill) that he'd had a raw egg on his steak tartare in München and enjoyed it. "*Mit Ei,* they call it there."

"You can enjoy it *here*," Joe said. "Mrs Pelissier!" he cried, not pronouncing her name as he usually did, but giving it everything it had, which was plenty, in French.

Joe and everybody (except Father Felix) urged Potter to have a raw egg on his steak tartare, as in München—*Mit Ei! Mit Ei!* But Potter wouldn't do it, although Mrs P. produced a dozen nice fresh ones, entering the study in triumph, leaving it in sorrow. Joe almost had one himself, for her sake. Potter came out of it badly.

Joe was hoping the Barcalounger would clear when he set forth with glass and plate, but Conklin was in it, and it didn't, and so he went and sat near Hennessy and Father Felix. "Never cared for buffet," he told them, and got no response. (Hennessy was saying that the monastic life was beyond one of his modest spiritual means, Father Felix that one never knew until one tried.) Joe tried the other conversation. (Potter was building up the laity, at the expense of the clergy, as was the practice of the clergy these days.) "Some of your best friends must be laymen," Joe said, and was alarmed to see Potter taking him seriously: that was the trouble with the men of Bill's generation—not too bright and in love with themselves, they made you want to hit them. "But what about the ones who empty their ashtrays in your parking lot?"

Potter smiled—*now* he thought Joe was kidding.

"Not much you can do," Conklin said. "Judah took possession of the hill country, but he couldn't drive out the inhabitants of the plain, because they had chariots of iron."

"That so?" said Joe, thinking, What *is* this? He tried his wine. "Not bad," he said to Potter and Bill (who still had their drinks from Bill's room), but he didn't get through to them. Potter was a talker.

"What kind is it?" said Father Felix.

Joe, speaking through his nose, named the wine.

"Grape," said Conklin, coming back from the table with the bottle from which only he and Joe had partaken so far, and sitting down with it, in the Barcalounger. "Anybody else?"

"No, thanks," Joe said, and was silent for some time— until he heard Conklin refer to Beans McQueen as Beans. "You a friend of Father McQueen's?"

"They taught this course together, at the Institute," Bill said. "Scripture for the Laity."

"That so?" said Joe.

And the talk went on as before, on two fronts, without Joe, leaving him free to go over to the table for the other bottle of wine. Hennessy wasn't having any, but Father Felix was. "Grape, you say?" Joe served Father Felix, and also himself, and left the bottle on the coffee table in front of him, but beyond his reach—not that wine, unfortified wine, was really alcoholic, not that *he* was. He just had to watch himself. He wasn't a wine drinker, but could see how he might have been one in another time and place—one of those wise old abbés, his mouth a-pucker with *Grand Cru,* his tongue tasting like steak, solving life's problems by calling people "my daughter" and "my son."

Potter was telling Bill and Conklin that the clergy should cast off their medieval trappings, immerse themselves in the profane everyday world, and thus reveal its sacred character.

"That why you're immersed in that shirt?" said Joe.

Potter just smiled and went on as before. It was odd the way Bill looked up to Potter, odder still the way they both looked up to Conklin—as *what*, a layman? It was a crazy world. Father Felix was telling Hennessy that the monastery should employ trained lay personnel in key positions, replace the kitchen, if not the laundry, nuns, and also certain brothers. "So Brother Gardener has to go?" said Joe.

Father Felix turned to Joe. *"You,"* he said, speaking with deliberation, as if the wine, and whatever he'd had in Bill's room, and the beer before that, had suddenly gone to his head. *"You. Covered. Up. Those. Flowers."*

"Flowers?" said Joe, and listened to the silence in the study. For the first time since the party began, he felt that others were interested in what he might say. He started to tell them about the leftover sod, but saw that they already knew about it, that he was already—the pastor's fate—being discussed before outsiders in his own rectory by the curate and the visiting priest, those natural allies. "Thought of putting the sod down around the flowers, if you could call 'em that—things like petunias. Have 'em growing right up out of the grass. Of course, you'd have to cut the grass by hand. I've always wondered about flower beds—who wants to look at a lot of dirt?" (Nobody else, it seemed, had ever wondered about this.) "Didn't realize you felt so strongly about petunias, Father. Strawberries, yes."

"Humph," said Father Felix.

"Excuse me," Joe said, believing that everybody was

against him, and went over to the table, where he had work to do. He had to fire up the chafing dish, pour the juice from the pitted Bing cherries into the top pan, or blazer, place it directly over the flame, bring the juice to a boil, thicken with ½ tsp. of arrowroot dissolved in a little cold water, but Potter was telling the others that family life was in such tough shape today because Our Lord had been a bachelor, and so, carrying a dead match to an ashtray, Joe appeared among them again, saying, "We used to ask a lot of silly questions in the sem. Would Our Lord be a smoker, drive a late-model car, and so on. Kid stuff—nobody got hurt. But I wonder about some of the stuff I hear today."

"So do I," said Hennessy. "That Our Lord was celibate is a pretty good argument for celibacy."

"No more. People today, living normal lives, can't identify with Our Lord," Potter said. "Or with *us*—because of the celibacy barrier."

"That so?" said Joe. "And where you *don't* have that barrier? I mean how well do *we* identify with Our Lord?" Joe put the question to Bill with a glance, skipped Conklin, and tried but failed with Father Felix, who was spearing kernels of corn with his fork, making a clicking noise on his plate— rather annoying, since it broke what otherwise would have been an impressive silence.

"He's got you, Pot," Conklin said, and then to Joe: "We may be closer than I thought."

Joe, not seeing why this, if true, which he doubted, should make Bill and Potter look so sad, said, "And when you consider we work at it full time, unlike the laity—well, it makes you wonder, doesn't it?"

"It did me," said Conklin.

Bill sighed, and Potter held out his glass to Conklin for wine—a highball glass with ice in it. Joe said nothing about a proper glass, afraid that Potter (who'd said earlier that he longed for the day when he'd be able to say Mass with a beer mug, a coffee cup, a small flower vase of simple design, because such things were cheap and honest and made, like us, of clay) would refuse a proper glass and, furthermore, would say *why*. In that way, Potter could easily evade the issue he'd raised, the celibacy issue, as he had the egg. Potter was tricky, had to be watched, but Joe was doing that—and then Father Felix had to butt in.

"There's been a lot of talk in the monastic community about family life, but whatever the future holds for you fellas, I think it's safe to say our status, or situation—some would say our lot—won't change. When you get right down to it, a monastery's no place for a family man."

"I'll buy that," said Joe.

"Oh, well," said Father Felix. "The community's family enough for me."

And that, thought Joe, is why you're here.

"When you get right down to it," Conklin said to Father Felix, "a monastery's no place for *you*. Priests weren't meant to be monks, and monks weren't meant to be priests—and *weren't* in the Age of Faith."

"We all know that," Joe said—Conklin sounded just like an ex-seminarian, or an educated layman.

"Times change," said Father Felix.

"Status seeking," said Conklin.

Joe gave Bill a look for grinning, and to make it absolutely clear where his sympathies lay, as between Conklin and Father Felix, who appeared to be wounded, Joe fetched the bottle. "Father?"

"All right."

Joe filled the monk's glass, also his own, and went back to the table, with Potter's voice following him. "Why put such a premium on celibacy—on sex, really? Think of the problems it creates."

"Think of the problems it *doesn't* create," said Joe, and while Potter and the others were thinking of those problems (Joe hoped), he poured the juice from the pitted Bing cherries into the top pan, or blazer. That done, he appeared among them again, saying, "The premium isn't on sex. It isn't on celibacy. It's on efficiency and sanctity."

"Oh, *no*!" said Conklin.

"Oh, *yes*," said Joe. "Even if we don't hear much about that aspect of the priesthood today." And, having given them more food for thought, Joe left them again, for he still had work to do, but before he reached the table the impressive silence his words had produced was cruelly violated.

"Father, how can we make sanctity as attractive as sex to the common man?"

Joe had to expect to hear that famous question even now from men of his era at the seminary—Potter's permissive pastor was one—but *not* from someone like Conklin, Joe thought, and showed it, saying, "Good thing I wasn't with you guys in Bill's room. You wouldn't have had anything to talk about."

"Got to talkin' . . . in Bill's room," Father Felix said, apologetically, and paused to watch his plate (which he'd been holding in a sloping manner) start down his outstretched leg, jump, and land on the floor, right side up. Once, twice, he nodded, as if to say no harm done, but his head hung down, finally, in an uncompleted nod.

Joe sprang into action. Others, nearer to Father Felix, had already sprung. But it was Joe who removed the fork (in the circumstances, a dangerous instrument) from Father Felix's hand and thrust it at Potter, who hesitated to take it by the greasy end, and it was Joe who deftly kicked the plate aside and told Bill to pick it up, and Joe who instructed Hennessy and Conklin, instead of foolishly trying to firm him up, to lay the helpless monk out on the couch. Joe then changed his mind about that in view of the sepulchral effect it might have on the party. *"Bed*room! *Bed*room!" he cried. *"Not* mine! *Not* mine!" Conklin and Hennessy, frog-marching Father Felix this way and that, didn't seem to know what they were doing. Then Joe saw what the trouble was. It was Conklin. Why, when there were plenty of clergy present, when the person in distress was himself one of them, why should a layman be playing such an important part? "Here, let *me*," Joe said, shouldering in, but the layman wouldn't let go. Joe ended up with Hennessy's portion of Father Felix. And so, borne up by Joe and Conklin, the helpless monk was removed from the scene.

18

Priestly

Fellowship

Concluded

When Joe got back from the guest room, he found that the juice, which he had yet to thicken with ½ tsp. of arrowroot dissolved in a little cold water, had already thickened, having been kept at, rather than brought to, a boil. Until then, he had hoped to serve cherries jubilee for dessert and to do the job himself, so Mrs P. wouldn't have to be present, but now he didn't know. The juice had definitely lost its liquidity, was hardening or charring at the edges of the top pan, or blazer. To go ahead now, with or without the arrowroot, might be a mistake. So, playing it safe, he blew out the flame, dished up the cherries as they were, room temperature and rather dry without their juice, and served them swiftly, with spoons. He said nothing, and nothing was said.

The conversation died away when he sat down with his dish and spoon. He had tuned in earlier, though, while serving, and was curious to know why Hennessy thought that Conklin shouldn't go on teaching at the Institute. "If he's reasonably competent, and if Beans wants him back— well, why not?" Joe said, feeling broad-minded. (Hennessy, too, had that effect on him.) No response. "I'll put it another way. What if he shaved off his moustache?"

Potter and Bill shuffled their feet and protested, but Joe ignored them. "Why not?" he asked, speaking directly to Conklin.

"You talkin' about the moustache or the Institute?"

"Both."

Potter and Bill protested again.

"It's a fair question," said Conklin. "About the Institute. You better tell him, Bill."

Joe looked at Bill. "Well?"

"Conk's lost his faith," Bill said.

"That so?" said Joe. He was sorry to hear it, of course, and felt that more was expected of him, but he also felt that condolences weren't in order, since some people, especially young people, regard the loss of their faith as a great step forward, and since he wasn't exactly rolling in the stuff himself. "I see," he said—now he saw why Conklin had been invited—why so much was being made of him by Potter and Bill—what was really going on. It was an old-fashioned spiritual snipe hunt, such as they'd all read about, with Potter and Bill, if not Hennessy, pleased to be participating, and also, it seemed, the snipe. That was the odd part.

"Conk just doesn't take God for granted—unlike some of us in the Church," Potter said, apparently to Joe. "That's been our trouble all along. Atheism and faith—true faith—have that in common. They don't take God for granted."

Joe looked cross-eyed at Hennessy.

"But Conk's not an atheist," Bill said to Joe. "Are you, Conk?"

Conklin smiled. "No, but I'm working on it."

Joe wanted to hit him.

"That's what I like about Conk," Potter said, grimly. "He's honest."

Bill nodded, grimly.

Joe sniffed. "What I don't get," he said to Conklin, "is why you want to go on teaching at the Institute if you've lost your faith. Just want to keep your hand in, or what?"

"Don't blame *Conk*," Potter said.

"*Conk* wants to quit," Bill said.

"He should," Joe said, and gave him an encouraging nod.

"*No!*" cried Potter, and stood up. "What matters in teaching is a man's competence, not his private beliefs, or lack of same. And that applies to Scripture and theology, if they're teachable, and *I* say they are. By agnostics, infidels, and apostates, you say? *Yes!* I say. And, thank God, some of our better institutions agree!" Potter sat down.

Bill stood up. "But how many of our *seminaries*, Pot? How can we go on calling theology the Queen of Sciences?" Bill sat down.

"How about Beans?" said Joe, without getting up. Joe was pretty sure that Beans didn't need Conklin, was just doing an ex-seminarian a favor, letting him keep his hand in, and maybe hoping for a delayed vocation. "*He* know about this? No? Better tell him, then, so he can find somebody else, if necessary."

Potter and Bill both stood up, both preaching, and Potter, of course, prevailed, but he was repeating himself.

"Look," said Joe. "The Institute isn't one of our better institutions." Even as an adventure in adult education, which was all it claimed to be, it probably didn't rate too high. "And it wouldn't be one of our better institutions if you guys pulled this off."

"It'd be a start," said Potter, sitting down.

"It'd be a stunt," said Joe, getting up. Going to the door, he took the tray from Mrs P., but on his return with his mind on the trouble there could be over Conklin at the Institute—factions, resolutions, resignations, and so on—he overran the coffee table, jarring it and cracking his shin. In some pain, he backed up and put down the tray, saying, "I worry about you guys." Pouring and handing around coffee, sloshing it, he spoke to them as he sometimes did to Bill alone, late at night.

HOME TRUTHS

He, at their age, he said, had dearly wanted to be a saint, had trained for it—plenty of prayer and fasting, no smoking, no booze ("Actually, I didn't drink anything but beer then"), and had worn a hair shirt for a while. At their age, *he* had worked out on himself, not on other people, and that was the difference between the men of his generation and theirs. One of the differences. "You guys even *want* to be saints? I doubt it. You're too busy with your public relations."

CHANGING STANDARDS

There might be worlds to be won, souls to be harvested, and so on, but not with stunts and gimmicks. He had been rather pessimistic about the various attempts to improve the Church's image, and he had been right. Vocations, conversions, communions, confessions, contributions, general attendance, all down. And why not? "We used to stand out in the crowd. We had quality control. We were the higher-priced spread. No more. Now if somebody drops the ball somebody else throws it into the stands, and that's how we clear the bases. Tell the man in the next parish [Ed Smiley] that you fornicated a hundred and thirty-six times since your last confession, which was one month ago, and he says, 'Did you think ill of your fellow man?' It's a crazy world."

STRANDED

There had always been a shortage of virtue in the world, and evil and ignorance were still facts of life, but where was the old intelligence? He had begun to wonder, as he never had before, about the doctrine of free will. People, he feared, might not be able to exercise free will anymore, owing to the decline in human intelligence. How else explain the state of the country, and the world, today? "We don't, maybe we *can't*, make the right moves—like those poor whales you read about. We're stranded.''

HUMAN NATURE

The Church was irrelevant today, not concerned enough with the everyday problems of war, poverty, segregation, and so on, people said, but such talk was itself irrelevant, was really a criticism of human nature. Sell what you have and follow me, Our Lord had told the rich young man—who had then gone away sad. That was human nature for you, and it hadn't changed. Let him take it who can, Our Lord had said of celibacy—and few could take it, then or now. "And that applies to heroic sacrifice of all kinds. Let's face it.''

BRUEGHEL THE ELDER

People, most people, lay *and* clerical, just weren't up to much. Liturgists, of course, were trying to capitalize on that fact, introducing new forms of worship, reviving old ones, and so on, but an easy way would never be found to make gold out of lead. Otherwise the saints and martyrs would have lived as they had, and died, in vain. Zero multiplied a million times is still zero. All this talk of community, communicating, and so on—it was just whistling in the dark. "Life's not a cookout by Brueghel the Elder and people know it.''

TOO FAR?

Sure it was a time of crisis, upheaval, and so on, but a man could still do his job. The greatest job in the world, divinely instituted and so on, was that of the priest, and yet it was still a job—a marrying, burying, sacrificing job, plus whatever good could be done on the side. It was *not* a crusade. Turn it into one, as some guys were trying to do, and you asked too much of it, of yourself, and of ordinary people, invited nervous breakdowns all around. Trying to do too much was something the Church had always avoided, at least until recently. At the Council, the so-called conservatives—a persecuted minority group if ever there was one—had only been afraid of going too far too soon, of throwing the baby out with the bath water. "And rightly so."

FLYING SAUCERS

The Church couldn't respond to all the demands of the moment or she'd go the way of those numerous sects that owed their brief existence to such demands. People had to realize that what they wanted might not be what they needed, and if they couldn't—well, they couldn't. Religion was a weak force today, owing to the decline in human intelligence. It was now easy to see how the Church, though she'd endure to the end, as promised by Our Lord, would become a mere remnant of herself. In the meantime, though, the priest had to get on with his job, *such as it was*. As for feeling thwarted and useless, he knew that feeling, but he also knew what it meant. It meant that he was in touch with reality, and that was something these days. Frequently reported, of course, like flying saucers, were parishes where priests and people were doing great things together. "But I've never seen one myself, if it's any consolation to you guys," Joe said, and paused.

Did the impressive silence mean that they were now seeing themselves and their situations in a new light, in the clear north light of reality? Bill, *finally*? Potter? Even Conklin?

Joe hoped so, in all cases. On the whole, he was satisfied with the response. The bath-water bit hadn't gone down very well (groans from Potter, "Oh, *no!*" from Conklin), and there had been other interruptions, but Joe had kept going, had boxed on, opening cuts, closing eyes, and everybody, including Conklin, looked better to him now.

He wanted Hennessy and Potter to come out again, and not just to discuss their problems with him (Joe), though that would be all right. He wanted them to come out whenever they felt like it, whenever they needed a lift, a little priestly fellowship. Actually, there might be more for them with him, and more for him with them, than with Bill—who, to tell the truth, wasn't much fun. It could happen, first Hennessy and Potter coming, then coming with others, and these in turn with others. There would be nights, perhaps when Bill wouldn't leave his room. "Where's Bill?" "Oh, he's listening to FM." Joe's rectory could become a hangout for the younger clergy, a place where they'd always be sure of a drink, a cigar, and if he put a table in the living room, never used now, a cue. Pastors at first critical ("Stay the hell away from there!") would sing his praises ("He sure straightened out that kid of mine!"). Time marching on, Hennessy seldom seen, a bishop somewhere, first, and last, of the old crowd to make it, but the others still around, pastors now with curates of their own—tired, wiser men, the age gap narrowing between them and their old mentor, not so old, really, and in excellent health, eating and drinking less. A few missing, yes, the others, though, still coming out to Joe's—in a crazy world, an asylum of sanity—for priestly fellowship, among them, perhaps, Father Conklin, old Conk, a pretty lonely guy for a while there, until he started coming out, shaved off his cruel moustache, found his lost faith, the road back, second spring, and so on.

"So what's the answer?" said Potter. "Watch the Twins?"

"Those bores," said Conklin.

Hennessy reproved them with a look, and spoke with his future authority. "What's the answer, Father?"

Eyeing Father Felix's glass on the coffee table, Joe said, "A few monks saved civilization once. Could be the answer again. Principle's sound. You'd have to work out the details. Wouldn't have to be monks. Could happen right here." Joe reached for Father Felix's glass, the last of the wine, and swirled it clockwise, counterclockwise, clockwise, denying himself before downing it. "Wanna see how Father is," he said. "Be right back." At the door, as he was about to leave them, he turned and said, "How can we make sanctity as attractive as sex? Answer I got was 'Just have to keep trying.' Not much of an answer. Nobody remembers it—just the question. Guess it's the answer to all these questions. Be right back."

The monk's eyes opened when Joe approached the bed. "Get you anything, Father?"

"All right."

"Drink of water?"

"All right."

Joe administered water to Father Felix, flipped his pillow, eased him down. "Want your shoes off?"

"Is the party over, Joe?"

"No, not yet."

"Then," said the monk, his eyes closing, "why is everybody leaving?"

"Not yet," Joe said patiently.

But when he returned to the study he saw that he was wrong.

Hennessy—he was the only one left—said, "How is he?"

"All right."

Led by voices to a window on the street side, Joe looked

down and saw Bill, Potter, and Conklin talking to a young woman—older than they were, though—in a convertible.

"Conklin had to leave," Hennessy said.

Joe came away from the window.

"Want to thank you, Father," Hennessy said.

"It was Bill's party."

"All the same." Hennessy seemed to know what it was like to be a pastor. "Oh, and I should thank the house-keeper."

"Good idea." Joe saw Hennessy, who'd go far, off to the kitchen, and came back to the window. The young woman moved over on the seat and the cruel moustache took the wheel. Potter and Bill then fell all over themselves saying good-bye, making it look hard to do. The convertible drove away. Then, to Joe's surprise—he had meant to say something about coming again, soon—Hennessy appeared below, having, it seemed, left the rectory by the back door. Without a word or sign to Potter and Bill, who stood together talking, Hennessy got into the driver's seat of the black sedan at the curb. Potter and Bill then parted, rather solemnly, Joe thought, and Potter got into the backseat of the black sedan. It drove away. A few moments later Bill entered the study, and Joe said:

"Who was *that*?"

"His mistress."

Joe stared at Bill. "Say that again."

Bill said it again.

"*That* what he calls her? How d'ya know *that*?"

"He told us."

"He did, huh?" Joe was thinking if he had a mistress he wouldn't tell everybody.

"He's honest about it, Father. You have to give him credit for that."

"I do, huh?"

Father Felix came in, looking much the same.

"You missed your bus," Joe said, and then to Bill, "Why don't they get married?"

"Complications."

"Like what?"

"She's already married."

Joe sniffed. "Great."

"Her husband won't give her a divorce. *He's* still a Catholic."

"Say that again."

Bill said it again.

Joe turned away. "And now you wanna get back to your monastery—right?"

"How?" said Father Felix.

"I'll drive you."

"Eighty miles?" said Bill. "Can't he stay overnight?"

"He wants to get back to his monastery. He's not happy away from it. And I need the air. Well, what d'ya say, Father?"

"All right," said Father Felix.

19
Bad News

Early in the evening on the following Sunday, after sending out for and enjoying a very tasty dinner with Father Felix and Bill, Joe took leave of them for a few days and drove off to the seminary to make his annual retreat, having explained that Bill was to carry on as usual, keep regular office hours, not throw any parties, or go to any, and not to give scandal ("i.e., stay away from Potter" *and*, it was implied, Conklin), and that Father Felix was to have the use of the pastor's office and study (TV) and was to act (implied) as turnkey in the pastor's absence.

At the seminary, in his room—it might have been better or worse—Joe right away opened his bag and hung two summerweight cassocks in the closet (a few wire hangers); opened the bottle of Airwick he'd brought along and started it off in the closet; opened one of the fifths of gin (not his usual brand but chosen for its handy cup cap, his answer to the glass problem at the sem). He poured himself a cup and sat down with it in the one sittable chair, his head nesting for a moment where another had nested during the academic year. He finished his drink standing, put the cup, now the cap, back on the fifth and it back in his bag, covering it with socks and underwear, thus uncovering, but covering again, the poker chips, the decks of cards, and hoped he wouldn't have to use them, would be invited to play elsewhere, as he had the previous year, and would do as well again.

The annual retreat for diocesan clergy (from which Bill was excused that year because he'd made one with his class before ordination) could be more of a social than a spiritual occasion for men of Joe's vintage and older, and since it was given twice in successive weeks so both pastors and curates could attend (the week coming up was the repeat) there was always an element of chance in it—as to who'd be there and who wouldn't—an element that Joe, by discreet, early inquiries, might have resolved to his advantage as a gambler but would not as a priest and also as a gambler.

He moved the Airwick to another location, the sittable chair, and went down to join the retreatants standing around in front of the Administration Building, to see who was there, to watch cars arrive and depart for the new parking lot (as Joe had) after the long-haired seminarian in overalls spoke his piece—"The Rector wants the entrance kept clear this year." Joe was in time to see Father Stock arrive in a flashy old black Chrysler and walk away from it with his Gladstone bag, ignoring the seminarian and everybody else, the sidewalk clearing for him.

Pogatznick, one of the little group, all pastors, that Joe had joined, said to the seminarian, "See if he left the key in it."

"You kiddin'?" said Schwinghammer, once a curate under Father Stock.

"Still," Mooney said, "you have to hand it to him for coming to the retreat at his age, retired and all."

"He comes for the group picture," said Schwinghammer.

Joe nodded, and asked, "What's the word on Po?" (The retreatmaster, an order man, was billed as Demetrius Po.)

"Not good," said Cooney.

"What I hear," said Rooney.

"*Not* what I hear," said Mooney.

"Hey, what kind of name's *that?*" said Schwinghammer.

"Well, there's the river Po," said Cooney.

"And Edgar Allan Poe," said Mooney, "but that's with an *e.*"

"Could be anything, a name like that," said Rooney.

"He could've changed it," said Schwinghammer.

"Shortened it, you mean?" said Pogatznick.

A black Continental pulled up to the entrance, which the driver, Monsignor Egan, after listening to the seminarian, appeared to agree with the Rector should be kept clear this year, and got out of the car. He asked the seminarian his name, his home parish, praised his pastor, and feared, he said, there were two large bags in the trunk, Rooney then coming forward for them. "Oh, thanks, Bob," Monsignor Egan said to him. "*And* Lawrence," he said to the seminarian. And nodding to some, greeting a few by name, among them Joe, and followed by Rooney with the bags, Monsignor Egan moved toward the Administration Building—from which the Rector swiftly emerged with his hand out—while Lawrence drove off to the parking lot with a funny look on his face.

The next ones to arrive, two country pastors in a dusty Chevrolet equipped with a long waving aerial and an outsize bug screen into which a small yellow bird had flown and stuck as if mounted there, were wary when told by Schwing-hammer and others that the Rector wanted the entrance kept clear this year. ("Yeah, sure"—"What about that old heap?") And seemed to doubt that Lawrence existed and would be right back. ("From parking a car?"—"Yeah, sure.") The Chevrolet, motor off and radio on (the Twins game), waited, and when a dusty Ford arrived, made common cause with it.

Joe had to leave the scene because Rooney came out of the Administration Building (which Joe had been keeping an eye on) and signaled to him with a card-dealing gesture.

*   *   *

So, that evening and thereafter, as at the last retreat, Joe and Rooney sat down with Monsignor Egan and his set, Fathers Keogh, Kling, and Moore, products of the twenties, solid, pink, white-haired or balding pastors, exactly the sort of men Joe had once scorned—too many like them cluttering up the priesthood, he'd thought—but now thought, when he saw them around a table at a restaurant, or, for that matter, around a green baize table at the seminary with their collars off and, in Kling's case, shoes, What an impressive group of men! And considered himself fortunate. Playing in ordinary company at the retreat could be debilitating and risky—last year at one of the conferences, which were held in the chapel, a man suffering from poker fatigue had fallen out of his pew—whereas playing with Egan's set was safe and salubrious: a man had maybe three drinks, began fasting at midnight, closed down at one, had a good night's sleep, and was ready for morning when it came, early. Joe liked the strict regimen—wished he could run his life on such lines the rest of the year—and he also liked playing in the distinguished visitor's suite, where the likes of G. K. Chesterton, Jacques Maritain, and Frank Sheed had stayed and where the Rector had put Egan again, with private bath, air conditioning, refrigerator, and *glasses*, and sent Lawrence up nightly with a platter of snacks.

So there were a number of advantages for Joe and Rooney as members (pro tem) of Egan's set—whose practice it was, however, to attend every conference, alas.

Father Demetrius, who worked in the peppery, hard-sell style of Walter Winchell, warned the retreatants not to expect much from him in the usual way of retreats, "moral, ascetics, liturgy, what have you," which sounded promising. A prison chaplain of many years' standing, Father Demetrius owed his current assignment to the state of the nation, he said. "I'm hot now, and if I know you bankers you're worried about the rising tide of crime." Insights, however, *positive* insights into the rising tide and practical suggestions as to how to stem it were not immediately forthcoming from Father Demetrius.

He devoted his first conference to reading statistics from the FBI and had everybody yawning. While some of the younger men said this was needed—a nonmythological approach to everyday problems—Joe had to admire Father Demetrius for not trying, as so many retreatmasters did, for a knockout in the first round. At the next conference, beginning again with the statement (soon to become tiresome) "The proper study of man is crime," and citing the case of Cain and Abel (having cited the case of Adam and Eve at the first conference), Father Demetrius told true-life stories from the pen, some of them pretty rough, some merely heartwarming. At the next conference, he told more stories. At the next, more.

The retreatants had expected to hear stories from an ex-chaplain, but not so many. What they came down to was that Father Demetrius, though part of the establishment as chaplain, had been closer to the inmates, the big fish and the small, some of whom had "formed the habit" of saying the rosary under his guidance— "Some, not all, life's not like that, my friends"—and were now doing very well on the outside, a surprising number as hoteliers, moteliers, and restaurateurs. "Come what may, *I'll* never want for bed and board"—this, with a bitter laugh, implied that the retreatants might so want, or that Father Demetrius was having trouble with his superiors. In any case, the man certainly knew a lot about prime cuts, shellfish, bar equipment, laundry service, pilferage, and protection, all matters in which Joe was interested. Most retreatants, however, seemed to feel that Father Demetrius' stories had little or no application to them—all those breaks, rumbles, and hits, all that gunfire, "Root-a-toot-toot!" But Father Demetrius was there, he said, to shake them up, which he occasionally did—"Floyd, a three-time loser, white slavery, as nice a fella as you'll ever meet on the outside"—and, sensing their disapproval, would refer them again to the parable of the Pharisee and the publican, associating himself with the humble publican, the retreatants with the proud Pharisee, and pharisaically seeing nothing wrong with that. The retreatants no longer smiled when he called them bankers.

Delinquency, always a problem, was rife that year, claiming those it never had before, iron pastors, responsible first assistants, and the kind of men who take notes (who were spelling each other). Most delinquents had the decency to stay in their rooms, out of sight, during conferences, but some of the younger men, the very ones who'd first said that the retreatmaster was following a course that would soon become clear, and then that he was simply doing his thing (not a bad thing, they said, since the Church was "overstructured"), *they* were all over the place during conferences, in the Rec Room shooting pool, out on the lake in boats, giving scandal to Lawrence and the kitchen help.

Joe had to keep telling himself how good it would be when the retreat was over, like this life, if one persevered now; that it wasn't the singer, or even the song, that mattered, that the Church wouldn't be the Church if she relied upon such things; that what mattered, what was part and parcel of reality, what could always be counted on to show itself in human affairs, the one constant, in which the Church had her reason for being, was the Cross.

It was good to see Egan's set accepting it, to see those old boys coming and going, never missing a conference, and good to be one of them.

The retreat had been mentioned among them (in Joe's presence) only once, one night two or three days out, between deals.

"Well, it's a change," said Egan.

"That's what I say," said Moore.

Keogh nodded.

"Queen bets," said Kling.

Joe and probably Rooney, in ordinary company, would have criticized the retreatmaster and the Chancery for booking him, but they said nothing, Joe enjoying, after a moment's discomfort, the strange sensation of not speaking his mind to no avail, and thinking there was something to be said for whatever it was, charity, or despair, or a blend of both—wisdom?—that moved old men to silence.

On the next to last day, the retreat, making for port like a crippled ship, hit a mine: word came that assessments for the ARF—the Archdiocesan Renewal Fund—had gone out from the Chancery, and all hell broke loose.

While the sound of a siren came and went, men milled about in the corridors, going from room to room, drinking from vessels of various kinds—a real glass crisis at the seminary. Of the men who managed to call home (the switchboard was overloaded), some immediately packed up and left, some stayed and raved as they would in their own rectories, some went quietly into shock, some tried to carry it off ("I knew this was coming"). Most were close-mouthed about their assessment (as Joe would have been if he'd known his), but some were not. The figures Joe heard were all sky-high and, quite apart from that, some were out of line, causing tension and worse between pastors of similar or adjoining parishes—Joe had to step between Mooney and Rooney, remind them that their quarrel was not with each other but with Toohey and the Chancery. Every pastor (and his flock) was in trouble, for now there would have to be *constant* strafing from the pulpit, house-to-house searches for pledges, and possibly the use of hardened mercenaries. But there could be none of that in Joe's parish, or Cooney's, under their fiscal system (unless they welshed on their parishioners). So Joe and Cooney were in more trouble than most, in that confused and confusing scene.

And yet there was Joe moving about with his bottle, his last one, sharing it with others, knocking back drinks from its handy cup cap, giving what succor he could to others, not once speaking of his own plight, which nobody else did either, even parenthetically, until . . .

"Boy, oh boy! Am I ever glad *now!*" cried Schwinghammer, who'd planned to install Joe's fiscal system until talked out of it, told in a nice way he just didn't have the parish for it, *by Joe.* Nothing about that now, no thanks, no sympathy, from Schwinghammer, just gloating, neighing. "Boy, oh boy!"

Examined by Schwinghammer, who was drinking from a murky cut-glass vase, and by a responsible first assistant with a bad cigar, Joe did his best to defend his system without running down theirs (Sunday envelope/special collections unlimited). "I try to budget for everything that comes along."

Pogatznick, coming along then, said, "You budget for *this*?" and set Schwinghammer to neighing again.

Serene, an example to them and to himself, Joe said, "A lot depends on my assessment, of course. What *that* is, I don't know—and don't want to, now." And added, hoping it wouldn't unduly annoy those who'd called home, and wouldn't sound as mealy-mouthed to them as it did to him: "I'm on retreat now." He drew aside for a moment in order to fill his cup, and was about to reenter the conversation when he changed his mind and moved on, hearing "Boy, oh boy!"

Sometime later, coming out of a room, he ran into Cooney.

"Joe, don't try to look so good. What d'ya mean you budget for everything that comes along?"

"Lou, I said I *try* to."

"Joe, you don't even try to budget for *this*."

Joe didn't like the sound of it. "You call home, Lou?"

"I did—and it's bad, real bad."

"How bad?"

"Not gonna tell you that."

"O.K., Lou. You don't have to."

"Tell you this. It's bad, real bad."

"O.K., Lou. I heard you."

"Joe, don't try to look so good. That's all I ask."

Cooney went off as he'd come, in a huff, weaving, and Joe moved on.

The last conference was a barnburner on the subject of the Good Thief, after which came solemn benediction, the papal blessing, and the group picture. This would show the retreatmaster, the Rector, the permanent members of Egan's set, and (for no reason that Joe could see) Mooney, in the first row. Joe was in the second row, between a country pastor and a responsible first assistant. Cooney and Rooney were nowhere—they'd checked out in the night. Father Stock was another—there were many that year—who missed the group picture, the siren heard the day before having been an ambulance's, sounding for him, and he was now doing as well as could be expected, it was said, in the hospital. (His car, about which there had been so many futile announcements in the refectory—"Will the owner of . . ."—was towed off by a wrecker, Joe and others watching in silence.)

Joe came away from the retreat a grand to the good, but was worried, despite appearances, about the future, i.e., his assessment.

20

The Moustache Job

The first thing Joe did on his return, late that afternoon, was sift through the pile of mail on his desk, but saw nothing from the Chancery, and went upstairs where he found Father Felix in the study having a beer and watching TV, a children's program.

"Ah, you're back, Joe."

"Where's Bill?"

"He's not downstairs?"

"No. His little car's gone."

"Then he's not back yet."

"Back from where?"

"That I couldn't say."

"How long's he been gone?"

Father Felix, shaking a voluminous sleeve of his forest-green habit to expose his watch, which had a black dial, said, "Should be back shortly," and resumed his viewing. A bear in a tux was slapping a double bass—he was good, but the background music ("Ain't Misbehavin' ") made him sound better than he was.

"What's it all about, Father?" Joe asked.

Father Felix, presumably thinking he was being asked about the program, chuckled.

Joe left him.

In the kitchen, hearing that Young Father had driven off before noon with Father Potter and Mr Conklin, Joe said,

"Oh, I see," as if things weren't as bad as Mrs P. seemed to think. And hearing that Father Potter and Mr Conklin had spent the night in the rectory, Joe nodded—the best he could do, since things *were* as bad as Mrs P. seemed to think. "Father, they drank *seventeen* bottles of beer! And that *crazy* Mr Conklin! Oh, *Father*!" Mrs P. turned away and ran water hard into the sink.

Joe left her.

What a homecoming!

Joe returned to the study, picked up his bag, which he'd put down while talking to Father Felix (from whom he now received a benign nod), and went into his bedroom, where he immediately inspected the sheets and pillowcase. Nice and fresh. But then Mrs P. would change them. Ask her. No, no. Ask Father Felix. No. The wily monk would continue to cover for Bill, and for this, perhaps, he shouldn't be blamed, although monks, Joe believed, had a vested interest in chaos, felt better about themselves if things went wrong in the world (since they'd renounced it).

When Joe came out of the bedroom, Father Felix inquired, "Bill back yet?"

"That I couldn't say," Joe replied, and kept going. He went down to his office and got busy—dusted his desk, dust-mopped the floor, threw out the mail. What he *wanted* to do was phone Holy Sepulchre, where Potter was the second assistant, but how do it without letting whoever answered— maybe the first assistant, Lefty Beeman—know he was looking for Bill? He didn't want that. SS Francis and Clare's wasn't that kind of parish, or hadn't been until now. And the odds were that Bill would show up for dinner, or at least would call and explain, though it was late for that now. Anyway, Joe did nothing—wisely, as it turned out after the phone rang.

"Hate to bother you, Joe, but Airhead called in from your

place last night. Got me out of bed. Said he was spending the rest of the night there. Haven't heard from him since."

"He's not here now, Lefty."

"Take it you haven't seen him."

"No, but I just came off retreat."

"Nijinsky's not back yet"—Lefty meant the pastor—"assuming he went."

"He was there."

"What'd you think of it this year, Joe?"

"Not a good year."

"No, but What's-his-name . . ."

"Po."

"He's not a bad guy if you can get him alone. I had a little talk with him. He's on cigars, you know. And hopefully . . ."

Joe was silent, waiting for clarification.

"Joe, did you know I gave up smoking?"

"No."

"You see, I've got this little rubber cigar. Got it from Horse. He got it from Beans. The idea's not to break the chain. I'm going into my third solid week. You still on cigars, Joe?"

"Wouldn't say I'm *on* 'em. Smoke one now and then. Babies."

"Like to have a little talk with you, Joe. And hopefully . . ."

Joe was silent, but not waiting for clarification.

"Joe, how's about us breaking bread sometime? Only let me know ahead. It's hard for me to get away. Nijinsky's never here, and Airhead's always out—and now he's disappeared. Joe, is Bill there?"

"Not at the moment, no. Should be back shortly."

"Had a little talk with Bill and What's-his-name. You know about *him*, Joe? And this married woman?"

"If you're talking about Conklin, I did hear something, yes."

"Did you hear they broke it off?"

"No, but I'm glad to hear it."

"Yes, but Airhead's trying to save the relationship—some relationship. And so's Bill, I guess."

Joe was silent.

"Sorry to be the one to tell you this, Joe. I know how you feel. I wanted to kick *all* their asses."

"It's a crazy world, Left."

"Joe, how're *things*?"

"O.K."

"What about this new drive? Were you badly hit?"

"Haven't heard yet."

"We got ours today, and it's rough—not that *I'll* lose any sleep."

"Didn't get ours yet."

"Joe, what happens when you do? With your system?"

"We'll see."

"I used to worry about money, Joe. No more."

"You will, Left. You'll get another parish."

"Nice of you to say that, Joe. Say, would you ask Airhead to call in if he shows up there?"

"O.K."

"And if Bill shows up here—"

Joe hung up.

At six o'clock he rose from his desk and stood by it for the Angelus, after which the phone rang—a question from the kitchen, Joe replying, "No, we'll eat at the usual time." He covered Bill's typewriter and went up to the dining room where Father Felix was waiting for him. "How was the retreat, Joe?" "Not a good year." During dinner, Father Felix spoke of outstanding men at the monastery, original thinkers but sound, some with parish experience like himself, ideal men to preach a diocesan priests' retreat, Joe occasionally inquiring, "That so?" Nothing was said about Bill, whose empty plate, though, kept saying to Joe, "Where's Bill?"

When the phone rang at 6:29 Mrs P. answered it in the kitchen, from which she came running. "It's Young Father, Father. He wants to talk to you."

"I'll take it in the study," Joe said, rising from the table, serene, an example to interested observers, unfortunately not noticing that he was wearing his napkin (tucked under his belt, out of *his* sight) until he sat down and picked up the phone in the study. "Thanks, Mrs Pelissier"—meaning she could and should hang up, which she did. "Bill, where the hell are you?"

"Father, I won't be home for dinner."

"You mean you *weren't.*"

"Can't make it, Father. Couldn't."

"Why's that, Bill?"

"Couldn't leave, Father. Can't."

"Bill, you sound tired."

"I am, Father."

"Bill, the thing to do when you're tired is come home."

"Father, I'm with others."

"Bill, just tell others what I said."

"Father, they're asleep."

"You mean passed out?"

"Father, I can't leave 'em here."

"Bill, where the hell are you?"

"In the city, in a place called the Bow Wow—it's a great big bar."

"Yes, isn't it? Look, Bill. They know how to handle a thing like this in a place like that. I know the management there. Ask the management—Dom, if he's there—to help you. Put others in a cab. Put yourself in one—*another* one—if you can't drive."

"I can drive, Father. I'm cold sober."

"Good. Then you should be back shortly."

Joe and Father Felix were watching TV when Bill's little car pulled into the driveway. Joe, saying nothing to the monk, left the study and was in the kitchen running water into the sink when Bill came in the back door—except for the way he was dressed (overalls and T-shirt), he appeared to be all right, just a bit drawn and embarrassed.

"Thought I'd make some coffee," Joe said. "Care for a cup?"

"Shower first, Father."

Joe was ready with the coffee in Bill's room and, to explain his presence there, said, "Father's in the study" (meaning we don't want the monk, who already knows too much, in on this) when Bill came out of the bathroom in his pajamas, though it was only eight thirty. Only, yes, but why had it taken Bill an hour and a half—at least an hour too long—to drive from the Bow Wow? Bill had a lot to explain, but he appeared to realize this and said:

"Father, it all started last night at Holy Sepulchre, but I wasn't there—I was here"—as if he deserved credit for that. He said that Potter and Conklin had been in the rumpus room at Holy Sepulchre when Father Beeman came in with Father Power ["Horse," Joe said]. There had been an argument about Conklin and the married woman—they were no longer seeing each other because of his infidelity ["*His,* huh?"], but Potter hoped to save the relationship, or, if not, that they'd all be friends ["All?"], Conklin, the woman, and her husband ["Bill, there used to be a thing called common sense"]. During the argument, Conklin had swung on Father

Power ["*What?* A layman hit a priest!"]. Helped by Father
Power, Father Beeman, who'd been doing some work on the
snooker table, going over the fuzzy places in the cloth with
an electric razor, had used this to shave off Conklin's
moustache, not all of it, just one side ["*Holy* Moses"]. Potter
and Conklin had then driven out to see Bill and stayed late
["Late?"]. In fact, they had stayed the night ["Where'd they
sleep?"]. They hadn't slept, had sat up all night talking in the
study ["Talking about what?"], about the Church, the clergy,
the moustache, Conk bitter about it, Pot blaming himself,
saying things like "There is no greater love, than one lay
down one's life for one's friend" ["Hallucinating, huh?"]. Bill
had been sympathetic at first, as had Father Felix ["*What?* I
thought *he* was in bed"], who, after a bit, had gone to bed
["Good"], as Bill had finally ["Good"]. Pot and Conk were
still at it in the morning ["Still in the study?"], still in the
study. Bill had said Mass ["What about Airhead?"], Pot
hadn't, and Bill, though tired, had gone to his office as usual
["Good"]. He had left Pot and Conk in the dining room
arguing with Father Felix ["Arguing?"] about the Age of
Faith ["Oh, *no!*"], when priests were priests and monks were
monks ["Gotcha"]. Father Felix had come down to the other
office with his breviary and closed the doors ["Hah!"], and
Pot and Conk had come down to Bill's office and sat around
["Great"] until they decided to go out for a beer ["*Out,*
huh?"]. To get rid of them, Bill had agreed to go along, but
in his car, so he could leave them as soon as possible
["Uh-huh"], but hadn't been able to, and later had to stay
and look after them ["What about earlier, Bill?"]. It had been
a mistake not to leave earlier. "Father, I'm sorry about that—
and other things." Bill had had too much to drink, and for
that he blamed himself. But it had been Pot's idea ["To have
too much to drink?"] to stay with, and stand up for, Conk (as

Pot had failed to do when Conk lost half of his moustache) should the necessity arise, as it had ["At the Bow Wow?"]. No, but before that, they had been in other places ["Like?"], like the Blue Forest, a strip joint ["In the afternoon?"], for the businessmen's matinee ["I see. How was it?"]. "Father, I've had it with Pot and Conk." ["Good," Joe was going to say, but said "Oh?"] Bill—this was something he should've mentioned earlier—had let Conk use a razor that morning to shave, but Conk hadn't done anything about his moustache, and was going around like that, with one handlebar, *telling* people ["Telling 'em what?"], " 'Catholic priests in good standing did this to me.' " ["I see. What'd people say?"] Some were sympathetic, some weren't—Father Felix was, Mrs P. [Mrs P.!] wasn't. It was like that everywhere—sort of fifty-fifty. ["And when he was *telling* people, what'd you guys say?"] Pot had been supportive [" 'Supportive,' huh?"], Bill hadn't been, had kept quiet, to his regret then and now. "I've really had it with Pot and Conk, Father." ["Let's hope so," Joe was going to say, but said, "So you put 'em in a cab?"] Bill, taking Joe's advice, had spoken to the management at the Bow Wow ["Fat guy with pimp sideburns? That's Dom—fairly big contributor when I was at Charities"], but Dom knew about Conk's moustache from the waitresses and he wasn't sympathetic, even when told that Pot was a priest (and that Bill was), not believing it until Bill mentioned Joe's name. Dom had changed then and had said it wouldn't show proper respect to put Pot in a cab and had wanted to call and pay for a limousine. But Bill had talked him out of that, had brought his bug around to the rear of the Bow Wow, and two kitchen workers had come out with Pot and helped him into the backseat ["What about Conklin?"]. Conk, who was able to walk, had come out minus—*completely* minus—his moustache ["No! What'd he *say?*"]. Conk hadn't said anything, not a word, until, at Holy Sepulchre, he gave Father Beeman a little plastic bottle—an imitation Old Grand-Dad whiskey bottle—that he'd got from one of those claw machines in an amusement arcade, when he'd said: " 'For you, Father, if thou wouldst be perfect, to go with your rubber cigar.' " ["What a hell of a thing to say to Lefty! What'd *he* say?"] Father Beeman said thanks. That was all. ["Poor guy. Still, he had it coming."] Then he and Bill had put Pot to bed. When Bill came downstairs, Conk was gone. Bill had then driven home.

"So that's it, huh?"

"More or less."

Less, Joe was afraid.

"Think I'll go to bed, Father, unless there's something you want to say."

"No."

"Thanks for not chewing me out. Or is that coming later?"

"No, not if I can help it. Just don't say *anything*—about *any* of this—to Father Felix."

"I won't."

"G'night, Bill."

"G'night, Joe."

It was the first time, Joe realized, that Bill had dared, or maybe cared, to call him Joe.

21

The Crunch

The next morning (Saturday) after the mail came, Joe closed the door between the offices and for some reason, maybe to get a hold on himself, dialed Time and Temperature. "Thanks," he said to the recorded voice. Then he opened and read the letter from the Chancery, stopped at *your parish is therefore assessed*, but carried on to the end, then started over. To be fair, he couldn't on the face of it assign the blame to Toohey, since the letter was on stationery and typewritten, or to the Arch, since it just didn't sound like him (manifest need, manifold purpose), though it was, of course, signed by him. It was manifest that the blame was manifold: Mayer, Mayer and Maher, of Chicago, by appointment consultants in finance and development to the Archdiocese and given office space in the Chancery, offered their special individualized, confidential services to you and your parish, be it large or small, and their Mr McMaster should be contacted by interested pastors without delay.

Joe read the letter again, and that was all he did that morning, again and again.

"Backlog of work, owing to the retreat. Won't be hearing this afternoon," he told Bill and Father Felix at lunch. He spent most of the afternoon in thought. But about an hour before dinner, he started typing—just a rough draft.

"Catching up with my correspondence. Won't be hearing this evening," he told Bill and Father Felix at dinner.

Hours later, after Bill and Father Felix had gone to bed, Joe was still at his typewriter, firing away.

He was in a dazed state when he put the final product in a protective folder and carried it upstairs. He stopped in the kitchen for ice, and after making himself a drink, settled down in his Barcalounger to give the final product its final reading, which took a while.

Well?

Well, allowing for the circumstance that it was his own work, discounting some for that, he found that he was still very favorably impressed—yes, it was quite a letter.

Why?

Well, it stated the facts, its language was well chosen, its tone was just right—courage in adversity and respect for authority. This was a letter that would not be read lightly and tossed aside. This was a letter that would certainly be pondered and possibly acted upon favorably.

Was this a letter that was, perhaps, a little long?

A little, perhaps, but then it had to be in order to cover the ground as it did, so well.

The odd thing was that when you finally came to the end of the letter you wished, well, you hadn't. And wanted to read it again. That was Joe's experience anyway. He read it again. And again. He made himself a drink and—guess what?—he wanted to read the letter again. And did. It was quite a letter all right.

Before he let himself read it again, he freshened his drink. It was then, soon after that, that he found himself first murmuring against the letter, then talking back to it, then mimicking it—"Thanking you in advance, Your Excellency, for any consideration you may see fit . . ."—literally incapable of reading it as it was meant to be read by the Arch, reading it, rather, as it might be read by, say, *Toohey*.

Oh, *no*!

Oh, yes.

Tearing the letter into small, flushable bits, and likewise the carbon copy, he bolted up from his Barcalounger to dispose of them and to freshen his drink.

He'd had a narrow escape.

The next day (Sunday), after the last Mass, Joe told Bill to look after Father Felix until it was time for his bus and to drive him to it. "Here," he said, and gave Bill a twenty. "See that you both have a very tasty meal. Don't count on me. Still have work to do, owing to the retreat."

"Anything I can do to help, Joe?"

"No." Short of robbing a bank. "Thanks."

So Joe went down to his office and, playing a longshot hunch, spent a couple of hours trying to write a *short* letter—" . . . difficult if not impossible in the circumstances, Your Excellency, but rest assured I'll"—and tore it up. Having made two trips to the kitchen he made a third for beer, this time picking up the paper (Bill and Father Felix had gone out), and returned to his office to read the one while drinking the other. His horoscope said: "Don't let irritation shake you from a methodical approach to a financial problem or property deal you are involved in. Your love life is confused but very happy now. Take thought." He lay down on the couch to take thought, or a nap, and was soon hotly engaged in conversation with Mayer, Mayer and Maher, their Mr McMaster.

JOE: Look. All I want to know from you is (a) are Mayer, Mayer and Maher taking their cut off the gross—projected or actual?; (b) what is that cut percentagewise?; and (c) is it deductible? Speak.

McM: Deductible from what, Father?

Joe: From my nut if I make it without calling in you frickers.

McM: Monsignor, Father called me a name.

Toohey: No, no, Mac. Frick, you see, wrote a textbook in use at the sem in our time. His name, for that reason, became a byword among us.

Joe: All right, Catfish. What's the cut and is it deductible?

Toohey: Busy here. Hey, Ordinary! It's frickin' Joe Hackett. You better talk to him. It's about you-know-what. Fry his ass.

Arch: Don't tell me you clowns sent that frickin' form letter to *Joe*! He's *special*! Thought you at least knew *that*! Hello, Joe. This is your Ordinary. About that letter, look, I'm *sorry*. It was never meant for *you*, Joe. A frickin' clerical error. Forget it, Joe, *if* you can.

Joe: I'll do my best, Your Excellency.

Arch: Just call me Arch, Joe.

Joe: Arch.

Arch: Or Albert.

Joe: I'd rather not.

Arch: Joe, though it does have its disadvantages at a time like this, I've long been an admirer of your system—did you know that our dear brothers in Abraham, in this as in everything else, were first in the field?—and I only wish more of my men had a modicum of your guts and pizzazz. Hell, send in whatever you can—spiritual bouquets if you're really strapped. Tear up that frickin' letter. O.K., Joe?

Joe: O.K., Arch. What about others in the same boat?

Arch: What others?

Joe: Smiley and Cooney.

Arch: Smiley? Is he still in the Church? Puts ice cubes in his beer.

Joe: I know. But he's got the same system I have, and likewise Cooney.

ARCH: Joe, we can't let *everybody* off.

JOE: Not exactly fair, is it, Arch?

ARCH: Not exactly, but that's life in the Archdiocese, Joe.

JOE: I'm not trying to tell you how to run the Archdiocese, Arch.

ARCH: Might not be a bad idea if you did, Joe. I don't say that to everybody in lower middle management.

JOE: I know. Thanks.

ARCH: Say, how's about us breakin' bread sometime?

JOE: Where?

ARCH: I'd say here. Only you know how it is here. Always a crowd.

JOE: Catfish, you mean?

ARCH: Ho, ho. Joe, there's something I've been wanting to ask you.

JOE: Shoot.

ARCH: Why do you call Kissass Catfish?

JOE: Because of his fat face, and big mouth, his little eyes. Started when we were kids. You know how cruel kids can be.

ARCH: "Shorty," you mean?

JOE: "Half Pint" and so on. However, where Catfish is concerned, there may be more to it than meets the eye.

ARCH: How so?

JOE: Catfish feeds on the dreck in organized religion— mummery, mobbery, robbery, finkery, fear. He's a bottom feeder, Arch.

ARCH: *Wham!*

JOE: Often wonder what you see in the guy, Arch.

ARCH: He has his uses, Joe.

JOE: Like the pilot fish.

ARCH: Don't get you.

JOE: Photo-essay in the paper today on pilot fish. Didn't you see it?

ARCH: Haven't seen the paper, Joe. Always let the house-keeper have it first.

JOE: Well, these pilot fish, they hang around big, person-eating sharks—great whites, hammerheads, and so on. Do odd jobs for 'em, point out prey, clean up the mess, and can't type.

ARCH: Joe, if he's a pilot fish, what does that make me? A hammerhead?

JOE: Don't push it too far, Arch.

ARCH: Joe, what's the trouble between you two?

JOE: It goes way back. His father worked for mine.

ARCH: "Hockitt's Cull Iss Hut Stoof."

JOE: Right. In grade school we were rivals—at least in his view—but the good nuns thought more of me. Understand-ably, what with free coal, capons at Christmas, and all those dimes and quarters for the Missions that came so easily to and from me. Not to mention my sunny disposition, my natural good looks (as a boy), and my athletic prowess. Can't blame 'em, the nuns. They're women, after all. Catfish couldn't keep up. He's had it in for me ever since. Oh, I know it's his job to be as excrementitious as possible within reason—probably I'd be the same, to some extent—but he goes too far. Why, when I call the Chancery and he answers, I want to hang up. And I'm not alone.

ARCH: Tsk, tsk.

JOE: He runs a lousy office, Arch.

ARCH: Joe, and I speak not so much as your pal as your Ordinary, if there's anything irregular about his conduct in future—anything at all—I want to know. Let me give you my unlisted number.

JOE: Let me give you an example, Arch. I thought, since you liked the new rectory so much, you might be interested in blessing it.

ARCH: Why not?

JOE: So I called the Chancery and got Catfish. "We bless one, we have to bless 'em all," he says. "Wait a minute," I said. "How many new rectories are there nowadays?" "You could start a trend. Bless it yourself," he says and hangs up. How 'bout that?

ARCH: Tsk, tsk.

JOE: Don't suppose he mentioned it.

ARCH: No, but I'm glad you did, Joe. Methinks Kissass needs a change.

JOE: What I was thinking, Arch.

ARCH: Up and out.

JOE: Hate to see him a bishop, Arch.

ARCH: In some respects, this is still an imperfect world, Joe. Ever think of going into administration yourself?

JOE: Who hasn't, Arch, in this diocese? But I'd like to see a new church out here before I move on, or kick off, which *may* come first.

ARCH: How *is* your health these days, Joe?

JOE: Not bad, everything considered—like ARF.

ARCH: ARF? Oh, you mean Arf. That's what we call it here at headquarters, Joe—after my dog.

JOE: "Arf" goes Sandy?

ARCH: Exactly. But you just forget the whole thing, Joe.

JOE: Thanks a mil, Arch. Fifty thou, I mean.

ARCH: My pleasure, Joe. Say, how's about us breakin' bread sometime.

JOE: Where?

ARCH: I'd say here. Only you know how it is here. Always a crowd.

JOE: Catfish, you mean?

ARCH: Ho, ho.

Joe woke up in the dark and was annoyed that Bill hadn't thought, or bothered, to look in on him. Or had he? Joe hoped not.

*   *   *

The next morning, after making a list, the first item on which required that he find out what others in his narrow category were thinking, Joe called Silverstream, learned that Smiley was attending a workshop in Chicago, and so spoke to the curate (Miller), which was better as things were in that parish since what the curate might say, if anything (that was the difficulty with the curate), would come from the horse's mouth, as would not have been the case with the pastor, far from it.

"Arf," Miller said. "It's a real problem for us, Father, and would be even if we didn't have the setup we have over here."

"We have the same system over here, Father. That's why I called."

"It's not working over here, Father."

"It's working over here, Father."

"The pastor's thinking of dropping it, I understand. At least for the time being."

"What d'ya mean, 'for the time being'? You either have it or you don't. You can't have it both ways, Father."

"Then we just might be able to handle our assessment"— Miller, ignoring Joe's objections, was used to dealing with Smiley—"like other parishes, Father."

"And bring in the mercenaries?"

"*Who?*"

"The fund raisers."

"It's my impression the pastor's thinking along such lines, Father."

"What about your good, loyal, paid-up people, Father?"

"They'd understand, I'm sure, once the urgency of the matter is explained to them. In any case, the decision rests with the pastor."

Joe had to respect the curate for playing the game. "So the pastor's taking a dive?"

"That's all I can say, Father, at this juncture."

"Nice talking to you, Father, at this juncture," Joe said, and hung up.

He called Cooney and told him that Smiley was taking a dive.

"I'm not surprised," Cooney said.

"*I'm* not surprised," Joe said. "Smiley's a reed."

"A what?"

"Shaken in the wind."

"Oh yeah."

They discussed ARF, saying that it wasn't the same for them as for others, that they might have been shown *some* consideration, that they might have been consulted beforehand, that they should not have been sent a frickin' form letter. They criticized its style ("Manifest!"—"Manifold!") and its content, saying that if there was such a money crisis in the diocese then things like the Institute should be closed down and not, for God's sake, expanded, that if there was such a priestpower shortage in the diocese, then men off getting degrees and men off serving in the armed forces and men off goofing off (on so-called leaves of absence, which usually ended badly) should come home and go to work. Cooney proposed a halt in all new construction, but Cooney already had a new church, and Joe, rather than spoil what until then had been a perfect meeting of minds, was silent— they'd got pretty far afield.

"Well, anyway, whatever others do, we won't, Lou."

"Won't what, Joe?"

"Take a dive." Joe wondered if they'd been cut off. "Lou?"

"Joe, what else can we do?"

After that, the conversation got confused. Cooney wouldn't admit that he was thinking of taking a dive, though obviously he was, and Joe really went to work on him. "Lou, you'll be letting your people down, your good, loyal, paid-up people. You'll be no better than Smiley. You'll be *worse*, Lou. Because, Lou, even if you"—in case this was going to be his out—"*don't* bring in the mercenaries, you'll know in your heart what you're doing, Lou."

"Look, Joe. It's *my* parish. They're *my* people."

"I'm sorry about that, Lou, for them *and* you."

"Joe, you don't know my assessment."

"And you don't know mine."

"Joe, what's your assessment?"

"I'd rather not say."

"I'll tell you mine if you tell me yours."

"I'll tell you this, Lou—it's a lot. More than double what I expected."

"And you think you'll make it by going after dp's?" Delinquent parishioners.

"I'm thinking of everything, Lou."

"Bank loan?"

"Everything, Lou."

"Swallow your pride, Joe. Do what I'm going to do. Put it to your people—*up* to your people, I mean."

"A distinction so fine as to make no difference. I'm sorry, Lou." And Joe hung up.

Addressing himself to his list—he had let irritation shake him from a methodical approach to his problem—he drew a line through (A) OTHERS?, underscored (B) PEOPLE, NO!, and circled (C) DP'S. And—knowing where he stood now, alone— tore up his list.

22

Roomy
Two-Hearted
Rectory

So Joe's evening routine had to change and did.

After dinner, as heretofore, he'd work a few innings in the yard with Bill and take a much needed bath, but then instead of retiring to the study he'd go off in his car with his list, having told Bill only "Some calls to make."

His list, comprising over a third of the families in the parish, was alphabetical. But his modus operandi, after a week, was still random: to cruise around until he sighted the man or woman of the house out on the lawn, or a child ("Hi, cowboy, what's *your* name?") who might lead him to them. Before he got down to business, he was not above saying where circumstances warranted it, "Heard you went to Europe," or "See you had the house painted," or "Thought only golf courses had mowers like that."

This, then, was what he'd come to, because he'd hoped to spare himself and his parishioners money talk from the pulpit. And because he who seeks to save his life shall lose it? And because, if an idle mind is the devil's workshop, the Chancery was an industrial park? He could hear it now. "Hey, Ordinary, 'member what Denver told you at the National Con and you laughed in his face? Says here he made it with half a mil to spare." "Well, I'll be fricked. Get me Denver, honey. Truck? Albert here. Congrats. Off the record, those numbers for real? O.K., *O.K.* Relax. I didn't *say* you're a liar. What's the story?

Use electric canes, or what? M, M and M, Chicago, huh? Will do, Truck, and thanks a mil—make that two."

He was averaging only three calls an evening. At first, he was slow to get down to business, and now, knowing that nothing much happened when he did, he was slower. He would begin by suggesting that failure to keep up payments, or to contribute at all, was probably an oversight—this was generally rejected, not, he thought, for its mendacity but for the obligation there was in it to do better in future. He was hindered, sometimes, by the absence of the spouse who ran the show (who, in one case, to judge by what Joe could hear of the telephone conversation, was being warned, for a change, *not* to come home right away). In any case, people had all kinds of reasons for being dp's.

"I'm gonna be transferred again, knew all along I would be"; "My wife's not a Catholic, Father"; "My husband's not a Catholic, Father"; "We don't know how long *this* marriage will last, do we, dear?"; "If the kids were school age, Father, it'd be different"; "Neither one of us is what you might call devout, Father, and with no kids"; "Just haven't got it, Father, and don't know what you can do"; "Glad you *don't* talk about money in church, Father, want you to know that"; "Father, you *should* talk about money in church—it'd be more like church—and I guess that's my advice to you"; "Sure, I signed up, but it didn't work out, and now I just contribute when and what I can"; "You find a five-dollar bill in the flower collection, Father, that's probably mine"; "Father, you say the Church always comes last, and you may be right about that, but not when you say people have money for *everything* else—*we* don't"; "My husband and I haven't recovered from the rectory yet. Pretty roomy, seems to us, for two bachelors. So you lived in a room in the school. Big deal. You should be living in a tent."

Yes, there were times when Joe felt like tearing his garments and, for an encore, singing "Laugh, Clown, Laugh."

After his last call, thank God, he sped home to his reward—a drink or two or three, maybe an old movie on TV, or the Twins if they were playing on the West Coast, and yes, priestly fellowship, in which Bill, for some reason, was showing more interest these nights, trying, it seemed, to *learn* from Joe. This was only as it should be in the pastor-curate relationship, but was new and different in theirs, making for more give and take, Joe doing his best for Bill, even if he sometimes lost by it, by telling the truth.

One night he confessed that, in the matter of taking up the collections on the day of his first Mass, he had attempted to buy off the pastor, and furthermore would do so again if he had his life to live over, but would not, he hoped, grab the empty envelope again, or hole up in the boys' washroom. " 'Joseph, you should be ashamed of yourself,' he said. Those were his last words. He hasn't spoken to me since." "But at your Mass you did take up the collection?" "Thanks to Toohey, yes. I didn't see any way out of it. I still don't."

One night, speaking of his first appointment, he was at pains to present Van as someone in a great tradition of the Church and not as some kind of nut, as Bill appeared to think when told of Van's horny knees. "He was trying to go all the way, Bill, and still is, I guess. I was like that myself—just a tenderfoot, though—when I went to Holy Faith. But I soon woke up, or gave up, however you look at it."

"What happened to your hair shirt?"

"I buried it."

"Joe, where do you stand on all that now?"

"I'm sitting down."

"That's how you look at it?"

"Yes, because that's how it is."

That night, talking during commercials, they were watching an old movie, new to them, in which Tyrone Power, employed by a carnival traveling through a part of the South that looked a lot like California, had drunk himself out of his good job as a barker and now, fit for nothing else and attracted by the pay, a bottle a day, had accepted the job of geek, which seemed to mean that he—yes—bit off the heads of live poultry. Ugh.

"That," Joe said, rising from his Barcalounger, "calls for a drink."

Bill, when Joe came out of the bathroom with their drinks, said, "Man here to see you this evening. A Mr McMaster."

"Who?"

Bill must have seen that Joe recognized the name, and did not repeat it. "Just a courtesy call, he said."

"Uh-huh."

"Said just to tell you he'd call again."

"Uh-huh. Thanks."

At the next break for a commercial, Bill said, "Everybody's talking about it, all my classmates."

"Alka Seltzer?"

"This drive. Arf."

"That so?"

"Joe, you think I don't know what you're doing these nights when you go out?"

Joe gazed straight ahead, at the tube, and said nothing.

"You're trying to raise money."

"So?" But not looking at Bill.

"You're in a bind."

"*So?*" Still not looking at him.

"Joe, I think you should've said something to me about this."

"Why?" Studying the action in a commercial for breakfast cereal, actually interested in it, a sack race.

"Why *not?*"

"Sack race."

"Yeah, I can see."

"Not a hundred-yard dash. Not a mile run."

"Joe, I don't know what *you're* talking about."

"It's a sack race, Bill. The priesthood."

"Yeah, sure. Joe, I think you should've said something to me, but I know why you didn't. You've got this thing about money and the priesthood, and I can see how you got it, what with your first Mass and all. I can see how you got the way you are, Joe."

Joe looked at him then. "How'd you get the way you are, Bill, or were?"

"All right, Joe." Bill blushed, remembering, it seemed, his reluctance to get involved in parish finance, his "Thanks" when Joe offered to handle the strong-arm stuff.

"Look, Bill. These may be the best years of your life as a priest, and as long as I have anything to say about it, as long as you're here, I want you to be just that, a priest—and not a bill collector. Time enough for that when you're a pastor."

"Sure, Joe, and thanks. But what if I want to help? I don't like it now, the way it is now, with you doing all the dirty work. I mean it, Joe. I *want* to help."

"We'll see," Joe said.

Joe had a pastor's concern for his curate, a father's wish for his son to have it better, and he also had qualms about revealing how many dp's there were in the parish—a reflection on his system—but since there were so many, and the servant, as Scripture says, is not superior to his master, and Bill was so willing to help, Joe decided to let him.

So the alphabetical list, lines drawn through the names of those Joe had failed with, halos around those, possibly three, he'd persuaded to try again, was split between them. And at nightfall, except on Saturday and Sunday, usually after a few innings and a bath, in Bill's case a shower, immaculate in black and white (Joe had read that the Wehrmacht in WWII wore its dress uniforms in battle), they'd (more like the RAF now) scramble their planes, Joe in his black bomber, Bill in his little caramel fighter, give each other a comradely salute, a slow wave from their respective cockpits, and take off on the night's mission.

For Joe, by now, it was more of the same, but for Bill it was new, and if Joe returned to the rectory first, if Bill was still out there somewhere, as he was on the first night (watching TV with the family of the breadwinner who was expected to arrive at any moment but didn't), Joe worried about him. He knew, from debriefing him, that Bill was catching a certain amount of flak—had been criticized for driving a foreign car, asked how much the rectory had set the parish back, advised that money matters should be discussed during business hours.

"Part of the trouble," Bill told Joe, "is we're calling on people during prime viewing time."

"I know," Joe said.

One night, after he'd been at it for a week, Bill said, "Parishioners in good standing could be used to do this job."

"You want out, Bill? If you do, I'll understand—no one better."

"No, I just mean they *are* being used in some parishes."

"For Arf, Bill, not for this. Don't mention Arf to people, Bill, even indirectly. As far as this parish is concerned, Arf doesn't exist. That's not the problem here."

"It's not?"

"It's a problem, yes, but it's not *the* problem." In admit-ting, in effect, that his system wasn't working Joe had lost ground with Bill, as he'd known he would, but what Bill had proposed, and was perhaps still proposing, would be wrong. "It wouldn't be fair to use parishioners in good standing for this, fair to them, or to the others, especially to them. It'd be like asking them to go to confession to a layman." And Joe cited the case of the dp who wouldn't talk to Bill because he was only the assistant, to which Bill nodded bleakly.

"On the other hand, Bill, this isn't what we were ordained for, and whether we succeed or fail is immaterial."

"Yeah, I know."

"It's not as if we were out trying to preach the Gospel."

"No."

"We're just a couple of bill collectors."

"Yeah."

"So don't take it so hard."

"O.K."

But Bill continued to take it hard, showing the weakness of his strength (innocence). Having done so well for his hairy missionaries, he may have thought he had a way with people. The trouble was, in Joe's view, that Bill's understand-ing of the Cross, like that of most young people today, was nominal, narrow, unapocalyptic, and so failure to him didn't, as it did to Joe, make much sense.

When they returned to the rectory, though, their evenings out, fruitless for Bill and nearly so for Joe, became something else—the best nights yet for priestly fellowship. Joe, if he returned first, as he usually did, would hand Bill a drink ("How'd it go?"—"Still batting zero"), and Bill, if he returned first, now followed that practice ("How'd it go?"—"Lousé"). Bill hadn't had occasion to make the drinks before, with Joe there, and need not have followed his example, but did. A little thing, yes. In other respects too, Bill was coming around—he'd entirely given up cigarettes for baby cigars and, almost entirely, the guitar (no little thing, in Joe's view).

But priestly fellowship, like love, is perhaps best measured in intangibles.

So often in the past, even at the best of times, Joe had sensed in Bill a prim disapproval of the kind of thinking and drinking that went on in the study at night, a stubborn, subterranean desire to be elsewhere. Not so now. So often in the past Joe had been afraid to get up and attend to their glasses, lest Bill get up too—and go to bed. Not so now. So often in the past conversation had become debate, one man arguing from received knowledge, the other from earned experience, each more interested in grinding his generation's axe than in arriving at the melancholy truth. Not so now.

Their evenings out, apart, had tempered and brought them together.

One night, before Joe could hand Bill a drink, Bill handed Joe a check, saying, "Apparently these people have been living in the parish since May, but never registered. The check's for more than it should be. I told the man, but he said, 'Forget it. I'll see you again in May.' How about that?"

"Uh-huh," Joe said, looking at the check again. It was for $750 and from Mr Lane.

"Is something wrong with it?"

"No, no." Joe, still under scrutiny—because he hadn't jumped up and down with joy?—moved over to the TV set, on which he deposited the check with due respect, and sat down with his drink. "How'd it happen, Bill?"

"I was next door, and when I left—no sale—the man was getting out of his car. He said hello and invited me into the house. After that, well, one thing led to another"—Bill glanced at the TV set, where the check reposed.

"Hmmm," Joe said.

"He's something in public relations at Cones. She—I met her—she doesn't say much. There are two other children—I mean, she's going to have a baby."

"Hmmm," Joe said.

"I told 'em they'd have to come in to register, one of 'em."

"You've seen 'em, Bill, so it can be done over the phone."

"They'll be glad to hear that." Bill removed his collar and coat, as was his practice, and collapsed on the couch with his glass from which he drank deeply while, as was *not* his practice, scuffing off his big black loafers and exercising his toes, *spreading* them, in his black socks. Ugh.

"You know what, Joe?"

"What?"

"I needed that."

"Uh-huh." Then, realizing that Bill—he'd glanced at the TV set—had meant the check, not the drink, Joe said, "Congrats."

23
Pastoral and
Homiletic

Browsing among the shelves in the Licensed Vintner's, Joe stopped to open the door for a truck driver with a dolly of canned beer, and then went up to the counter with a bottle of red table wine—he had to buy something—and paid for it. "Thought Mr Barnes worked Saturday mornings."

"Not today, Father." The Licensed Vintner's wife, in mobcap, peasant blouse, and dirndl skirt (approved dress for female employees in the Mall shoppes), put the bottle in a parchment-look bag and slapped it. "There you go, Father." But not without being preached at. "Have a good day!"

"Uh-huh," Joe said.

He was getting into his car when the truck driver came up behind him and said something.

"How's that again?"

"The old man. They let him go."

"Mr Barnes?"

"Hey, don't tell 'em I told you."

"Don't worry."

"He's workin' out to Badger now, in the liquor store."

"I see. Thanks."

Browsing among the shelves in the Great Badger's liquor store, Joe was accosted by a small humpbacked man in a grey business suit and a black sombrero with silver balls around its brim. "Don't see what you want, sir, just ask for it. If we haven't got it, we'll be happy to get it for you."

"Thanks. I'm waiting for Mr Barnes."

"Your customer, Mr Barnes."

"Yes, sir." When he'd finished with his other customer, Mr Barnes, in a dark blue blazer with badger rampant on its breast pocket (certainly an improvement on the red shirt, white sleeve garters, and blue leather-look apron he'd worn at the Licensed Vintner's), came nodding over to where Joe was, by an island display of gin.

"Case of this, Mr Barnes."

"Yes, sir."

"And a case of my beer. Case of empties outside."

"Yes, sir."

Joe, having paid by check, which he'd never done at the Licensed Vintner's, never having bought a case of anything there except beer, held the door open for Mr Barnes, who had the gin and beer on a dolly, and opened the car trunk for him. Mr Barnes nodded at Joe's nice clean case, then went to the not-so-clean one on the dolly, opened it, and there, lying on its side, was a fifth of brandy (Christian Brothers).

"Compliments of the management, sir. That was Mr Brock himself who spoke to you."

"The Great Badger himself?" (The truth was, the man's face—hat, actually—had been known to Joe from reading the discount house's shopping news.)

"Yes, sir."

"I see. Well, be sure and thank him for me."

"Yes, sir."

Mr Barnes then switched the beer bottles, the full ones for the empties, to Joe's nice clean case, Joe helping in this operation, in the end laying the fifth of brandy down on its side, and that was it.

"Thanks, Mr Barnes. Glad to see you here."
"And you, sir."

Joe was about to drive away when he saw, coming out of the Great Badger, of all places, of all people, Barb, and was seen by her. She rushed (but with a slight skiing movement of her left leg) up to his car and gasped: "Where can we talk?" And like Lot's wife, she looked back as if they might safely return whence they'd come, perhaps to the coffee shop. Swiftly, before she turned into a pillar of salt, Joe opened the door on the passenger's side for her.

"Father, it's about Greg. His induction notice came today, but he says he won't go. 'You quit school, so now you *have* to go.' But he says no, he won't. 'What'll your dad say? You'll break his heart.' Father, this war means so much to Brad—me, too, with Scott in it. But, Father, what I'm really worried about is Brad. Things aren't good for him these days. They don't appreciate him at the paper. They won't let him go to Saigon—too controversial, they say. They killed his story on that poor family that lives next to the dump—too controversial, they say. They want him to quit, he says. Father, he's going through hell these days. And now this. Father, will *you* talk to Greg?"

"Have him come and see me, Barb."

Shortly thereafter, from the tire swing in the Gurriers' yard, Joe, viewing the herd of old cars grazing in the tall grass, said, "Jim, what d'ya mean you're looking for a 'buyer' for your 'inventory'? What's it worth?"

"Plenty. Even as scrap."

" 'Even'?"

"Just one of my options."

"What're the others, Jim?"

"Kids buy up these cars. Couple spoken for."

"What about the rest? Let's say you *don't* find a buyer."

"Get me a rig in here like they haul new cars on."

"I see. And what'll that cost you?"

"Not so much."

Joe got out of the swing. "You might break even, huh?"

"Wouldn't pay me," Jim explained, "just to break even."

"I see. Haul 'em where?"

"That's the trouble—I might not have room for 'em if we move back to the city."

" 'If,' Jim?"

"We might *not* move back."

"Oh? Why's that?" If the proposed expansion of the dump went through, the Gurriers would receive some compensation—on which Joe had assured them he'd make no claim—and they could be back in the inner city where they wanted to be and the action was.

But before Jim could explain, Nan came out of the black house with drinks garnished with mint, which grew on the outer banks of the dump and had also, in the Gurriers' Holy Family period, cropped up in one of Joe's sermons—which Nan, it seemed, remembered. "Praised be God for green things," she said, improving on Joe and Gerard Manley Hopkins. "Jim tell you about this reporter, Father?"

"No."

"Didn't get around to it," Jim explained. "Talkin' about my inventory."

"Reporter from the local paper, Father." Nan was obviously pleased to be the one to tell him the good news. "He's doing a story about us maybe losing this place. He was real uptight about it."

"Family man himself," Jim explained.

Joe, wondering how he could tell them the bad news, decided not to, and used the sprig of mint in his drink to stir the ice cubes in it, then tried it—yes, the red table wine. "Where're the kids, Nan?"

"At Badger, Father. Registered nurse in the playroom."

Jim explained, "It's not free. You have to show a sales slip."

Nan said, "But I don't like to park *our* kids there too long, Father."

Joe nodded, gravely, in tribute to motherhood, and wanted to depart on that note, but couldn't, not yet. "Look. If I were you people I wouldn't count too much on a story in the local paper."

"Oh, we don't," Nan said. "Not on *that*."

"The wire services'll pick it up," Jim explained.

"And TV," Nan said.

Joe sniffed. "This reporter tell you that?"

"No, but that's how it works," Jim explained.

"You see it all the time," Nan said.

Joe sniffed. "Look. I thought you people *wanted* to leave."

"We did, but now we don't," Jim explained.

"And why's that—Nan?" (Joe preferred, but only slightly, talking to her.)

"Father, until this reporter interviewed us and the kids, and took pictures, I guess we just didn't know how we really feel about this place."

"And how's that, Nan?"

"Father, it's our *home*."

"I see. That how you feel too, Jim?"

"Plus I have to think of my inventory."

"I see."

*   *   *

That night when Joe returned to the rectory (having been summoned to the city by the little hospital nun who watched over Father Day) Bill and Father Felix were drinking beer in the study with Greg, a muscular, long-haired type in a (to look on the bright side) *plain* white T-shirt, but in overalls and sneakers, these with fuzzy worn places around the toes and laces dangling, picking up germs.

"Asked Greg to wait," Bill said, "but didn't think you'd be so long."

"Took longer than I thought." Joe hadn't said where he was going, only "Some calls to make," which, though, had turned out to be the truth by the time he'd tracked his old confessor back to the hospital and found him snoring in his bed. "Sorry, Greg."

"No harm done," Father Felix said. "Gave us a chance to rap."

Joe, thinking the word would soon be obsolete but not soon enough, seated himself in his Barcalounger—it was warm. Bill? Father Felix? Bill.

"Greg was telling us about his draft problem," Bill said to Joe.

"Care to tell *me* about it, Greg?"

"You already know. Barb told you."

Barb, huh? "Your mother didn't tell me much. I didn't ask her to. Thought I'd wait and ask you."

"Against war, is all. Lotta shit."

"Now, now," said Father Felix. "We're all against war, if it comes to that, Greg."

"*If?* You mean *until.*"

True, Joe thought.

"It hasn't come to that yet," Father Felix said. "This war is still undeclared, Greg."

"For you, not for me."

True, Joe thought.

Bill said, "Greg told us he was a language major before he dropped out of college, Joe."

"So?"

"So we were wondering if he could maybe go on with his education in the service—maybe learn Russian."

"Or even Chinese," said Father Felix.

Joe, sorry but not surprised to see Greg close his eyes and shake his head in dismay as seen on TV, said, "Not his immediate problem, is it—going on with his education?"

"Maybe not," Bill said, "but I understand only one in ten sees action."

Greg opened his eyes. "I don't intend to be one of the ten, *or* the nine. And I don't intend to throw myself on the mercies of *my* local draft board as a c.o."

"You'd be wise not to do that," Father Felix said. "Greg, if it's such a matter of conscience with you and worst comes to worst shoot at their legs. That's what I'd do."

"I can't tell—is he kiddin'?" Greg said to Joe.

"Afraid not." Joe got up to go to the bathroom, saying, "I've heard that one before, though not recently. In the seminary. It's a crazy world."

"That may be," Father Felix said, his voice following Joe into the bathroom, "but there's more than one way to be against war *and*—what's more to the point—to work for peace."

"Shoot over their heads?" said Greg.

Joe, listening to their conversation while he made himself a drink in the bathroom, appeared among them again, still listening.

"Greg, have you thought—*enough*, I mean—of your folks?" said Bill.

"And your brother in Nam?" said Father Felix.

"Don't forget the fuckin' neighbors," said Greg.

Joe—he'd heard enough—spoke then.

WITH SOME AUTHORITY

Since he was (and the fathers, here, weren't) Greg's pastor, and since he had given some thought to the subject of war, more than most people and certainly more than most clergy ["Humph!" said Father Felix], including St Thomas Aquinas and the late Cardinal Spellman ["Dear me!" said Father Felix], he (Joe) spoke with some authority and wished, if possible, to be heard ["Humph!" said Father Felix].

HOPING FOR BEST

The fathers, here, wanted Greg to go on with his education and to enjoy the benefits he'd have coming to him, not least the respect and gratitude of the nation—"It says here"—and of the copulating neighbors ["Joe, this is a serious business," said Father Felix, and Bill nodded]. The fathers, here, also wanted Greg to realize that if he followed another course he'd be giving himself, and those near and dear to him, a lot of grief. He'd be in jail, or on the run, marked for life. So Greg should be in no doubt that the fathers, here, meant well by him and hoped for the best.

INVIDIOUS COMPARISON

But then the fathers, *there,* in Italy and Germany, during the Second World War and before—Abyssinia and Spain—had also meant well by their people and hoped for the best.

"An invidious comparison!" cried Father Felix. "The Italian and German clergy were placed in a very unfortunate position in the Second World War."

"As they were in the First World War," Joe said, "enemies then, marching to different drummers, actually the same one, not hating each other, though, only hating each other's *ideas*. Used to hear that one a lot during the last war—last but two, I mean."

"I didn't," said Father Felix.

"Never heard it?" said Joe.

"Rarely," said Father Felix. "In any case, Joe, judge not, lest ye . . ."

"Gotcha. Dresden, Hiroshima, Nagasaki."

PASSING THE BUCK

For the faithful to have followed another course in Germany would have meant, as it did mean for a few, the axe— literally. Heroic virtue had been called for, and this for most people, paralyzed or galvanized by nationalism, the bad wine of the country, was unthinkable—literally. ["Don't blame the clergy," said Father Felix.] The German clergy, knowing what people are like in wartime and not being so different themselves—as we aren't—had once again passed the buck, which was passed on to their dear brothers in Christ in, for a start, Czechoslovakia, then Poland, then France. *Dulce et decorum est pro patria mori!* How sweet and meet it is to die for my country! And to take a few with me, with ecclesiastical approbation. That the faithful—faithful to what?—expect no more from themselves and the Church, this is the world's worst and longest-running scandal. ["Don't blame the Church," said Father Felix.]

JESUS WEPT

Those words were said to be the saddest ever written, but that was before the conditions for a just war were written. Namely, that there be grave and just cause for war, that it be declared and conducted according to law, that it not be protracted, that the peace be just, and so on. These conditions, written in the days of "the Christian Prince" (who'd reigned only in the minds of theologians), hadn't been met then, and today, more than ever before, were unmeetable, and yet were still serving as an out. ["Don't blame the theologians," said Father Felix.]

PRIMACY OF CONSCIENCE

The just-war theologians would have a lot to answer for in the next world. In holding that conscripts could usually presume that their country was right, and if in doubt could prudently acquiesce because the civil and ecclesiastical authorities were probably right, and if wrong could not be blamed if acting in conscience, St Thomas and others had dated badly. But what they had said about the primacy of conscience ["An *informed* conscience," said Father Felix, and Bill nodded], informed or not, if sincere, was still true. The authorities today could no more vouch for the consciences of others than the Christian Prince could in the Thirteenth, the Greatest—or Hitler or Mussolini could in the Twentieth, the Crappiest—of Centuries. Or FDR. Or JFK. Or LBJ. "Think of *him* closeted with his advisers, agonizing over meeting the conditions for a just war." The Church's problem, however (though you'd never know it), is not the odd conscientious objector, or even the unconscientious objector to war but the mass of conscientious, not so conscientious, and unconscientious acceptors of war— and herself. The Church, in playing footsie with the powers that be, from Constantine to LBJ, had been remiss.

"*Remiss?*" said Greg. "You mean *chicken.*"

"O.K.," Joe said. "I'll buy that."

"No, no," said Father Felix.

"Joe," said Bill.

DISHONEST DIOGENES

He (Joe) and a couple of others at the seminary had decided to refuse deferment as divinity students, to register as conscientious objectors, but the Rector had got wind of this and had registered them himself. When they received their deferments and might have objected, they had said the hell with it. They had let it ride. "I still think about it. So whenever I run across somebody like Greg, which isn't often, I feel like Diogenes—a dishonest one."

"The Rector did the right thing," Father Felix said. "You must've thought so too."

"That so?" said Joe.

"If not, why'd you let it ride?"

"For the same reason I still think about it. I was remiss— chicken, I mean." Joe turned to Greg. "As your pastor, I had to tell you what I have. In a way, I wish you'd say the hell with it and report for induction—I don't want to be blamed for what may happen to you if you don't. (You could, yes, maybe go on with your education, become an officer, have your uniforms custom-made and your hair cut.) But I have to follow my conscience, informed or not, and you do. *That*, despite all the evidence to the contrary, is the mind of the Church."

Father Felix said, "I don't say you're wrong about that, Joe, in principle, but I do say you may have given Greg the wrong impression. Commentators have often remarked on Our Lord's kindness to the military. If he disapproved of their calling, why didn't he say so, admonish them? Remember, in the Garden of Gethsemane, how he admonished Peter for cutting off the ear of the high priest's servant? 'Don't you know I could call on my Father in heaven and he would send me more than twelve legions of angels?' Strange words indeed from one supposedly opposed to anything military?"

Joe, looking cross-eyed, got up. "Beer, anyone?"

"No, thanks," Bill said. "It's late."

"No, thanks," Father Felix said. "Have to hit the sack."

"Beer, Greg?"

"No, thanks. I'll have what you're having. No, just kiddin', I'm leaving."

Father Felix and Bill said good night to Greg—"You mean *good-bye*"—and Joe walked him to the front door where they shook hands and Joe would have liked to give him his blessing.

"Poor Barb," Greg said. "She had you all wrong."

"Don't blame your mother for that, Greg. Before you go, do me a favor, will you?"

"Sure. What?"

"Tie your shoes."

Greg looked at Joe. "Why?"

"Just as a favor to me," Joe said.

Greg dropped down to tie his shoes, and while he was down Joe secretly blessed him.

The next day, Sunday, between Masses, Joe got a phone call from Barb.

"I just called to thank you, Father. You did your best."

"Greg say that?"

"Yes."

"I see."

"He's gone, Father, but Brad doesn't know yet. So if you should see him . . ."

"I won't say anything, Barb."

"Thanks, Father."

24

An

Inspector

Calls

"*Signal* when you throw that thing," Joe said, having fumbled what was practically a wild pitch, snatched up the ball, shook it at Bill to settle him down, and whipped it back. *Plunk.*

The temperature was in the high eighties, but they'd had ice cream for dessert and were working it off, Joe in the shade of the rectory, Bill in the shade of the garage, the sun between them—a problem too in old outdoor ball parks, Joe thought, the sinking sun, the creeping shade.

Bill signaled with a flick of his gloved hand and threw another fast curve, a slider. *Pop.*

"That's better." *Plunk.*

"Somebody asked me if we were taking donations to Arf." *Pop.*

"Who?" *Plunk.*

"Mr Lane." *Pop.*

Plunk.

"I said I'd let him know." *Pop.*

"You know the answer to that." *Plunk.*

"I guess I was thinking of our assessment." *Pop.*

"Bill, if somebody wants to donate to Arf, O.K., but not through the parish. It would reflect on others." *Plunk.*

"Joe, what if others *wanted* to?" *Pop.*

"No good, Bill. Not through the parish. It'd make *others* look bad. They're protected against that." *Plunk.*

"Yeah." *Pop.*

"People slip you a donation, Bill, or try to, for something like Arf and think they're not only building themselves up with you, which may be so, but performing an act of true charity, an almsdeed—not so. Or when they contribute to the support of the Church, when all they're doing is paying for goods and services." *Plunk.*

"See what you mean, Joe. An almsdeed should be in secret. 'And thy Father, who sees in secret, will reward thee.' " *Pop.*

"Right. Otherwise, apart from the material good it might do, it's money wasted." *Plunk.*

"Wow, Joe." *Pop.*

"Hardball, Bill. Scripture's rough and tough and hard to stay with. People can't have it both ways, and we—the clergy—can't, though God knows we try." *Plunk.*

"Be a lot more charity—true charity, Joe—if everybody looked at it like that." *Pop.*

"And a lot less strong-arm stuff like Arf." *Plunk.*

Pop.

Plunk.

"Man I ran into last night, Joe, said he talked to you about registering, but didn't get around to it. Name's Gumball." *Pop.*

"Oh, yes. Phoned. Never came in." *Plunk.*

"Said to tell you he's sorry about that, Joe." *Pop.*

"So when's he coming in?" *Plunk.*

"Joe, I told him he wouldn't have to, in the circumstances ["*What* circumstances?"], since I'd seen him and all his free time goes on the house. Hers too. They're redoing the place from scratch. But he said he'd put a check in the mail." *Pop.*

"Great." *Plunk.*

"How d'ya mean, Joe?" *Pop.*

"I tell man he, or his wife, has to come in to register, and you tell him forget it." *Plunk.*

"I thought, in the circumstances . . ." *Pop.*

Plunk.

Pop.

"You want to be the good shamus, Bill." *Plunk.*

Pop.

"And you want me to be the bad one." *Plunk.*

Pop.

"No way to run a parish, Bill." *Plunk.*

Pop.

Plunk.

Pop.

"O.K., Bill. Man won't have to come in." *Plunk.*

Pop.

"But only because I don't want you to look bad—and the Church." *Plunk.*

Pop.

Plunk.

Pop.

Plunk.

"*Ow!*"

On seeing the new patient at his front door—this was, in fact, their first meeting—Dr Wylie had said, "Oh, shit," but had turned off the TV within and rushed the patient over to the clinic next door, turned on the TV there, and ministered to him silently during the rest of "Gunsmoke."

Now that the air had cleared, physician could consult with patient. "Mind telling me how it happened?"

Joe did mind, some. "Playing catch in the yard. Hard ball."

"No shit? In that getup? You don't look it."

Joe, immaculate in black and white, found this line of questioning hard to take from a professional man of his generation (and, incidentally, short stature) who wore cowboy boots, overalls, no shirt, and a lavaliere. "Had a bath and changed before I came here." And also had a drink—should've had two.

"Hard to dress yourself, wasn't it, with one hand?"

"Yes." And to make a drink.

Dr Wylie blew smoke in Joe's face, saying, "Well, that's what you get for playing catch in weather like this."

"Just trying to keep in shape."

"*Keep?* You sure as hell don't look like you're in shape to me."

"Let's just say I'm trying to keep my weight down."

"*Keep?* Down to *what*? You're twenty pounds overweight."

"Let's just say I don't want to be thirty."

"Sure as hell will be if all you're doing about it is playing catch with kids. Had a physical lately?"

"No."

"Who's your regular quack?"

"Don't have one—haven't since I was a kid."

"About time you had one then. But don't think I'm looking for business. Mind if I ask how old you are?"

For some reason, Joe did mind. "Forty-four."

"Yeah? Guess how old *I* am."

"Why?"

"Go ahead, guess. I won't bill you for it."

"Thanks. You're about my age, maybe younger."

"Like hell I am. I'm *fifty*-four." Dr Wylie stubbed out his cigarette. "How do I do it, huh?"

"You're on some new special diet?"

"Diet, shit. I eat like a horse, drink like a fish." Dr Wylie lit a cigarette. "Try again."

"You smoke a lot?"

Dr Wylie, as if he'd underestimated Joe, looked at him with qualified respect. "Smoking can be a factor in weight control, and to that extent it's a plus, but there are minuses too. The Surgeon General has determined that smoking is dangerous to your health."

Joe nodded.

"But smoking, or nonsmoking, could never account for this." Dr Wylie, seen now in profile, hands hooked and pulling against each other, biceps and pectorals tumescent, lacking only grease, posed like the late Charles Atlas.

Joe nodded.

Dr Wylie relaxed then, only to expose a muscular calf and flex it.

Joe nodded.

Dr Wylie slapped his belly, which was tight as a drum, and glanced at Joe's, which was embarrassing.

But Joe nodded.

"How do I do it, huh?"

"You pump iron?"

"Iron, shit."

Joe nodded.

Dr Wylie laughed. "O.K., I'll tell you. Last thing I do at night—drunk or sober—is go for a little ride."

In case this meant what Joe thought it might and he was about to be tempted to have sex on medical grounds— celibacy was still the Church's trump and why the heathen rage—Joe waited for clarification and did not nod.

"Sleep like a log."

Joe did not nod.

"Wake up bright-eyed and bushy-tailed."

Joe did not nod.

"See that horse in the lobby?"

Joe looked in the direction indicated, trying to see through the cinder block wall, but couldn't. "Horse?"

"Mechanical horse—for kids. Have 'em in supermarkets."

"Oh, yes."

"Have one in my bedroom. Muscle model. Runs on two-twenty current. Knock the shit out of you. What you need."

"That so?"

"If you can pass a physical, which I doubt."

"That so?" Joe—he'd had enough of this—rose to go, but noticed his thumb, numb in its pink plastic sheath thing, and wondered what the prognosis was for it. "Won't be deformed, will it? *Gnarled?*"

"Shit, no," said Dr Wylie.

Joe, dying for a drink when he got back to the rectory, had to deny himself, for Bill was in the study with a big, heavy, white-haired, red-faced type in a summerweight business suit with flared trousers.

"Mr McMaster," Bill said. "Mayer, Mayer, Maher, Chicago."

Mr McMaster, having heaved himself up from the couch with his right hand out, put it away. "Hurt your hand, Father?"

"Thumb."

"Car door?"

"No."

"Sorry," Bill murmured to Joe, nodded to Mr McMaster, and left them alone.

Mr McMaster was sitting down again, but Joe—significantly, he thought—remained standing.

"Nice place you've got here, Father."

"Thanks. Nothing special about it except the office area— in the basement but surprisingly bright and airy."

"So I've been told, Father."

Joe, hoping to hear more, sat down in his Barcalounger.

"Understand you built the rectory, Father."

"Also the school and convent."

"*That* I didn't know." Mr McMaster, in dismay, his big fat head cocked back, his pop eyes popping, then winked one of them. "And all paid for, Father?"

"*No.*"

Mr McMaster smiled, nodding, as if he could never be so blunt and honest but would certainly like to be. "Father, wherever your name comes up—for example, at the Chancery—I've heard nothing but good."

"That so?"

"Indeed. Oh, indeed."

Joe—he'd had enough of this—said: "What can I do for you, sir?"

Mr McMaster, in dismay again, said: "Father, you took the words right out of my mouth!"

"That so?"

"Indeed. It's part of my job, or I wouldn't dare ask, but how's the program going here?"

"If you're talking about Arf, Mr McMaster, there's *no* program here."

Mr McMaster was obviously in pain. "Why's *that*, Father?"

"Thought you knew." And still thought so. "My assistant didn't tell you?"

"I wasn't here very long, Father, before you came."

So Joe, though doubting it was necessary, explained his fiscal system to Mr McMaster. "You must've run across something of the sort in your travels."

"Yes and no, Father. Exceptions are often made when it comes to a big-ticket item like this. Pastors, God love 'em, aren't so rigid then."

"Sell out, you mean."

"Father"—Mr McMaster shaking his big fat head—"I couldn't—and *wouldn't*—say that about any of the many fine men like yourself it's been my good fortune to meet."

Joe sniffed. "I try to budget for everything that comes along. There'll be no thermometer on *my* church lawn."

"*That's* optional!"

"Not here."

"Father, how can you budget for *this*?" In his professional capacity, Mr McMaster would know Joe's assessment.

Joe had weakened at the thought of it. "Fortunately, it's spread over three years."

"Three *years*! You could wrap it up in three *weeks*!"

"Sorry. I'll do it the hard way."

"Too bad." Mr McMaster was staring at Joe's thumb. "Keeps you from saying Mass?"

"Afraid so." Not many laymen would have thought of that, it occurred to Joe. "Look, Mr McMaster."

"Just call me Mac, Father. All my other friends do."

"Uh-huh. Look, Mac, we can't do business, but I can make you a drink." To say nothing of myself.

"Thanks. Bourbon, if you've got it, and water."

While Joe was occupied in the bathroom, with the door open, Mac spoke to him of a certain Monsignor Pat ("in another diocese, Father, so I'm not talking out of school") who, being shafted with a ball-breaking assessment and being a poor administrator for a pastor in the modern world of today, had spurned outside help (Mac?) and had then suffered a massive stroke—which, however, had become the balls of the program in his parish. "Over the top, Father."

Joe, who'd had his hands—hand—full making drinks, brought them out of the bathroom on a tray. "How about Monsignor Pat? He make a miraculous recovery?"

"No, I'm sorry to say." Mac bowed his big fat head in grief, but snapped out of it, scooted forward on the couch, the toes of his tasseled loafers pointing at Joe. "Father, in my humble but expert opinion—and they don't call me the Grand Old Man of Fund-Raising for nothing—an exception could and should be made here. This is a hardship case. Sometimes, Father, it's the *little* things that count." Mac was staring at Joe's thumb.

Joe poked it at him. "What if I told you I got this little thing playing catch? Hard ball."

Mac merely nodded. "So what? It's not the same, no, as a massive stroke. But, Father, the fact is—You. Can't. Say. Mass. Can *you* think of anything worse for a priest? *I* can't. Everybody in the parish with kids, or without 'em—everybody who was *ever* a kid—would get behind you and the program. It'd fly, Father, believe me. Over the top!"

"Sorry, Mac."

"Father, could I say something—with your kind permission?"

Joe kindly gave it with a nod.

"Father, go ahead, go it alone—it's no skin off my ass. But whatever you do, Father—go it alone, or go with the program—I want you to know my hat's off to you." Turning over his grey enameled straw hat, which was cooling upside down on the end table by the couch, Mac raised it to Joe and let it drop right side up on the table as though resting his case. "Father, if it's not asking too much, I'd like to see the office area before I leave."

"Why wait?"

So, carrying their drinks, they went down to the office area, with which Mac was anything but unimpressed (unlike some of the clergy), as he was ("Indeed! Oh, indeed!") with

Joe's office/offices lecture, after which, saying it had made him think, he appeared to be depressed.

"Father, I'm worried about the Church these days. So many changes, and not all of 'em, I'd say, for the best."

"Hardly any, I'd say."

"No, but *I* shouldn't say it."

"Why not? Who cares?"

"Father, I'm a convert."

"Hard to believe." (Mac, smiling, appeared to take this as a compliment.) "Convert from what?"

"Nothing much."

Joe nodded. "In that case, you should feel right at home these days."

Mac grinned. "Not many left like you, Father."

"Oh, I don't know, Mac."

"*I* do, Father—going from diocese to diocese, the things I hear and see."

"We just have to hang in there, Mac." The phone rang. "St Francis."

"Father, I know it's late and I don't want to say who I am, but my husband and I, we're not regular contributors, and now we wonder if we should be. The other one was here a while ago and said if people give to the church and anybody knows about it, except God, it's not true charity. That's what he said, Father." (A man, presumably her husband, came on the line: "If you ask me, the other one's full of shit.") "We thought you should know this, Father."

"I'll make a note of it. Anything else, ma'am?"

"No, Father."

"Thanks for calling. G'night."

Unfortunately, before Mac could leave he had to return to the study for his hat, with which he then—having to rest for a moment to catch his breath from climbing the stairs—sat fanning his face. "For some reason, Father, I keep thinking of my friend Lou."

"Lou?"

"Cooney."

"*Cooney?* Oh, you mean *Father* Cooney." Joe had expected this to have (on a layman and a convert of Mac's vintage) more of an effect than it did.

"That's right. Lou, if you don't know, Father, had your system, but he couldn't sleep nights. A bad case of the shakes—*moneywise*, Father. The same with Lad—Ladislaw, Lou's assistant. Poor guys, Lou and Lad. Out every night beating the bushes for bucks, trying to make their assessment." (Mac shook his big fat head.) "It's not a ballbreaker like some—like yours, for instance, Father—but it's still a nice piece of change. Naturally, I wanted to help, but Lou can be a very stubborn individual, Father. I left my card. 'Call me if you change your mind, or even if you don't—we can always have a drink.' A couple of days later Lou did call me—in the middle of the night. I got dressed and went to see him. Something I'd said made him rethink his situation, he said, namely that it wasn't hopeless, that he could wrap it up in a matter of weeks without really going against his system— against the letter, maybe, but not the spirit. *That's* what counts, as I understand it."

"Uh-huh."

"So Lou's all fixed up now. He's got a twelve-man pledge team—three of 'em women, a nice mix—who, for the purposes of the program, take the names of the twelve apostles and wear badges to that effect, which they get to keep. One of my ideas."

"Who's Lou—Judas?"

Mac answered the question substantially. "Lou and Lad

don't go out, Father—just the 'apostles,' all parishioners in good standing."

"I see. And how're the *others*—the other parishioners in good standing—taking it?"

Mac answered the question with a nod and asked Bill, who'd come into the study, "How'd it go, son?"

Son, thought Joe, how'd *what* go?

From the bathroom, where he was making himself a drink, Bill said, "Not good."

Mac shook his big fat head.

So, thought Joe, he knows.

Mac then heaved himself up from the couch and had the nerve to leave his card on the end table. "Sorry about your hand, Father, but it could be a plus, if you know what I mean. Call me if you change your mind, or even if you don't—we can always have a drink, Joe."

Joe, thought Joe.

Joe saw the man out, returned to the study, poured himself a much needed drink, settled himself in his Barcalounger, and after a moment of silence, another, another, spoke to Bill. "O.K. Let's have it."

"Only made three calls," Bill said, looking up from *Sports Illustrated.* "Went 0 for 3."

"Not talking about that. Why'd you let that man, of all people, know how we spend our evenings?" Now the interested, the oh so interested clergy ("How'll you handle this one, Joe?") would also know. *Poor guys, Joe and Bill. Out every night beating the bushes for bucks, trying to make their assessment.* Ugh. And all—like Joe's thumb—Bill's fault.

"I just told him the truth, Joe. You *ashamed* of it?"

"As a matter of fact, I am. You think I want the Chancery, Catfish Toohey, Judas Cooney, and everybody to know we're out every night beating the bushes for bucks?"

"But we *are*, Joe—most nights. I'm not ashamed of it."

Joe sniffed. "It's not the same for you, Bill."

"No?" As if Joe didn't appreciate him, what he went through most nights.

"All I mean is I'm the pastor here, you're not. The joke's on me, not you."

Bill looked as though he'd like to, but couldn't, argue with that. "I'm sorry, Joe, if that's the way you see it."

Joe sniffed. "Is there another way?"

"Look, Joe. You made a promise to your parishioners—no special collections, no matter what—and you're keeping it. The clergy respect you for this—maybe they don't want to, but they do. Even that man respects you, Joe. His hat's off to you, he told me."

"His hat's off to everybody."

"O.K., Joe, for what it's worth, *I* respect you. And so do *you*, Joe. So who cares who the joke's on?"

Joe was silent, thinking that respect for him might not be as widespread as Bill said, might not, in fact, go beyond the two of them, but that it was certainly good of Bill to say it did, that Bill hadn't known what he was doing when he gave them away to Mac, that Bill might have done so even if he had known, that discretion, not loyalty, was what Bill lacked, that Joe, not Bill, would pay for this, would be, to the clergy, for all their respect for him, if any, a figure of fun, and that there would be justice in this, justice exacted by the very ones he'd tried to deceive ("I try to budget for everything that comes along"), retributive justice . . .

"Am I right, Joe?"

"I guess so."

"So there you are." Bill finished his drink and stood up. "G'night, Joe. Oh, how's the hand?"

"Thumb. Numb." But starting to feel, to hurt.

"My fault, Joe, but I'll say your Mass until such time as you can."

"Thanks."

"G'night, Joe."

"G'night, Bill."

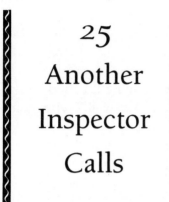

25
Another
Inspector
Calls

Joe reached for the phone, switched hands, and got it with his good one. "St Francis."

"Barb, Father. The FBI was here."

"That so?"

"Nice young man, southerner, very polite and friendly—his name's Tom—but I thought I'd better warn you, Father."

"You're a little late." Joe assumed she'd had a cordial or two first.

"I'm sorry, Father."

"O.K. I'll talk to you later. Somebody here now." Joe hung up and nodded to Tom. "You were saying?"

"Shame we can't get in touch with Greg, sir."

" 'In touch,' huh? So you can lock him up?"

"Not necessarily, sir. Fine family and all—Brad I haven't met, but Barb I have, and with Scott already serving it's possible the court would be lenient with Greg, sir, providing he reports for induction."

"Why would he do that? That's why he's on the run."

"He could change his mind, sir. Hopefully, he already has."

"That I doubt. It's a matter of conscience with him."

"Sir, can you tell me why he didn't register as an objector?"

"I can. I asked him. When he registered for the draft, he said, he didn't know what he was doing, and later, when he did, he didn't want to upset his folks. His father's mental about the war."

"Sir, how do you mean that?"

"He's very enthusiastic about it."

"A lot of people are, sir."

"A lot aren't. I'm not. Greg was hoping it would just go away. A lot of people were. General Maxwell Taylor, some years ago, gave it six months."

Tom changed the subject. "Barb says you did your best with Greg, sir."

"That's what Greg told her."

"You didn't do your best, sir?"

"I did. But that wasn't what his mother thinks it was."

"May I ask, sir, what it was?"

"You may. I don't have to tell you, but I will. I advised Greg to follow his conscience, not that he was inclined to do otherwise. I'd tell you—or anybody who came to me for advice—the same thing."

Tom smiled. "Fortunately for me, sir, I've come to you for information, not advice."

"You've had it, anyway."

Tom shrugged. "No idea, then, how we can get in touch with Greg, sir?"

"No, I can't help you there."

"Would you, sir, if you could? That's just a hypothetical question."

"Not if it meant Greg would be put away—as it would. That's just a hypothetical answer."

Tom smiled. He stood up and went for his briefcase, which was on the desk. "That'll be all, sir."

"Not quite."

Tom left the briefcase on the desk and sat down. "At your service, sir."

"Is my phone tapped?"

"Not that I know, sir."

"Would you know if it is?"

Tom shrugged. "I'll be frank with you, sir. I might, but I don't."

"O.K. I'll be frank with you too. If my phone's tapped and I can prove it, I'll sue your ass off." But how? "How about the mail?"

Tom shrugged.

"Likewise," Joe said.

"Likewise, sir?"

"I'll sue your ass off." *How?*

"Look, sir, you may not believe it, but this is a national emergency." As if this, much as Tom wished he could go on being very polite and friendly, might bring Joe to his senses.

Joe sniffed. "You really believe that? Or's that what you have to say?"

"I really believe that, sir."

"Shame you're *here* then."

"If called, sir, I'll go."

"Great. Not much chance of that, though, is there?"

"I wouldn't know, sir." Tom stood up. "If that's all, sir." Joe, switching hands, beat him to the briefcase. "What I said about the phone and the mail goes for this thing too, if it's wired." With his good hand Joe then shoved the briefcase across the desk to Tom.

"Thank you, sir. Have a good day, sir."

"I'll think about it. That's the best I can do."

The next morning, throwing out the mail, Joe came upon a postcard from Canada: "Tell mom and dad I'm all right—not to worry. Have good job. Eating balanced diet for them, tying shoes for you. G."

"Oh, it's you." Barb seemed unhappy to see him—had Tom been in touch with her?—but she unlocked and opened the screen door. "Oh, your poor *hand*!"

"Thumb."

Barb seemed to think he'd come to tell her about it, and so he did, briefly. "Oh, you poor *man*!" Barefooted and in shorts—not bad but with a slight skiing movement of her left leg—she led him down into the sunken living room where they sat across from each other in leopardskin-look chairs. "Brad's not here, Father."

"Didn't think he would be." It was only a little after three. "Should he be?"

Barb made a face—no, dear God, she was *crying*. "Father, they let Brad go yesterday, but he went back this morning to clean out his desk, and that's the last I saw of him. When I called the paper around noon—'*He's no longer with us.*' Oh, *Father*! What if it's *true*!" Barb broke down then, wailing.

Joe had to raise his voice to be heard. "Why *wouldn't* it be true?"

"Father, what if he's no longer with *us*?" Barb broke down again.

Joe had to yell to be heard. "Shut up! He stopped for a drink. He ran into friends. He'll be here any minute. You'll see him all too soon."

"Father, I've been so *worried* about Brad."

"I know. You told me the other day. Trouble at the paper."

"But *then* I didn't know *why*."

"Brad's too controversial, you said."

"No, it's all *my* fault, Father. Brad told me last night—

they've had it in for him ever since my accident at Badger."

Joe, though he didn't doubt this (and had been shocked the other day, and was perhaps not the only one—parking lots have eyes—to see Barb, of all people, at Badger), said, "That I doubt, Barb. Brad's just too controversial. It's as simple as that."

But Barb knew better, it seemed, knew he was trying to absolve her, and broke down again.

This time Joe didn't interrupt her, waited in silence.

"Father, how can people be so shitty?"

"It's how they're—we're—made."

Barb broke down again, and Joe waited.

"Father, did you ever think life would be like this?"

"Not exactly, no."

Barb suddenly got up and padded over to the picture window.

"What'd I tell you?" Joe said, and thought, watching Barb return to her chair looking cross, That's humanity for you.

Brad came into the living room, tossed a couple of magazines on the sectional sofa, and then, only then, noticed that he wasn't alone. "Hey, look who's here! I mean *me*. Ho, ho, ho."

"Brad, you said you *wouldn't*."

"And *didn't*, Buttercup. But now I will. What can I bring you, Padre? Hey, what's with the hand?"

"Thumb." Joe told him about it, briefly.

"Well, well. Let's hope you don't lose it. In the meantime, what can I bring you?"

"Just a beer, if you've got one, *and* a glass."

"I shall return," Brad said, which he did with drinks on a tray—a shot glass and a bottle of Kahlua for Barb, to whom he said, "Ho, ho, ho."

"*Brad.*"

Having thoughtfully served others before himself, Brad sat down on the sectional sofa and raised his highball to them, saying, "To me."

"I'm sorry, Father."

"Barb, I think Brad's trying to tell you something."

"Clever people, these Romans," said Brad. "O.K. I'll begin at the beginning." He said he'd cleaned out his desk and kissed the other cheap help good-bye and was about to leave the office for the last time when the phone rang. Could he have lunch that day with the personnel manager of a large local concern in its canteen? He could. [Barb: "What concern?"] "Wait." So there he was with the p.m., not a bad-looking woman, another with a game leg, when who should join them in their booth but the c.e.o. himself. [Barb: "C.e.o. of what?"] "Wait." The p.m. finished her tea and green salad and excused herself—significantly, Brad thought, but after she left, the conversation continued as before, on very general lines. As it did when the c.e.o. showed Brad around the various departments—in automotives, they sat talking in the backseat of a car that was in for a lube job, even when it went up on a lift—"I kid you not"—and in home furnishings they lay talking on water beds, first on twins, then on a double. They were getting to know each other and, at least in Brad's case, getting to like each other. But the conversation was still on very general lines and going, as far as Brad could tell, nowhere. In the end, though, they had holed up in the c.e.o.'s office. "And well, the upshot is I've accepted the editorship of the Great Badger's *Shopping News*."

"Oh," Barb whispered, *"no."*

"Wait. At more—quite a bit more—than I made at the paper."

"No, Brad."

"Wait. I'll have my column under *my* name, and it won't be *cut*. My readership will go up—*way* up."

"Readership! Nobody *reads* that thing."

"Nobody *does*, Buttercup, but everybody *will*."

"Because of your column? Oh, *Brad*."

"No, Buttercup. *Not* because of my column. *Not* that it won't help."

"What else?" Joe asked.

"Wait." Brad got up and went off with his glass, saying, "I shall return."

"Oh," Barb whispered, *"God."*

"Wait," Joe replied. He felt that more than met the eye, more than Badger's policy of employing the elderly and handicapped—proselytism at the Mall's expense might figure in Brad's case (as in Mr Barnes').

"I'll tell you what else," Brad said when he returned. "Plenty." The *Shopping News* would be renamed and restructured, would become the *New Shopper* and a tabloid. It would still run Badger's ads, of course, but ads as well from other local concerns and (these at cost) from the general public—classifieds, wedding announcements, obits, eck cetera, eck cetera. "Wait." [Barb was making noises.] Why would other local concerns and the general public advertise in the *NS*? Circulation. Yes, the old *SN* had had *that*. Circulation, yes; readership, no. The *NS* would have *both*. It would have circulation because, like the old *SN*, it would be a throwaway, and it would have readership because, unlike the old *SN*, it would have readability, would be unthrowawayable. The *NS* would not be like the lousy *Universe*, full of crap about the school board and widening the highway. The *NS* would give people what people want, in easy-to-take capsule form, from the world of politics, sports, crime, space, women, TV, dieting. Furthermore, the *NS*, unlike the old *SN* and the lousy

Universe, would be controversial. "Controversial but fair," to quote Dave (the c.e.o., Mr Brock). "He reads *these*"—Brad held up the *Nation* and the *New Republic*. "He reads *books*."

"Hmmm," Joe said.

Barb was silent, perhaps coming around.

"Now hear this," Brad said. "Dave wants me to go to Nam for the *NS*. 'See what's going on over there, Brad, and while you're at it see your boy.' Earlier, I'd told him about Scott."

Barb clutched her head. "I hate to say this, Brad, but what about . . ."

Brad shuddered. "Hardest thing I ever had to do, Buttercup, but I thought I'd better and I did. I told Dave about Greg. And you know what? He was *very* understanding. How about *that*?"

Joe nodded in approval—what he'd dropped in to tell Barb could now be told to Brad, thanks to Dave, or could it?

Barb poured herself a shot of Kahlua.

Brad tossed back what was left of his drink. "You know what else Dave said? 'Find out how high up she is and how big around, and we'll do better.' He was talking about the *weather ball*."

"*Oh* oh," Barb said.

"Oh," Joe said.

Brad got up, saying, "I shall return."

"Wait," Joe said. "I've had word from Greg—just a card." Standing up, switching hands, Joe got the card out of his coat pocket but held onto it, keeping the view of Montreal toward him, his fingers clamped down over the stamp and postmark, while Barb and Brad read the message and had the reference to shoes explained to them.

"Yeah, yeah," Brad said, going for the card. "Where the hell *is* he?"

Joe, shaking his head and moving away, put the card in his pocket.

"I don't get it," Brad said, looking from Joe to Barb.

"Brad, he's afraid if he tells us where Greg is we'll tell Tom."

"Yeah? You know what? I think we *should*. Come on, Padre. Give."

Joe, not caring for this at all, sniffed. "I don't know how you—or Tom—can get in touch with Greg. I don't have his address. If I did, I wouldn't tell you. This is how Greg wants it, and my responsibility is to him. He asked me to tell you he's all right. I've done more than that."

"*We're* his parents," Barb said. "What about your responsibility to *us*?"

"Yeah," Brad said. "What about *that*?"

"I was coming to that." Joe then came to it. "I thought Greg would tell you this, but he didn't—probably for my sake. I advised him to follow his conscience—in this matter, as in others. Not that he was inclined not to. And Tom knows this, so you don't have to tell him."

Brad, it seemed, was under so much stress he had to sit down, which he did, croaking, "Advised him *not* to report for induction?"

"I'm sorry," Joe said to Barb. "I should've told you this before."

"You didn't have to tell *me*," Brad said. "I knew it in my bones. And you know what else, Padre? Padre, hell! The trouble in Nam'd be all over now if it weren't for pricks like you!"

Joe, rising swiftly, said, "If I hear from Greg again, I'll let you know," and swiftly departed, hearing them call after him:

"Don't bother!"

"*Do!*"

26
Another
Inspector
Calls

There hadn't been any more anonymous complaints about Bill. In fact, one night after he'd gone to bed, there had been an anonymous compliment for Bill, which Joe, remembering it the next night, passed on to him. "Some woman phoned to say the Church could do with more young priests like you, Bill. And *old* ones, I told her. She agreed wholeheartedly." Bill: "Joe, you're not so old." This, though well meant, hardly needed saying, Joe thought, and got up *immediately*, which he hadn't meant to do, to freshen his drink. He didn't know what had appealed to the woman—she'd told him only what he'd told Bill—but he was afraid it might be the same thing that had scandalized the other woman (and her husband), "true charity." If so, if this thing got going, parishioners, and not only dp's, would be asking themselves and each other, "Hey, whose writ"—the pastor's or the assistant's—"runs here?"

Speak to Bill? And say what? Just tell him in a nice way to go easy on Scripture. Just renege in a nice way, you mean. You're the one who set him off, you know, with your Scripture's rough and tough and hard to stay with, people can't have it both ways, and the clergy can't, though God knows we try. And thy Father, who sees in secret, will reward thee—right, Joe? Not necessarily, Bill. You see, we have to distinguish between what we might call acts of true charity and simply contributing to the support of the Church, the former *not* to be performed at the expense of the latter. The faithful are obliged to maintain the Church's mission, ministers, real estate, and so on, according to divine positive law. *The Lord ordained that they who preach the Gospel should live by the Gospel*—1 Cor. 9:14. This, if read both ways, covers laity and clergy alike. This is also one of the Precepts of the Church, Bill. Joe, *I* know that. We had it at the sem, right after finger painting. But if people can't afford to *pay* the going rate, let 'em *give* what they can—it's better than nothing, isn't it? And if it's done on the qt so much the better—thy Father, who sees in secret, will reward thee. Go easy on *that*, will you, Bill? Joe, I only say it to those who can't pay the going rate. What's wrong with that? Let God, who numbers the hairs on our heads, do the bookkeeping, Joe. Great, Bill. But if this thing spreads, if paid-up parishioners get wind of it, what happens to our fiscal system—the *parish*? Joe, you mean the parish *as we know it*, don't you? Well, yes, Bill, I do. Oh, *that*. One of the turning points in ecclesiastical history, Your Holiness, Your Eminences, Your Excellencies, a case, you might say, of an idea whose time has finally come—and none too soon for me. I'd never been happy with the business side of the Church. Even as a child, when an altar boy and my mind was often elsewhere during sermons, I still heard too much about the Dollar-a-Sunday Club—an upgraded version of the envelope system, up from a dime ("A few lire, Your Excellency"). The day I celebrated my first Mass in my home parish will live in infamy. So, when I got my own parish, meaning to spare myself and my people all talk of money from the pulpit ("*Why*, Your Excellency? I guess you might say I'm funny that way"), I installed the country club, California, or game sanctuary system (also known as the table d'hôte). With this I did as well as could be expected but not well enough, owing to the greed of the Archdiocese. Desperate to make my nut and deaf to the siren song of the fund raiser, thanks to the prophetic counsel of my curate (as His Eminence then was), I installed the honor system, that is, no system at all, which, need I say, is now in use by dioceses everywhere and by not a few civil governments inspired, perhaps, by the success of our own IRS? We all know *how* this system works, but a word on *why*. People—and not just deep-seagoing saints and mystics—have always tried to make contact with God, especially in time of trouble. But most have had to settle for the ordinary, the all-too-ordinary, consolations of religion, among these the respect and sympathy of other believers (once a minority). Religion, in our time, had lost its clout, had become the victim, as "science" was the beneficiary, of changing fashions in credulity. Who, then, would have dreamed that religion could become what it is today—a matter of giving blindly, of sacrificing secretly, for the love of God? Could this be what the Great Bookkeeper—so jealous of his prerogatives and oh so mum since Old Testament times—has been waiting and hoping for? My view is that bookkeeping is bad for people, for those who do it and even for those who don't if they take pleasure in thinking they aren't like those who do. A plague on both your houses, I say. *Sursum corda*, folks!

"By the way, Bill, any ideas about those fives and tens in the flower collection lately?"

"No. But that's good, isn't it?"

"I guess."

Thanks to the honor system and to my young curate (as he then was) for his faith in it, in me, and in people (of whose magnanimity I confess I saw only the tip of the iceberg), I now have no money problems, I let God do the bookkeeping, I eat like a horse, I drink like a fish, I sleep like a log, I wish everybody did, or, anyway, wouldn't call me at all hours of the night. "St Francis."

"*You're* St Francis, *I'm* Lyndon B. Johnson."

"It's a deal. What's on your mind, Lyndon?"

"Been readin' the Good Book and don't like how you're runnin' things over there."

"That so?"

"Hate your methodology."

"I'm beating my breast. What else can I do for you?"

"Ask not what you can do for me. Ask what you can do for yourself."

"O.K. What?"

"You need a role model. We all do. Yours may not be mine. Mine may not be yours."

"Who's yours?"

"Talkin' about *yours*. Know who it should be?"

"Offhand, no."

"Give you a clue. He's right out of the Good Book and so's his methodology."

"Hit me again, Lyndon."

"*You* should be *his* assistant."

Joe pushed the button, terminating the call, and left the phone off the cradle. "The Repeater," he said to Bill, and then, since Bill was going to bed: "Some woman and her husband phoned to complain about you—and true charity."

"Yeah?"

"Yeah. I'd go easy on that if I were you, Bill. Remember what Our Lord said about celibacy, and what somebody else said about reality—not that they're the same, though maybe they are—few can take it."

Bill, after a moment of introspection, nodded. "See what you mean, Joe. Thanks. Actually, I *knew* that. G'night, Joe."

"G'night, Bill."

* * *

The next afternoon, a few minutes after Joe called a number and gave his own to the answering service and hung up, his phone rang. "St Francis."

"Dom, Father."

"Oh, Dom. Say, a friend of mine wants the price on Gene."

"For the nomination, Father?"

"And the election."

"*Both*, Father?"

"Both, Dom."

"Father, how much your friend want?"

"Just a g, Dom. He's got a cash-flow problem."

"Hold on, Father."

Joe, holding on, heard a knock, but it was next door.

"Come in," Joe heard Bill say.

"You Hackett?" Joe heard a man say.

"Me Schmidt—*Father* Schmidt," Bill said. (Nice going, Joe thought, hit him again.) "*Father* Hackett's in the other office."

"Entrez," Joe said to the knock at his door—a young man with a briefcase. "Sit down. I'll be with you in a minute. Yes, Dom."

"Nomination ten, election even, Father."

"Hmmm. My friend was hoping you'd do better, Dom— on the election."

"Sorry, Father. But that's where your friend could collect."

"Dom, what about a parlay—a double?"

"Hold on, Father."

"What's on your mind?" Joe asked the young man.

"State Board of Health." The young man got up, with his wallet out, evidently meaning to show Joe his identification.

Joe waved him down. "Dom, would you mind repeating that?"

"Eleven and six to five, Father."

"That's it, huh?"

"Best I can do, Father. Vigorish."

"You'd lay it off?"

"The second leg, if there is one, Father. Your friend know something?"

"Just what a little bird told him, Dom. I don't put much stock in it myself."

"Father, if I have to insure it I won't get no six to five."

"O.K., Dom. My friend wants in."

"One g on Gene, eleven and six to five, parlay."

"Right. Nice talking to you, Dom."

"Nice talking to you, Father."

Joe, doing some calculations, found that he stood to win a little better than a third of his assessment. "Sorry," he said, "to keep you waiting. What is it? Something about the school?"

The young man got up again, though Joe waved him down, and flapped his wallet open for Joe to read.

"George Z. Barnhart," Joe read, aloud, and asked, "What's the Z for?"

Mr Barnhart, saying "Mind if I close this?" closed the door between the offices.

Whereupon Joe said, "No, go right ahead," but couldn't see that this had any effect on the man, obviously one of the new prehistoric types. "What's it all about, sir?"

Mr Barnhart had sat down and unzipped his briefcase, from which he took a document. "I am authorized to read you the following regulations. 'Gonorrhea, syphilis, and chancroid, hereinafter designated venereal diseases, are hereby declared to be contagious, infectious, communicable, and dangerous to the public health. It shall be the duty of every person who makes a diagnosis of, or gives treatment for, a case of gonorrhea, syphilis, or chancroid, to report immediately to the State Board of Health on a form supplied for the purpose, the name and address, age, sex, color, occupation, marital status, and probable source of infection of such diseased person together with such other information as may be required. Local health officers are hereby directed to use every available means to ascertain the existence of, and immediately to investigate, all known or suspected cases of gonorrhea, syphilis, or chancroid, within their respective districts and to ascertain the sources of such infections. In such investigations said health officers are hereby vested with full power of inspection, isolation, or quarantine, and disinfection of all infected persons, places, and things. It shall be a violation of these regulations for any infected person knowingly to expose another person to infection with any of the said venereal diseases or any person knowingly to perform an act which exposes another person to infection with venereal disease. All persons reasonably suspected of having a venereal disease shall submit to an examination as shall be deemed necessary by the State Board of Health, provided that where such examination is of a personal nature it shall be made only by a licensed physician. All persons infected with a venereal disease shall continue under treatment or proper observation until no longer able to transmit the infection. In the case of chancroid this shall be until all ulcerations are completely healed. Whenever a case or suspected case of venereal disease is found on premises used for immoral purposes, or whenever a case of venereal disease is found upon premises where it cannot be properly isolated or controlled, or where the infected person will not consent to removal to a hospital or sanatorium where he or she can be properly isolated or controlled during the period of infectiousness, the health officer or representative of the State Board of Health shall put in a conspicuous place on the entrance to the premises where such venereal disease exists, a notice in words as follows: Warning, Venereal Disease Exists on These Premises, Posted by order of Health Officer (name and date). Such notice shall be printed in black boldface type upon a red card with the words Venereal Disease in letters not less than three inches high.' " Mr Barnhart produced such a red card from his briefcase and flashed it at Joe. "Any questions?"

"Many. If you're talking about somebody else, why are you talking to me? And if you're talking about me, what's it all about?"

"I'm talking about you."

"You think I have VD?"

"You're a suspect."

"And why's that?"

"Your name came up in connection with another case."

Joe sniffed. "*Another* case, huh?"

"We have to follow all leads."

"Somebody with VD mentioned me as a likely prospect?"

"Suspect."

"*Who?*"

"That has to remain confidential. The Board has to protect all cases, or they wouldn't cooperate. *You* can understand that."

"Not quite. What if you're wrong? What if I'm *not* 'another case'?"

"We have to follow all leads. It's the law. I'm just doing my job."

Joe sniffed. "I'll put it another way. What if this is a dirty trick, somebody's idea of a joke?"

"It's no joke."

"I agree. I'll put it *another* way. Has the Board ever been sued?"

"Sued?"

"For causing people needless, grievous embarrassment?"

"It can't be helped."

"Can't, huh? Why not write a letter? What's wrong with that?"

"Some people wouldn't answer a letter."

"O.K. *Then* go and see 'em. Why come out here and throw your weight around? Some people would feel insulted, as I do, but wouldn't be so polite. The Board could be sued. You could get your ass kicked. I'm surprised it hasn't happened before now, *if* it hasn't."

"I am authorized to inform you that you are suspected of having a venereal disease, and that you have forty-eight hours to provide the Board with medical proof to the contrary." Mr Barnhart then got up with his briefcase and left his card on the edge of Joe's desk. "What's wrong with your hand?"

"Thumb," Joe said. "Ulcerations."

After the young man departed, which he had immediately, without a word, Joe sat on at his desk, wondering *Who?*

So that evening, by appointment, Joe visited Dr Wylie. After an X-ray was taken of Joe's thumb—he wouldn't have to wear the splint but would have to be careful—he stripped down to his shorts and was given a physical.

"That's it," Dr Wylie said, blowing smoke in Joe's face. "Get dressed, for God's sake."

"What about VD?"

"What about it?"

"I thought I'd be tested for it."

"Whyn't you say so?"

"I thought, the way things are today, it was part of having a physical."

"You thought wrong. If you're worried about syph, it'll show up in your blood test. You worried about clap, or what?"

"No, I just want medical proof that I'm A.O.K."

"*A.O.K.? You?* You want to see A.O.K., look at *me.*" Dr Wylie, that evening, wore overall cutoffs and cowboy boots (with, Joe thought, elevator heels), and as before was bare above the waist except for his lavaliere.

"I want medical proof I haven't got VD, in case I decide to become a chaplain."

"Do that, you should have your *head* examined." Dr Wylie kicked a metal stool over to where Joe was standing, and sat down. "O.K., let's see what you've got. Whip it out."

Joe exposed himself, saying, "If this and the other—the blood test—are negative, would you put it in writing?"

"Sure, for the Commander in Chief. Milk it down."

Joe did as directed, wondering again, but more poignantly than ever before, who had caused him this needless, grievous embarrassment.

"Again."

Joe did as directed, wondering again, *Who?*

Dr Wylie said, "What you *should* be worrying about is this corporation of yours. It'll only get worse, you know. You guys are always going on about the primrose path and the wages of sin. Boy, *this* is it. Give the horse any thought?"

"Horse? Oh, yes. Some." Humor the man.

"One more time."

Joe did as directed.

"Clean as a whistle. Get *dressed.*" Dr Wylie turned away

in disgust and lit a cigarette. "Tell you what. The wife's home, and she hates the Catholic Church, but we'll go up to my den and have a few. I'll show you my horse. Maybe let you try it on walk or canter."

"Thanks a lot, but some other time," Joe said, wondering again, *Who?*

27
August

They took a few nights off from their mendicancy to watch the Democratic Convention on TV. This was educational for Bill, with Joe there to tell him who was who, what was what, and to comment on the fashions of the day—these at an all-time low. "Walter Cronkite's wearing a four-in-hand bib." "Get a load of the pimp sideburns on Sander Vanocur." By the end of the second night, the realities of political life, the effects of original sin, were emerging in Chicago, and Joe, who'd been hoping that a groundswell would somehow develop for Gene, was drinking more than usual (Bill too, not, however, the same thing) and feeling mean. "Is *this* the best we can do?" he'd inquire from time to time, and exclaim, "Get those hillbillies out of the government!" His stock of booze, which he'd let run down—wisely or unwisely, depending on when he thought about it, in the morning or in the evening—had been liquidated the second night. The next morning, with a head of lead, he had resolved to swear off, or anyway cut down, if only for Bill's sake. So that evening they were drinking beer.

"Actually," Bill said, "I prefer it."

"In hot weather," Joe said, and reached for the phone, on the floor beside his Barcalounger. "St Francis."

"Father Schmidt, please."

"One moment."

While Bill, who'd turned down the TV sound, took the call, Joe viewed without comment (more hillbillies) and listened in on Bill.

"My fault, Herb. We've been so busy here. No, I'll ask him tonight and get back to you tomorrow. Right. G'night, Herb." Bill turned up the sound and went to his chair. "That was Mr Lane, Joe."

"Herb?"

"He wants me to call him that."

"What else does he want?" Both kids in the school?

"That was about the Cheerleaders."

"The what? Oh."

The Cheerleaders, whose sole purpose it was to have their picture taken with the principals of new enterprises and construction in Inglenook, and who showed up in beanies and sweaters with "I" on them, with megaphones, pennants, pompons (if female), and a bass drum with a smile painted on it, were in reality Mall-based merchants and professional people, invariably described in the *Universe* (where the pictures ran when space permitted) as "that congratulatory group."

"They'd like to come here, Joe."

"What for?"

"Joe, you know what for."

Yes, to congratulate him on his new rectory. Either it hadn't occurred to them to do so before, or they'd known better before Lane came along. "Sorry, Bill, but the answer has to be no. Nothing doing."

Bill appeared to question his pastor's judgment. "All right, Joe. I didn't promise anything. But I didn't think you'd mind, actually."

Joe sniffed. *"Actually,"* he said, reaching down for the phone, "I'd rather bite the head off a chicken. St Francis."

"Joe, you doing anything?"

"No. Not much."

"Like to talk to you."

"Go ahead."

"Not on the phone. If it's all right, I'm coming out. I'm at Horse's, so I won't be long. I won't stay late, Joe."

"O.K., Left."

Joe searched his bedroom and the bathroom for bottles possibly mislaid, and returned to his chair, his beer, and the convention. He was troubled, however, by thoughts and pictures of the Cheerleaders. "Bill, if Lane wants to know why not, tell him you don't know—which you apparently don't. Or tell him to ask me—which he won't."

"All right, Joe."

"If Father Beeman comes before I get back, tell him I won't be long." About to depart, Joe waited for the convention to be gaveled to order by the chair, a southwesterner, said, "Get those cowboys out of the government," and left.

Backing out of the driveway, Joe was almost sideswiped by a dented black Impresario, and spoke to the driver. "The back door's unlocked. I won't be long. Bill's in the study."

"Bill? Want to talk to *you*."

"Ride along then."

Lefty squeezed into Joe's car and was still gasping from the effort when Joe turned the corner and Big Mouth and Patton came into view, the latter heavily engaged on the rectory lawn.

Lefty yelled out the window: "Church property!"

Big Mouth, nodding and smiling, waved.

"How *about* that?" Lefty said to Joe. "Parishioner?"

"What else?"

"Kick ass, Joe. That's what I did when—whenever—I was a pastor. I still do, but not as much."

"You're learning, Left. What's on your mind?"

"Oh." Lefty opened and shut the glove compartment. "Joe, I don't know how to tell you this. But maybe you already know."

"You've been offered a parish. Cathedral?" Cruel.

"Joe, this is serious. You *sure* Bill didn't tell you?"

"What could *Bill* tell me?"

"Plenty."

Joe turned onto the highway, into the slow lane. "Like what?"

"Joe, remember the day I phoned to ask if Airhead was at your place—*or* Bill?"

Joe was silent.

"The day you came off retreat, Joe. Remember?"

"Not all the details."

"Did you know those clowns were with this creep Conklin?"

"Not when you phoned. Bill told me later. He told me Conklin was bitter about the clergy—something about losing his moustache, half of it."

"Joe, I'm sorry about that, and so's Horse. We got carried away. Conklin's really hard to take, though I will say this for him—Airhead's worse. Joe, did Bill tell you where they went that day?"

"More or less."

"He tell you what they did—maybe not Bill but Airhead and Conklin?"

"Not exactly, no."

"Airhead was lucky, but Conklin caught a dose."

Joe shook his head, turned into the Great Badger's parking lot, came to rest near the liquor store, and shook his head again. "It's a crazy world, Left."

"There's more, Joe. Some shit from the state department of

health wanted to know if I had VD. Said my name came up in another case. '*What* case?' I said. He wouldn't tell me. That's how it works, Joe—the burden of proof is on the innocent. You're supposed to offer to take a physical. 'You think I'll do that, that's where you're wrong,' I said. 'You don't, there'll be a sign on the front door,' this shit says, and shows me the sign. It got kind of wild then. I got carried away, Joe."

"It's a crazy world, Left."

"That's not all, Joe. I *now* know the same thing happened to Horse. Only *he* caved in and took a physical."

Joe was silent.

"Poor Horse. Instead of keeping it to himself and eating his heart out—they say he's a slob, and he is, but he's a *sensitive* slob—he should've come to *me*."

"Come to *you*," Joe swiftly replied. "How was he to know he wasn't alone? Why didn't you come to *him*?" And *me*?

"Joe, I *did*, but by then it was too late."

"Look. What if Horse *had* come to you?" Or *I* had?

Lefty, from the breast pocket of his black summerweight suit, produced a rubber cigar. "Joe," he said, speaking around it, through his teeth, "I broke the case."

Joe just looked at him and the cigar.

"Blew it sky high, Joe. The same day this shit called on me. At dinner that night—and, fortunately, Airhead was present—I told Nijinsky I'd sue the state if the sign went up. You know how pale the man is anyway, Joe. Well, he got paler. I felt sorry for him in a way. (This is only his first pastorate, you know.) I offered to take a physical if the case went to court, doubting, I said, that it would. I even offered to take a physical the next day, the result, though, to be my secret until, and if, the case went to court. But nothing seemed to help. Nijinsky was still what I guess you might call speechless. He got up and left the table. So did Airhead then, and drove off. It was around midnight when he knocked on my door. (I was in my skivvies having a nightcap and soaking my dogs—Joe, I have one of these Massagic footbaths.) Well, Joe, Airhead came clean, told me what I already told you, Joe, about Conklin catching a dose and himself being lucky (not that he won't have to take a physical now) and also why Conklin brought Horse and me into it: on account of his moustache, Joe, half of it."

Joe nodded, wondering, though, why he'd been brought into it.

"You know what else, Joe?"

"What?"

"Conklin asked Airhead to beg my forgiveness. 'Ask him to beg it himself,' I said, 'and then we'll see.' I'd still like to kick his ass."

"What about Horse's forgiveness?" And mine?

"Also Horse's. And you know what else, Joe?"

"What?"

"Airhead's under the impression he laid down his life— his *spiritual* life—for his friend, than which there is no greater love."

Joe was what he guessed you might call speechless.

"Some shit, huh? And you know what else, Joe?"

"What?"

"Airhead says Conklin was also out to get *you*. Why, I don't know. Do you?"

"No."

"I'll try to find out if the creep comes around to beg my forgiveness."

"Don't bother. Forget it."

" 'Forget it,' he says. You wouldn't talk like that, Joe, if this'd happened to you—and I'm not thinking of myself so much as I am of poor Horse."

"I know."

"Joe, it's odd Bill didn't tell you any of this. Well, maybe not."

"Far's I know, Bill hasn't been in touch with Potter and Conklin lately." Joe opened the door of the car. "I'll be right back, Left."

"I'll trail along, Joe."

When Joe opened the door to the liquor store, he saw two youths go out the other door and heard one of them yell, presumably at the sight of clergymen in clerical attire, "Spooks!"

Lefty went after them.

"No, no," said Joe, thinking there was reason to be annoyed, as he was, yes, but not to kick ass, and, following Lefty, was in time to see an old car, one of those with its rear end obscenely cocked up, roar off.

"Gone," said Lefty.

"Good," said Joe.

Lefty glanced at Joe and then away in disgust. "Wake up, son. That was a heist."

They went inside where Mr Barnes, who'd been standing at the cash register before, was releasing three customers— two middle-aged men and an older woman—from the walk-in cooler. Mr Barnes and the customers, particularly the woman, were grateful to Lefty and Joe, in that order, to the former, the real hero if there was one, more than to the latter, for coming on the scene when they had—in the nick of time, Mr Barnes said, because the robbers, as he called them, had got nothing, "thanks to you gentlemen."

The real hero if there was one said modestly, "Too bad the assholes got away."

After the three other customers, whose names, addresses, and phone numbers were taken down, had left (the woman slow to leave, seeming to regard Lefty and Joe as a couple of colorful TV-type troubleshooters), Mr Barnes politely declined payment for a bottle of bourbon and two of gin, saying the management, Mr Brock, wouldn't want it otherwise. Joe paid for his gin, but Lefty didn't for his bourbon, and went into unnecessary detail about his address with Mr Barnes. "Holy Resting Place, it's called now, but Holy Sepulchre will always get me."

On the way home, Joe switched on the car radio, the convention, and Lefty got out his cigar.

"Afraid Gene won't make it, Joe."

"Could've told you that, Left." Uh-huh. One grand.

When Joe switched off the convention, Lefty put away his cigar.

"Joe, did you know—your old pastor's in the hospital."

"Dollar Bill. He's been in for some time."

"No, Van."

"Oh, *Van*."

"They've got him in an oxygen tent."

Joe, after a moment of reflection, said, "He's been in one for years." Cruel.

"Joe, I'm not so sure about that as I used to be. I've just about had it with life here below. More and more, I find, my heart's in the highlands, my heart's not here."

"I know what you mean, Left." Joe turned into his driveway, giving the accident-prone Impresario a wide berth, and came to rest in the garage, where he turned off the car lights and said in the dark: "Look, Left. I may've given Bill the idea I was cutting down, and I don't want him to think I made a special run. So we won't say anything about the holdup."

"We won't, huh?"

"No, we'll just say you brought 'em—the bottles."

"You know what, Joe?"

"What?"

"I'd hate to be a pastor again, with a candy-ass assistant."

"You will be, Left."

"You *hear* something, Joe?"

"No."

"Oh."

As it happened, nothing was to be gained by misrepresenting the bottles to Bill, for he was on the phone in the study with (he whispered to Joe) Security at the Great Badger. Joe took over then. "No, offhand, I'd say they were Caucasians. No, I doubt it was stolen, from the look of it. Model? That I couldn't say. No, he's right here. No, no"—Security, it seemed, had already spoken to one of the other witnesses—"he's not my *partner*." Lefty took over then. "No, if I saw 'em again—and the wheelman I *didn't* see—I wouldn't recognize 'em—just assholes. The heap I would. Old Biscayne four-door, green repaint, and no plates I could see. That's right, Holy Sepulchre, but for the next hour or so I can be reached at this number."

While Joe made drinks (Bill stayed with beer), Lefty told Bill about the attempted holdup . . . but worse things were happening in Chicago, on TV, police rioting in the streets, peaceniks, innocent bystanders, and even media people getting beat up, Senator Ribicoff (D., Conn.) protesting these outrages from the convention platform and being barracked from the floor by Mayor Daley and his claque.

Lefty got so worked up over what was happening inside and outside the convention that he, now occupying the Barcalounger and over Joe's tacit disapproval, called Chicago, the Cardinal ("You *know* him?" said Bill—"What's *that* got to do with it?" said Lefty), but somebody else answered the phone, and while Lefty was willing to identify himself

("Don't worry, Monsignor. I'm a priest in good standing. I'm in the *Directory*"), he wouldn't entrust his message to anyone but the Cardinal, would only say it was a matter of faith and morals, was put on hold, lost the connection, called back ("It's not a matter for my Ordinary, Monsignor. It's a matter for *yours*, the Cardinal. Why d'ya think I'm calling him? *Retired?* Who you kiddin'? Oh, gone to *bed*. No, if he's in delicate health, don't wake him. First thing in the morning then. Here it is. Quote: Respectfully submit, indeed urge, that His Honor and others of the Faith among the police and National Guard be exhorted privately to do public penance for their sins against society or be duly excommunicated. Unquote. Monsignor, what's happening in Chicago tonight, I hope I don't have to tell you, is a scandal to the jaybirds"), lost the connection again, but didn't call back because Bill, who must have heard the doorbell, brought two deputies into the study. After Joe offered them refreshments (politely declined) and he and Lefty were questioned by them, Lefty, now out of the Barcalounger and walking the floor like some great caged beast with a drink in one paw and a rubber cigar in another, lectured the deputies on the crimes of the fuzz in particular and of the establishment in general ("Sure, I'm a radical, but what's *that* mean—look it up—it means going to the roots of the problem"), after which, having heard Lefty prophesy revolution, "Red or green, take your choice," and heard Joe, who was watching the convention, exclaim, "Get those mothers out of the government," the deputies soberly left, escorted by Bill, who, it occurred to Joe later, hadn't returned to the study.

In Bill's absence, Joe and Lefty, both collarless and in one case shoeless (always, Joe thought, a sour note somewhere, even when this life was most harmonious), blasted off into the empyrean of priestly fellowship. Confiding in each other

as they ordinarily wouldn't, they spoke the truth, the language of God, which was all the more cleansing and refresh-
ing after what they'd said to each other, and not said, earlier.
Lefty admitted that he wouldn't mind being a pastor again,
indeed desired it, and to that end when appearing before the
Arch (Nijinsky having booked a hurry-up appointment for
him) had appeared to bow before superior wisdom as well as
authority and to forswear his declared intention to sue the
state, which he'd already to himself, at the moment he'd
broken the case, forsworn. "I could see it made Big Albert's
day, but I don't feel so good about it, Joe. Pretty tricky,"
Lefty confessed.

"You're too hard on yourself, Left," said Joe, absolving
him.

"Not hard enough, Joe."

Moved by such probity and given an unfair moral advantage he wished to neutralize in the interest of truth and
priestly fellowship, Joe admitted that he too had been
approached by the state department of health and—"Left,
here's why I didn't tell you"—had gone and taken a physical.
"Like Horse, I caved in, Left. I should've come to you," Joe
confessed.

"Sure, but, like Horse, how were you to know you
weren't alone, Joe?" said Lefty, absolving him.

Lefty spent the night at Joe's, ultimately in the guest room.

The attempted holdup was featured in the *NS*, where the
emphasis was on the heroism of Joe and Lefty, in *that* order,
and on the robbers' panic-stricken flight. " 'Spooks!' they
gasped when confronted by the doughy [sic] clergymen.
Sheriff Shorts Morsberger, when asked if the wanted persons
are thought to be devout Catholics, said: 'We can't rule it out.

We're looking at all the angles.' " The story, ignored by the *Universe*, was picked up nationally and internationally. Brad phoned to say he was proud of it, except for the typo ("*Doughty*, Father"), and hoped Joe would take it as "a peace offering, like." Joe, trying to change the subject but perhaps revealing his concern that the story would damage him with the Mall crowd, inquired after Barb's left leg.

28

The Geek

Act

When Joe came in, the Arch, in his usual chair, looking up from his reading matter, cried out, "Hail, the conquering hero!"

Joe, blushing, made for his usual chair and barber, murmuring rather stagily, "Oh, oh," when the Arch asked if anyone there *hadn't* read about the abortive holdup out in Inglenook, his barber interpolating, "Sir, it was on TV too," other barbers confirming this and, where necessary, filling in their clients.

"Over here!" cried the Arch, after speaking to the barber belonging to and sitting in the next chair.

So Joe and his barber moved over to it.

"Well, well, Father. How's it going *otherwise?*"

"No problems to speak of, Your Excellency." Joe was relieved that he wasn't being asked for a firsthand account of his heroism—that it had happened where it had and not, say, in a bank was probably as incriminating in the eyes of the many who didn't know him (and Lefty) as it was in the eyes of some doughy clergymen who did, they thought, know him (and Lefty) all too well.

"Hmmm," said the Arch. "Arf?" he barked.

Joe, trying to relax, tightened up. "We're doing as well as can be expected in our circumstances"—a veiled, double-barreled reference to his system and his assessment.

"What's *that* mean?" Blunt.

"No problem." Brazen.

"Good. You run a tight ship, Father."

"Thanks, Your Excellency. I try."

"You must be doing more than that."

Well, yes, I am—at the moment I'm lying in my teeth. "No problem, Your Excellency."

"Music to my ears these days, Father."

"That so?" Was the Arch in trouble with Arf? Joe hoped so, and while he hadn't expected the Arch, an Ordinary's Ordinary, moderate in all but moderation (and extortion), to reel off the names of delinquent pastors, he *had* expected his concerned "That so?" to be acknowledged in *some* way—the ensuing silence was embarrassing to Joe.

Presently: "Little bone to pick with you, Father."

"Oh, oh." The bad publicity arising out of his heroism? The bad company he kept (Lefty)? His refusal to cooperate with Mac? With Tom? With—but surely not, for even if the Arch did know of Joe's involvement with the state department of health, which was doubtful, he, Joe, like Horse but unlike Lefty, had done the right thing, had caved in, had gone and taken and, furthermore, passed a physical . . .

"Thought you'd invite me out to bless your new rectory."

"Oh, oh. Well, you see . . ." You see, I called the Chancery about this very thing, Arch, and Catfish turned me down flat. Bless one, have to bless 'em all, he said, to which I—mindful of the material as well as the spiritual well-being of the Church—in this, if only in this, like you, Arch—sadly replied, How many new rectories are there nowadays? Busy here, bless it yourself, snapped he, and hung up. Typical. "I'm sorry, Your Excellency."

"Bless it yourself, Father?"

"No, not yet."

"Like me to come out sometime?"

"Of course."

"It's a deal. Monsignor Toohey'll let you know when."

That I doubt, Joe thought, tempted again to tell all, to *get* Toohey. "Thanks a lot, Your Excellency."

The Arch, descending from his chair in the odor of witch hazel and talcum powder, dropped his reading matter in Joe's lap, *Forbes*.

A couple of days later, Bill, having learned only that evening (when Potter called him) that Joe had been under suspicion at the state health department but was now considered "clean," was able to explain why Conklin had borne false witness against Joe. It went back to that bad day at the Bow Wow. What Bill had told Joe at the time was substantially true, but not the part about Bill waiting in his little car for Conklin to come out of the Bow Wow—Bill had gone in after him; and Bill had omitted the next part entirely, the part where Dom called Joe a saint "in no uncertain terms" and Conklin laughed in Dom's face. That was when Dom and the kitchen help completed the job begun by Father Beeman and Father Power on Conklin's moustache. "Bill, what d'ya mean, Dom called me a saint 'in no uncertain terms'?" "He put it very strongly." "C'mon, Bill." "Joe, he called you 'a fuckin' saint.' " "Yeah? What if Conklin was laughing at *that*?" "No, I think it was the whole idea, Joe." "Yeah, it *is* funny, in a way." Bill had minimized Dom's loyalty to and respect for Joe because Bill hadn't wanted Joe to feel responsible for even one of the day's events. "Thanks." Bill hadn't foreseen the consequences—had, in fact, regarded the final, total loss of Conklin's moustache as a good thing—and had been shocked to hear (from Potter) that Conklin had blamed *Joe*, along with Father Beeman and Father Power, and to hear that even in *their* case he'd taken such revenge.

"The thing is, Joe, I feel responsible for what you've been through. After all, Conklin was—is, I guess—*my* friend."

"Forget it, Bill."

"I'd like to, Joe, but I can't. And Pot says to tell you Conklin wants to personally beg your forgiveness."

"That won't be necessary. He has my forgiveness, tell him. No, tell *Potter* to tell him."

Joe got up to freshen his nightcap, and bet himself, when the phone rang (considering the hour), it would be LBJ, but lost. It was Mac, in his cups. "Joe, my hat's off to you . . . if I can *ever* be of *any* service . . . my hat's off to you, Joe."

Joe managed, in a nice way, to terminate the call. "Mr McMaster," he told Bill. "His hat's off to me."

"The holdup?"

"What else?"

Joe's heroism had been commented on by others far and near. Mrs P., Steve, Big Mouth, Patton. Dave Brock, in a letter of thanks. The Licensed Vintner's wife (after Sunday Mass): "We miss your custom, Father, but it's all *his* fault for letting nice Mr Barnes go." Nan Gurrier, whose Jim still had his inventory and house, but was now *gainfully* employed in Shipping at Great Badger, owing to the intercession of the editor of the *NS*, which stood ready to mount an all-out campaign against it should there again be talk of expanding the dump: "We see you and the whole wide world with new eyes these days, Father." Earl, another family man soon to better himself by making a change, by moving to Great Badger, Home Furnishings, in a managerial capacity, having responded to an ad in the issue of the *NS* that featured the holdup story: "Wow, Father. Hey, when it came out in the interview that I knew you personally and did your rectory, I was *in*." Smiley of Smiley's Shell, whose brother, Ed, pastor in name only, had eloped in July and of whom Smiley had then said, "Ed wasn't fit to wear the uniform he didn't wear," and now said (of the holdup), "Nice going, Father. It may interest you to know Ed's back in uniform—got himself a desk job with the Seattle P.D." Father Day: "Joe, what a gas! By the way, Dollar Bill and Van, they're both doing poorly." Joe's folks, now living year round in Florida, who'd advised him, in effect, to let the robbers have it next time, life being more important than moola. Likewise Sister Agatha, in a note (with holy card enclosed), from retirement in her order's motherhouse and possibly living in the past: "God bless you, my boy." Uncle Bobby, in a wire from Honolulu, currently his base of operations: POUND THAT BEER. From LBJ, though, before Joe hung up on him again: "They caught you red-handed, huh?"

"No word from Toohey," Joe said to Bill. "Well, I'm not surprised."

Bill stared at Joe. "You expected *him* to say something?"

Joe stared at Bill and gradually understood. "About the holdup—hell, no. About the Arch coming out."

"Oh."

"To bless the rectory—I told you that."

"Oh, sure."

"Look. I'm not surprised. I don't see how Catfish could queer the deal, but I never made it better than even money he wouldn't."

At first, Joe had wondered how Toohey, when and if he called, would eat crow. Would he act as if he hadn't said no earlier, or not disguise the fact that he had and be hard-assed about it, or would he get someone else at the Chancery— maybe one of the women—to do the job? At first, Joe thought he'd just wait and see. But with each passing day he thought it more likely he'd just wait and not see. Call the Arch, tell all, *get* Toohey? This was a recurring fancy, building up, gathering force when, suddenly, early one morning, Catfish was calling.

"Don't know what the hell you're up to now"—alluding to Joe's heroism?—"but we'll be out there tomorrow. Eleven A.M. That's *sharp*. He'll do the other first. Five minutes for that. No more. Then the blessing."

" 'The other'? What 'other'?" Joe was saying when Toohey hung up.

Later that morning when Bill arrived at his office—he'd had a tooth pulled—Joe went over to see him.

"Any pain?"

"No, not yet."

"Good. I had a call from Toohey."

"Oh?"

"Oh?" Had Bill been given a mind-altering medication? "The Arch's coming out to bless the rectory. Remember?"

"Joe, I guess I figured since it hadn't happened, it wouldn't . . . like the end of the world."

"Yeah? Well, it's happening. Tomorrow. Eleven A.M."

"Joe"—Bill still seemed to find it hard to believe—"you want me to be present?"

"If you don't mind," Joe said with, he thought, sarcasm, which didn't seem to get through to Bill. Joe told him about the conversation, such as it was, with Toohey. "Any idea what he could mean by 'the other'?" But Bill was no help.

So Joe retired to his office to do some thinking, which went on, off and on, all day. Just before closing time, he called the Chancery, hoping to get an explanation from someone else if Toohey wasn't there, but determined, if Toohey was there, to get it from him, and if hung up on, to call, or maybe go and see, the Arch and tell all—I'm tired of covering for that horse's ass, Your Excellency.

But Toohey was there, and when Joe, his tone intimidating, asked about "the other," Toohey was surprisingly civil.

"Some group he's supposed to have his picture taken with. Wait a minute. Here it is. 'Mr Lane, Cones, Casing,' it says here. 'Cheerleaders.' Cheerleaders?"

Joe was silent.

"That mean anything to you?"

Joe was silent.

"You don't know *anything* about this?"

"I didn't say that," Joe replied, and hung up.

Joe's first thought was to call the Arch right away and let him know what he'd be doing if he had his picture taken with the Cheerleaders: repudiating one of his best men ("You run a tight ship, Father"), who'd said no to the Cheerleaders for much the same reason that some aborigines, he'd read, refuse to be photographed, fearing loss or diminution of being.

Joe's next thought was not to call the Arch right away, but to try to understand what was going on, and so he made a list:

a) Arch doesn't know what he's doing, that I turned down Cheerleaders.
b) Arch knows what he's doing, that I turned down Cheerleaders, but thinks I was wrong to do so.
c) Arch, in either case, probably aware of my infamy (in eyes of Mall crowd) and hopes, by having his picture taken with me and mine with him and Cheerleaders, to improve my image (in eyes of entire community).
d) Arch, in *any* case, doing business as usual—P.R.

*   *   *

Joe decided to leave well (lousy) enough alone, not to call the Arch, and for the next few hours he tried to be himself, which, in the circumstances, was hard for him. In the evening, as usual, he visited dp's, forcing himself to do this, as he'd have to force himself in the morning, if by then he found the strength or the weakness—which would it be?—to do "the other." Could something like this, for all its absurdity, be of divine or diabolic origin, a trial of humility or a temptation to pride, meant to build him up or tear him down? Or was it just more of the same, just *nothing*—in that case perhaps diabolic?

At last! A saint for today! Blessed Joseph of Inglenook, help of victims of P.R., pray for us!

As it happened, except for forcing himself to visit dp's, he gained nothing by it and returned to the rectory in a state of acute dehydration. He was on his second drink when Bill returned, came in from what he called "chores," and after taking a phone call in his room, reported to the study with a beer.

"Bad news, Joe. Al Fresco's in the hospital. Bleeding ulcer."

Joe was sorrier than he would have thought to hear this, but said, "What he gets for eating beans out of the can."

"Frucht's afraid Al won't be back."

"Don't need two men at Holy Cross. Slum parishes aren't what they used to be. Somebody should tell the Arch."

"He's got the shakes."

"*Who?*"

"Fruchtenberg. He's in *charge*."

Joe sniffed. "What's the difference in a parish like that?" And got up to make a drink. He was back to thinking of his own trouble, of ways out, trying to see this as one of those situations from which the wise pastor ostensibly retires and handles through his assistant—"Father flew to Florida, Your Excellency, to be at the bedside of his parents ["*One* of his parents, Bill"] and deeply regrets he can't be with us today"—and was still getting nowhere. Oh, the humiliation there'd be for him when he told Bill, who really should be told, the Cheerleaders were coming—assuming Bill didn't already know this (from Lane?) and hadn't meant anything ominous by it when, presumably speaking only of the Arch's engagement to bless the rectory, he'd said what he had ("I guess I figured since it hadn't happened, it wouldn't . . . like the end of the world"). If Bill did know the Cheerleaders were coming (and if he did, why didn't he say so?), the humiliation for Joe would be even greater when, if . . . no, don't. Don't tell Bill. Let it ride. Let it all happen in the morning . . . like the end of the world. No, Bill should be told even if he already knew, for Joe didn't know that, and therefore when he came out of the bathroom with his drink he said:

"Bill, I called Toohey."

Bill just looked at Joe.

"About 'the other.' Remember?"

Bill nodded, sort of.

"Bill, what it is . . . *is.*" Joe shook his head and was, though he'd been about to go through with it again, silent again, looking down into his glass.

"Joe, I *know* what it is—and I'm sorry."

Joe looked up from his glass, blushing.

Bill, also blushing, tried to explain. He said that Herb had met the Arch at some affair in the city and had got him to say yes to the Cheerleaders, but that this had happened before Joe said no to them, at which point *Herb* had been in a bind. Then, when, later, the Arch promised Joe to come out and bless the rectory, *Bill* had been in a bind. But had been hoping—"You said there was a good chance, Joe"—that Toohey would somehow queer the deal. "If *that* had happened, Joe, there wouldn't be any problem. I mean, Herb would understand—he's not a bad guy, Joe. *He* thought you'd be pleased. *I* wasn't so sure. But I didn't think you'd mind—to this extent."

"Whyn't you tell me this before?"

"Herb asked me not to. He said if you found out he went to the Arch before he went to you, you'd think he'd gone over your head. You would've too."

Joe, not saying so but agreeing, was silent, wondering whether he'd have had the guts to say no if he'd known the Arch had said yes, whether, in fact, since that *was* the situation now, he had the guts to say no now.

"Joe, as I see it, when the Arch said yes to Herb, the whatchamacallit was cast."

"The die."

"Right. Joe, what is this *die*?"

"It's the singular for dice."

"I see. So what's the deal on tomorrow, Joe?"

"We'll see."

Bill finished his beer and rose to leave, which was all right with Joe that night—it wasn't that he was sore at Bill, it was just that there was nothing to say. "See you in the morning, Joe."

"Uh-huh." In the morning. What a thing to say, even if Bill hadn't, and he hadn't, meant anything ominous by it.

"Joe, I don't know if you've thought of it or not, but as I see it, you ought to try to see this as a, well, *cross*."

Joe sniffed. "Some cross," he said.

"G'night, Joe."

"G'night, Bill."

*　*　*

A couple of drinks later, around midnight, Joe did what he should have done earlier, hours earlier, called the Arch and heard him say:

"Hello. This is a recorded message. Please identify yourself and state your business briefly. If necessary, I'll get back to you. Go ahead."

"Father Hackett, SS Francis and Clare's, Inglenook," Joe said, making an effort to speak effortlessly. "This is about tomorrow morning, Your Excellency. I think you should know, if you don't, that I said no, nothing doing, to the Cheerleaders, that congratulatory group. This is such a low-grade operation that I don't think a priest, and even less a bishop—the Church, Your Excellency—should have anything to do with it. So, when I learned, as I did only this morning, that it's on and that you're in on it, well, to put it mildly, Your Excellency, it came as one hell of a shock to me. I realize it's late, but not too late, I hope, to call off your visitation tomorrow, even if this means postponing the blessing. That's all I have to say. Thank you. G'night."

That "G'night" could sound silly in the morning, perhaps *alcoholic*, Joe thought, and was about to go into the bathroom with his empty glass when he didn't, surprising himself but not much (the next time might be different). He wandered over to the windows and seeing the weather ball—red—wished he had the whole message back. Would that have been—to have said nothing—to despair? noo, said the water tank. Was this—to have said something—to hope? noo. Did anything mean anything? noo. Was that the phone? noo.

"St Francis."

"*You're* St Francis, *I'm* Lyndon B. Johnson."

"Not tonight."

*　*　*

In the morning, Joe got up with difficulty, with a head of lead, but wasn't sorry (had feared he might be) that he'd called the Arch so late. For now there was a sporting chance—he rated it two to one—that the Chancery would call to say the Arch was indisposed, in which case, if the Cheerleaders had to be so informed, Bill ("Herb would understand") could handle it. So, before going over to church for his Mass—naturally, when he could have used the sleep, he had the early one—Joe told Bill (still in bed) to be sure and find out, if word came from the Chancery of the Arch's indisposition, whether the Cheerleaders had been so informed. "And don't let Toohey hang up on you. Take a firm line with him. That's what I do."

After Mass, when Joe asked him, Bill said there hadn't been any word from the Chancery. It was still early, too early, Joe told himself. He had orange juice for breakfast, while scourging himself with thoughts about cutting down on his drinking, then went and sat in his office. When the time was now or never, you'd think, to call off an eleven o'clock engagement—one involving, among other things, a big bass drum—there was still no word from the Chancery. The odds had gone up to five to one, and these were Joe's odds—any other bookmaker would have doubled them. Then—it could be anybody, though—the phone rang.

"St Francis."

"This is just to confirm he'll be out there at eleven sharp," Toohey said, and hung up.

For the next hour, with the door closed between the offices, Joe was in a state, walking around in circles, shooting out of orbit from time to time to do some dusting, until, to get away from Bill's typing, music to Joe's ears these days but that day deafening, he went upstairs to his halloween bathroom where, standing before the open medicine cabinet, having already had four aspirins, and an eyecup catching his eye, he changed his prescription, poured himself a small gin and knelt down (the frosted window was up a bit) to see if he'd heard what he thought he had in the street, yes, at the curb, disembarking from their cars, their drum from a station wagon, the Cheerleaders in full fig (male and female made he them, but for this?), and a heavily armed photographer, no, two, oh, *no*, Brad . . . all of them, a hellish host, advancing on the rectory, and then, sliding into the breach of the driveway, the archiepiscopal car of hearselike length and breadth and hue, the rocket trail of mud splashmarks on its flank giving it a sinister GHQ look to Joe, who, rising from his knees, joints buckling, staggered away from the window and poured himself another small gin and, hearing the doorbell, seated himself on the toilet, its lid down not for the purpose it then served, not for sitting on while sipping an aperitif, but on general principles, and heard, as he'd known he would, Bill come for him, announce through the bathroom door, calmly, the end of the world.

"The Arch's here, Joe, and Toohey's in a hurry."

Silence.

"Joe?"

Silence.

Bill tried the door—locked.

Joe, afraid he was getting in too deep, replied, feebly, "Not feeling well, Bill."

"Not feeling well, Joe?"

"Awful."

"Indigestion?"

"You might say."

"Joe, you need a doctor?"

"*No.*"

"O.K., Joe. I'll tell 'em what you said."

Thinking how *that* would sound to the Arch and Toohey if they'd both audited his nocturnal message, or if the Arch hadn't and Toohey had broken it down for him—"Don't be surprised, Bishop, if he's indisposed"—Joe rose up, took a swig of Lavoris for his breath's sake, and would have rushed out the door if it hadn't been locked, unlocked it, and rushed out.

When he came to the front door and heard the voices on the other side, he was tempted to go down to his office, to the lavatory *there*, but didn't. He went out the front door and was warmly received by the Cheerleaders—Herb, however, not among them—and by the Arch, who called to Toohey (who stood apart, with Brad, in the shade of the rectory), "What'd I tell you, Monsignor?"

"Thought we'd do it here on the steps," the *Universe* photographer said to Joe.

"That so?"

The *NS* photographer, coming out of the shade, said to Joe, "They say we can't shoot it, Father."

"That so?"

"Say they have your permission."

"That so?"

"And we don't."

"O.K. You've got it."

"Thanks, Father. You won't regret it. *We're* shootin' *color.*"

If the Cheerleaders and the man from the *Universe* (who, though, didn't seem to give a shit) had expected Joe's decision to be reversed by higher authority, they were mistaken, since there is no higher authority on earth than a pastor in his parish, and the Arch, knowing this and smiling away, was obviously pleased with Joe for being so masterful, so pastorful, as Joe was, while aware that all he'd done, in the interest of fair play, was assure that the task at hand be performed by both executioners.

"Thought we'd do it here on the steps," said the one.

"Where the hell else?" said the other.

So—with the Arch in the middle, and next to him Joe and Bill, and next to them two females, with four males behind, and kneeling down in front, alongside the drum, two more, one of whom struck the drum before each take (three takes), making for smiles and merriment all around, with one grim exception—the deed was done.*

Joe, first to break out of formation, was approached by Toohey, who said, "Hope you're ready for him inside," or, as Joe construed it, Look, Shorty, if it's slipped your mind what else he's here for, better round up some holy water and a candle.

"The curate took care of everything," Joe said.

They stood together in uneasy silence, watching the Arch and the Cheerleaders, the Arch giving them one and all a lube job. "Get on with it," Toohey muttered. And the Arch, as if in response, finished up, looked around to see where he was now, and came over to Joe with his hand out, which Joe shook, the Arch saying to him:

"Nice group, Father. Oh, there's something in what you *said* last night, but a lot more in what you *did* this morning."

"That's what I'm afraid of." *Wham!*

The Arch smiled frostily.

Joe had been hoping for more of a response, believing as

---

* In the color photo that appeared in the *NS*, the Arch, Joe, and Bill were all smiling broadly, especially Joe, and the Cheerleaders, with all their pomps, were nowhere to be seen.

he did that the separation of Church and Dreck was a matter of life and death for the world, that the Church was the one force in the world with a chance to save it (but first, "Physician, heal thyself!"), and he was still hoping for more of a response when Toohey intervened, "We're running late, Bishop," and so they went inside and got on with the blessing.

III

29
September

Joe sat in the sanctuary of the cathedral with Egan's set and others either eminent or, like himself, associated in some way with the deceased. Hardly any laity present, and few of the clergy went on to the cemetery. After the prayers at the grave, about to go to his car, Joe was detained by a layman of scholarly mien, well dressed in black but much too tall, who said, "I was instructed by the deceased to give this to you here, in the cemetery, Father. I'm his lawyer."

Joe accepted the envelope, reading on it, in shivering blue-black script, *Courtesy Mr Von Keillor*, and asked, "What if I hadn't been able to come to the cemetery?"

"I was instructed to get in touch with you."

"And if I hadn't been able to come to the funeral?"

"The same."

So the deceased had considered that possibility too, as Joe had. He wanted to open the envelope then and there, out of curiosity, and so didn't. "Thank you, sir."

"Good day, Father."

In the seclusion of his car, Joe opened the envelope and read:

Dear Joseph—
You were right.

I was wrong.
Pray for me.
Wm Stock

A few days later a letter came from Mr Von Keillor saying that the deceased had made a bequest in the amount of $10,000 to Joe. Wondering if the deceased had said *why*, Joe phoned the long lawyer, who, though, couldn't or wouldn't help him in that respect but suggested he get in touch with Father Butler. Joe had already thought of doing this, and now did, by phone.

"I understand you're Father Stock's executor."

"That's right."

"So you know he left me ten grand."

"Yes."

"There were other beneficiaries?"

"Yes. The pastor remembered all his assistants still living."

"Still in organized ball, you mean."

"Yes."

"Including Father Day?"

"Yes."

"That's good. He earned it. How about Beeman?"

"Who?"

"Lefty Beeman. He did time there briefly."

"Oh. No, none of those. But housekeepers and janitors, or their survivors. Most of the estate went to the Sisters."

"That's good. They earned it. Everybody did. I was wondering, though, why me?"

Silence.

"Anything in the will that would explain it?"

"No."

"Anything you might know that might explain it—me being boy from the parish, maybe?"

"No, not that."

"He leave Toohey anything?"

"*Monsignor?* No, Father."

"That's good. Look, Father, here's what I want to know. Did you, by any chance, tell the man I made a contribution to his purse?"

Silence.

"Could he have *known?*"

Silence.

"I mean, the *exact* figure?"

Silence. And then, with a rush: "Father, I was *new*. Nothing—just nothing—was coming in until . . . he *made* me tell him—*you* know how he was . . ."

"I do, I do, and I don't blame you, Father. That's all I wanted to know. Thanks."

So it was as Joe had thought: he had been paid back at the biblical rate of exchange, a hundredfold. Although the money, in view of its source and its suitability, would have to go into the parish account and thus to ARF, Joe would still profit by it greatly—as his benefactor was now, wherever he might be, in a better position to appreciate. For the rest of the year, if not, alas, for the foreseeable future, Joe and Bill could and would suspend their evening operations with dp's.

That, then, was the good news in September.

The bad news began on a Sunday with a sermon, the salient parts of which Joe caught while pacing back and forth where once petunias had bloomed . . .

"The story is told of a certain man punished for working on the Sabbath and other holy days. Which is not to say that circumstances don't, sometimes, alter cases. Contrary to what the Pharisees of old believed, *they* having had the nerve to rebuke Our Lord for allowing his hungry disciples to pick corn on the Sabbath. What, replied Our Lord, of David and his men when they were hungry and went into the house of God and ate the holy bread? 'The Sabbath was made for people, and not people for the Sabbath.' Be that as it may. A certain man, though repeatedly cautioned by the local clergy, and by his neighbors, against working on the Sabbath and other holy days, persisted in his fell course. And on one such day, going into his vineyard in Cocaigne, or perhaps it was Champagne, in what is now known as France, had scarcely put foot to spade when, lo and behold, his head was twisted around backwards and locked, so to speak, in this ungainly and painful position, so that he was perforce looking out behind him. Something like this, only more so, *all* the way around. Ouch. Well, my good people, you can imagine the effect of this on the man's neighbors and their children. To say nothing of his own wife and children. Yes, indeed. Fortunately, the poor man's repentance was so sincere that he was cured of his affliction in a matter of days. Whereupon he gave public thanks to God and St Avit, the latter a holy abbot who flourished in the sixth century and whose feast day (a holy day of obligation in the region) it was when this occurred—the affliction, not the cure—and who, it was generally believed, had worked both miracles."

Joe hadn't thought much of or about the sermon at the time. During the week, though, he heard here and there that the Mall crowd—many of them, of course, parishioners—had taken the sermon as a warning to concerns doing business on Sunday, particularly the Great Badger, since it had been first, and was foremost, in the field locally. Joe, the following Saturday when he met Father Felix's bus, mentioned the sermon, the flak, and was told, "Flak schmak. Nothing could've been further from my mind, Joe, but if the cap fits, I always say, wear it." Words singularly ill chosen, it seemed to Joe, since the monk, who liked to see the world when away from his monastery, and who, some weeks before, had accompanied Bill on a fast shopping trip for boxer shorts, was now wearing the glossy black straw hat presented to him on that otherwise unmemorable occasion by Dave Brock. But Joe said no more about the sermon, hoping it would die a natural death—which it wouldn't.

In the week after its delivery its effect on the student body of Joe's school, now in session again, had been woeful, with kids throwing their necks out of joint all over the place, a girl and three boys requiring medical attention, the former now the envy of all in her cervical collar—Joe was glad the old Duke of Brunswick, with his "Pass that to thy neighbor," had been visited upon the parish during summer vacation.

The effect of the sermon was still being felt in the second week, Bill and Sister, the school principal, both reporting to Joe that children, more girls than boys, were having nightmares about the man with his head on backwards. "That so?" Joe said, sorry to hear it, of course, but not knowing (any more than Bill and Sister) what could be done about it.

On Friday of that week, Bill reported to Joe that a sixth-grade girl, kept after school, had *seen* the man with his head on backwards going, apparently frontwards, into the girls' washroom, but that Sister herself, who had heard the girl's screams and had been the first one to investigate, had found the washroom unoccupied.

*   *   *

What was called assembly, or even convocation, in some schools was called convention (after the Constitutional Convention) in Joe's, his first principal (now serving in the navy) having had a fixation on the Constitution, bringing in speaker after speaker to talk about *it* to grade schoolers—another example, in Joe's view, of the U.S. Church's patriotism, nationalism, inferiority complex. But convention, once a monthly pain in the ass to the student body and faculty, had changed, now booked other attractions—missionaries, magicians, acrobats, dieticians, folks singers.

Some of *these* were down for September, and since this was the first convention of the year, Joe put in an appearance, arriving late with the idea of leaving early. He'd expected to find the folks in their prewashed, stone-ground overalls, and they were, but he hadn't expected to find Bill in *his*, to see and hear him up there on the stage with his guitar, playing and singing along.

While they were doing "Ol' Man Mose"—not very well, Joe thought, remembering Louis Armstrong's version—the bad weather, which had been carrying on in the distance for the last hour or so, arrived in a big way with thunder and lightning only seconds apart, but the folks, with presence of mind, kept at it even after the lights went out and a child somewhere in the auditorium, in the sudden dark and confusion, screamed:

"I *saw* 'im! I *saw* 'im!"

"Stay in your seats!" Joe heard Bill yell, to no avail. "Pray along with me! Hail Mary, full of grace—"

"*Stop!*"

Joe, it seemed to him later, had lost by that. Although nobody had been seriously hurt in the exodus from the auditorium, several students were subsequently removed from the school, which might have happened anyway—the night-mares continued—and which in any case made it possible to enroll both Lane children, this matter handled by Bill and Sister. Oddly enough, the child who'd screamed when the lights went out and who was questioned by Sister and Bill, had not seen, she said, the man with his head on backwards but ol' man Mose—a relief, in a way. Joe, of course, had to explain his action to Bill. "I don't say it was wrong for you to pray, Bill, or for those hillbillies to switch to a hymn. It was just that kids were running for the exits." "So when you said 'Stop,' you meant the *kids* should, Joe?" To this, after a moment, Joe nodded for Bill's sake. The truth was, though, Joe had been scandalized that prayer was being offered, and this quite apart from the fact it wasn't working, as a tranquil-izer. Did Bill sense this, consider it precious of Joe in the circumstances, and resent it? Did the nuns? (Certainly one of them did: "I don't know *what* Our Lady must think of you, Father.") It did seem to Joe there was an anti-Joe feeling in the air. He wondered if this might not be one of those times when the wise pastor takes off for a week or two, in the hope of absence making the heart grow fonder, if he can find, but not through the Chancery ("Die"), a replacement. The first one to come to mind—but not the first one called, or the second, or the third—said he just might be able to get away from his monastery for a week. "Or possibly two, Joe."

30
October

Joe, so he wouldn't have to put up with people, was traveling in mufti, a dark grey suit and a light grey sport shirt, the latter so he wouldn't have to wear a tie, which he (and other priests of his generation at that time) thought was carrying camouflage too far, the next thing to cross-dressing.

He entered Canada late in the afternoon, drove another hour, and checked into what appeared to be the only *ho*tel in a fair-sized town. After a poor meal in the dining room, he dropped into the adjoining bar and there he stayed—too long. The next morning he was having a triple order of orange juice in the coffee shop when joined by Duke, somebody he'd met in the bar the night before, who'd right away asked him if he happened to be a Catholic and when told, "Well—yes," had said, "Takes one to tell one." Duke was in uranium, Joe in life insurance. ("What company?" "Eternal." "Oh yes.") It had been a long night: and among other things they had discussed massage chairs and, in that connection, "one of God's gentlemen," as Duke called a certain Father Antoine, of the Blue Friars (Friars Missionary of the Society of St Louis), or Blues, who had a massage chair, a late model Niagara, he'd be only too glad to show Joe if Duke vouched for him, which Duke would be only too glad to do, he'd said, and for some reason remembered that morning (as Joe didn't at first).

"Joe, if you're still heading east, stop and see old Tony. Watch for the blue sign. It's right on your way, the friary."

"Sorry, Duke. I might turn myself in." Joe shook his head of lead.

"Morning sickness?"

"You might say."

"Hmmm. The trouble is I already gave Tony a ring. He's expecting you, Joe."

"Better give him another ring, Duke."

Duke went away, and came back, frowning. "Joe, I told him what you said, but he's getting on, you know, and I'm afraid he's still expecting you."

"I'm sorry, Duke."

An hour or so later, seeing the blue sign, Joe changed his mind, turned off the highway, and drove through woods that cried out for forestry before he came to the friary, a nondescript red-brick affair, circa 1900—and likewise Father Antoine. Joe saw him in his room, which said PROCUREUR-PROCURATOR on its door, in a chair much like Joe's inanimate Barcalounger in appearance. "How's Duke keeping?" After that, to which Joe had nodded in a thoughtful manner, Father Antoine fired up his pipe, and his inquisitorial manner, in Joe's opinion, ill became one of God's gentlemen.

"Married, Joe?"

"No."

"Ever been?"

"No."

"Expect to be?"

"No."

"Kind of work you do?"

"Oh, office work."

"Office manager?"

"Yes. Branch office."

"Big concern?"

"Well, we're multinational."

"Hah. So are we." Father Antoine, settling deeper into his chair, blew a smoke ring. "Tired of it all, eh? You were thinking of coming in as a brother?"

Joe was thinking of kicking Duke's ass. "Not exactly."

Father Antoine appeared to be, if anything, *more* interested in Joe. "You've heard of our program for late vocations—to the *priesthood*?"

"Can't say I have, but it's a thought."

Father Antoine, just as Joe in his place might have done with a layman, let him have it. "It's *quite* a thought, *mister*."

"Look, Father. I'm only here to see your chair."

"My *chair*?" Father Antoine, it seemed, didn't understand, and then, it seemed, he did. "Oh."

"I'm sorry, Father."

Father Antoine nodded, but more to himself. "Duke didn't mention the chair. I somehow got the impression you were interested in . . . more than that. I'm sorry, Joe."

"No, *I'm* sorry, Father. I'm not as concerned about missionary work as I probably should be."

Father Antoine—he might have done something with such an admission from a layman—said: "In that case, how about a cold bottle of beer?"

"All right."

"And while I'm up, try the chair." While Father Antoine was up, taking two bottles out of a small brown refrigerator ("Duke gave me this"), Joe switched from an ordinary club chair to the Niagara, which Father Antoine had to turn on for him. "I don't use the power much. Oh, sometimes at night if I can't sleep. But you can *drift* off, so at night I always buckle up."

"According to Duke," Joe said, vibrating nicely, "the Niagara was invented in Pennsylvania and the belts under the seat run on the same principle as the ones for screening coal."

"I wouldn't be surprised." Father Antoine, having polished the glasses with the skirt of his blue-black habit and poured with a practiced hand, served Joe his beer with a quivering head on it. "No, no, don't move."

So Joe stayed put, beer in hand, and it too now vibrating nicely. "My—" he said, and about to say *curate*, started over. "A friend of mine sent a check to your men somewhere in Africa—for a milch cow. They needed one. Also reading matter and T-shirts."

" 'Milch cow'? Yes, that does sound like our Irish province—it serves Africa and Asia. But when *was* this?"

"A few months ago."

"Well, if the check hasn't cleared yet, better tell your friend to stop payment and write another. You see, we're— they're back in Ireland. Forced to leave by the new government."

"Too bad."

Father Antoine sighed. "We're pulling in our horns these days."

"That so?"

"Yes, but there's plenty to be done in Ireland. Oh, plenty. *And* on this side of the water." Father Antoine, perhaps concerned that such candor might be shocking to a layman, was watching Joe closely.

"Here in Canada, you mean?"

"Or thereabouts. Hah." Father Antoine clapped his glass to his mouth and finished his beer.

So Joe did the same, turned off the Niagara, and stood up with the firm intention of leaving, and held to it firmly when invited to have another "brew" (a word he disliked without knowing why), saying "Thanks, Father, but I have to drive"—sounding mealy-mouthed to himself, in view of his tolerance for alcohol (if beer could be called that), his morning-after thirst, and the old friar's undoubtable hospitality.

"Split one then."

"All right."

After serving Joe (now back in the club chair) and himself, Father Antoine returned to the Niagara and spoke of the Society's work in Latin America, which he said was going about as well as could be expected. Or not very well, Joe gathered, and was moved to sign a traveler's check, which was gratefully accepted, and then to ease his conscience further:

"Father, there's something I have to tell you. You know how it is when you're traveling if you're dressed as a priest—people pounce on you."

Obviously Father Antoine did know—he was of a generation that hadn't gone in for camouflage—but he said, " 'Pounce'? I wouldn't say that, Joe. People generally mean well."

"All right, Father. I don't say they don't. But there's still something I have to tell you—I'm a priest myself."

"*Are* you now?" (Joe had expected more surprise, less anxiety, and thought the question loaded, that what he was really being asked was, "Are you *now*?") "Religious or secular, may I ask?"

"Secular, but in—as we say—good standing. I can show you my driver's license"—Joe felt for his wallet—"and you can look me up in the *Directory*."

"No, no, Joe, Father. I believe you. Where *are* you? What diocese?"

Joe told him.

"Well, you fooled me, Joe, but I will say this for myself, Father. I thought there was something funny about you right from the start, something that didn't quite click—from what I'd been given to understand by Duke, but then . . . Poor Duke."

"Yes, and I'm sorry about that, Father."

"Joe, it couldn't be helped, Father. No harm done. I love company these days. And now that I know where you—*we*—stand, there's something I have to tell you. Duke was one of us, no, *is*. 'Thou art a priest forever.' "

Joe nodded to that.

"If not perhaps"—Father Antoine sighed—"in good standing."

"Duke just left, or what?"

"Just left. Why, I can't say. Not women, I think, or even drink, and money's not enough. I really can't say." Father Antoine sighed.

"About all you can say, Father, is there's a lot of it going around."

"Never heard it put so well. It's my theory—and that's all it is—that Duke now disapproves of himself and is trying to make amends. You're not the first one he's sent my way, and probably won't be the last. (So far, no takers.) I can't say a lot for Duke's head, but he has a good heart. He gave me this chair." Father Antoine sighed. "Poor Duke."

Joe nodded to that. "He may be back."

"My hope, of course, and speaking of that, should *you* ever . . ."

"Thanks, Father, but I don't think I'm cut out for missionary work."

"Well, keep us in mind. For someone like you, it wouldn't necessarily mean *Latin* America. You see, we have this program, though it's only in the talking stage, to begin operations in the States. Unquestionably, there'd be a great deal of sentiment and support up here—among people generally, of all creeds or none—for such a move."

"That so?"

"Unquestionably. It's true the U.S. is no longer classified as a missionary field, but hopefully something could be done about that, with things as they are down there and becoming more so. The problem may be the U.S. hierarchy—they'd have to apply to Rome for reclassification and they may not be ready *yet*."

"Possibly not."

"Joe, how do you yourself feel about such a program, Father?"

"I'm all for it," Joe said, "and I'll see what I can do about the U.S. hierarchy." With that and a smile, Joe got up to leave.

"Joe, it's going on eleven, Father. Why not stay for lunch? We'll have time to talk and time for a brew."

Joe shook his head, which, he noticed, had lightened and loosened up some. "No, I'd better not, Father. I have to drive."

"My thought exactly, Joe. Get some *food* in you, Father."

Joe shook his head, denying himself, his thirst, and also, he was afraid, Father Antoine his love of company these days. "Well, all right, Tony."

At the end of his vacation, doing the last eleven days in Montreal without a drop except for wine at his daily Mass and though staying in a hotel, working long hours, sometimes as a priest, at the Catholic Worker house where Greg had what he'd called (on his first postcard) a good job, Joe took leave of the loving and, yes, lovable derelicts, giving them, since they asked for it, his blessing, and went out to his car, which had come in handy during the eleven days and had been puked in twice.

"Do *me* a favor," Greg said.

"Sure. What?"

"Keep it up."

"What?" Joe said, though he knew what.

Greg just looked at him.

"We'll see," Joe said then, and drove away.

The morning after the night he got back, and was still keeping it up, though he'd stopped at the friary again, he went to see the Arch.

31

November

Joe had driven out to Brad's place that Sunday afternoon with misgivings, afraid what Barb had said on the phone ("We hope to see you here at two P.M., Father—it's important") might mean that Brad had decided to join the Church. But Joe had been wrong. He had simply been tricked into attending a surprise party for himself, a cookout. Already there, sitting or milling around the campfire with the host and hostess, were (in the host's words) "All your friends, Padre"—Mr Barnes, Earl, Earl's wife and their kids, the Gurriers and theirs, Father Felix, Lefty, Bill, and Father Day, who'd been picked up at the hospital by Bill, who said Mrs P. couldn't make it, but sent her best. Joe kept moving around—to give everybody a shot at the guest of honor—and was in, or listened in on, a number of conversations. There was some talk of the national election, in which Joe hadn't voted and about which he had nothing to say, and much more about Brad's coming trip to Nam, about which Joe also had nothing to say. Barb, catching Joe alone, said, "I asked him *not* to mention his trip, but you know how he is, Father." Joe said he did and told her he'd seen Greg, something of the good job he had, and how good he was at it, which Barb was glad to hear. "But don't say anything to Brad, Father." "No, I won't," Joe said, and moved on, since Barb had left him for the grill. "Oh, *no*," he said, hearing Bill tell Father Felix that Conklin had not only found his lost faith but was thinking of studying for the priesthood again. "Where?" said Father Felix. "He doesn't know yet—*not* here," Bill said. "Have him drop me a line," Father Felix said, "or—what's his address?" Joe moved on. The kids had a football. Before and after eating—steak—he worked out with them, showed them how to get their punts to spiral, and said, inscrutably, the time before the game, when the punters warmed up, was the best part of it. He and the kids had soft drinks again, and he looked cross-eyed and said "Hic" and made them laugh, not as much, though, as he had at first. When it was time for him to leave—so soon, yes, but not too soon—he took Father Day by the arm, walked him out to the car, and settled him in the front seat. Lefty, who'd stood by during this operation in case he was needed and who had then circled the car, pointed out that *all* its hubcaps were missing. "Yeah, I know," Joe said. "Dear God," Lefty said, speaking of Bill, who could be seen and heard with his guitar, leading the singing around the campfire, "look at my candy-ass assistant." "Yeah, I know," Joe said—he now had none. A pickup truck pulled into the driveway and Dave Brock, sans sombrero, got out. Joe, because he'd sort of met Dave once and had had a letter of thanks from him after the abortive holdup, introduced Lefty to him, then excused himself, saying, "I have to leave," and hurried out to his car parked at the curb, his passenger having disappeared from view. When Lefty called after him, "*Sure* you don't want that *chair*?" Joe shook his head and kept going, calling back, "*Yes*," and when Dave called after him, "Where is it you're stationed now—Holy . . . Faith?" Joe shook his head and kept going, calling back, "*Cross.*"

A NOTE ON THE TYPE

The text of this book was composed in Palatino, a type face designed by the noted German typographer Herman Zapf. Named after Giovanbattista Palatino, a writing master of Renaissance Italy, Palatino was the first of Zapf's type faces to be introduced in America. The first designs for the face were made in 1948, and the fonts for the complete face were issued between 1950 and 1952. Like all Zapf-designed type faces, Palatino is beautifully balanced and exceedingly readable.

Composed by
American–Stratford Graphic Services, Inc.,
Brattleboro, Vermont

Printed and bound by
R. R. Donnelley & Sons,
Harrisonburg, Virginia

Designed by Marysarah Quinn